Conceit &
Concealment

Abigail Reynolds

White Soup Press

Chapter One

Sir William Lucas, his usually jovial face grim, strode into the sitting room at Longbourn. "Bad news," he told Mr. Bennet without even pausing to greet the ladies first. "Robinson has been arrested."

Mr. Bennet's eyes widened. "Arrested? What crime could the old fool possibly have committed? Losing his way?"

"He contested Captain Reynard's plan to commandeer his house. The good captain has taken a fancy to it and wants it as his residence, and does not care that it has been in Robinson's family for generations. When Robinson declined to be evicted and threatened to make a complaint to General Desmarais in London, the captain ordered his soldiers to search the house. They went through his newspapers and found a copy of *The Loyalist*. They say that is treason."

"When did reading *The Loyalist* become treason?" asked Mr. Bennet mildly. "It is anti-French and illegal, to be sure, but a small bribe will convince the officers to look the other way. If reading it is treason, they will have to hang half the town."

Elizabeth Bennet looked up from her mending, unable to keep silent. "I imagine it is only treason if you happen to possess something Captain Reynard wants. What is being done to help Mr. Robinson?"

Sir William mopped his brow. "That is why I am here. Bennet, I need your help. Captain Reynard has given me three days to talk sense into Robinson, and if he still will not give up his claim to the house, he will be hanged. Robinson is more likely to listen to you than to me. There is a small cottage at Lucas Lodge where he can live until he finds something else."

Of course Captain Reynard would do whatever he wished, and the only question was how to convince Mr. Robinson to submit to the yoke. Under her breath, Elizabeth said, "If only I were a man…"

Her sister Kitty gave a derisive snort. "If you were a man and did all the things you say, you would have been hanged long ago."

"Just think how much easier that would have made your life!" Elizabeth retorted.

Mr. Bennet pinched the bridge of his nose. "This situation is difficult enough without having squabbling geese underfoot," he said sourly.

Elizabeth looked away. Her father might be able to accept everything the French did, but she could not. It had been easier in the first years after the French invasion when she and Jane had lived with the Gardiners in London. She could almost have imagined nothing had changed – nothing except blue uniforms taking the place of red coats and people wearing clothes two seasons out of date owing to Napoleon's levies to pay for his war. Not only did the English suffer defeat at the hands of the French, but they had to pay for the privilege.

In Meryton, she could not forget the existence of the French garrison for more than a few hours. French soldiers were everywhere, pestering any girl they saw, exacting non-existent fees and fines to line their own pockets, and strutting about as if they owned the town. It was painful to watch them and say nothing, especially with all the suffering her poor sister Jane had endured.

"Will you help me convince poor Robinson to give in?" Sir William asked.

Mr. Bennet frowned. "I suppose I must."

"Capital! I will drive you there." Sir William lowered his voice. "On a happier note, I have met Mr. Bingley, our new neighbor at Netherfield. He is young and unmarried – a fine thing for our girls. A most amiable fellow, I would say."

"Is he English?" asked Mr. Bennet.

"Indeed he is." Sir William's usual good nature seemed partially restored by indulging in gossip. "His money is from trade, so the French have allowed him to keep it. He has two sisters who do not care to leave the social whirl of London. Of course, before the French came, their breeding would not have been good enough, but now they can mix with the highest circles. He will not be alone at Netherfield, though. A friend of his, a gentleman, will be arriving soon for an extended stay."

"Is his friend unmarried, too?" asked Kitty eagerly.

"He is not married, but his young sister will accompany him. She is half-witted, they say."

Poor fellow! It was good of him to keep his sister with him rather than sending her to an asylum. "Is he in trade also?" asked Elizabeth.

"Nooo," said Sir William, dragging out the single syllable as if reluctant to say more. "He is from an old family with aristocratic connections. He owns a large estate in the north."

A traitor, then. The French had taken their revenge on the English aristocracy and the landed gentry after the invasion by confiscating all the grand estates. The only exceptions had been for property owners who agreed to cooperate with the invaders. So much for pitying the man! But she should make certain she had not misunderstood. "He still owns his estate?"

"He does." Sir William waggled his eyebrows meaningfully.

Mr. Bennet removed his spectacles and polished them with his handkerchief. "Well, we can all guess the price he has paid for keeping it. Lizzy, you must take care if you meet him. Kitty, I am sure you care nothing for his politics since he is rich and wears trousers, but I would urge you not to trust him. I even begin to doubt this Mr. Bingley for having such a friend."

Sir William nodded. "I quite agree with your caution, but I will withhold judgment for now. Perhaps this fellow and Bingley went to school together. Or it might have been his father who made the decision and he has but inherited it."

"I do not think I could remain friends with someone who accepted such an arrangement," declared Elizabeth. "It is hard enough to remain *sisters* with —"

"Lizzy!" snapped Mr. Bennet.

Kitty tossed her head. "If you wish to be a fool and throw your life away dreaming of the past, do not let me stop you. Some of us want a future, and it is obvious where that lies. You may not like what Lydia has done, but you are happy enough to enjoy the benefits of it."

"That is not true. You know perfectly well I would rather go into exile in Scotland with nothing but the clothes on my back than to accept luxuries under these circumstances." How she envied the fortunate Scots who had nothing Napoleon wanted and therefore could keep their own country. "I would do more than go into exile to be free of French rule."

"That is easy to say while you still have an excuse. You are just jealous of Lydia because she was the first of us to marry."

"Jealous? Now *that* I can assure you I am not. How long until you decide to sell yourself, Kitty? Are you holding out for a higher price than Lydia?"

Mrs. Bennet bustled in. "Oh, you have no consideration for my nerves! Arguing like this where the servants could hear you! Would you have us thrown out into the hedgerows, Lizzy? Begone from my sight, you wicked girl!"

Elizabeth gathered her dignity around her and ignored Kitty's smirk. "Happily!" She stalked away, her shoulders aching with tension.

Elizabeth carried the tea tray from the kitchen across the courtyard, past the empty stalls of the stables to the former tack room which had been converted for Jane's use. She knocked three times — *rat a tat tat*— and waited while Jane raised the bar across the inside and opened the door.

"Teatime," Elizabeth said brightly, carrying the tray into Jane's tiny sitting room. "Not the swill that is all we can buy these days, but the last of the chamomile I picked and dried last summer. I had it hidden in my room."

Jane's face lit up. "Bless you, Lizzy! I do not like to complain, but I can barely swallow some of that so-called tea. I think it must be tar and sawdust with a few leaves added to fool us into thinking it is real tea."

"I cannot disagree." There was no point in telling Jane that the tea Lydia served tasted just as tea should. Even so, every drop of it threatened to choke Elizabeth whenever she drank it. How could she enjoy tea purchased by a French officer?

Jane's brows drew together. "What is the matter, Lizzy? There is no need to put on false cheer for me."

"Nothing of importance. I quarreled with Kitty again. I should not let her provoke me, I know, especially since none of it compares to what you suffer every day. I do not know how you bear it!"

"It is not hard. Things could be much worse. After all, I have everything I need right here." Jane poured out the tea into two cups.

"Except the freedom to leave these rooms!" Elizabeth said hotly. "Oh, I could just kill that man!"

"It would not help me for you to be hanged for murder. One of these days Captain Reynard will be transferred elsewhere and I will be able to go back to my old life. In the meantime, I have your visits and Charlotte's to look forward to. It is not so bad."

"I wish you did not have to be alone so much." Elizabeth forced herself to swallow her rage. All it did was upset Jane, who had already suffered enough. "How is the tea?"

Jane lifted her teacup to her mouth. "Heavenly!"

Mrs. Bennet expressed a wish for fresh pastries from the bakery in town, so naturally her middle daughter Mary had to display her sense of charity by offering to fetch them. Unfortunately, that meant Elizabeth and Kitty were obliged to go with her. It was unsafe for a woman to walk alone these days, so perforce they had to escort each other. It had not always been that way. Elizabeth could remember taking long walks in the countryside with no company but her own, but that had been before the French came.

She did not mind the walk, only the company. If there was one thing worse than suffering Kitty's chatter about the officers, it was enduring Mary's constant admonitions about loving their enemies. At least Mary truly believed forgiving their enemies was the right thing to do. Kitty only wanted the financial advantages the enemy could provide her. What did it matter to Kitty why the officers were in Meryton so long as she could flirt with them and accept their little gifts?

Elizabeth paid little attention to her sisters as they walked, instead girding herself for battle. Not the kind of battle which could be fought openly, but the painful battle within herself whenever she met the officers in their fancy blue coats. Even after all this time, it was a struggle to force herself to smile at them and converse pleasantly. But her parents relied on the goodwill of the French soldiers, and Lydia's husband could not single-handedly protect them if Elizabeth made a show of resistance. Still, it stung. How it stung!

"Miss Kitty! Miss Elizabeth!" Lieutenant Bessette hailed them as they entered town, a fellow officer by his side.

Kitty, her eyelashes fluttering, said, "*Bonjour*, Lieutenant Bessette, Sous-Lieutenant Gareau."

"*Bonjour, mesdemoiselles*," said the lieutenant. "How charming to meet with such lovely ladies! Have you heard about the *Assemblée*? *Capitaine* Reynard says all the young ladies must attend and dance the night away."

"I will look forward to it," said Elizabeth, who would do nothing of the sort. Lieutenant Bessette might be more tolerable than most of the other officers, but he was still a French soldier.

"*Merveilleux!*" cried the lieutenant. "May I have the honor of the first dance, Miss Elizabeth?"

Her other choices for a dancing partner would likely be worse. "Of course. I would be delighted." At least she could count on Lieutenant Bessette to behave properly.

A drumroll sounded from the market square, and Elizabeth's hands clenched. The lieutenant seemed to notice the change in her bearing and said, "There is no need to concern yourself, Miss Elizabeth. A sous-lieutenant is being promoted. That is all."

That was much better than the other occasions for drumrolls – a public flogging or, even worse, an execution – but there would still be the usual problem. The second drumroll came, followed by the inevitable chorus of "*Vive l'Empereur!*"

Just as inevitably, a voice not far behind Elizabeth cried, "God save Her Highness!" A young boy, from the sound of it.

The lieutenant turned to give chase, but Elizabeth caught his sleeve in her hand. When he rounded angrily on her, she gave him her warmest smile. "Remember, Lieutenant, that you were once a boy and loved your country."

His expression softened slightly. "*Mais oui.* Boys will be boys." But he set off after him anyway, albeit at a slower pace.

He did not get far. Townspeople began pouring into the streets, apparently doing nothing more than talking to their neighbors, sweeping the pavement, or carrying buckets to the well. And, coincidentally, forcing the soldiers giving chase to slow down and weave around them. The French were never fooled by these tricks, no matter how much the townsfolk denied hearing the treasonous shouts.

There was so little the people of Meryton could do to resist the invaders. Even this small gesture warmed Elizabeth's heart.

Mr. Bennet pushed himself to his feet as his guest entered the library. "Why, Mr. Bingley, how good of you to return my call so quickly. How are you finding Netherfield?"

Bingley sat down across from Mr. Bennet. "It is very much to my taste, and I am enjoying meeting my neighbors."

"Good, good. I understand you have a guest coming to stay with you." Mr. Bennet watched him closely.

"Yes, an old friend. He arrived two days ago."

It was time to test the amiable Mr. Bingley's loyalties. Mr. Bennet poured out two glasses of port. He handed one to his guest and then, one eyebrow cocked, held out his own glass as if to make a toast.

Mr. Bingley looked startled, but did not hesitate. He clinked his glass against Mr. Bennet's. "Her Highness. God save her." It was the established toast since the invasion, ambiguous enough to mislead the French, yet understood by all loyal Englishmen. God save Her Highness Princess Charlotte, the mad king's granddaughter and heir – and England's last hope.

"God save her," Mr. Bennet echoed quietly. Apparently Mr. Bingley was a Loyalist despite being the friend of a French sympathizer.

"I have just come from a visit with Sir William Lucas. What a fine fellow he is! He asked for my assistance in a small matter, although it clearly went much against the grain for him. Still, when times change, we must change with them. His daughter has been invited to an assembly with the French officers. Refusing is not an option, I gather, and Sir William says fathers are not welcome to attend."

Mr. Bennet curled his lip. "It is true. They prefer our daughters to be unprotected. I suppose Sir William is in a difficult position now that his son has been conscripted into Napoleon's *Grande Armée*. He escorted Charlotte in the past."

"You have perceived his difficulty! Sir William asked if I would be kind enough to escort his daughter in place of his son, purely as a matter of her safety. Naturally I was happy to oblige." Bingley paused to take a sip of port. "He also hinted I might wish to speak to you about the matter."

In general Mr. Bennet preferred to pretend that particular problem did not exist. Still, if Sir William was going to make this simple for him, the least he could do was to oblige. "I imagine he was thinking of my Lizzy. I have a married daughter, but her husband, I am sorry to say, is a French officer himself." It was not worth the trouble of explaining that Mary was not invited and Kitty had no desire to be protected.

"My friend would no doubt be happy to escort your daughter if it would help to keep her safe."

Mr. Bennet raised an eyebrow. "I am certain you mean well, but who is to protect my daughter from your friend?"

Frowning, Bingley leaned forward. "Sir, I do not know what you have heard, but you misjudge him. Darcy would never take advantage of a young lady. He has a young sister and is well aware of the dangers to ladies in these situations."

"Softly, my friend, softly! If you say he is honorable in this regard, I will believe you. I understand, though, that his estate and fortune were not forfeit to the Emperor, so apparently his honor does not extend to remaining loyal to England."

Bingley set down his port. "I have known Darcy for years, and I trust him implicitly. If he has agreed to cooperate with the French, I have complete certainty it was because the other options open to him were even less honorable. We have all made compromises with our enemies, all of us who have chosen to remain alive rather than fighting to the death. You also still own an estate. Should I assume you are disloyal?"

Mr. Bennet snorted. "Anyone in Meryton can tell you the price I paid to keep Longbourn, and most likely they have already done so. But in case they have not, I will tell you myself. The French took this house and used it as a barracks until a year ago, at which point they offered it back to me at the cost of my youngest daughter, who fortunately was quite eager to be sacrificed. But the French know I am not their friend."

"I am not criticizing you, sir, merely noting we have all made such arrangements. The French are perfectly happy to tolerate me while my factories keep producing caissons and limbers to transport their artillery, and I can justify it to myself because it protects the Englishmen who work in those factories from being conscripted to fight in Europe. But you and I are both living in glass houses, so let us not throw stones!"

Mr. Bennet inclined his head. He did not agree with Mr. Bingley on this point, but Lizzy would be safer with a gentleman to escort her, even one who had struck a deal with the French in the past. "We have all made difficult decisions. If you believe your friend is trustworthy and would be willing to provide an escort for my daughter, I would be obliged to you and to him."

Darcy could find no particular fault with Netherfield Park. The house was spacious and pleasant. The grounds were well kept. The rolling hills surrounding it kept the landscape interesting. Bingley was a gracious host. His cook produced tasty meals. And after two days, it was slowly driving Darcy mad.

He had spent hours calming Georgiana's anxieties about being in a new place. He had walked with her around the gardens and listened to her practice her music. The previous night he had stayed up late drinking brandy with Bingley, something he had been looking forward to. But instead of finally being able to talk freely to his friend as he had hoped, he had hidden everything.

Today Bingley had gone to visit a neighbor, and Darcy was too restless to keep his attention on a book. The only distraction he could find was to work on his billiard game. At least it was quiet in the billiard room apart from the clicking of balls striking and the satisfying thump when one dropped into a pocket.

Bingley appeared in the doorway, apparently done with his visits. "Practicing again? As if you need it to thrash me thoroughly!"

Leaning over the table, Darcy sighted along his cue stick. "It passes the time."

"If it is time you wish to pass, I have volunteered you to join me in a charitable duty."

Without raising his head, Darcy flicked his eyes up at Bingley. "Why do I suppose I will not like this?"

Bingley chuckled. "It is true; you will not like it. The local regiment is having an assembly and has commanded the presence of all the young ladies. I agreed we would escort two of them who would both be unprotected otherwise."

Darcy dropped the cue stick and straightened. "Bingley, the last thing I want is to be giving some local girl expectations I will never be able to meet."

"There will be no expectations. Their fathers arranged it purely as a matter of their safety. So many of the local men have been conscripted that there are few left to provide escorts, leaving the ladies to the mercies of the French officers."

"I suppose we must, then," Darcy said grudgingly. Had he not already given up enough for his fellow countrymen? But the same answer always resounded in his head. Many had been forced to give their lives for their country, and he had not. Yet.

He would only go to this damned dance because if he refused and anything happened to those poor girls, he would bear that burden forever - along with so many others. Sometimes he wondered if a clean death in battle would not have been preferable. But Georgiana needed him, so that was not an option.

Bingley clapped him on the shoulder. "No need to be so glum, old fellow! You might even enjoy yourself a bit. From what I gather, you are getting the young and pretty one. Mine, according to her loving father, is all but on the shelf and 'not what I would call pretty, but a good girl, a good girl.'" His voice had deepened into an imitation of an older man's.

"Most likely yours will at least manage some interesting conversation. What is the name of my insipid miss?"

"Miss Elizabeth Bennet. Her father already dislikes you, so you should be safe from expectations."

"Dislikes me? I have not even met the man."

Bingley grinned. "Oh, you are in a mood today! It is the usual complaint. I did not hesitate to point out his own failings in that regard. But look – the sun is finally showing its face. You should go for a ride and clear your head."

He had been longing all day to do exactly that. "You will stay here if I do? I do not like to leave Georgiana alone in a new place."

"Of course. Now go. Get out of here!"

A quarter of an hour later, the stable master regarded Darcy as if he were a being from another planet. The Netherfield staff had not yet accustomed themselves to their guest's eccentricities, such as saddling and bridling Hurricane himself. But Hurricane was the one luxury he had insisted on keeping at a time when he had given up so much else. He had raised and broken the horse himself, and Hurricane always understood him. Darcy hated allowing anyone else to handle him. Even the process of saddling him and the feeling of Hurricane's warm flanks under his hands brought him some much-needed peace.

They set off at a trot down the lane and jumped a fence before cantering across a pasture. The sun had not yet burned off the dampness in the spring air.

Darcy had loved springtime when his mother was alive. She had taught him the names of each spring flower in the Pemberley gardens, encouraged him to watch each stage of leaves unfolding, made wishes with him over the star-shaped wood anemones, and taken him on adventures in Pemberley's magical bluebell wood. She had died in the springtime, too, just as the bluebells were fading away to nothing. And then there had been the terrible spring of 1805 which had cost him his father and more relatives and friends than he could count, as well as his freedom and his country.

Spring had once been a time of beginnings for him. Now it made him think of all he had lost.

These thoughts were not helping to clear his head. He laid a hand on Hurricane's neck, feeling the tautness of his muscles beneath his shiny coat. Hurricane was still with him – loyal, steady Hurricane.

At Pemberley he could gallop for miles over the empty moors, but Hertfordshire was more settled. He spotted a copse in the distance and made for that, hoping to find some semblance of untamed nature there. He skirted the edge until he found a path leading into it, but before he even entered the copse, a familiar floral scent transported him into the past. It was a bluebell wood.

On impulse, he dismounted and tied Hurricane's reins to a tree. Ahead of him bluebells swayed in the dappled sunlight. He strode towards them as their almost otherworldly scent enveloped him, raising goose bumps on his skin. The spring green of the wood was the perfect frame for the sapphire flowers. Magic, his mother had called the bluebells.

His pace slowed. How long had it been since his last visit to a bluebell wood? He could not even recall. The bluebells seemed to dance around him with a ripple of laughter. But no – that was human laughter, and it was followed by a squeal of pain.

15

"That hurt, young man! Or young woman, if that is what you are." A woman's musical voice seemed part of the magic, drawing him towards it with a seductive enchantment of its own. Where was she, the woman of the rippling laughter? He searched for a side path through the flowers. His mother had taught him never to trample bluebells.

There it was, so faint it could barely be called a path, just grass dividing a sea of bluebells. Carefully he stepped along it.

He could see her now. Tendrils of dark chestnut hair escaped their binding to riot across her long neck in exuberant curls. She sat on the ground, her legs curled up beside her, and she was surrounded by... puppies? Yes, puppies, crawling over her lap, nipping at her skirts, and rolling over for petting. She picked one up and kissed its head. Fortunate puppy!

His lips curved. A poet would call her Titania, queen of the fairies, in the flesh. More woodland magic.

She must have heard his footsteps, or perhaps the yapping of a puppy alerted her, because she looked back over her shoulder. At the sight of him, she twisted around and scrambled backwards.

In the dappled sunlight, his Titania's face was alive with energy, full of fine sparkling eyes and kissable lips.

And she was pointing a fully cocked pistol at him.

He took a step back and opened his hands to show they were empty. "I mean you no harm." The sound of his own voice startled him.

"English?" Her voice was sterner now.

"Yes. I am visiting from Derbyshire. Or, if you prefer, I will say it – *Theophilus Thistle, the thistle sifter, sifted a sieve full of unsifted thistles, thrusting three thousand thistles through the thick of his thumb.*" It was the tongue twister no Frenchman could pronounce, no matter how accentless his English might be.

Her lips quirked, but she kept the pistol leveled at him. "Well, Theophilus Thistle from Derbyshire, why are you following me?"

"Because I was walking through an enchanted bluebell wood when I heard the dulcet tones of Titania, queen of the fairies, which enspells any mortal man." He swept her a full court bow.

She chuckled. "Lovely words, but perhaps you should avoid sudden movements when I have a pistol trained on you."

"Do you know how to use it?"

"Of course. You could have been a French soldier out hunting for game." The distaste in her voice made it clear what kind of game the soldiers hunted here.

"Good. I trained my sister to shoot for the same reason." One of the puppies began to crawl in his direction.

"Ah." She lowered the pistol but did not put it aside. "If I am Titania, perhaps I will cast a spell on you instead. It would be much less bloody."

"Since I would prefer not to have the head of an ass, perhaps I should leave you in peace. Or at least as much peace as you can find with all these puppies." He could see the mother dog now, a springer spaniel lying in a hollow between two trees and nursing two more puppies. "Which was the one that nipped you?"

She pointed to the brown puppy squirming his way toward Darcy. "That little wild thing."

He took a slow step forward and held out his hand to the puppy, who sniffed it eagerly. "May I?"

At her nod, he picked up the puppy. The mother dog raised her head and growled.

"You need not worry," his Titania said to the dog. "He is wearing brown, not blue." She looked up at him again. "I am training her to attack soldiers who come too close to me."

"I will keep that in mind." He turned the puppy over in his hands and examined him. "If you were still wondering, he is a young man. Definitely a young man." He held the puppy up to his shoulder and

17

scratched its ears. Pushing back against his hand, the puppy licked his chin. Repeatedly.

Her eyes sparkled when she laughed. "I should have known as much since he is a troublemaker already!"

Darcy cuddled the puppy for another minute, taking pleasure in his warmth and the softness of his fur, then reluctantly set him down. "Back to your mistress, young Puck," he told the puppy firmly. "And now I will leave you in peace. Farewell, proud Titania."

She set down the pistol at last, picked up the puppy, and waved a tiny paw at him. "Theophilus Thistle, I grant you safe passage through my domain." She crinkled her nose at him.

He made his way back through the sea of bluebells, smiling for what felt like first time in years. His mother had been right; there was magic in a bluebell wood. He would not wait so long to revisit one.

Perhaps he would bring Georgiana here. She was even more in need of a dose of magic than he was.

Chapter Two

Darcy's improved spirits lasted through the following day, even when it came time to depart for the assembly. He had resigned himself to the prospect of spending the evening with a silly, chattering girl. After all, he did not have to listen to what she was saying, did he?

Miss Lucas, whom they collected first, was a pleasant surprise, or at least a relief. While living up to her father's description, she was soft-spoken and seemed sensible and, more importantly, showed no embarrassing intention of flirting with either Bingley or Darcy. She was a peaceful presence. If he had to spend an evening escorting a woman, someone like Miss Lucas would suit him well.

He was less sanguine about the prospect of Miss Elizabeth Bennet. Miss Lucas described her as much younger, with a lively wit and a strong will. Not the sort of comfortable companion he would prefer.

Still, he managed to be civil through his introduction to Mr. Bennet and even to ignore that gentleman's slightly scornful coolness.

Then a familiar face appeared, one whose eyebrows shot up in surprise. "Theophilus Thistle!" she exclaimed.

Now he was smiling like a fool again as he bowed. "Proud Titania."

Mr. Bennet looked amused. "Lizzy, I would present Mr. Darcy to your acquaintance, but I perceive you have already met."

19

Bingley asked, "How could you have met? Darcy has barely stirred from Netherfield since he arrived."

Darcy said solemnly, "We have a mutual acquaintance, a young man with a taste for making trouble."

Bingley looked more baffled than ever. Mr. Bennet wore a quizzical look.

Titania – no, Miss Bennet – had a mischievous glint in her fine eyes. "And a taste for licking Mr. Darcy's face."

"That as well," Darcy agreed.

With a sidelong glance at her father, Miss Bennet said, "One of Rose's puppies."

Mr. Bennet pushed his spectacles up the bridge of his nose. "Are dogs performing introductions these days? Quite remarkable. Perhaps they are taking on the civility so many Englishmen have abandoned of late."

The amusement faded from Miss Bennet's face. "Indeed," she said coolly. "I suppose we must not keep the French officers waiting, should we, Mr. Darcy?"

No. Not his Titania, too, turning away from him because of his association with the damned French. Why did the one bit of joy he had discovered have to be quenched by those damned assumptions he could not contradict? His stomach churned.

Well, so be it. He had agreed to the sacrifice himself, and he would do it again in the same circumstances.

But sometimes it was simply not fair.

It simply was not fair. Elizabeth did not want to like Mr. Darcy. How could she like a man who put his own wealth and possessions before his love of his country? True, he had been far from the only man to do so, but she was prepared to hate every last one of them.

But she had liked Theophilus Thistle. How long had it been since she had the opportunity to exchange witticisms with an educated young Englishman? He had displayed a sense of humor and an ability to laugh at himself, and he was unquestionably pleasant to look at. He even liked to cuddle puppies. Why did the best prospect for flirtation she had met since the invasion have to turn out to be a French sympathizer?

Oh, if only she could stamp her feet in frustration! She should have realized who he was and not allowed herself to dwell on him. It was not as if young men of wealth and education suddenly appeared from nowhere. But it had been such a pleasant interaction that it had never crossed her mind he could be a traitor to England.

And now he was being unfair again, not only engaging her playfully, but then having the gall to look injured when she treated him as coldly as he deserved. Did he think his bloodstained wealth would influence her? If he had to consort with the enemy, the very least he could do was to behave like an unpleasant fellow. Before his arrival, she had been prepared to dislike the unknown Mr. Darcy, and dislike him she would, regardless of whether he cast puppy dog eyes at her. She certainly would not tell him she had named the mischievous puppy Puck in his honor.

Fortunately, she had a great deal of practice at being coldly polite.

Mr. Darcy declined to take the hint. "Miss Bennet, might I have the honor of the first dance?"

"I am afraid it is already promised." It was just as well. If she had to spend half an hour close to him right now, he might start seeming like the delightful Theophilus Thistle again. That would be a mistake.

"Perhaps the second, then, or whatever you might have open?"

"If the second dance would suit you, I will be pleased to dance it with you."

Once in the carriage, Mr. Bingley rubbed his hands together. "What should we expect from this assembly? Since it is given by the officers, will the gentlemen outnumber the ladies?"

Under her breath, Elizabeth said to Charlotte, "It depends on how you define 'gentlemen.'"

Charlotte pretended not to hear her, but judging by Mr. Darcy's raised eyebrow, he had made out her words, too.

Tactful as ever, Charlotte said, "It is likely they will, although not by much since there are so very few Englishmen left here. Lizzy and I will be the envy of many ladies for having English escorts."

Mr. Bingley seemed somewhat embarrassed by that. "Will it be English dances or French?"

"Need you ask?" said Elizabeth with a lightness she did not feel. "They may have an English reel or two as a token gesture, but most will be waltzes and quadrilles. They are particularly fond of waltzes."

"London balls are much the same," Bingley confided. "Even those given by Englishmen seem designed to please the French."

"There is no surprise in that," said Elizabeth.

Mr. Darcy, of course, said nothing.

The first dance was indeed a waltz, and Elizabeth feared the second might be more of the same. To her relief, the musicians struck up a reel for it. That meant less opportunity for speech with Mr. Darcy, less ability to gaze into his eyes, and she did not have to spend half an hour with his arms around her. A pity – she had imagined the pleasure of waltzing with Theophilus Thistle, but that had been before she discovered who he truly was.

When they reached the end of the set and had to wait to rejoin the dance, he said to her, "I hope your first set was enjoyable."

"Waltzing with Lieutenant Bessette? It was tolerable, I suppose. His manners are better than many of the other officers and he never tries to take advantage of women, so I cannot complain."

"He is a favorite of yours, then?"

She shot him a sharp look. "I suppose, in the same way that I prefer fleas to lice. Though that is unfair; if the lieutenant would simply return to France, I would think him a fine fellow."

He spoke in a low voice. "Do you see all the French in England as being detestable, then?"

"Yes," she said rashly. "And you do not."

"I see them as men, some good, some bad, and I have yet to meet a single one who wishes to be here. They are following their Emperor's orders, and they would tell you that we were the ones who started this war." He glanced around as if to see if anyone might be listening.

Detestable man! "Only after they had invaded other countries! But I should have known you would take their side."

"If you think considering them as individuals faced with a situation not of their choosing is taking their side, then yes, I do."

With a huff, she turned to watch the dancers. No matter how handsome and amusing Mr. Darcy might be, he was a traitor, pure and simple.

At the end of the dance, she gave him only the curtest of thanks before Mr. Bingley came to claim her for the third dance.

Mr. Bingley brought her lemonade during the break before the fourth dance, returning just as Lydia descended upon them in all her glory, clad in a fashionable silk dress dripping with lace. She tapped Elizabeth's arm with her fan. "La, Lizzy, is that not last year's dress?"

"It is three years old, as you know well," said Elizabeth, but she bit her tongue before saying anything further about the source of Lydia's lovely gown. No matter how much she disapproved of Lydia's decision, she could not deny it had made her family's life more comfortable. Not that Lydia cared about anyone's comfort but her own, of course.

When Lydia moved on to preen her extravagant feathers in front of the other officers' wives, Bingley said, "Is that your youngest sister, then?"

"Sadly, it is. Forgive me for not introducing you. She is not fully respectable."

"I thought she had married a French officer."

Elizabeth flushed and moved closer to him so she could speak quietly. "She went through a marriage ceremony with him, it is true, but he has a wife and children in France. All indications are that he intends to return to his French wife someday, though Lydia is certain he loves only her and will never leave her."

"I suppose your parents had no choice but to allow it." Bingley sounded bitter.

"They did not try to stop it. He was quartered at Longbourn at the time, and Lydia was perfectly happy to succumb to his blandishments."

"Taking over our country was quite bad enough, but how dare they behave as if our women are their playthings!" said Bingley with some heat.

"Do you have sisters, Mr. Bingley?"

"I do, but they have protected themselves, at least to the extent they wish to. They have been very successful in French society circles in London. No, it is more that I hate watching how the French officers swoop in on the nearest pretty girl and treat her as their personal property." His scorn was strong enough to make Elizabeth wonder if he once had a *tendre* for one of those pretty girls.

Just then, Captain Reynard began to move in Elizabeth's direction. "Oh dear," she said softly to Mr. Bingley. "This may not be pleasant."

Miss Bennet – Darcy was going to have difficulty not thinking of her as Titania – had an odd, stiff expression when the captain of the garrison asked her to dance, and she did not move with her usual smoothness as the music began. Something was amiss. Was there going to be trouble? Darcy watched closely, just in case.

The trouble started almost immediately. The captain was holding Miss Bennet too closely as they waltzed. She had been light on her feet when she danced with Darcy, but now she looked clumsy. Her face was in shadow, perhaps because she was looking down. The captain was speaking to her at length, but her replies appeared to be no more than a word or two.

Then the captain slid his hand downward from her waist to her hip. Judging by the pleased smirk on his face, it was no accident. Darcy's hands wanted to clench into fists, but he forced them to relax and gritted his teeth instead. Visibly clenched fists could raise suspicions.

He could not afford to draw attention to himself by interrupting the dance, but he took a few deliberate strides until he was only a few steps away from the dancers, making it clear he was watching. Unfortunately, his mere observing presence seemed to have no effect on the captain's behavior.

Miss Bennet was practically stumbling over her own feet. Damn the man! Darcy would give it another minute or two, but then he would have to intervene, even if it did draw the wrong sort of attention.

Then she tripped while turning. With a sharp cry she staggered backwards, favoring her left foot.

"How clumsy I am! Pray forgive me, captain; I seem to have twisted my ankle." She began to hobble toward the seats by the wall.

The captain put his arm around her, his hand trespassing to a spot where it had no right to be. "Allow me to assist you, *ma chérie*."

Rage clouded Darcy's vision. Without stopping to consider his actions, he cut between them and scooped Miss Bennet up in his arms. "That is very kind of you, Captain, but I am sure Miss Bennet would not wish to be any trouble to you." He carried her towards the entrance to the hall.

She hissed, "Put me down! My ankle is fine."

He did not slacken his pace. "I know. I saw it all." Carefully he set her down in the chair nearest the door and gestured to a servant. "Have my carriage brought around immediately."

Elizabeth's face was flushed. "There is no need for any of this."

That was hardly news. Why had he reacted so angrily when the captain attempted to take liberties? Simply stepping in and saying something might have sufficed to stop it, and it would have drawn far less attention to him. Now he might well have made an enemy he could not

25

afford, all because he had not been able to tolerate that man touching a woman Darcy hardly even knew.

No, it was not just that. It had been the half hidden look of despair in Miss Bennet's fine eyes. It made him willing to do anything to rescue her, even if it meant forgetting his other responsibilities which ought to have taken precedence in his mind.

Now those fine eyes sparkled with irritation at him. Most likely she did not realize yet the consequences of what he had done. If he was luckier than he deserved, perhaps she never would. With a bow, he said, "I apologize if I overreacted." He could say nothing more, not with all those ears listening to his every word.

The dance behind him ended. A minute later Miss Lucas joined them, still breathing quickly from the exercise. "Is something the matter?"

Darcy spoke in his most authoritative voice. "Miss Bennet has injured her ankle. I think it best to take her home directly." From the expression of the nearby officer, his words had been noted, as he had intended.

Miss Lucas said something quiet into Miss Bennet's ear and received a nod in response. Her lips tightened. "Shall I inform Mr. Bingley?"

"I suspect there is no need. He is already headed this way." Of course he was; no one could have missed the little scene Darcy had made.

After Darcy made a quick explanation to Bingley, a servant informed him the carriage was outside. This time Darcy let Miss Bennet lean on his arm as she limped to the carriage. He handed her in, followed by Miss Lucas.

Their dark heads bent together, the two women were already conversing in low tones when he followed Bingley into the carriage. He rapped his cane on the roof to signal the driver to start up.

"Thank you for your assistance," said Miss Bennet, as if the words pained her. "It was a difficult situation."

"What happened?" asked Miss Lucas.

"Captain Reynard, of course. He asked me to dance and of course I could not refuse. It was dreadful, just like what happened to Jane. First he asked about Jane and said what a pity it was, then he told me I was almost as pretty as Jane, but in that horrible suggestive way he has. He said he wished to know me better, and he started to....Well, never mind. You can imagine."

"Oh, Lizzy, I am so sorry." Miss Lucas moved closer to her friend.

Miss Bennet said in an unsteady voice, "I do not think the consumption story would work twice, but I will think of something."

Bingley cleared his throat. "Might I inquire who Jane is?"

The two ladies looked at each other. Miss Bennet, apparently reaching a decision, said, "Jane is my elder sister. She is very beautiful and the captain decided to pursue her. He was not offering marriage, and he threatened to force our family from Longbourn if she did not agree."

"Despicable, completely despicable!" Bingley cried. "But I was told your elder sister was in the last stages of consumption."

"That is what you are supposed to think. She did not want to be his mistress nor to injure our family by refusing, so she decided to have consumption instead. We shaved her head and told everyone her hair had fallen out, and I painted her face so it would look as if she had sores all over it. I stained handkerchiefs with blood from my arm, and Jane would pretend to cough into them. She now lives in isolation and the only people who see her are my father, Charlotte, and me. The rest of my family cannot be trusted."

"That poor girl!" Bingley said. In a lower voice, he added, "That *brave* girl."

"We have been hoping he would be transferred away. Unfortunately, it has not happened." Her voice trembled.

Bingley leaned forward. "Do not despair. Darcy has bought you some time. The captain is unlikely to act while he thinks Darcy has an interest in you."

"Devil take it, Bingley!" snapped Darcy. "Enough of that."

27

"Why?" demanded his friend. "Should I let her live in terror to protect your precious privacy? You have done her a good turn; now let her have a little peace of mind."

"It is not that simple!" Darcy avoided Miss Bennet's eyes.

After brief silence, Miss Bennet spoke in a level, restrained voice. "It seems I owe you more thanks than I knew. But why would a captain in the French army defer to you?" Apparently even in a situation this unpleasant, she was reluctant to be indebted to him.

Darcy said dismissively, "It is all foolishness. The French are under the impression that I am single-handedly preventing rebellion in Derbyshire."

"And are you?"

"You must not be acquainted with the people of Derbyshire if you believe that I or any man could convince them not to rebel if they truly wished to." His voice was sharper than he had intended.

"Why do the French think it, then?"

His temper snapped at her obvious disbelief. "I cannot tell you why they believe it but I can tell you this – that I would indeed stop a rebellion there if it were in my power, and it has nothing to do with favoring the French. A rebellion would be a pointless endeavor, apart from making the rivers run red with blood when the French took their inevitable reprisals. I would not want another Newcastle massacre or the burning of Portsmouth on my conscience."

"Do you favor giving in to our conquerors to avoid risk?" Her voice was sharp.

"No. I favor keeping Englishmen from throwing their lives away when there is no chance of victory," said Darcy.

"Lizzy," said Miss Lucas in a low voice.

Miss Bennet shifted back on the bench, took several deep breaths and folded her hands in her lap. "My apologies, Mr. Darcy. We have all found our own ways to live with the French, and it is not my place to criticize the choices others have made. If you have spared me, even temporarily, from an untenable situation, I am grateful." But it was easy to see her words were recited rather than coming from her heart.

"You have no need to apologize for your loyalty." But his words were stilted. If only they could go back to the simplicity they had found in the bluebell wood! Rashly, he said, "I think I liked it better when I was Theophilus Thistle and you were pointing a pistol at me."

Her lips twitched. "I am sorry I cannot oblige you by doing so again, but the pistol does not fit into my reticule."

"If you did have it, I hope you would have used your bullet on a more deserving target at the assembly."

"Do not tempt me!" But she smiled as she said it.

Miss Lucas, apparently deciding this was as much of a truce as she could hope for, began to discuss the weather in a determined manner.

As the carriage pulled up to Longbourn, Darcy said, "Miss Bennet, if it would be better for your family to believe you truly did injure your ankle, my walking stick is available for you to employ as you hobble in."

She cocked her head to one side. "Thank you. It indeed would be wiser, and I would be glad to have your support for my story."

He had plenty of practice at false stories, after all. Once upon a time, disguise of every sort had been his abhorrence. Now he could hardly recall when he had not worn a disguise.

As he handed Miss Bennet out of the carriage, she looked at him seriously and said, "Theophilus Thistle, you puzzle me exceedingly."

He raised her gloved hand to his lips. "Queen Titania, if you should ever discover the answer to the puzzle, I hope you will share it with me."

Her scent of lavender lingered even after she was gone.

Elizabeth continued to limp for the remainder of the evening, but in the morning she declared her ankle much improved. Otherwise her imaginary injury might prevent her from visiting Jane, and she did not want that.

She was still in the house when Mr. Bingley called to inquire after her recovery. It was a remarkable civility on his part, given that he knew she had not been injured at all, but Elizabeth was not inclined to complain.

Mrs. Bennet could not contain her excitement at this apparent sign of interest in her least favorite daughter, so after the briefest possible conversation, she suggested that Elizabeth should show Mr. Bingley the gardens. He accepted with alacrity.

Once outside, Elizabeth said, "I apologize for my mother's assumptions. Pray be assured I have no expectations of you or anyone else." Would he realize she was referring to Mr. Darcy?

He laughed good-naturedly. "How could I have expectations when we established last night that Darcy has staked a claim to you?"

"Do not mention that! It is beyond embarrassing," cried Elizabeth.

"He would have come with me today except that he dislikes leaving his sister alone in a place she does not know well. After going out last night, he felt he should stay with her today."

Elizabeth raised an eyebrow. "He sounds like a most devoted brother."

"He is. He keeps Georgiana with him wherever he travels. She feels safer that way."

Elizabeth was in no mood to hear praise of Mr. Darcy, but Mr. Bingley's words gave her an idea. "I too have a sister to whom I am devoted. I wonder if I might take advantage of your amiability to impose upon you to meet my sister Jane. She is so very isolated, you see, and the sight of a new face would cheer her immensely. I daresay she is quite sick of Charlotte and me."

"I cannot imagine that to be true, but if you think it would please her, I would be more than happy to provide whatever amusement I may."

"I thank you. It will brighten her day. But I pray you, do not tell her about the events of last night. It would upset her greatly."

"Of course not."

When they reached the empty stables, Elizabeth told Bingley to wait at a distance before she knocked three times at the door.

Jane opened the door with a smile. "Good morning, Lizzy!" She stepped back to allow her sister to enter.

"Actually, Jane, I have a surprise for you. Would you like a visitor?"

Jane stiffened. "Is she someone you trust? Should I prepare?" She ran her fingertips down her cheek to indicate putting on makeup.

"No. *He* knows the truth, and yes, I do trust him."

Her sister's cheeks grew pink. "In that case, I would be delighted to meet him."

Elizabeth signaled to Mr. Bingley. He came forward with his customary amiable smile, but then his face took on a stunned expression which gave Elizabeth great satisfaction. Jane's hair had grown back enough to frame her face with golden curls. It suited her, and in a few months it would be long enough to pass for one of the fashionable cuts popular in London. And nothing could disguise the beauty of her face and form.

"Jane, dearest, may I present Mr. Bingley, who has recently let Netherfield Park? Mr. Bingley, this is my sister."

He bowed. "It is a very great pleasure to meet you, Miss Bennet, and an honor. Your sister has told me of your courage."

Elizabeth led the way into Jane's sitting room. "Mr. Bingley and his friend, Mr. Darcy, were kind enough to escort Charlotte and me to last evening's assembly. I had the presence of mind to turn my ankle rather than dance with a particularly unpleasant partner, and as a result I learned that Mr. Bingley has a great deal of sympathy for ladies whom the French attempt to misuse. I am most obliged to him and to his friend for their assistance."

31

Jane's eyes took on a warm glow. "Then I am also in your debt, Mr. Bingley. I thank you for helping my sister."

Mr. Bingley looked down at his feet. "Darcy deserves more credit than I do. It was his quick thinking that saved the day."

"Then I owe him my gratitude as well. Would you care to sit down? I am sorry I have nothing to offer you in the way of refreshment."

"That is my fault," said Elizabeth. "I should have gone back for a tea tray, but I did not wish to lose the opportunity to introduce you."

"And I am glad you did!" declared Mr. Bingley.

It was long past the half hour typical of the morning call when Elizabeth finally escorted a reluctant Mr. Bingley outside. With a hint of mischief, she said, "It was very kind of you to give so much of your time to Jane's entertainment."

He shook his head bemusedly. "It was far from a sacrifice. Your sister is an angel. That she should be forced into hiding and still retain such essential sweetness! I would not have believed it possible."

"Jane has always possessed the talent to see the best in any person or situation. It has served her well of late. I think I am more angered by her position than she is."

"You may be certain I am angry about it, too!" Bingley frowned. "Is there no other choice for her?"

"None that Jane would consider. If she were to leave Meryton for any reason, Captain Reynard would punish my father, so she chooses to stay."

"Would it..." He hesitated, his cheeks reddening. "Would it be possible for me to visit her again? Only if she would like it, of course."

"I think she would like it very much. I would be happy to accompany you there whenever you choose."

"You are very kind."

"You may ascribe that virtue to me if you like, but in truth I am thinking more of Jane. Her days are long and tedious, and I could see how much having a new visitor today improved her spirits."

Mr. Bingley's pace slowed. "If having visitors is helpful to her, I know someone who might equally benefit from making her acquaintance."

Not Mr. Darcy, please! "You do?"

"Darcy's sister. She is also limited in her acquaintance."

Did he truly think Mr. Darcy's half-witted sister would be good company for Jane? Carefully she asked, "Would she have much in common with my sister?"

"I imagine quite a bit." He must have seen something in her expression, for he added, "Oh! You have heard she is half-witted?"

Elizabeth looked away. "Someone mentioned it, I believe."

"Miss Darcy's half-wittedness is very much like your sister's consumption."

"But how...? Oh, I see. Yes, I imagine she and Jane would have a great deal in common." It also might explain why Mr. Darcy seems to hover over his sister so much. What was he protecting her from? Was it a situation like Jane's? "I am sorry to hear she has faced similar difficulties."

"I do not know the details, but she had an unfortunate experience during the invasion which has left her quite fearful. The sight of a French uniform sends her into a fit of terror, so she never goes out without Darcy. He is the only one who can calm her. I am one of the few people outside their family who has even met her. Darcy hopes visiting me at Netherfield will be good for her. She has never stayed in someone else's home this long."

"Poor girl. Perhaps Jane would be a good influence on her."

"I will speak to Darcy about it. If he does not object, I would be happy to introduce them." Mr. Bingley beamed at the thought.

Elizabeth suspected Mr. Bingley would seize any excuse to come back to see her sister.

Chapter Three

Darcy knew he was going to regret this. He had brought it on himself with his actions at the assembly, and now he had to follow through with the appearance of interest in Miss Elizabeth Bennet. Even if Bingley had not been so insistent about taking Georgiana to meet his new angel, Darcy would have had to make this journey to Longbourn.

But he could have traveled alone then, and that was half the problem. Elizabeth Bennet disturbed his peace of mind, yet he found himself craving her presence. He could not afford this sort of emotional turmoil. And he wanted to be alone with Elizabeth, not observed by Georgiana.

He had dreamed of her last night, of his Titania in the bluebell wood, but in his dream she had no pistol. Instead she held her hand out to him, beckoning him with that impish smile of hers. And he was all too ready to be beckoned.

Best not to think of the rest of that dream, though, not when he was about to be face-to-face with her. If Elizabeth ever discovered the content of that dream, she would slap his face and refuse ever to see him again. But even then, he would not go, because she was his Titania. Good God, now he was confusing dreams with reality!

Georgiana was watching him already, her finely arched brows drawn together in puzzlement as she twisted a ringlet around her finger. It was no wonder; he was not behaving like himself.

But the coach was drawing up in front of Longbourn, and it was too late to say anything now. "Georgiana, I suggest you remain here while I invite Miss Bennet to join us on a walk. I would rather avoid her sharp-eyed father at the moment, and her mother is not to be trusted."

"Very well," said Georgiana. "But if this makes you uncomfortable, perhaps we should not plan to repeat the visit."

"Let us see how it goes." The rational part of his mind – the small, overwhelmed rational part – considered the visit a good idea. Georgiana had been chafing at the bit this last year, longing for the company of other young people and frustrated by her isolation. An overly serious and solicitous elder brother who watched her every move was not the sort of companion any young girl would wish for. But what else could he do? He had to keep her safe.

Perhaps an acquaintance with the two eldest Bennet sisters was what she needed. What he needed did not matter. He had given up the right to consider his own needs.

After the carriage drew to a stop, a footman opened the door and flipped down the steps. Georgiana carefully rearranged her expression into her well-practiced façade of placid bovine stupidity.

It was wrong that a fifteen-year-old girl should have to learn so well how to wear a mask. But there was so little right in their world. Why should one more wrong matter? When he tried to remember his own carefree days before his father left, it was as if they had happened to someone else a long, long time ago.

He jumped out and rapped the head of his walking stick on the door of Longbourn. Elizabeth had used that stick the night of her supposed injury, and now he could not forget she had touched it. When a manservant opened the door, Darcy handed him a card and said brusquely, "My sister and I wish to inquire if Miss Elizabeth Bennet would do us the honor of joining us on a walk."

"I will ask, sir. Would you care to come inside?"

"I prefer the fresh air." It was impolite but he did not care. He could not leave Georgiana alone in a strange place.

The sun seemed to shine more brightly when Miss Bennet appeared wearing a bonnet and spencer. Good. She must be planning to join them. But he must remember to call her Miss Elizabeth, not Miss Bennet, since her elder sister was the true Miss Bennet. Miss Elizabeth. He liked the sound of it. And he liked seeing her altogether too much. He must not let anyone guess how much her mere presence lightened his heart.

"Good morning, Mr. Darcy." Her smile was cautious.

"Thank you for joining us. May I present my sister to you? Georgiana, this is Miss Elizabeth Bennet."

Georgiana descended from the carriage and curtsied clumsily. She spoke in the strange, flattened voice she employed when playing the half-wit. "It is a pleasure to meet you."

Had he not made it clear to her that Bingley had already told Miss Elizabeth the truth? Then he looked back over his shoulder. The manservant stood in the doorway watching them. Georgiana was simply being careful, just as he had taught her.

Darcy turned back to Elizabeth. "Bingley told me you enjoy long walks but often lack the company to take them. We came to offer our services in that regard. May I hope you will consent to accompany us?"

"I would be very glad to do so. I am indeed a great walker when I have the opportunity, which is not as often as I would like." There was an odd wistfulness in her voice.

Why could she not take walks? "It is my special pleasure, then, to share one of those rare occasions. Since I am new to the area, I do not know the best walks hereabouts. Perhaps you could recommend a route?"

"I would be happy to. One of my favorite walks begins this way." She gestured towards an old track which disappeared behind a row of trees.

As they set off together, she added in a low voice, "If Mr. Bingley sent you, I assume you must be here to meet my sister. Is that correct?"

"We hope to meet her, but she is far from the only attraction here." Despite Bingley's praise of the mysterious sister's beauty, Darcy could not help thinking he would prefer his own Titania.

Miss Elizabeth looked past him towards Georgiana, who had dropped her half-wit role. "Tell me, Miss Darcy, does your brother always flirt with the ladies he meets?"

Georgiana's quick shake of her head showed her disbelief. "William? He never flirts. Ever."

"Truly? How interesting. What say you, Mr. Darcy?" The teasing glint in her eyes was a challenge.

His lips twitched. "It would depend upon the lady. I am quite selective."

"And thus you answer my question! Now, if you will come this way, Jane's rooms are at the back."

He followed her past a series of empty stalls. Had they built a new stable or were all their horses taken by the French? Most likely the latter.

A golden haired woman opened the door that Miss Elizabeth knocked at. For once Bingley had been correct about Miss Bennet's beauty, although Darcy preferred more liveliness in a woman's expression. He fought the urge to rest his eyes on Miss Elizabeth. He should be focusing his attention on Georgiana.

As Elizabeth made the introductions, his sister seemed to manage well in the conversation despite her limited experience with strangers. Until the last year or so, she could not be trusted not to blurt out something inappropriate or dangerous.

Miss Bennet seemed a safe sort of acquaintance, especially as she was not in a position to spread gossip. She was almost maternal in her behavior towards Georgiana, gently drawing the girl out. If Georgiana liked her, this could indeed be a step forward.

After a short time, Elizabeth said, "Mr. Darcy, you are very quiet. I hope we are not boring you." It was a challenge, no doubt about it.

"Not at all. I simply prefer to admire the   conversation rather than to participate in it."

Georgiana bounced in her chair. "He means he is too busy watching over me. Do go away, William! I do not need to be hovered over every moment."

He did not know if he was more annoyed by her presumption or pleased to see her show some liveliness. He gave a slight bow. "If you wish."

Miss Bennet said hurriedly, "I have hardly had a chance to exchange a few words with your brother. If he is to leave now, I hope we will have another chance to meet soon."

Georgiana bit her lip, a stricken look in her eyes. No doubt she was worrying, as she always did, that someone would be angry at her for any slight mistake.

Elizabeth rose from her chair with a laugh. "Whereas I thank you, Miss Darcy, for sending your brother away, for now I can insist on his taking me on that long walk he promised earlier."

Darcy inclined his head. How neatly she had turned that situation around! "It would be my very great pleasure. Georgiana, if it is acceptable to Miss Bennet, I will return later for you."

He followed Elizabeth out of the stable. "Is there anywhere in particular you would like to walk, Miss Elizabeth?"

She studied him for a moment. "We should not be gone for too long, so it cannot be a lengthy walk. Might we visit the puppies? I have not had the opportunity to check on them for several days."

The air around him seemed to lighten. "Queen Titania, your humble servant would be delighted to escort you to your bower."

Elizabeth stroked Rose's furry head as the bluebells danced around them. "You have been doing an excellent job," she told the dog.

Darcy looked up from the puppy who had engaged him in a ferocious game of tug-of-war over a stick. "Is this her first litter?"

"Yes, and it cannot be easy to manage with so many puppies." She picked up a particularly tiny puppy and put it to nurse on its mother. "But not, I imagine, as hard as caring for a girl at the most difficult age. Have you been responsible for your sister for long?"

"Almost six years, ever since my father left. He had planned for Georgiana to live with my aunt and uncle, but when my uncle suffered an apoplexy, I had to take over. And she is right; I do hover over her."

Six years ago? He must have been little more than twenty himself. Then his words struck her. "Your father left?"

Mr. Darcy gave her a long serious look. "Yes. He went to Canada in '05."

A large landowner moving to Canada? It made no sense. Unless... "With *her*?"

The corner of his mouth twitched down. "It is not illegal to say her name. Yes, he accompanied Princess Charlotte when she was spirited away to Canada for safety, poor girl."

"I have wondered who went with her. At such a young age, it must have been very hard for her to leave her family and country."

"Yes, and now the family she left behind no longer exists. Her grandfather, King George, is a madman imprisoned in France, ruling in name only. The princess would have been executed like her father, the Prince Regent, had she remained here. But she still has lost her place in the succession with Napoleon's brother declared heir to the throne in her place and married to King George's youngest daughter as a sop to English pride." Darcy's upper lip curled.

"I do not accept that, nor does anyone I know. According to English law, Princess Charlotte is still heir to the throne."

"But there is no English law now, only a scared little girl half a world away with the entire country waiting for her to save them when neither the king nor the military and naval might of England could do so. Perhaps they think she will bring the French to their knees by throwing her dolls at them." Bitterness edged his words.

Was that his true opinion, or was he repeating his father's words about the princess? She supposed Darcy had a right to be bitter, having been left to raise his young sister alone and to care for the family estates in the face of an invasion. "Is your father still in Canada?"

"He died last year." He sounded indifferent, but she had already learned he had hidden depths. "I should not have told you any of that. As far as the world knows, my father died in the invasion."

"You may be certain I will say nothing, but I am sorry for your loss." She understood his desire for secrecy. If his father's actions were known to the French, both Darcy and his sister would have been in grave danger. Others had been guillotined for less. Still, it was baffling. His father had been loyal enough to go into exile rather than live under French rule, but his son had become a turncoat. It did not make sense.

"It is better if everyone believes he died long ago. It is simpler that way." He wrestled the stick away from Puck, who immediately started yapping.

There was something missing from this puzzle, but Elizabeth had already pried far more than was polite. "I cannot believe how these puppies have grown in just a few days! I wish I could see them every day to watch how they change."

"But you cannot?"

She picked up a puppy and kissed its head. "I do not travel this far from Longbourn without the pistol, but often it is not available to me."

It was just a fact of life. Why did it make him frown so ferociously?

Darcy minded his tongue as he and Elizabeth returned to the stable. He had already told her too much, and it had to stop. No matter how well-meaning Elizabeth might be, she was not in the habit of disguising her feelings or considering what she said before it left her mouth. But she was far too easy to confide in.

When had he started thinking of her as Elizabeth?

It was hard to see anything at first when they entered the dim stables from the bright sunshine. Elizabeth halted beside him with a sharp indrawn breath.

"Is something the matter?" he asked.

She put a finger to her lips and gestured towards one of the stalls, now occupied by a large bay. "Someone has been here."

In this at least he could reassure her. "That is Bingley's horse."

Her shoulders lost some of their stiffness. "I see." But her voice still trembled. She had been well and truly frightened. A rush of anger filled him. She should not have to worry so much.

Bingley was, of course, in Miss Bennet's tiny sitting room and looking as enamored as Darcy had ever seen him. Georgiana appeared to be at ease. A good sign.

Elizabeth halted in the doorway. "How lovely to see you with all this company! I will fetch your tea tray."

Was she displeased to find Bingley there? He could think of no other reason why she would try to leave the moment she had arrived. But only three chairs were available in the room. Perhaps she was being tactful.

"Might I accompany you?" asked Darcy.

She paused in the process of leaving. "If you wish." But she sounded puzzled.

"Yes, I wish," he said firmly.

Once outside, she turned to face him. "This is a perfectly safe walk. I do it twice a day."

"I do not doubt it. But neither Bingley nor Georgiana wish to divide your sister's attention with me. This was a simple way to give them their wish."

"Oh." She sounded satisfied by his answer. "Is it your opinion Mr. Bingley might continue to call on my sister? Not as a suitor, of course, but as a friend?"

Had she not seen Bingley's besotted look? "I would be surprised if he did not."

She hesitated. "Could you give him a message from me?"

"Certainly."

She bit her lip. "It would not do for word to get out that Jane has regular visitors, and it will look suspicious if Mr. Bingley is seen regularly traveling past Longbourn. Could you tell him that if he continues down the track by the stables it will rejoin the road without passing the house? I do not intend to suggest he should visit her illicitly, just without fanfare."

"I will tell him so and assure him this is not an attempt at entrapment."

Now she looked shocked. "How could it be? Jane cannot marry. That would be tantamount to refusing Captain Reynard. We would all suffer for it."

"Are you still worried about Captain Reynard on your own behalf as well?"

She hesitated. "I have heard nothing further from him."

That was not the question he had asked. "If Georgiana wishes to visit your sister again, is the route you mentioned passable by carriage?"

"I would have to check. Parts of it are somewhat overgrown."

"What if she and I called to invite you for a walk as we did today?"

"That would not be a problem, but it might take up a great deal of your time."

"You forget I will be calling on you in any case to keep up appearances." He tried to say it lightly.

She frowned and said nothing, but perhaps that was because they had reached the kitchen door of Longbourn. When she reemerged with the tea tray, he took it from her. Watching her do a servant's work was intolerable.

After the visitors had left, Elizabeth said to Jane, "I hope you found your visitors diverting."

"Oh, very much so! The day has gone so quickly. I am grateful to you for finding new friends for me."

"I am glad. What did you think of Miss Darcy? I did not have much chance to observe her."

Jane hesitated, but then she smiled. "I like her very much. She seems to be a sweet girl, even if she is unaccustomed to speaking to someone she barely knows. It seemed to be shyness rather than pride. Did you know she fences? I have never known a woman who fenced before."

Apparently Mr. Darcy had unusual ideas for women's education! "It is a rather shocking idea, but not without its appeal. Her brother told me she practices shooting, too."

"She also has ladylike accomplishments. She talked so enthusiastically about her love for Mozart and Haydn and how much she enjoys playing the pianoforte. Mr. Bingley said she has had little opportunity to spend time with ladies, and he thought it would help her to know me. He is such a kind, thoughtful gentleman."

"I thought you would like him." Elizabeth tried not to sound smug.

"Oh, very much! If only I had met him before all this I think I might be falling in love with him."

"After only two meetings?" Elizabeth teased.

Jane's expression grew dreamy. "Sometimes you just know."

Elizabeth quickly put on her bonnet and gloves when she saw the Darcy coach approaching Longbourn the following day. Once again, she and Mr. Darcy escorted Georgiana to Jane's rooms before taking a walk. Charlotte Lucas was already visiting Jane, so it was easy for Elizabeth to excuse herself to walk with Darcy.

When they were by themselves, Darcy cleared his throat. "I find myself in a dilemma. There is an item I greatly wish you to have at your disposal, but it would be improper for me to give you a gift. Would you perhaps be willing to consider it as a sort of permanent loan?"

Elizabeth drew back slightly. How puzzling! He sounded very serious, not at all as if he planned to flirt with her. "I suppose it would depend on what the item is and why you wish me to have it."

"That seems fair." He reached into his pocket and handed her a small muff pistol with an engraved barrel. "I think you know why I wish you to have it. For the sake of the puppies, if nothing else."

She turned it over in her hand, admiring the carved ivory handle. Such a lovely object to be a dangerous weapon! But of course Mr. Darcy would have the best. "I do not know what to say." Especially as owning pistols was illegal, for him as well as for her.

"You could say you will accept it. Come, do you know how to load it?"

"It is not muzzle loaded, then?"

"No." He took it from her and unscrewed the barrel from the handle. Turning the handle section to face up, he pointed at the opening where the barrel had been. "Black powder here, and then a ball. Do not tamp it down; just screw the barrel back on." He demonstrated, then pointed at a tiny opening beneath the flashing pan. "A touch more black powder here and you are ready to fire."

What was a lady to say when receiving the gift of a pistol? *Thank you, it is very lovely? Thank you, I will do my best to shoot only villains with it? Thank you, there is nothing I like better than a lethal firearm? Thank you, I promise not to turn you in for possessing an illegal pistol?*

Perhaps it was simplest to avoid thanking him at all. "I am certain the puppies would be grateful to you."

"You will accept it, then?"

"Are you certain you do not need it? I cannot imagine you have spare pistols lying about waiting to be given to hapless damsels in distress."

He muttered something under his breath. It sounded like "You would be surprised." Aloud he said, "I have others." He handed her a cloth bag and small embossed flask. "Powder and shot."

Both hands now full, she looked up at him mischievously. "I will do my best not to employ it."

"If you need it, use it."

She smiled up at him "I know just the place to keep them – a cubbyhole in the stables. It might be difficult to explain their presence if someone found them in my room!"

To the delight of Mrs. Bennet, Mr. Darcy and his sister continued to call on Elizabeth on days when the weather was clement.

"Lizzy, I cannot believe you have attached a single English gentleman with a fortune! What luck, with so few available! Providence is watching over you. Such pin money you will have! Such dresses! Such carriages!"

It was a novel experience for Elizabeth, who had become accustomed to her mother's constant disapproval, but her attempts to lower her mother's expectations failed. "I believe he comes primarily because he wishes for his sister to have female companionship, not for his own pleasure. And he is still a French agent – no fortune can wash that stink away."

"Nonsense, Lizzy, how you do go on! Of course he wishes for you to be friends with his sister before making you an offer! I shall go distracted if I think of it."

As it happened, Miss Darcy was a common topic of conversation on Elizabeth's walks with Mr. Darcy. There were so many topics to be avoided that Elizabeth clung to the few that remained, and Mr. Darcy seemed to be glad of the opportunity to hear a woman's view of his sister.

"She has lived almost in seclusion since the invasion," Darcy told Elizabeth. "I have only just begun introducing her to other people in the last year. She has had a music master, of course, and a woman who taught her to paint watercolors, but even those were difficult for her."

"What of servants? Surely she must have dealt with them."

Darcy looked away. "She is uncomfortable with servants and does not trust them. This is why your sister has been a godsend. Georgiana feels safe with her precisely because your sister's life is as constrained as her own. It is a step forward for her to be so comfortable with both Bingley and Miss Bennet."

"It seems you spend a great deal of time in her company. If she has difficulty being around others, does not that limit your ability to socialize?"

He ran his hand along the needles of a fir tree they were passing, keeping his gaze upon it. "It does, but that is of no great importance to me. I have little interest in the events of the *ton,* and I can be happy spending the evening in the company of a good book. When we are in London, there are events I am obliged to attend, but it is difficult for Georgiana to be alone so many evenings, and she is glad when we leave the city."

What sort of events could make him feel he had no choice but to attend? It was most likely wiser not to ask. "To think that sometimes I feel sorry for myself because seeing to Jane's needs limits what I can do! You show me how little I have to complain of. And indeed, I am happy to be able to help Jane."

He turned a searching gaze on her. "What would you do if you did not have to tend to your sister?"

What was it about his eyes that made her mouth go dry and her body flood with warmth? Her fingers itched with the urge to explore his face. She pulled her attention away from him before she could respond. "Most likely I would go to Scotland."

"Is that what you would do if Captain Reynard persisted in his attentions to you?"

Her cheeks grew hot and she looked down at the footpath. "Yes," she said in a low voice. "I am not proud of it because I know full well how selfish it would be to abandon my father and Jane here to suffer Captain Reynard's displeasure. But I am not Jane; I cannot sacrifice myself for them."

Darcy halted, and when Elizabeth turned to see why, he put his finger under her chin and lifted it until she had no choice but to meet his eyes. "You are not being selfish. It is your father who is selfish if he would want you to pay that price for his comfort. He should be taking the entire family to Scotland. What would you think of me if I were willing to allow Georgiana to degrade herself in that manner merely so I could remain in my home?"

The intensity of his gaze made her swallow hard, her lips tingling. "I cannot imagine you doing that."

"Do you think it is right for your father to allow your sister to hide in the stables all this time?"

She looked away. "Jane could stay in the house if she chose, but it would mean pretending to be sick all of the time. It was her idea to move to the stables, claiming the doctor said she needed complete quiet. My mother was happy to agree since Jane's coughing irritated her nerves."

He shook his head. "How long has that been going on?"

Elizabeth touched the tip of her tongue to her dry lips. "Almost a year."

"God in heaven!" he swore. "Is your family so little to be trusted?"

47

"My sister Mary, perhaps, but we cannot be certain. My mother supports the French because it means Longbourn will stay in our family. Under English law it was entailed away, and the French civil code breaks the entail. She would urge Jane to do as the captain wishes."

"Does your father know?"

"Yes, but he has never been a man of action. His nature is to be indolent and to avoid conflicts. That is why Jane and I were sent to live in London after the invasion."

Frown lines appeared between Darcy's brows. "I do not understand."

"The French had taken Longbourn for one of their barracks, so we had to move into our steward's cottage. Jane was sixteen and I was almost fifteen. The cottage was crowded with all of us, and the soldiers were always trying to corner Jane or me. Rather than demand that they leave us alone, my father sent us to live with our uncle in London. It turned out well for me; in London there were fewer French soldiers since they could enforce the peace with the cannons of the warships anchored in the Thames. But even so, I longed to come back to Meryton. When the French no longer needed Longbourn and returned it to my father, Jane and I came back, and now I wish we had not." Why had she told him all that? She could have answered his question with far fewer details.

The corners of his mouth turned up. "I have the opposite reaction to London. When I am there, I am constantly in company with the French – those unavoidable obligations. I can avoid them much better when I am in the country."

Any desire to respond froze in her throat. Why did she keep forgetting that he cooperated with the French? Or not precisely forgetting, but more wishing for it not to be true. But it was true. "I can see why you would not enjoy that sort of obligation," she said coolly.

His lips tightened, the warm look fading from his eyes. "I do what I must, just as you do."

The brief intimacy was over, cut short by the reminder of his betrayal of England. How could she be so drawn to such a man?

"Lizzy? Did you hear a word I said?" Jane asked.

Startled, Elizabeth shook her head. "My apologies, Jane. My mind was wandering."

A smile brought light to Jane's eyes. "Did your body not wander far enough today? You and Mr. Darcy were gone a long time."

Elizabeth shrugged. "We walked to Oakham Mount."

"He seems to enjoy your company."

"Not you, too! Mama keeps telling me he will be making an offer soon, and she will be sadly disappointed when it does not come to pass."

"Is it so impossible that he might like you?"

"He likes me, yes, but to choose me out of the thousands of women who would be delighted to marry an Englishman with a large fortune when both single Englishmen and large fortunes are in short supply? I think not."

"You are out of sorts today, Lizzy. Now I begin to wonder if you might like him better than you wish to."

Elizabeth did not dare to meet her sister's gaze. Jane had come too close to the truth. "He is clever and pleasant company, but there is no point in thinking more of it. Even if he did make me an offer, I would have to refuse him. I will not marry a French sympathizer."

Jane's brows drew together. "It is odd. Both Mr. Bingley and Miss Darcy seem to think him an honorable man, and he shows concern for your well-being. Many good men have assisted the French simply to protect their families. If the French were to take Mr. Darcy's land and money, how would he care for his sister?"

"It is rare for the French to take everything. They took Longbourn at first and most of father's money, but they left enough for us to survive on and a cottage where we could live until they were done with Longbourn." Elizabeth could not permit herself to accept excuses for Mr. Darcy.

"But Mr. Darcy might be treated more harshly because he has aristocratic connections. The Earl of Matlock, or perhaps I should say the former earl, was his uncle. The French hate the aristocracy."

"Jane, you will always believe the best of everyone. I cannot do so." Especially since then she might not be able to suppress certain feelings she could not afford to feel.

She had realized long ago she was unlikely ever to marry. There simply were not enough single men. So many men had been killed during the invasion, and a large portion of those who had survived it had been conscripted into Napoleon's army. Perhaps someday a small number of them might return, but even that would make little difference. Marriageable gentlemen were few, and they could take their pick of well-dowered beauties. Even men with injuries from the war were quickly surrounded by eligible women. Some English women preferred a French husband to no husband at all, but Elizabeth would sooner cut off her own hand. But she also did not wish to spend her life longing for something she could not have. It was easier to accept that all she would ever have in terms of romance were occasional flirtations. There was no point in wishing for more.

Why did Mr. Darcy have to come to Meryton and meddle with her plans and dreams? She had spent more time in conversation with him than she had with any other man apart from her father and uncle. He listened to what she said, studying her with dark, intent eyes that raised those longings she had so carefully packed away. He had awoken feelings in her that were best left dormant, a yearning to step closer to him, to gaze into those dark eyes and to trace her fingertip along the edge of his lips. Would they feel as firm as they looked, or would they be soft and warm? Then she would caress the line of his jaw, so clearly defined and strong. How would he react? Would he look shocked or dismayed, or would he possibly be pleased?

She had to stop thinking this way. He had betrayed England by supporting the French. He was undeniably handsome, well-educated, witty, kind, and protective – and he was a traitor.

Briskly she said, "I have been gone too long. I should return the tea tray before someone comes looking for me."

She would stop allowing Darcy's image to float before her at odd moments. She would not think about the way he tilted his head to the side when he was contemplating an idea. And she would not count the hours until she might see him again.

Darcy was spending far too much energy counting hours until the next time he would see Elizabeth. His heart beat faster each time they approached Longbourn.

But on the next fine day, Elizabeth did not greet him with her usual warm smile. No, her expression was a shadow of that smile, a mere curving of her lips in an attempt to appear socially pleasing. Worse yet, her eyes were red-rimmed. She carried a basket over her arm. "Good day, sir. I hope I can persuade you to walk with me to Lucas Lodge. I have an errand to discharge there." She indicated the basket.

He bit his tongue to stop himself from demanding to know what was wrong. What would have made Elizabeth cry? If the captain had been bothering her again, Darcy would rip him limb from limb. But propriety demanded that he restrict himself to polite nothings. "I will be happy to escort you wherever you wish to go."

After leaving Georgiana with Miss Bennet, they proceeded down the lane. Usually Elizabeth would find something to tease him about as they walked, but today she did not look at him. His attempts at conversation were met with brief responses.

Was she angry at him? Perhaps it was about his supposed French sympathies, but she had known about that all along. As they neared Lucas

Lodge, he could not hold himself back any longer. "Has Captain Reynard been troubling you?"

At least she turned her head towards him this time as she spoke. "I have not heard from him since the night of the assembly. I hope he has made no difficulty for you."

"Not at all." But that still did not explain her distress.

The gatehouse of Lucas Lodge was decked in black bunting. Darcy shot Elizabeth a look. "May I ask for whom they are mourning?"

"No one you have met. Charlotte's brother John." Her voice hitched. "In Spain, of course. They received an express yesterday."

That must be the brother who had been conscripted into Napoleon's army. Had his death been the cause of Elizabeth's tears? The idea of her crying over another man stung. "I am grieved to hear it. You knew him well?"

"Yes."

When she said nothing further, Darcy asked, "Is this a condolence call, then?" It would leave him in an odd position.

"No. I called on them this morning. I offered to visit Mr. Robinson to spare Charlotte the effort. Usually the task falls to her."

"It is kind of you to do it."

"Ah, but was it kind of me to force you into helping?" This time her smile was genuine, if small.

Darcy had never been so grateful to be teased.

After they left Mr. Robinson's cottage, Darcy said, "I had assumed you were making a charity visit to a poor tenant. I was surprised to discover the object to be an elderly gentleman instead. He reminded me of my grandfather."

"Mr. Robinson? He is a neighbor who has fallen on hard times. He is a good-hearted man, even if he is forgetful, and we are trying to help in his time of troubles. Sir William Lucas has generously allowed him to live here."

"What happened to him?"

Elizabeth scowled. "Captain Reynard decided Mr. Robinson's house would suit him as his residence. Mr. Robinson refused to leave, so he was arrested for treason. For reading *The Loyalist*, to be precise. Captain Reynard agreed to let him go if he gave up the house. Of course, all his goods and money were still forfeit because of the so-called treason. Now he has nothing to live on but charity."

"Damn the man!" Darcy's face grew pale. "For what little it is worth, I have sent a letter to London complaining of his behavior, and I hope they will investigate soon. But there are too many like him, Frenchmen who have risen beyond their station and look at this country as their personal property to pillage at will, and I cannot request an intervention on every single one."

"I thank you for your attempt to help," said Elizabeth. "But I do not understand you. If you feel so strongly about the French misusing us, why are you helping them?"

Darcy's nostrils flared. "Because life is not simple. Because when the choice came before me, whatever I did would betray something or someone I loved. My aunt, Lady Catherine de Bourgh, was killed when she refused to allow the French on her lands. Her invalid daughter now lives in Pemberley under my care. My uncle, the Earl of Matlock, suffered an apoplexy after the French took everything he owned, and he and his wife also came to Pemberley. Although he has left this earth, his wife still needs a roof over her head. My tenants and all my servants would otherwise face conscription and ruinous taxes. Should I have betrayed my family and my tenants for the sake of my precious honor as an Englishman? Or was I right to sell a portion of my soul so I could protect them all? My death would serve no one. It would not save a single inch of English soil." He paused to stare at her searchingly. "But it does not mean

I have to like it when I watch Napoleon's dogs use Englishmen as their slaves."

Taken aback by his sudden ferocity, Elizabeth said, "I did not mean to suggest you had no reason for your choice —"

"Yes, you did mean to suggest that, and ever since we met you have been implying that all I care about is money and my estate. The price I paid is far higher than money or land." His hands were clenched and he was breathing hard. "Should I have let my invalid cousin die on the streets? Should I have left my aunt and uncle homeless and destitute? What would have happened to Georgiana? Starvation or selling herself to the French? Tell me you think I should have allowed those things to happen to protect my honor as an Englishman. Tell me straight out that you think I should have fought back at the price of all those lives. Tell me that, if you can!"

She hesitated. Could she have done it? She was willing to have her family lose Longbourn to protect her from Captain Reynard, but they had relatives who could take them in, and she had never feared they might starve. Slowly she shook her head.

"You see?" Darcy's eyes seemed to pierce her. "It costs you nothing to speak against the French. Nothing. No one will kill the people you love if you do. You cannot possibly understand my choices."

Elizabeth's throat tightened. "I... I am sorry. You are correct that I do not understand. I have seen so many gentlemen cooperate simply to maintain their standard of life. Even the Prince Regent accepted their rule as long as he could live in luxury at Carlton House."

"And where is Prinny now? Guillotined after the London uprising. We have no army, no navy, no government, only a mad king held hostage in Paris – and we face the greatest military genius the world has known. One day Napoleon will die and his empire will disintegrate under its own weight, but until then, all we can do is to try to survive and be prepared to reclaim our country when we can." He halted, rubbed his hand over his mouth, and turned away.

Apparently the controlled Mr. Darcy had hidden passions. But it hurt to see him suffer, knowing it was her fault, that she had pushed him too hard and created this pain. "You are right," she said, her voice low. "I do not like to admit how hopeless our situation is. I hate seeing our people bending their necks to the French yoke and groveling for favors from our conquerors. But there are no good choices."

Still he kept his back to her. Should she say something else or would it only make it worse? Oh, why had she kept pressing him on his connections with the French?

Finally, when she thought she could not bear it another minute, he turned back to her. His face was devoid of all expression. "I apologize for my unseemly outburst. I freely chose my lot, and I have no reason to complain of it."

"Mr. Darcy, I would prefer to have you scold me than to pretend nothing has happened."

"I wish I could oblige you, Miss Elizabeth; however, some matters are better not spoken of. Perhaps we should return to Longbourn now."

They did not usually turn back so early, but Elizabeth nodded her head jerkily. She did not trust her voice. Only now that he had withdrawn his warmth and teasing did she realize how much it had come to mean to her. She wrapped her arms around herself as if she were cold, despite the warm spring day.

She waited to see if he would speak to her again as they walked, but he was firm in his silence. Should she say something? Would a new subject be better or would that make things worse? If only she knew what to do!

Instead she formed a desperate resolve. When they reached the stable and he held the door for her, she stepped halfway through and turned to face him, her heart pounding. "Shall I see you again after today, Mr. Darcy?"

His mouth twisted. "No doubt." It sounded more like a penalty than a choice. "You would oblige me if you would forget every word I said today."

With a weak attempt at a smile, she raised a hand to her ear and mimed pulling something out of it. Opening her fingers as if to release the imaginary item, she said, "Poof! Gone." Hot tears gathered in the corners of her eyes, and she blinked them back.

But apparently he had seen them already. "No. I pray you...I cannot!"

She lifted her chin. Swallowing hard, she said, "Well, as usual, I cannot understand a thing you say. But Jane will be waiting." She turned on her heel and walked quickly towards the back of the stable.

She did not look at him again even after they were with the others.

Chapter Four

In the carriage, Darcy's fingernails dug into the palms of his tightly clenched fists, but he kept them out of Georgiana's view. What in God's name had possessed him to open his soul to Elizabeth Bennet? After all these years of hiding his motivations from the world, he had been within an inch of telling her everything. Was he out of his mind?

What did it matter if she thought him the worst kind of traitor to his country? So did many other people. He knew the truth and nothing else mattered. Or at least it had not until Elizabeth Bennet looked at him with those accusing eyes.

All the reasons he had given her were true. They simply were not the real reason. If only he could tell her all of it! But there was too much at stake, far more than she could ever imagine.

Georgiana said timidly, "I am sorry if I have done something wrong. I do not mean to make you angry."

He forced his hands to relax. "You have done nothing wrong, and I am not angry with you," he said warily.

"I know I am not always easy to be with or ladylike enough, but I will try harder. You do so much for me, and I have done little enough to deserve it. I am very grateful to you." The words seem to rush out of her mouth.

How he hated it when she became anxious like this! "Truly, Georgiana, this has nothing to do with you. If you must know, I quarreled with Miss Elizabeth. She disapproves of my politics." He could not help saying it bitterly.

"Oh, no! That is the most unfair thing in the world! Should I tell her the truth?"

He froze. "Absolutely not! You are never to tell anyone the truth!"

She shrank away from his anger. When had he become such a bully? He tried again. "I apologize; I am simply in a bad temper today. Perhaps I need more of a walk to settle my mind. Would you mind if I got out in Meryton and walked the rest of the way? You would be perfectly safe with John Coachman."

If he left the carriage in Meryton, he would not subject Georgiana to more of his temper. Perhaps he could even find a trinket for her in one of the shops. That might reassure her a little.

"Whatever you think is best, William."

He forced his voice to be gentle. "Truly, I am not angry at you."

The only problem was that it was not the truth.

He *was* angry with Georgiana, angry for all the secrets he had to keep on her behalf, angry at the compromises he had to make because of her, and above all angry because he could not have a future with a woman because of her. Because of Georgiana, Elizabeth Bennet was as far out of his reach as if she were on the moon.

There it was. And he was angry.

But it was not Georgiana's fault. She had not asked for this situation any more than he had, and the price for her was just as high. And she needed him.

When they reached the town, Darcy rapped on the roof of the carriage to tell the coachman to stop. "I will see you back at Netherfield soon," he told Georgiana.

"I promise you I will stay out of trouble. I will practice my music the whole time." Her eyes beseeched him.

He patted her arm as he opened the coach door. "I will look forward to hearing you play, but I am still not angry at you."

He waved as the carriage pulled away. He needed to give her more independence. After all, what could go wrong in the two mile drive to Netherfield?

Highwaymen. A squad of French soldiers who would overcome John Coachman and the groom. A broken axle that would leave her stranded by the side of the road.

Now he wanted to race after the carriage and keep Georgiana under his eye for the rest of her life. But that was ridiculous. She needed to be more independent, and this was a good time to practice that. If it made her nervous, that was something they would need to discuss. He needed a little freedom, too.

Or was freedom truly all he wanted? Had he agreed to let Georgiana visit alone with Miss Bennet because it was in her best interest or because he wanted to be alone with Elizabeth?

He knew the answer to that question. He had been selfish.

He ducked his head under a low lintel as he stepped into the milliner's shop. Without much thought, he chose a shawl for Georgiana in her favorite shade of green. He turned his eyes away from the silver one shot with red ribbons that would suit Elizabeth so well. She always dressed in drab colors, her hair pulled back without ornament. No doubt it helped her avoid unwanted attention from the soldiers, but Darcy wished he could see her when she was not deliberately hiding her attractiveness, when her dress and her hair could match the beauty of her fine eyes.

But there was no point in dreaming. Darcy made his purchase and left the shop, crossing the street to avoid a group of drunken French soldiers who were calling out at two young women whom he sincerely hoped did not understand French. He started off in the direction of Netherfield.

He had not even reached the edge of town when a familiar mocking voice came from behind him

"Well, well, well! If it is not the great Fitzwilliam Darcy trudging down a provincial road. How the mighty are fallen!"

Slowly Darcy turned on his heel. "Wickham." He allowed his eyes to drift down over the French uniform his childhood friend was wearing and tried not to curl his lip. "I had not known you were in Meryton."

"Or you would not have come here yourself? Is that any way to greet an old friend? And you cannot ignore me when I am in uniform." Naturally Wickham would enjoy that power.

Darcy raised an eyebrow. "How did you arrange to avoid being sent to the front like all the other English conscripts?"

With a cold smile, Wickham said, "I am more useful here as a translator, thanks to the gentlemen's education your father gave me, both in French and how to speak with a proper accent."

"A favor which you repaid by betraying his location," Darcy said icily. It was a shot in the dark, but of all the people who had known where to find his father, Wickham was the most likely culprit.

"Unkind of me, I know, but I had to save my own skin first. Besides, I gather he escaped before the troops found him. Where did he go?"

It had been Wickham after all. Darcy shrugged. "Killed in the first assault, we assume, and buried in an anonymous grave."

"While you made a deal with the French! I would never have thought you would bend that stiff neck of yours, but perhaps we have more in common than I thought."

Years of practice allowed Darcy to ignore Wickham's insinuations. "As you say."

"I hear you are at Netherfield along with your sister. How is dear Georgiana? Perhaps I should take the opportunity to call on her." Wickham's eyes glittered.

He could not allow Wickham to see Georgiana, no matter the cost. "Georgiana is not out yet and cannot receive gentleman callers, even ones in uniform. It is not worth your while in any case. Her dowry went to pay Napoleon's special levy in '08."

"Raiding your sister's dowry? Darcy, I am shocked at you!"

"Apparently you do not know me as well as you think," said Darcy evenly. Someday he would strangle the life out of Wickham, but it would not be today. "Is there anything else?"

"Not for today, Darcy, not for today. But I will be keeping my eye on you, and I have Captain Reynard's ear."

"How fortunate for you." Wickham and Captain Reynard were birds of a feather.

"It is not pleasant to be the one without power, is it? I can carry tales about you, and you can do nothing. Quite the change from Cambridge. I have the upper hand now."

Apparently Wickham was not as much in the French inner circles as he claimed, if he thought Darcy had no power left. "It seems to please you to believe so."

Wickham smiled with the air of a cat that had cornered a mouse. "You still have a few claws left. What a pity they will not protect you." He tipped his military cap, smirked, and turned away.

Damn him! Damn the man! Openly admitting he had betrayed Darcy's father to what he assumed to be his death? It had been mere luck that Darcy's father had set off with the royal party for Canada before the troops came.

He strode out of town, failing to return the nods of people he had met. If only he could crush Wickham under his boot like the miserable insect he was! Bile rose in his throat. He could not let fear get the better of him.

But he had to think. Wickham's presence was a problem. Darcy's secrets were well hidden, but Wickham always had a talent for finding Darcy's weak point. The last thing he needed was more attention from the French. Now he would need to take even more care to protect Georgiana. Wickham had not seen her since she was a child and likely would not remember her well enough to cause difficulties, but Darcy could take no risks.

He knew what he had to do. He had to take Georgiana away from here. They had left other places for less than this. But this time something inside him twisted in agony at the idea.

Georgiana would not want to leave her friend, Miss Bennet, but he could convince her it was necessary. It would be harder to convince himself to part from Elizabeth. The loss of her companionship that made him remember the man he used to be was the least of it, painful as it would be. No, what he could not abide was the fate he would be abandoning her to. His presence was all that kept Captain Reynard away from her. Once Darcy had gone, Elizabeth would face the nightmarish choice of becoming the Frenchman's mistress or allowing him to ruin her family.

Darcy pressed his palms against his forehead. He could not do it to her. He had no choice but to do it to her.

Darcy was no nearer to a solution by the time he reached Netherfield. His neck was unpleasantly sticky underneath his cravat, an odd contrast to the block of cold lead sitting in his stomach.

There was no point in trying to reassure Georgiana right now; she would most likely take one look at him and think the world was coming to an end. It certainly felt that way.

Bingley caught him on his way upstairs. "Darcy, I am glad you are back. I was beginning to think you had forgotten our dinner guests."

Darcy groaned. "I did forget, but I must beg off. I am in no mood for company."

"But they are coming particularly to see you! Do you not remember? Mr. and Mrs. Goulding from Haye-Park are bringing their guest, the one who knew your father and wants to meet you."

"Damnation! I suppose I must, then, but I will not be at my best."
Bingley frowned. "What is the matter? Has something happened?"
"I will tell you, Bingley, but not now. Not now."

Somehow he kept up a façade of politeness during dinner and made appropriate conversation with Mr. Tomlin – "formerly Lieutenant Colonel Tomlin," as he had said. Darcy had even eaten a few bites, but mostly he pushed the food around on his plate.

But now Mrs. Goulding and Georgiana had withdrawn, leaving the gentleman to their port. Darcy had already started to feel the wine at dinner going to his head; he would have to take care not to overindulge. Perhaps he would be fortunate and the evening would end early.

Tomlin sent the Netherfield servants from the room, leaving only his own batman, and took on a serious, almost military air. "Darcy, I last saw your father in '05 when we were working together to plan a government-in-exile."

Apparently he truly had known Darcy's father. "His part in that is not well known, and perhaps it is better that way."

"I suppose so. Afterwards I returned to being Wellington's aide-de-camp, and by the time of the surrender, I had lost track of your father. Recently I came into possession of some information which could be of use to the government-in-exile, but like everyone else, I do not know how to contact them."

"That is unfortunate," said Darcy blandly. He could see where this was going.

"Some time ago, an old friend mentioned your name as someone who might be aware of how to reach the government-in-exile. When I heard you were visiting here, I decided to ask you directly."

Darcy attempted to look surprised. "I cannot imagine why anyone would think I have some special knowledge. I am sorry to disappoint you, but your old friend was misinformed."

"Precisely what I would expect you to say. But I am willing to prove my bona fides and the value of my information. In addition to what I know, I now have a contact in the occupying army who is giving me information about their weaknesses. He is apparently an old acquaintance of yours."

Darcy sat up straighter, dread filling him. "Are you perchance referring to George Wickham?"

"The very man!"

An image of Wickham's smug smile rose before him. "Wickham is not to be trusted. He is a traitor and for sale to the highest bidder. If he is giving you information, it is because he hopes to earn a reward when he turns you in."

Tomlin leaned forward with a frown. "You are certain of this?"

"Quite certain. He was the one who betrayed my father to the French; he has admitted as much to me." It was reckless talk on his part. A day ago he would not have said it, knowing there was a good chance he would be signing Wickham's death certificate. Today he did not care.

"You are quite, quite sure?"

"Yes. It might be wise for you to leave the vicinity in case he has already passed along your name to the authorities."

Tomlin gestured to his man, another soldier by his stance. Darcy's suspicion was confirmed when the man saluted Tomlin, nodded and left the room without a word.

Darcy would not feel sorry for Wickham. He had brought this down upon himself. But how could he feel nothing when they had played together as children? At least his father had not lived to see this day or to know his beloved Wickham had betrayed him without a second thought.

Tomlin's lips were twisted in an expression of distaste, one Darcy recognized because he saw it in the mirror all too often. The man was loyal and honest; Darcy would bet on that. The remarkable thing was that he had survived this long.

After a swallow of port, Tomlin said, "It will be back into hiding for me, then, at least until the scent is cold. Darcy, I am obliged to you for the warning."

It was too much. Elizabeth's distaste for what she saw as his treason. Georgiana's fear of abandonment. Wickham's implied threats and smirks. Worst of all, knowing he would be forced to abandon Elizabeth to her fate. And now this.

For six years he had kept Georgiana safe by dint of staying silent while the French ransacked England, never even sharing the little he knew that could help the rebels. There had been no choice, but by God, he was sick of it!

He had to do something. When the gentlemen left to join the ladies in the drawing room, Darcy took a quick detour to Bingley's study. He found a blank paper in a desk drawer and wrote a few words. After tearing off a small section of the paper with the words, he secreted it in his hand and left the study.

In the drawing room Bingley was involved in a lively discourse with Mr. and Mrs. Goulding while Georgiana sorted through sheet music at the pianoforte. Off to one side Tomlin wore a brooding look.

Darcy sidled up to Tomlin and said in a low voice, "You wanted something earlier." He opened his hand so the words were visible, if slightly smudged.

Tomlin's eyes widened. "That is it?"

"Look closely. You see the tiny crown drawn above the letter N? You must include that. You have it?"

Tomlin gave a sharp nod. "I thank you."

"Tell no one." Darcy crumpled the paper in his hand.

"Wait! In case my letter does not reach them, this is the message: they must contact the harbormaster in Milford Haven. It is very important."

Darcy shook his head. "Do not depend upon me. I am not in contact with them."

"If you ever are, remember that. The harbormaster at Milford Haven."

It was easiest just to nod. As Darcy crossed the room towards Georgiana, he unobtrusively tossed the scrap of paper in the fire.

It was an unspeakable relief to finally do something after all these years of waiting.

Now he just had to find a way to save Elizabeth.

Chapter Five

Elizabeth studied the sheet of fine notepaper. "It is from Miss Darcy. She is unwell and will not be able to walk with me today, but invites me to spend the day with her at Netherfield. She has sent the carriage for me in the hope I will join her." Odd. Had Mr. Darcy refused to bring his sister to Longbourn because of their quarrel on his last visit? Her stomach twisted into a knot.

Mrs. Bennet patted her hair. "You must go, of course. You cannot miss an opportunity to catch the eye of Mr. Bingley or Mr. Darcy!"

"Of course not," said Elizabeth dryly. More importantly, she needed to know if Mr. Darcy would still receive her. Otherwise she would face another sleepless night of self-recriminations.

Her heart was racing when she finally reached Netherfield and asked for Miss Darcy.

The butler bowed and said, "This way, Miss Bennet." He showed her to a book-filled study.

Miss Darcy was not there. Her brother sat behind an imposing desk, his face drawn as if he had not slept either.

Elizabeth took an involuntary step backwards. "Forgive me. Your sister sent me an invitation to visit her. I did not mean to interrupt you."

Mr. Darcy waved the butler away and closed the study door. "I know. I asked her to do so. I could not think of another way to arrange a private meeting with you."

What could he be thinking? If they were found alone together in a closed room... "Well, here I am," she said with more lightness in her voice than she felt.

"Yes." He frowned at a pile of books as if they had personally offended him. "Georgiana and I will be leaving Netherfield tomorrow morning."

She had not expected that, and it felt like a blow. "Will you be returning at some point?"

"No." He continued avoiding her gaze.

Her mouth was dry. "Does this have something to do with our disagreement the last time we met?"

"What? Oh, that. No, nothing at all. This is something quite separate and urgent."

"I see," she said, although she did not.

"Unfortunately this leaves you in a difficult position regarding Captain Reynard. In my absence it is likely he will renew his demands on you."

Her throat seemed to have turned to stone. Of course he would. It was only Mr. Darcy's presence that kept the captain away. She squeezed her eyes closed before sudden tears could escape. "I am grateful to you for giving me a reprieve." There. Her voice had hardly shaken at all.

"I cannot tell you how sorry I am to leave you in this position. If I could, I would offer to take you with us, but that is impossible. The only thing in my power is to give you this." He held out a small pouch.

She did not reach for it. "What is it?"

"Money enough to see you to Scotland, and the name and direction of a contact in Newcastle who can help you across the border safely. Please memorize it and then burn the paper; it is not safe to have it in writing." He tucked the pouch into her hand.

The warmth of his hand still clung to the leather bag, and the touch of his long fingers seemed to leave an imprint on her hand. This was a final goodbye, not just to him but eventually to her life in Meryton.

Somehow she lifted her eyes to his face. "Why are you doing this? How do you know someone who can help me escape?"

"I cannot tell you that. I am sorry." His voice was rough.

A movement beyond him caught her eye and she turned to the window. "Does it have anything to do with that?" She held out a trembling finger to point at the troop of French soldiers marching towards the house.

He hurried to the window. "No. Hell and damnation, no. I am a fool. We should have left yesterday. May God forgive me." It was the voice of complete despair.

"What is the matter?" Now she was truly afraid.

He turned back to her, took a deep breath, and grasped her shoulders. His eyes were haunted. "There may not be much time, and you must listen to me. Everything depends upon it. If they are here to arrest me, I must ask you to care for Georgiana and take her away from here."

"Of course, if you wish. She will be welcome at Longbourn."

He shook his head fiercely. "No. I am asking you for more than that. Take her far away. Do not tell your family you are leaving, and do not return."

She could not have heard him correctly. "Are you mad? I am happy to help your sister, but you are asking me to leave everything behind for a girl I hardly know!"

A violent pounding came from below. Darcy opened the door a crack and listened. A distant French accented voice said, "I have a warrant for the arrest of Mr. Fitzwilliam Darcy."

Instantly Darcy closed the door and turned the key in the lock. "No, I am not mad. I will have to trust you."

She stared at him in bewilderment. He moved closer until he could speak directly in her ear. "Listen carefully. I have not seen my sister in six years, not since she boarded a ship for Canada, where everyone believes she is Princess Charlotte. Need I tell you who has been pretending to be my sister and going by the name of Georgiana Darcy?"

Elizabeth's mouth dropped open. "Surely you cannot mean she is —"

He pressed his hand over her mouth. "Do not say that name, not ever. I will do everything in my power to keep that information from the French, but I can be broken by torture like any other man. That is why you must take her and go."

Elizabeth's head was spinning. "But where? How?"

"Georgiana knows what to do. We have prepared for this. But God help us, she is still too young to travel by herself, and so I must beg you to help her. Do not stop for anything, not even to see your family."

"Of course." Stunned by his revelation, she could not even think through the consequences of what she was agreeing to.

"Good girl." He winced at the sound of boots marching up the stairs. "Since I am damned anyway, and now that you know I am not a traitor..." Taking her face between his hands, he lowered his head towards hers.

He brushed his warm lips gently against hers, and then, when she did not protest, with greater firmness. His simple touch held a thrilling magic, creating in her a delectable sensation she could never have imagined and an aching hunger that spiraled through the deepest parts of her. As he nibbled at her lower lip, all vestige of rational thought deserted her. Instinctively she arched herself towards him, seeking something to fill this new need inside her.

Then it was over, leaving her trembling and more confused than ever. His dark eyes, only inches away, were fixed on hers, and he looked as overwhelmed as she felt. His lips soundlessly formed her name.

Could it be her heart pounding so loudly? No, the noise came from the study door.

With a deep breath, Darcy raked his hand through his hair, lifted his chin, and somehow transformed into a facsimile of his usual calm self. He turned the key and opened the door, feigning surprise at finding soldiers outside it.

Lieutenant Bessette was in the lead. "Mr. Fitzwilliam Darcy, you are under arrest for the murder of George Wickham."

Darcy raised his eyebrows. "I am afraid you have the wrong man," he drawled. "Wickham may have deserved to be murdered several times over, but I cannot claim credit for it." He repeated his words in French. One of the soldiers guffawed.

Lieutenant Bessette glanced at Elizabeth, then back to Darcy. "You must come with us," he said firmly.

Darcy replied in French too rapid for Elizabeth to understand.

This time even Lieutenant Bessette smiled. "*Bien sûr!*"

Darcy returned to Elizabeth's side. Raising her hand to his lips, he held it there for a moment beyond what was proper, and whispered, "Courage, proud Titania." Then he turned on his heel to face the soldiers. "Gentlemen, I am at your service."

Frozen, Elizabeth watched his retreating back, first down the passageway and then out the window, taking some vital piece of her with him. She touched her fingers to her tingling lips. How hard she had fought not to care about him because of his political beliefs! Only now, when she might lose him forever, had she learned he was everything she could have wished for – and more. She might never have the opportunity to tell him of her regrets. His life might be counted in days, leaving her to grieve for the opportunity she had lost.

She swallowed hard and forced that thought out of her head. She could think about him later. Right now she needed to focus on the impossible task he had passed on to her. Darcy had put his royal charge ahead of everything else, even when it meant working with the French, even when it might cost him his life. Now it was her turn to make his sacrifices worthwhile.

Her breath caught in her throat. Could the girl who had visited Jane in the stables and drank ill-tasting tea with her truly be Princess Charlotte, the rightful heir to the throne? Of all the possible explanations for Mr. Darcy's inconsistent behavior, this was the most inconceivable, but her instincts told her it was true. It made sense of everything that had puzzled her. She shook her head in mingled bewilderment and wonder.

And now Mr. Darcy was likely to die for his loyalty, and part of her would die with him.

But there was no time to dwell on his fate. She had a princess to rescue. She rubbed her damp hands against her skirt and hurried downstairs to find a servant, but the echoing rooms were empty. Had the servants disappeared when the French arrived? Finally she located a footman who told her Miss Darcy was in the library.

She found the girl she called Georgiana curled up in an armchair reading a book, one of her golden ringlets wrapped tightly around her finger. Her concentration was such that she did not even notice when Elizabeth approached her.

The truth hit Elizabeth like a blow to the stomach. This girl was the heir to the throne. Princess Charlotte, the hope of England, the one mentioned in every toast between Englishmen. And now she was Elizabeth's responsibility. It was terrifying.

How was she supposed to tell the girl what had happened and that they must leave? Yesterday she would have had no difficulty telling Georgiana Darcy what to do, but that was when she had not known the truth. Now she was royalty, so far above Elizabeth that she hardly dared to speak. Part of her wanted to disappear, but Mr. Darcy had been clear in his directions to her.

"Georgiana?" she asked with more timidity than she cared to admit.

The girl jumped. "Oh! I had not realized you were here already. I heard some noise earlier but did not think much of it." As she spoke, she closed her book and surreptitiously slid it under a stack of other volumes.

Elizabeth bit her lip and forced herself to speak. "I do not know how to tell you this. Mr. Darcy was just arrested by the French. Before they took him, he asked me to take you away from here as quickly as possible."

Georgiana paled. "They took William? I knew something must be wrong when he said we had to leave!" Her eyes filled with tears.

There was no time for this. The French might return at any moment. "He said you would know where to go and what to do."

"Oh! Yes. We have practiced this. We must leave at once. I have to collect my satchel for my room, then I will be ready."

"Good. I will ask for the horses to be hitched to the carriage again."

"No, not the carriage. The curricle. That is the plan." The girl hesitated, then grabbed her book from under the pile.

"Would not the carriage be more suitable for traveling a long distance?"

Georgiana shook her head. "More suitable, but we do not want people to think we are going a long way. William says taking the curricle helps to throw off the scent."

"I see. Is there anything we should do to assist your brother before we go?" Of course, Mr. Darcy was not Georgiana's brother. Oh, this was just too confusing!

Now tears were beginning to escape the girl's eyes. "No. He would want us to go straight away. But should I leave a note for Mr. Bingley and ask him to contact William's friend in London? He might be able to use his influence to help him. But William would tell me not to take that time, that it is too risky." Her breathing was growing rapid and shallow.

The poor girl. Even if royal blood ran in her veins, she was still a terrified fifteen-year-old who needed help. "Yes, you should do that. Where can we find paper?"

"In my room." Georgiana dashed her tears away.

"Then let us go there." She did not dare let the girl out of her sight.

On the way upstairs Elizabeth found the lone footman and told him firmly to have the curricle prepared for an immediate departure. Then she watched as Georgiana quickly wrote a note, her racing pulse counting out each second that prolonged their danger.

After finishing the note quickly, the girl pulled out a small trunk from the wardrobe, opened it and produced a large satchel. She shoved her book inside it. "Very well, I am ready." Her voice barely trembled.

"Then let us go." Asking a servant for help would only waste precious minutes, so Elizabeth picked up the surprisingly heavy satchel.

When they reached the curricle, Elizabeth stopped short. The grooms were just finishing harnessing a pair of grey thoroughbreds to it. "Georgiana, I have never driven anything larger than a donkey cart."

"I can drive it." She sounded forlorn. "William thinks of everything."

"I am certain he will be released soon," she said with a confidence she did not feel. If she thought too hard about Mr. Darcy she might lose her composure, and that might tip off the grooms that something was amiss.

Georgiana's lower lip trembled. "I hope so." Then she stepped up into the curricle and took the reins from the groom. Elizabeth swung herself up on the opposite side, her heart pounding.

Was she truly going to do this? Vanish without a word to her family? Would they think she had run off, or would they suspect foul play? Poor Jane would be devastated, never knowing what had happened to her.

But she had a duty to her country as well. How could she ever live with herself if she allowed Princess Charlotte to be taken by the French owing to her inaction? She had dreamed of an opportunity to do some service for England, but she had never considered it might come at such a price. How much had it cost Mr. Darcy over the last six years?

She could think about that later. It was not as if Elizabeth could have remained at home long anyway, not once Captain Reynard found out Mr. Darcy was no longer there to protect her. This had only changed the time and the means of her departure. She took a deep, steadying breath.

Georgiana shook the reins and the horses set off down the drive.

Heaven help her. Elizabeth did not even know where they were headed. "Are we going to Scotland?"

"No, Oxford. Do you know how to get there?"

A bubble of hysterical laughter rose in her chest. No doubt Mr. Darcy had memorized the entire turnpike system of England in case of this eventuality, but Elizabeth had not. "I suppose we should head west on the Hatfield road. There will be signposts when we reach the Old North Road." It might not be the best route, but at least the general direction was correct.

"The Hatfield road? Where is that?"

"I will direct you. At the end of the lane we should go right. No, left. Right is faster, but it would take us through Meryton and people would see us. But wait – will Mr. Darcy not know you are headed to Oxford?" The French might be in pursuit of them sooner than she had thought.

Georgiana shook her head. "It is a secret. Even William does not know my emergency destination. They could make him talk, you know."

The thought of Mr. Darcy in a cell, his elegant hands bruised by chains, made bile rise in Elizabeth's throat.

The girl stole a glance at Elizabeth. "Did he tell you? About... me?"

Elizabeth gripped the curricle bar to hide the shaking of her hands. "Just before they took him away. I had no idea. I do not even know what to call you now."

The question seemed to steady the girl. "You should call me Georgiana and never even let yourself think that other name. Otherwise you may slip and say it when you should not. That is what William always did."

"Very well, but I do not understand why you are playing this part. Why the masquerade, and why Mr. Darcy? He must have been quite young at the time of the invasion." Far too young for a responsibility of this sort, just like Elizabeth herself was now.

"I was not supposed to be in his care, but my original guardian had an apoplexy, and the one who was his substitute was executed. William was all that was left, so he took me in." Suddenly she seemed very young. "My grandfather – King George, that is – commanded that I remain here in England. He said if I grew up in a foreign land, I would never be accepted as fully English, just as his father and grandfather had not been accepted. His plan was to keep me with him and retreat to Wales, believing Napoleon would make it no further than London. Lord Matlock and William's father saw the danger – and indeed I would have been captured if I had gone with my grandfather – so they carried me off secretly. They feared Napoleon would spare nothing in the effort to

75

capture the person he thought to be me. The ship to Canada was a decoy to draw his attention away from me."

And so the girl had been taken away from everything and everyone she had known. Even her name was no longer her own.

Now she was Elizabeth's responsibility – a terrifying thought. "Might I inquire who is in Oxford?"

Georgiana shrugged. "Someone who can be trusted to take care of me. I have never met him." Her voice was flat.

The poor girl must feel like a package that was passed from hand to hand. *Poor girl* – was that not what Mr. Darcy had said about Princess Charlotte? No wonder he had expressed such strong feelings! But if there was someone in Oxford who would take over Georgiana's care, perhaps Elizabeth could go back home then, at least long enough to tell them she was leaving for Scotland. Jane would only have to worry for a few days.

Georgiana's voice interrupted her thoughts. "Is there a private lane or someplace we could be hidden for a few minutes?"

Elizabeth glanced behind them to make certain they were not being followed. "There is an area ahead where the hedgerows are high. If we turn past them on a track, we would not be visible from the road." Probably the girl needed to relieve herself.

Georgiana slowed the horses. When they reached a lane, she turned down it and stopped the curricle. "Can you hold the reins?" she asked Elizabeth.

"Of course." That much she could manage.

"You will need to stand."

Mystified, Elizabeth obeyed.

Crouching on the floor of the curricle, Georgiana ran her hand below the edge of the seat. "There. Elizabeth, you should look at this in case you need to find it someday. See, there is a little hook here." She lifted up the leather seat, exposing a hidden compartment beneath it. The girl folded back the oilcloth and revealed a tightly packed space. She took a pistol from the top of it. "Do you know how to shoot?"

"Yes. I have a pistol already. Your brother loaned it to me." Elizabeth jiggled the large reticule pinned to her waist. She had taken the precaution of bringing it with her to Netherfield, not knowing whether she would be returning to Longbourn in the carriage or on foot. Now the reticule also held the money Mr. Darcy had given her to pay her way to Scotland. It would serve to take the two of them to Oxford.

"You should load it. We should each have one ready to fire." She retrieved a pile of clothing and a pair of scissors from the compartment. "I must change. Will you assist me?"

"Of course." Elizabeth followed Georgiana out of the curricle and behind the hedgerow. "Is this another part of your brother's plans?"

"Yes." Georgiana presented her back to Elizabeth. "If anyone is trying to find us, they will be looking for two women, so I will be a boy."

Elizabeth's fingers paused in undoing Georgiana's buttons. "Men's clothes?" She tried not to sound horrified.

"Do not worry; I have practiced in them many times before. William says this is the simplest disguise, provided I know how a boy walks."

"But your hair!"

Georgiana removed her hairpins and shook out her hair, then handed Elizabeth the scissors. "You must cut it." Her voice did not even tremble.

Elizabeth looked down at the scissors in dismay. "Cut it? Are you certain?"

"It is part of the plan. Do it quickly, before I lose my courage."

Gingerly Elizabeth took a lock of the flaxen hair between her fingers. Royal hair. Could this truly be necessary? She thought of Mr. Darcy's face before the soldiers took him away. Yes, it was necessary. She took a deep breath and began to snip away long locks of hair. It felt like a desecration.

Stepping back, she examined her handiwork. "It is not perfectly even, but it will do for now."

The girl's face looked more angular now. Tears were gathering in her eyes.

Elizabeth straightened her shoulders. "Excellent," she said with false cheer. "I tried to leave enough length so it could be made into one of the cropped cuts fashionable ladies wear and some short ringlets in the front. With a curling iron and a ribbon, you will look like you stepped out of a fashion magazine!" She tossed the stray locks of hair into the hedgerow. "Some fortunate bird will be delighted to find such excellent padding for its nest. Perhaps your hair will cradle baby robins."

Georgiana swallowed hard. "I would like that," she said bravely. She stripped off her dress and petticoat. A few minutes later, a young man in a waistcoat stood before Elizabeth. The new angles of her face fit in perfectly. No one would recognize her as Miss Darcy.

Elizabeth tried to shut her mind away from the shocking idea of Princess Charlotte wearing trousers in public. "What else is hidden in your supplies?"

"Ammunition, knives, money, cloaks, oilcloth, a little food – dried fruits and nuts, mostly – a map, bandages. All sorts of things. William is very thorough." Georgiana tugged at her coat to straighten it. "And travel permits, of course."

"It sounds more like preparation for battle than a journey," said Elizabeth.

Georgiana fingered her cropped hair, her expression pained. "We are at war, you know."

Of course they were. "I am only sorry you have had to live with this fear every day."

The sympathy made Georgiana's lips tremble. The girl had sounded so sure of herself a minute earlier when talking about Darcy's plans, but apparently that confidence was just a veneer.

In the hope of distracting her, Elizabeth asked the first question that came to her mind. "Do you have a hat tucked away somewhere, too?"

"In my satchel. It is a small one." The girl sounded a little calmer.

"Now I will have to think what to call you, since you no longer look like a Georgiana!" Elizabeth tried to sound as if she were teasing.

"William calls me George, sometimes even when I am being a girl. It is easy to remember." She made a valiant attempt to smile. "And the name does run in my family."

Had she actually made a joke about her situation? "I suppose it does at that." Her father, grandfather, great-grandfather, and his father before him had all been named George. "Well, it will be easier to stop at an inn for the night with George than with Georgiana. Two women traveling alone together would draw attention. And I must say you make quite a fetching boy!"

Georgiana found a pen and a bottle of ink in the curricle's hidden compartment. "To fill in the travel permit. It is signed, but otherwise blank. What names should we use?"

"I do not know – anything, I suppose. Perhaps Elizabeth and George Gardiner?" Her uncle's name was the first that came to her mind.

"Good. Travelling to Oxford, dated today and tomorrow, then?"

"That sounds right." Elizabeth did not know how her legs were still holding her up. Possessing a forged travel permit was a hanging offense. It was one thing to exchange jibes with her younger sister about being hanged and another to actually risk it.

When Georgiana picked up the reins again, the loaded pistols and travel permit sat between them, a brutal reminder of the danger they faced. How had Mr. Darcy carried this burden alone all these years? No wonder he sometimes appeared grim.

"Who else knows about you?" Elizabeth asked quietly.

"In England? Only William and Lady Matlock, and now you. Lord Matlock knew, of course, but he is dead now. William says that if you want a secret kept, you must tell no one at all."

How very alone they both must have felt!

When they reached the road to Hatfield, Georgiana brought the horses to a full trot. They would make better time now, but they would also be more conspicuous. If someone were pursuing them, this would be one of the first roads to be checked. And since Hatfield was a common stop for travelers on the Old North Road, they would have to travel beyond it tonight if they were to avoid potential pursuers.

As it was, they would no doubt be stopped in Hatfield by soldiers checking their documents. Elizabeth picked up the permit Georgiana had produced. Her eyes widened when she saw the signature. General Desmarais. What had Mr. Darcy been thinking to use the name of the supreme commander of all the French troops in England on his forged permits? She hoped the soldiers would not look too closely at the papers.

But even if they made it past the checkpoint, they would still need a place to spend the night. "Did your brother have a plan for choosing an inn?"

"Not that he told me. He always chose the inns, and I assumed we would be together if we ever had to flee. William insisted on teaching me what to do in case I was alone when problems arose, but he almost never leaves me, so I did not worry about it." She made a sound halfway between a gasp and a sob.

Elizabeth could not afford to let herself feel anything about Mr. Darcy right now. "It sounds as if he has been very devoted to you."

"More than I deserve. He did not ask to be given charge of me, and I was often difficult at the beginning. I was accustomed to people waiting on me and to being the center of attention, and I did not understand why that had to change. I made mistakes, bad mistakes, at first. He ought to have hated me for disrupting his life. He dislikes subterfuge, and because of me he must pretend to be someone he is not. And now he has been arrested because of me." Tears began to run down her cheeks, an odd contrast to her boy's clothes.

How could she reassure the girl? "It might not have been because of you. The warrant for his arrest was for murder."

"Is that what they arrested him for?" Georgiana wrinkled her forehead. "Who was the victim?"

"I had never heard of him. George Wickhurst, I think. No, it was Wickham. Your brother seemed to know who he was."

"Wickham? I do not know the name. Perhaps he is someone from Cambridge or from Pemberley. William has not been able to go back to his home because of me, either. People at Pemberley remember what the real Georgiana Darcy looks like. He misses Pemberley, though he would never admit it to me."

How badly she had misjudged Mr. Darcy! "As I said, perhaps his arrest has nothing to do with you at all." But that left another horrible possibility. Could it have been caused by Darcy's decision to protect Elizabeth from Captain Reynard? The captain was fond of taking revenge. Darcy might now be suffering as a result of his decision to help her. Her stomach tightened uncomfortably.

"Perhaps." But Georgiana did not sound convinced.

Elizabeth tried to put on an air of confidence as she requested rooms for herself and her young brother at the first inn they passed in St. Albans, grateful to have the satchel to show they were respectable travelers. She was even more grateful to escape any prying eyes when they were finally alone in Georgiana's room.

The girl opened the satchel and began to unpack its contents. Like the hidden compartment in the curricle, the satchel held more than Elizabeth would have thought possible.

Georgiana unrolled a bundle of pale green fabric which miraculously turned into a simple day dress. She shook it out and held it up in front of Elizabeth. "I think this should fit you. William chose dresses a little big for me in case I grew before the next time he replaced them. There should be another in here." She dove back into the satchel.

"I appreciate his forethought." But wearing the same dress again tomorrow was the least of her worries. Now that the details of their day's travel no longer preoccupied her, fear had begun to fray her composure.

Good God, she could be hanged three times over for what she had done today!

"I think this is the other dress. There are stockings, gloves, and a spare shift. And more money, should we need it."

"I have money, too. Your brother gave it to me." The sum Darcy had given her that morning was more than Elizabeth had ever seen at one time, but money would not tell her how best to hide and protect Georgiana. Darcy had chosen Elizabeth for the task because she was the only person available when he needed help, not because she possessed the necessary skills.

She could not afford these unsettling thoughts, so she picked up the book Georgiana had brought with her, expecting to see a popular novel. She flipped open the cover, revealing the French title. "*Art de la Guerre*? Interesting reading material."

Georgiana looked up at her solemnly. "It is very interesting. It is an ancient Chinese book on tactics. Napoleon always carries a copy of it with him. I need to know how he thinks and what he will do next. I can already see how he uses some of these tactics in battle."

Yet another side of this girl – the future monarch. A shiver ran down Elizabeth's spine. "It is wise to know your enemy."

"I intend to kill him someday, or at least give the order for it." Georgiana's lips tightened, making her look older than her fifteen years.

"Many Englishmen would be happy to join you in that." Elizabeth sat on the bed beside the satchel.

"Many would, though few have more reason than I do. He killed my parents and my uncles, imprisoned my grandfather, and forced my aunt to become his brother's whore in a mockery of a marriage. I will kill him for that." The girl's voice was growing louder, her eyes over-bright.

"Hush. He has done your family great wrong. It is no wonder you want revenge."

"And I shall have it!" Georgiana said fiercely.

Elizabeth's head was spinning. There had been so many shocks today. Mr. Darcy had turned her world upside down, and now this mercurial girl was proving unexpectedly challenging. She needed time to think, both for her own sanity and to decide what to do next. "I do not know about you, but I am quite tired after today's events. I think I shall rest in my room before dinner, if you do not mind."

At her words, Georgiana shifted from vengeful murderess back to frightened girl. Her breathing quickened as she said, "Must you go? You could rest in here. I can put everything back in the satchel. Or I could go with you to your room. I will just sit in the corner and read, and you will not even know I am there."

Mr. Darcy had said his sister was easily frightened, but Elizabeth had not expected her to fear being left alone in a room. It was hard to believe Georgiana was nearly Lydia's age, but the two girls had been raised so differently. Lydia had never been discouraged from her attempts at independence, even when some rules might have done her good. The stakes were much higher for Georgiana. If she made a mistake, she would face imprisonment at best and execution at worst. It was more than enough to make anyone fearful.

"Of course I can rest here if you would prefer."

"Thank you." Georgiana spoke barely above a whisper.

But lying down and closing her eyes provided Elizabeth no relief. Her mind whirled with the consequences of her actions. What would Jane and the rest of her family think when she did not return from Netherfield? They would discover soon enough that Mr. Darcy had been arrested. Perhaps they would think she had fallen into the hands of French soldiers or been taken captive while trying to return to Longbourn. Or she might have met with an accident. They would be scouring the fields and woods for her tonight. It might occur to Jane that she could have run off, but she would find it difficult to believe Elizabeth would have gone without a single word to her or without collecting the items she had stored in the stable in case she ever had to leave in a hurry.

Jane would worry herself half to death even if Elizabeth returned in a few days.

What was she thinking? It was comforting to believe she could go home, but she had been fooling herself. The damage was already done. Even if Mr. Darcy revealed nothing about Georgiana's identity, Elizabeth would have no acceptable explanation for her absence. Everyone would assume the worst. She would be ruined, a burden to her family and an even easier target for Captain Reynard. She would have no choice but to flee to Scotland immediately, leaving her family to once again suffer through losing her.

And if Mr. Darcy had been forced to talk, the French would be waiting to pounce on her as soon as she appeared. They would leave no stone unturned in their efforts to find Georgiana. No, her family was lost to her. The best she could hope for was to someday get a message to Jane to tell her she was alive and well. Poor Jane would be even lonelier and more isolated now. Would anyone trouble to bring her tea? What would happen to her if Captain Reynard forced the family out of Longbourn entirely?

If she kept thinking about her family, she was going to burst into tears. Perhaps she should consider her future instead. Scotland was still the obvious choice since so many English Loyalists had formed their own community there. It was what she had always pictured doing if she ran off. But she knew no one in Scotland and would be all alone there with no family, friends or status.

But none of that needed to be resolved now. Tonight all she had to decide was the plan for tomorrow's journey to Oxford.

Unsurprisingly, Georgiana asked Elizabeth to share her room that night. It was even less of a surprise when Elizabeth was awakened in the night by the sound of muffled sobs. She took the girl into her arms as if she had been one of her sisters, feeling close to tears herself.

"All will be well, you will see," she told Georgiana. "Tomorrow night you will be safe in the hands of someone you can trust."

"Will you stay with me? At least for a while? Otherwise I will be with a total stranger." Another sob shook her.

"If you like, I will be happy to stay with you." Could remaining with Georgiana be an alternative to Scotland? Even if Mr. Darcy should return – she could not bear to think of it as only a possibility or the tears would begin to flow – Elizabeth could make the argument that Georgiana desperately needed a female influence in her life. Elizabeth could be her companion and thus be of service to England at the same time. It would be risky, of course, but going to Scotland would be dangerous, too. If she changed her name, no one would know that Georgiana's companion had once been Elizabeth Bennet.

Georgiana swallowed another sob. "But you will leave, too. Everyone leaves. William was the only one who stayed, and now even he is gone."

"We do not know that. His friend in London may be able to have him released, at least if they have not discovered about you."

"I... I have never been apart from William this long before." The girl dissolved anew into heartbroken sobs.

Mr. Darcy must have been a very devoted guardian indeed if he had never spent a night apart from her in six years! "It is not the same, but I am here with you, and I will not abandon you."

"Not now, but someday you will." The girl's despair seemed to overwhelm her.

"Perhaps someday you will no longer feel a need to have me stay with you, but if you do need me, I will stay, unless..." She had been about to say unless she fell in love and married. The image of dark, intent eyes rose in her memory. She had to blink hard to keep back the tears.

Georgiana froze. "Unless?"

Thinking quickly, Elizabeth said, "Unless I have the opportunity to travel to Africa to see the elephants. I have a great desire to see elephants. And the tigers in India, but I suppose I could take you with me to India since it is more civilized. I would dearly love to see the kangaroos in Australia, but it is such a lawless place I think I shall have to survive without them. A pity, though, since I simply cannot imagine how an animal that large can possibly hop. But apart from the elephants in Africa and the tigers in India, you may depend upon me."

The girl giggled. "There are elephants in India, too. You could even ride one of them in a canopy chair. I have seen pictures in books."

"That would simplify matters," said Elizabeth with mock seriousness. "Africa is a very large place, after all. In India we could purchase dozens of those beautiful shawls, and be the envy of everyone we know when we return."

"Oh, yes! And some of those lovely jeweled silks, too."

"Perhaps we could disguise ourselves and go down to one of the native markets to find the best silks. We would have to darken our faces, of course, or everyone would know we were foreigners. They must have the most amazing fruit there, things we have never tasted, more exotic than even a pineapple." Elizabeth continued to spin the tale until her silliness distracted Georgiana enough that she fell asleep. But Elizabeth lay awake much longer, wondering what the mysterious man in Oxford would be like and how he would respond to taking in Elizabeth as well as Georgiana.

She could not bear to think of the man she had left behind.

"How is Mr. Tennant of Pennington Hall to know who you are?" asked Elizabeth as they neared Oxford.

"I am supposed to tell him I have a package from the governor of Jamaica."

"Jamaica? How does Jamaica come into it?"

Georgiana shrugged. "I do not know, but that is what I am to say."

"I thought no one knew you were in England. Is Mr. Tennant aware you are here?"

Georgiana's brow furrowed. "I do not believe so. William would not have agreed to let anyone into that secret. Even the government-in-exile believes I am in Canada."

"It is possible Mr. Tennant may be inclined to be dubious."

"Why? You seemed to have no trouble believing it."

Elizabeth hesitated. It was a good point. Why had she immediately believed Darcy when he told her the implausible tale about his sister being the heir to the throne? Well, she had known him, at least to some degree, and generally trusted him – except when it concerned the French. More importantly, the story made sense of several things which had puzzled her. But perhaps the most convincing point had been the intensity of his concern for Georgiana when he was the one about to be arrested and quite possibly executed.

Mr. Tennant of Pennington Hall would have none of these advantages when two strangers appeared on his doorstep. How were they to convince him? What if he did not believe them? For that matter, what were they to do if he was away? He might be in London.

She was still pondering that question as they approached Pennington Hall, having received directions at a nearby inn. The gatehouse was not difficult to spot along the country lane. Georgiana reined in the horses at the wrought iron gates and called for the gatekeeper.

The man who stepped out of the gatehouse wore a French uniform.

Georgiana, in her disguise as George, rose to the occasion. Pitching her voice in its lower ranges, she said, "We are travelers who thought to call on Mr. Tennant. Is he no longer here?" At the guard's blank look, she repeated the question in French.

The soldier shook his head. "No more."

"Do you know where we might find him?"

The soldier grinned, showing blackened and missing teeth. "Chez Madame Guillotine." And in case they might have misunderstood this, he drew the back of his thumb across his throat.

Chapter Six

Darcy forced himself not to look back at Elizabeth as the soldiers marched him away. It would accomplish nothing and would undercut his efforts to make his arrest seem no more than a laughable error. Instead he pretended to joke with the soldiers about Wickham's bad habit of failing to pay his gambling debts. A few of them began to look uneasy, no doubt recalling how much Wickham owed each of them, money they would now never see.

But behind the amused façade his mind was racing. Had Elizabeth believed him? If there had only been more time, he would have offered more explanation than the basic facts. It must have sounded ridiculous. She had seemed to accept his story at the time, but now she must be questioning it. Could he truly expect her to abandon her family and everyone she knew for a mad story with no proof? What sensible person would risk so much on trust? And she had never trusted him because of his history with the French.

But perhaps she would still do something. Even if she simply took Georgiana to stay with her sister in the Longbourn stables, that would be safer than leaving her at Netherfield. Still, he knew about those stables, and anything he knew could be extracted.

But what if this arrest really was for Wickham's murder? As soon as he had realized the soldiers were coming for him, he had assumed they had discovered his true crimes against the French. Since he had not committed any other crimes, it never occurred to him it might be for something completely different. Perhaps the murder charge was simply a cover for putting him to the question for other suspicions they might have.

He should have asked Elizabeth to send word to General Desmarais. If Demarais knew about his arrest and it truly was for Wickham's murder, Darcy could expect to be released within hours. Without Desmarais's help, his situation could become desperate.

It was up to Darcy to save himself. He stepped up beside the officer who had laughed at his joke earlier. "Lieutenant," Darcy said in quiet French, "A man who sent word of my arrest to General Desmarais in London could expect to be well rewarded."

The lieutenant straightened. "You know General Desmarais?" At Darcy's nod, he added, "Just the facts of your arrest?"

"Just the facts. It is not a secret, is it? But he would be most unhappy if he were not informed. You could write to his aide-de-camp, Colonel Hulot, at Carlton House." Seeing the lieutenant hesitate, Darcy added, "It might be worth a transfer to another unit. I have already written to the general to inform him of your captain's interesting disciplinary practices." No need to say his letter had been more about the captain's behavior towards Jane Bennet.

The lieutenant's eyebrows shot up. *"Merci bien, Monsieur.* I see I will need to attend to my correspondence tonight."

"A fine idea." It was a double relief. First, that the lieutenant would write for assistance, but more importantly, he would have shown more concern if Darcy's arrest was also for suspicious activities.

Apparently Darcy's status as a gentleman still made a difference, for when they reached the town hall, he was taken to a spartan room with a door that locked rather than a gaol cell. The waiting guard said, "His hands must be tied." He pulled out a rope and yanked Darcy's arms behind his back.

Darcy's new friend the lieutenant stepped forward. "I will handle that." He took the rope and gestured to Darcy to put his hands in front of him. When Darcy obeyed, the lieutenant looped the rope around them so loosely it would take little effort to extricate himself.

"I have one question," said Darcy. "Why do you think I killed George Wickham?"

The lieutenant gave a Gallic shrug. "He said if anything happened to him, it would be because of you."

"Is that all?" Darcy asked in disbelief.

With a gap-toothed grin, the lieutenant said, "That, and the captain, he does not like you. Something about a girl, of course." He winked at Darcy before he left.

Now all he could do was to wait and worry – and remember the pleasure of kissing Elizabeth Bennet. Would he ever have the opportunity to do so again?

Elizabeth stared at the French soldier. Mr. Tennant of Pennington Hall had been executed? What were they to do now? "What a pity!" she said quickly. "Mama will be sad to hear it. Come, brother, in that case we must be on our way."

"Oh! Yes." With a quick twist of the reins, Georgiana turned the curricle in the narrow lane.

"*Non*! *Attendez*!" shouted the guard.

Elizabeth hissed to Georgiana, "Go!"

The guard made a grab for the bridle of the nearest horse, but the pair was already moving at a quick trot. He was still shouting in French as they rounded a curve that took them out of sight.

"Do you think we are safe?" Georgiana asked.

"I do not know." Elizabeth turned to watch the lane behind them.

They were nearly to the main road when she spotted a cloud of dust behind them. It was horses, several of them. "They are coming!"

Georgiana paled. "Hold on tight! I will try to outdistance them."

Elizabeth grasped the bar in front of her with both hands as the horses took off at a canter. The curricle bounced over a surface not designed to be taken at such speed and tipped precariously as Georgiana took the turn onto the main road. "They will have seen which direction we turned!" Elizabeth shouted over the wind.

"No matter. If they are on ordinary horses, we will be able to outrun them, at least for a time." Georgiana's eyes were glowing.

"Be careful! There is a barouche ahead!" And they were gaining on it at a frighteningly rapid pace.

Georgiana did not slow the horses. Was she out of her mind? Then Elizabeth saw her intent expression. Surely she was not planning to pass it on this narrow road?

Just as Elizabeth braced herself for an imminent crash with the barouche, Georgiana turned the horses. She was going to try to pass! If anyone was coming the other direction, there would be no way to avoid a disastrous collision. Elizabeth squeezed her eyes shut.

Nothing happened. The curricle kept speeding along. Georgiana had won her gamble.

"They will not be able to see what we do with the barouche between us." Georgiana had to speak loudly to be heard over the rushing wind.

Elizabeth only hoped to live to see the next village.

The horses could not maintain that pace for long. As they began to tire, Elizabeth searched the road ahead. Placing her hand on Georgiana's arm, she pointed to a long barn up ahead. "If we could get behind that barn, we might be able to hide as they go past."

Her companion nodded. She waited until the last moment to slow the horses. The curricle tipped again as they turned in at the barn. Fortunately the yard was paved, with a track continuing beyond it. Georgiana pulled the curricle into the tall grass behind the barn.

As soon as it stopped moving, Elizabeth jumped out and scuffed the grass which had been bent by their passage. It would be impossible to completely disguise where it had been crushed by the wheels, but she managed to cover their tracks fairly well. Her heart pounded. If this did not work, if the French caught them here...

Across the paved yard an older woman with a broom stepped out from a cottage. Cold sweat pricked at Elizabeth's neck. Had she seen their arrival? Elizabeth held her breath as the stoop-backed woman hobbled slowly toward the road and began sweeping dust from the paved yard.

Elizabeth dared to breathe again. The woman was covering their tracks! Had she guessed the French were after them and decided to help them?

But now they had bigger concerns. She hurried to Georgiana who was holding the bridle of one of the horses and whispering to it.

"Georgiana, you must hide. If they stop to look here, they must not find you."

"But they will arrest you! What would I do without you?"

"You would find someone else to help you. You are far more capable than you think. Here, take this money. As long as you have that, you will manage somehow. Now hide!"

"But —"

The old woman hobbled around the corner of the barn. "Those Frenchies just rode past without a second glance. You're running from them, aren't you?"

"Yes, we are," said Elizabeth. "They will likely come back this way later when they give up on catching us. May we remain here until then?"

"Of course, dearie. Stay as long as you like. I wouldn't turn over my worst enemy to those cursed Frenchies!"

"I thank you, again and again. In truth, we have done nothing wrong. Our only crime was to ask them the wrong question."

"All Frenchies are moon mad, dearie, and there's no accounting for any of them. You just rest here."

Elizabeth took a deep breath. "May I ask one favor? It is very important to keep my friend out of their hands. I am not important, but she is. Is there somewhere she could be hidden?"

The woman's eyebrow flew up. "She?" She looked up and down at Georgiana's male attire.

Bother! She had slipped up already. It was too late to cover her mistake. "Yes, she is in disguise," she said ruefully.

"Well, then! You come into the house with me, young man or young lady, whichever you are, and you can keep watch out the window. If you see hide or hair of those Frenchies, we'll pop you into the root cellar. No one would ever think to look there."

"The horses need to cool down," said Georgiana. "Can you take care of that, Elizabeth?"

Elizabeth had no idea how to cool down horses. "Of course I can." She watched Georgiana's retreating back and sank down onto the ground until her pulse returned to something close to normal. It did not happen quickly.

The sun was growing low in the sky when the old woman came behind the barn again. "They've gone past again, so all should be well. You must come inside and share some bread before you go. No need to travel on an empty belly!" she said to Elizabeth.

Stiff from the long wait, Elizabeth gratefully followed her into the sparsely furnished cottage. Georgiana was perched on a stool, listening intently to a gnarled old man with tufts of white hair standing out from the sides of his head.

The woman said, "Here is your friend, safe and sound! She went into the root cellar when the Frenchies rode past, but they never stopped."

As Elizabeth thanked her, Georgiana looked up. "Mr. Simmons has been explaining how life has changed here since the arrival of the French."

94

The old man puffed on his pipe. "Aye, and I have been telling her that she would do better to sleep in our barn tonight and leave at first light. Them French bastards may still be watching the roads now, but they're slugabeds, the lot of them."

Elizabeth had been worrying about this very thing. Stopping at a nearby inn for the night would be risky. "I thank you for your offer and gratefully accept it."

Georgiana surveyed the hayloft. "This will be a new experience."

Elizabeth spread the blankets Mrs. Simmons had given them in an area where the hay was thick and even. "It is better than staying at an inn where we might have encountered some of those soldiers." At least Georgiana was not complaining about their humble lodgings as Elizabeth had feared she might.

"I am glad to stay here. I need to learn how the common people live."

"Is that why you were asking so many questions?"

"Of course!"

Perhaps she had underestimated the girl. "You certainly made the old man happy by providing such an attentive audience. I am glad to see you in such good spirits." Even if it puzzled her.

The girl plopped down on her blanket. "I am. I cannot explain it, but I have spent all these years terrified that something would happen to William and that I would be found by the French. Now it has happened, and it is almost a relief. If only I knew William was safe..."

The same events had left Elizabeth feeling at least a decade older and exhausted. "We were very fortunate today."

"We were." Suddenly Georgiana's expression turned sober. "But what should we do now? The plan did not include what I should do if I could not find Mr. Tennant."

Elizabeth's heart sank. "You have no other names?"

95

Georgiana shook her head. "No one. I have an address I can write to for help, but it is in Jamaica, so it would take months to get a response. There is Lady Matlock, but it would be dangerous to try to reach her. She is watched by the French."

Elizabeth wrapped herself in her blanket. "The first thing to do is to find out what happened to your brother. If he has been released, we may be able to find a way to contact him, but I see no safe way for us to discover that on our own without potentially revealing our location."

"What can we do?" Georgiana's breaths were coming rapidly again.

Apparently Elizabeth's habit of thinking out loud was making the girl more nervous again. Doing her best to radiate certainty, she said, "Our best course is to go to London and take lodgings. My uncle there is very trustworthy, and he can go to Meryton to discover if there is any news of your brother. We have enough money to live on while you send a letter to Jamaica and wait to hear back from them. It may not be as luxurious accommodations as you are accustomed to, but it will do. And if that fails, there is always Scotland." She hoped she was choosing to ask her uncle's assistance because it was the wisest thing, not because she wished for the consolation of some member of her family knowing what had become of her.

"I do not mind simple accommodations," said Georgiana. "I would like to go to London. When I was there with William, he would take me to museums and sometimes for a walk in the park, but I never met anyone or did ordinary things." Her voice hitched. "I miss William."

Elizabeth missed him, too. More than she cared to admit.

The following morning, their hosts fussed over Georgiana to the point that Elizabeth half wondered if she should not just leave the girl there. Mr. Simmons had harnessed the horses while his wife plied their guests with bread and preserves that likely they could ill afford to share. Elizabeth pressed a coin into her hand.

"There's no need," protested Mrs. Simmons. "We are happy to help anyone fleeing the Frenchies."

"I beg of you to take it," said Elizabeth. "You have done us a far greater service than you can imagine."

Mr. Simmons stepped back inside. "All harnessed up and ready to go, no worse for their run yesterday. Handsome beasts, those."

His wife said, "Best of luck to you both. I will be praying for your safety. I only wish I could someday see you in a dress, young lady!"

"And so you shall." Georgiana spoke with an assurance Elizabeth had never heard from her before. The girl tugged off one of her rings, placed it in Mrs. Simmons's hand and closed the old woman's fingers over it. "In the meantime, pray keep this ring as a remembrance of the day you saved Princess Charlotte from the enemy. And I promise you, someday I shall return here wearing both a dress and my rightful crown."

Mrs. Simmons stepped back unsteadily, pressing her hand against her chest. "You... You are... Her Highness? And I let you sleep in the hayloft!"

With a poisonous look at her companion, Elizabeth interjected, "We are very grateful for it."

Georgiana said warmly, "King Charles had to spend a day in an oak tree when he was fleeing the Roundheads. I am certain your hayloft is far more comfortable than a tree."

The old man looked from Georgiana to Elizabeth. "Is this true?"

There was little point in denying it; the damage had been done. Elizabeth took a deep breath. "It is, but I beg of you to tell no one, not even your closest friends or family. If even a rumor of the princess's return were to reach the French, it would lead to good men dying, and our chance to reclaim our country may be lost."

"No one will hear a word of it from us," Mrs. Simmons said, tears shining in her eyes. "I'm just that glad to know Your Highness has returned. I could die happy today."

The girl took her hands and kissed her wrinkled cheek. "I would rather you lived long enough to see England free once more."

Mr. Simmons said gruffly, "Now, off with the both of you before those Frenchies wake up."

"Yes, it is time," said Elizabeth firmly.

The old couple followed them out to the curricle. As Georgiana stepped up into it and Elizabeth followed her, the old man said, "God save Your Highness."

The girl gave him a long, serious look which somehow reminded Elizabeth of Mr. Darcy. "God save England," she said. Then she shook the reins, and they were off.

Elizabeth could not trust herself to speak, so instead she stared straight ahead and fumed. Had the girl been planning that little speech, and had she thought even for a second about what it could mean?

"Are you angry at me?" It was Georgiana's timid voice again.

"I am furious at you!"

"Because I told them? But it made them so happy."

"Very well, two people are happy. Now think, for just a minute, of what your brother has suffered on your behalf, sending his real sister and father halfway around the world where he might never see them again, and dedicating his own life to protecting that secret you so freely shared with two people you hardly knew! Think of him in prison, and what will happen if someone puts together the disappearance of Georgiana Darcy and the reappearance of Princess Charlotte."

"The two of them will not tell anyone; I am certain of it!"

"I hope you are correct, for you have wagered your brother's life and quite possibly my own based on your impression of them."

"I must reveal myself someday!"

"Naturally, but this was done without forethought or consultation with anyone else who might have a stake in whether you live or die. Even if I abandoned you today, I cannot go back to my family. I have lost Jane, my parents, my home, and all my friends for your sake. I did it of my own free will, but with the expectation you would be careful not to make my sacrifice meaningless!"

Georgiana did not reply this time. Now she was the one staring rigidly ahead. Elizabeth's anger was still burning, but it helped calm the fires to see the girl taking in her scolding. Perhaps she might even learn something.

But it was also amusingly ridiculous. She, Elizabeth Bennet, was sitting beside the heir to the throne, having just delivered a tongue lashing that reduced the girl to blinking back tears! Had she read a scene like this in a novel, she would not have thought it credible. Who would believe it? Mr. Darcy had come to her neighborhood, and from that first moment they met, one event had led to another until here she was.

Georgiana still wore a stony expression, the reins loose in her hands. Most likely it did not matter, given how well-trained the horses seemed to be, but it was not a good habit. Elizabeth reached over and gently took the reins from her. She might not be nearly as fine a driver is Georgiana was, but she could most likely manage to stop or to turn the horses if needed.

The girl's frozen distress tugged at Elizabeth's sympathy. Had anyone ever spoken to Georgiana in that way before? She could not imagine the controlled Mr. Darcy doing so, and perhaps Georgiana might not have given him a reason to be angry since he hovered over her and allowed her so little contact with other people. But he might have restricted her contact precisely because Georgiana had a tendency to speak first and think later. Her brother's overprotectiveness might have been warranted after all – one more way in which she had misjudged Mr. Darcy.

Georgiana burst out, "I wish they had taken me to Canada in the first place!"

It sounded a bit too much like a tantrum for Elizabeth's taste. "It is not too late. We could buy your passage on a ship. I imagine the real Georgiana Darcy would be thrilled to come home," Elizabeth said coolly.

"William would likely be happier that way. After all, she really is his sister," Georgiana said wistfully. "And I ruined his life. He must hate me." She covered her face with her hands as her shoulders began to heave.

Elizabeth slid closer and placed her arm around the girl's shoulders, hoping the horses truly were as well-trained as they seemed. "Now that is just silly. I never had the impression he was anything but concerned and caring about you. Why would he hate you?"

"Because he lost his father and sister because of me, and even his brother no longer speaks to him, again because of me. He never does any of the amusing or sporting things other gentlemen his age do, and that is because of me. He hates that everyone thinks he is a traitor when he only works with the French to protect me. Now he is in prison or maybe even dead because of me, and he might be happier being dead because if I am ever restored to the line of succession, I will ruin the rest of his life!"

There was no point in telling the girl she was being silly; it might provoke one of her nervous spells. "I think he would be very happy to see you take your rightful place."

"No doubt he would, at least until he realized it meant he has no choice but to marry me. He does not think of me that way, and I can think of no man who would hate life in the public eye more than he will. All he wants is to go back to Pemberley, not to have everyone watch his every move."

Elizabeth's stomach twisted in a knot. "Why should he have to marry you? Everyone would expect you to marry a foreign prince!"

The girl shook her head miserably. "That would have been true before the invasion, but now England would not stand for a foreigner as Prince Consort. It would be too much like Bonaparte's brother marrying

100

my aunt. And then there is the question of propriety. I have been alone with William for years, and he is an unmarried gentleman. Everyone will insist we must marry to preserve my reputation. And he will detest that, especially after everything else he has given up for me."

They were approaching the turnpike. Elizabeth needed both hands to stop the horses, so she removed her arm from Georgiana's shoulder. Numbly she drew up the reins and handed a coin to the staring gatekeeper. He opened the gate as if there were nothing unusual about a sobbing young gentleman being driven along the road.

Elizabeth shook the reins as she had seen Georgiana do, but the horses did not move. Mortified, she elbowed the girl. "I need you to drive," she said gracelessly.

"Oh." Georgiana took the reins and did exactly what Elizabeth had done. Naturally, the horrid horses moved immediately into a trot. It was not fair.

Mr. Darcy marrying Georgiana. That was not fair either, and it hurt far more, as if a knife had cut her insides wide open. Rising nausea made her wonder for a few minutes if she might actually be ill and how she could possibly explain that. Or if she cared. A future of watching Darcy married to Georgiana, whether he willed it or not, would be her own personal hell. Two hells, one where the French kept control of England, and one where Georgiana assumed her rightful place and Elizabeth would be forced to hear about the queen and her prince consort every day of her life. What irony – she had finally found something that felt even worse than having the French occupy England.

She could not even argue with Georgiana's analysis. Once it had been pointed out, it was obvious. Darcy was going to have to marry her whether either of them liked it or not. He must know it, too. Why else would an eligible young gentleman avoid flirting? Georgiana was no doubt right in her other conclusion as well. He would be miserable as Prince Consort.

She hated the thought of Darcy marrying the girl beside her, hated it with a passion beyond her loathing of the French. His rare playful moments would disappear completely.

Suddenly she would have given anything to hear him call her proud Titania again.

She could not bear to talk to Georgiana about this, not now. Even letting herself think of it was risking her composure. Instead she said briskly, "I am of the opinion Mr. Darcy does care about you as he would his own sister. But right now we have another problem on our hands. I think you had best give me a lesson on how to drive this team so I can manage them if I need to."

The prospect of something concrete to do seemed to cheer Georgiana. "Of course. I would be happy to."

If only Elizabeth could have relieved her own agony as easily!

When they stopped later at an inn a short distance outside of London, Elizabeth asked for use of paper and pen. Taking them up to her room, she sat down at the small desk and tried to think of what to say. There was so much she wanted to tell her uncle, and little of it could be safely put in writing.

It took her almost an hour to compose a letter she was content with. It began without salutation.

I beg of you to say nothing about this letter to anyone. It is more important than you can possibly imagine. Your missing niece is alive and well but in great need of your assistance. I am at the location the bearer will reveal to you, and I beg of you to come here as soon as you can so I may explain the situation to you more fully. I will remain here three days in the hope of seeing or hearing from you. Again, not a word to anyone, neither friend nor family, about this. I apologize for being mysterious, but you will understand when I can explain it to you. Ask for Miss Gardiner.

The pen dropped a spot of ink on the end. Elizabeth did her best to blot it up, but the stain remained.

She hoped she was not making a dreadful mistake.

Chapter Seven

Three days after Darcy's arrest, General Desmarais's aide-de-camp strode into his cell and stopped short. "*Mon Dieu!* What happened to you?" The friendly lieutenant trailed behind him.

Darcy hoped his bruises looked as bad as they felt. "Captain Reynard heard I was a fine boxer, so he decided we should have a match – with my hands tied. He enjoys that sort of game." Darcy could have pulled his hands out of his bonds and defended himself, but had decided a few bruises would be a cheap price for making certain Captain Reynard was removed from command. At least he had not knocked out any teeth.

The aide-de-camp spat. "*Canaille.*" He snapped his fingers for the guard. "Fetch your captain at once. Darcy, we will have you out of here immediately, and I apologize for this insult to your person."

Lieutenant Bessette untied Darcy's hands without being told.

"I thank you for coming so quickly, Colonel. I see you have already met Lieutenant Bessette. He has been of great assistance to me, treating me with respect while following all regulations for keeping me under guard. I can also say in his favor that one of the young ladies of the town, one who usually has nothing kind to say about any Frenchman, pointed him out to me as an honorable man."

The lieutenant's expression brightened, and he bowed to Darcy. "*Monsieur* Darcy is most kind."

Monsieur Darcy was not feeling in the least bit kind, but he paid his debts. All he wanted now was to get away from this place and find Georgiana and Elizabeth.

Two hours later Darcy left Meryton on a borrowed horse lent to him by the embarrassingly grateful Lieutenant Bessette, now Captain Bessette and acting commander of the Meryton garrison. He headed straight for the Longbourn stables.

Bingley's horse stood placidly in one of the stalls. Darcy put his borrowed mare in the neighboring stall and strode to the end of the stable, remembering at the last minute to use the special knock Elizabeth had shown him.

A worried looking Bingley opened the door. "Darcy! They released you? But what did they do to you?" He peered at Darcy's face.

Darcy waved his concern away. "Nothing serious."

"I tried to see you, but they would not allow me to visit."

"I appreciate the effort. Is Miss Bennet here? I must speak to her."

With apparent reluctance, Bingley stepped back to allow him to enter. Jane Bennet, her eyes red-rimmed, curtsied to him. "Miss Bennet, I am sorry to interrupt you at what appears to be a poor moment, but I thought you would wish to know Captain Reynard has been taken to London to answer charges and has been replaced here by one of his lieutenants. You are free to leave these rooms and to go wherever you wish."

Miss Bennet pressed her hand over her mouth, her eyes wide, but it was Bingley who said, "Is this true? Are you certain?"

"Quite certain. I provided evidence against him, and he was foolish enough to leave visible proof." Darcy tapped his bruised cheek.

Bingley's eyes lit up. "But this is wonderful news! It changes everything!" Then he sobered. "But all is not well. Miss Elizabeth is missing."

Elizabeth had believed him and had left with Georgiana! Relief flooded through him. But he must remember that he should have no knowledge of that. "Missing?"

"The same day you were arrested. The servant said she was with your sister and the two of them departed in your curricle. Georgiana left me a note saying you had told her to go to Pemberley, but not a word about Miss Elizabeth. I assumed Georgiana had simply taken her home to Longbourn, but neither of them have been seen since. A curricle is not suited for a long journey, and they did not even take a servant with them, so how could they have gone to Pemberley? And why would Miss Elizabeth have failed to tell her family?"

"One question at a time, if you please. I have been in a cell all this time and know nothing. What has been done to discover them?"

"I sent servants along the North Road to ask if anyone had seen them, and there are men searching the area between Netherfield and here. There has been no sign of them, neither the curricle nor the horses."

All according to plan, although it was deuced inconvenient now. "Miss Bennet, can you think of anywhere your sister might have gone?"

She shook her head. "You do not understand. She did not leave voluntarily. I know that because her emergency satchel is still here. It was packed with everything she would want if she had to leave unexpectedly. I checked that first thing." A tear slipped down her cheek.

That was a difficult point to counter. "Perhaps you are right, but if she had to leave so quickly that she could not even afford the time to fetch her satchel, where would she go? I do not want to leave any stones unturned."

Miss Bennet hesitated. "I would have said she would go either to Scotland or to my uncle's house in London, but my uncle has not heard from her." She lifted her chin. "Mr. Darcy, I understand you knew nothing of this until now, but you seem remarkably calm about your sister and mine being missing. I would have said you are not even particularly surprised by it." She met his gaze steadily, with a surprising hint of steel in her eyes. "I must ask what you know about their disappearance."

Bingley frowned. "Yes, Darcy, what do you know?"

Devil take it! In his preoccupation with finding Georgiana, he had handled this badly. He lowered himself into a chair. "I confess I am neither particularly surprised nor particularly worried about Georgiana's disappearance. There has always been a very real possibility I would be taken by the French, so we had an escape plan for Georgiana to employ if that happened. The curricle is always filled with supplies, including pistols. My sister is a crack shot, Miss Bennet, and well able to defend herself. If she has followed the plan, she should be fine." He believed it, too. Not just because the French were not hunting them, but because if something had happened to Elizabeth, he would know. He would feel it.

Miss Bennet shook her head. "That did not explain my sister's absence."

"No, it does not, but since they were seen leaving together, I can only assume Miss Elizabeth decided to accompany Georgiana. I cannot say why she would have left no message for you and not taken her satchel, unless she had some reason to disappear without a trace." Darcy gave Bingley a significant look.

Bingley snapped his fingers. "Captain Reynard! Had you told her you were planning to leave Netherfield? That would have left her at his mercy – unless she disappeared."

"That could explain it," said Darcy.

Miss Bennet's eyes were downcast. She said slowly, "I would rather believe she disappeared deliberately than that she has come to harm, but somehow it does not make sense. Something is not right."

Darcy put on his blandest, most innocent look. "What is that?"

"I cannot put my finger on it. But wait – perhaps I can. Why did you have elaborate escape plans for your sister when you are in high favor among the French?"

Damnation! He should have realized Elizabeth's sister would be clever enough to spot that hole in his story. "At present, yes, but these things can change very rapidly. The escape plan was also for me. I had assumed she and I would go together. Unfortunately, there was no opportunity for that."

Bingley said harshly, "Darcy is an agent for the government-in-exile. That is why he is worried about arrest and has an escape plan."

Astonished, Darcy stared at his friend. "Where on earth did you get that notion?"

Bingley met his gaze without flinching. "I have suspected it for some time. You are not the sort to sell out your country merely for your own comfort. The night when the Gouldings came to dinner, I saw you show their friend a bit of paper, and you burned it afterwards. That was when I knew."

Darcy sat back, drumming his fingers on the armrest of the chair. It was better to have them believe him a spy than to guess at the truth. "I deny it, but then again, I would deny it whether it was true or not. But what I can tell you, Miss Bennet, is that I will not rest until I have found my sister and hopefully yours along with her, and when I have done so I will endeavor to inform you somehow as to Miss Elizabeth's safety."

"All you need to do is to go to Pemberley," grumbled Bingley. Was he cross because Darcy had not admitted to his charges?

"Unfortunately, it will not be so simple. Part of the escape plan was to lay a false trail. I do not know where Georgiana is, except that it is not Pemberley. I will have to search for them, and it will not be simple or quick. Georgiana knows how to hide her tracks."

"I can help," Bingley offered.

Darcy shook his head. "I appreciate the offer, but it is better for me to do this alone. There is too much I cannot tell you, and it could endanger both of us. I would feel much easier knowing you are here and can pass along to me any news Miss Bennet may receive." He attempted a smile. "And without Miss Elizabeth or Georgiana here, someone should remain with Miss Bennet."

His friend considered this. "Will you inform me if you do need help?"

"That I will be happy to do, and I am glad to know I can rely on you."

"Of course you can. Dammit, Darcy, I do love England, too. You do not need to hide things from me."

"It is not up to me, Bingley. Too many lives are at risk." And he had been right not to tell Bingley anything, given how quickly his friend had shared his suspicions with Miss Bennet. A secret was only a secret as long as it was kept.

Miss Bennet folded her hands in her lap. "Mr. Darcy, did my sister know anything of your...other activities?"

Darcy weighed his options. "Not until the very end when I needed her to carry a message to Georgiana." It was an admission, but he suspected Jane Bennet knew how to keep a secret even if Bingley did not.

"Good," said Miss Bennet. "She found you very confusing. At least now she has an answer to her questions and will no longer blame you for your choices."

She was not the only one who was glad. It had been surprisingly painful to keep secrets from Elizabeth. And he would never forget the warmth of her lips against his.

Elizabeth sent a boy with the message first thing in the morning, praying her uncle would read it and understand. She had always considered herself an independent person, but her constant fear of being captured by the French and her responsibility for Georgiana made her long for the presence of someone older and wiser. Her uncle would make everything better.

It was not yet noon when she spotted Mr. Gardiner riding in on a sweating horse. Her heart swelled at the sight of his familiar face. She hurried outside to greet him, followed by a worried Georgiana.

Her uncle dismounted and tossed the reins to a groom, seeming to notice her only at the last minute. Then he hugged her so hard she gasped for breath when he finally released her. "Thank God!" He grabbed her shoulders. "But what in God's name were you thinking? Do you have any idea what you have put us through by disappearing like that?"

Tears came to Elizabeth's eyes. "I am sorry. I did not want to leave, but I had no choice."

Mr. Gardiner's face grew grim. "Who was it? Who took you away?"

Elizabeth shook her head. "No, it was not like that. It was my duty, but I wish there had been a way to prevent my family from suffering for it. But I cannot tell you about it here. There is a garden behind the inn where we can talk."

"Very well." Mr. Gardiner followed her into the inn and out through the rear door. Georgiana trailed after him.

They sat on a stone bench some distance from the inn, while Georgiana waited near the doorway. The words burst from Elizabeth. "Is my family safe? I have been so worried about them."

Her uncle's brows knitted. "As far as I know."

"The French have not evicted them from Longbourn?"

"Not that I have heard of, and they would have told me. But why did you leave?"

Elizabeth breathed a sigh of heartfelt relief. "I needed to help her escape." She gestured towards Georgiana.

Mr. Gardiner looked around them. "Of whom are you speaking?"

Elizabeth glanced back at Georgiana. "That youth over there. She is a girl dressed as a boy. Do you remember my letters about Mr. Bingley and Miss Darcy, the new friends who were visiting Jane? That is Miss Darcy.

Or that is how we were introduced to her, but it is not her name. Her brother had been keeping her hidden from society much as we did with Jane, but he was not really her brother at all. Then he was arrested, and because I was the only person there, he told me the truth—"

"You are making no sense, Lizzy. Why did you run off without a word?"

"It is not why, but who." She whispered in his ear, "She is Princess Charlotte."

He crossed his arms and glared at her. "Ridiculous. I do not know if you have gone mad or are merely the victim of a clever hoax, but that girl is no more Princess Charlotte than I am King George. You cannot believe everything you are told!"

"That is not fair! It was not simply believing what he told me. For weeks I spent hours every day with Mr. Darcy and his sister, and the entire time I felt there was something I was failing to understand about them. Jane felt it, too. When he was forced into telling me who she was, suddenly the entire puzzle made sense."

Her uncle sighed heavily. "Somehow I am certain he wanted something from you when he concocted this fable."

"He was being arrested. He wanted me to protect her, to take her away."

"He told you the thing that would make you most likely to do as he asked. Lizzy, I know how much you have wanted to contribute something to the cause of England's freedom, but he took advantage of your trusting nature to accomplish his own ends."

"My trusting nature? You are confusing me with Jane! Can you not even consider that I might be telling you the truth? I have spent four days and nights with her, and I am certain beyond a doubt of her identity. For heaven's sake, this is a girl who reads French books on military strategy for pleasure!"

Mr. Gardiner simply shook his head. "I am sorry, Lizzy, both for your disappointment and for all the pain this deception has caused."

Elizabeth pressed her arms tight against her sides as she forced her anger down. Finally she stood and said, "Very well. I know better than to think I can change your mind when it is made up. I will ask only that you not repeat anything of what I have told you to anyone, for the sake of my safety, if nothing else. She and I will leave here today."

"This is ridiculous! What of your father and mother, not to mention your aunt, who are all desperately worried about you? You must return to them."

A cold numbness spread through Elizabeth, but there was only one course of action open to her. "I did not ask for this burden, but I have a duty to something larger than my family. If it will console them, I will send you a letter saying I am safe in Scotland, and you may show it to them."

He opened his hands as if he wanted to take her by the shoulders, but he made no move to touch her. "Is that where you will be going, then?"

"I do not know yet, but we will disappear completely. I have mastered that particular skill in the last few days." She hated sounding so cold when this was likely the last time she would see her uncle, but if she did not focus on what she had to do, she would start to cry.

His hands fell to his sides. "I can only pray someday you will see reason and return to us. I can give you a little money if that would help."

She made a harsh sound in the back of her throat. "Thank you, but I have more money than I know what to do with."

Georgiana's voice came from beside her. "Elizabeth, may I speak to your uncle privately for a few minutes?" She sounded calm and confident, much as she had when she had revealed her identity to the old couple near Oxford.

Elizabeth lifted one shoulder. "If he is willing to speak to you, I have no objection. I will pack the satchel; we will be leaving as soon as possible." She left without a word to her uncle. Her lower lip did not begin to tremble until she was inside the inn.

Half an hour later, Georgiana returned to Elizabeth's room. "Go to your uncle," she said. "He wishes to speak to you."

Elizabeth turned a pained gaze on her. "Did you convince him?"

"I think so. He asked me a great many questions."

Bile rose in her throat. Had her uncle believed a stranger when he had not trusted Elizabeth? She was not certain she wished to know the answer.

Mr. Gardiner was still sitting on the bench behind the inn. No doubt her red and swollen eyes were obvious, but there was nothing she could do about that. "Georgiana says you have something to tell me," she said coolly.

He rubbed his hand over his mouth. Beads of perspiration edged his forehead. "I cannot believe it! But I must believe it. She knows too much, and the way she carries herself..."

Elizabeth held back a bitter laugh. Her uncle had never seen one of Georgiana's nervous attacks. "You should not judge upon that. Sometimes she is quite different. I have come to the conclusion that she is very good at being that other person whose name I will not say, but she is not well suited to being meek, obedient Georgiana Darcy."

"But that this burden should fall onto you! My hands are shaking just thinking of what might have happened to her and to you. I am sorry I disbelieved you, Lizzy."

She thawed a little. "I still wake up in the night disbelieving it myself."

"That a secret of this magnitude could be kept for so long!" He mopped his brow with a handkerchief. "But you said in your letter that you were in urgent need of help. If it is not money, how can I assist you?"

Elizabeth sat down beside him. "She was supposed to go into the care of another Loyalist, but he has been executed. We do not know where to take her next. Only Mr. Darcy or someone in Jamaica would know that.

We need to discover what has happened to Mr. Darcy, but very quietly, so no suspicions are raised." At least her voice had not trembled while speaking of Mr. Darcy.

Mr. Gardiner said, "I can write a letter to your father and ask about him, or I could travel there myself. Or I could send someone to ask questions."

Elizabeth shook her head. "It is more difficult than that. There can be no direct questions or involvement of anyone else. No one must know you have any interest in Mr. Darcy. If he was forced to confess, they will be watching my family and on the lookout for strangers inquiring after him. You would have to visit Longbourn, but I know it would look suspicious if you left your business and go there for no reason, so we may have to wait."

Mr. Gardiner blinked several times before responding. "I see. I will have to set up a family visit, but you are right. It would raise questions if I appeared suddenly."

"We also need help finding somewhere to stay, especially if Mr. Darcy can no longer help us and we have to contact the government-in-exile for instructions. It will take months for a letter to travel across the Atlantic and back, and we cannot stay at inns indefinitely. Too much attention is paid to travelers."

Her uncle nodded. "I can assist you with that. We will have to discuss what type of situation would be safest."

Elizabeth felt a weight lift off her shoulders. "Secrecy is paramount. You are only the fourth person in England to know the truth, but that is already too many." But she was glad for her own sake that he knew it. It had been a heavy responsibility to carry alone.

Elizabeth looked curiously at the pile of parcels Mr. Gardiner set on the small writing desk in her room at the inn. "What have you brought us?"

"Mourning dresses," said her uncle. "Do not worry; no one has died. They are costumes for the role you will need to play in your new situation."

"You have found us lodgings?" asked Georgiana.

"Of a sort. It was more challenging than I anticipated. I looked at several flats before discovering that Hangman Lamarque requires new lodgers to be reported to the French. If your Mr. Darcy has confessed, they might be watching for two young people in search of lodgings, so I decided to look at other options."

Elizabeth raised an eyebrow. "Hangman Lamarque?"

Mr. Gardiner looked at her in surprise. "You have not heard him called that before? I suppose the nickname has not yet traveled outside the city. Monsieur Lamarque, who became head of London police last year, suspects all Englishman and considers almost everything a hanging offense."

Elizabeth nodded. "I read in *The Loyalist* that London arrests and executions had increased."

"There is one of Lamarque's hanging offenses for you – possessing a copy of *The Loyalist*."

"Hanging just for that?" cried Elizabeth. "Why, when the French commander in Meryton arrested someone for that, we all thought it was just a ploy."

"Not in London. You will find life in Town quite changed since his arrival. Everyone is afraid of him."

Georgiana's brows drew together. "Can no one stop him?"

Mr. Gardiner shook his head. "Rumor has it that General Desmarais attempted to persuade him that a frightened populace is a dangerous populace, but Lamarque is not under his command. He reports directly to the Emperor."

Elizabeth placed a calming hand on Georgiana's arm. The girl's hatred for Napoleon was too close to the surface as it was. "What shall we do then? Would it be safer to seek lodgings elsewhere? We could go to Bath or Brighton, I suppose."

"It would be much harder for me to arrange, and more difficult for me to communicate with you if I discover anything about your Mr. Darcy. I have a better idea. The widow of a man I did business with has a good heart and a large house, but she rarely goes out because she is confined to a chair, and she has no family who visits her. When her husband was dying, he asked me to check on her from time to time, so I usually call on her once a fortnight or so. She said she would be very happy to assist me by taking in two young women, distant connections of mine, who were recently orphaned in a tragic fire which destroyed all their belongings, thus explaining your limited luggage. The French would never know, and since you would be in mourning, you could avoid any callers she might have. Then, if it proves necessary in a month or two, we can take lodgings for the two of you when the French might be paying less attention to new tenant reports."

Elizabeth considered this option. "But would she not mention us to my aunt?"

Mr. Gardiner shook his head. "They are not acquainted. I only met her through her husband, and she is not someone we would invite to our house. Your aunt likes the company of clever, educated people. Mrs. Landon is neither of those, just a simple, good-hearted lady."

"It may be to our advantage that she is not clever," said Elizabeth slowly. A recent bereavement would explain Georgiana's fears and timidity. "It sounds like a good plan. What do you think, Georgiana? Can you play the role of a bereaved girl?"

"It would be much easier than pretending to be a half-wit," declared Georgiana. "That is exhausting."

"Excellent," said Mr. Gardiner. "I can bring you there today, hence the mourning clothes. I purchased pre-made dresses in several sizes, so you can pick which fits best."

"What will we do about the curricle and horses?" Elizabeth had grown remarkably attached to the carriage, the only constant in their travels.

"I will arrange for a livery stable to care for it," said Mr. Gardiner. "Under a false name, I think, as it is hardly the sort of vehicle I could afford to keep. But your aunt has agreed to write to your mother to suggest that we visit Longbourn next month. I told her I was feeling in need of some country air. The wait is longer than I would like, but it would look odd if we tried to go sooner."

A month until they could hear what had happened to Mr. Darcy. It was going to be a very long month.

Elizabeth and Georgiana had only been at Mrs. Landon's house for a week before Mr. Gardiner came to call. After visiting with Mrs. Landon for a time, he asked to speak to Elizabeth privately with the suggestion that it was a matter concerning her supposed father's will.

When they were finally alone, Elizabeth asked quietly, "Do you have news?"

"Not of your friend, but we received a rather surprising letter from your sister Jane yesterday. I had hoped to show it to you, but I could not find an excuse to bring it with me."

"What does she say?" After missing Jane for so long, the idea of a letter from her nearly brought tears to Elizabeth's eyes.

Mr. Gardiner frowned. "This may come as something of a shock to you as it did to us. She told us she is engaged and will be married as soon as the banns are called."

"What?" It made no sense. Jane was supposed to be grieving. Elizabeth recovered herself enough to say, "Engaged? To Mr. Bingley, I suppose. There is no one else. But how can she leave her hiding place safely?"

"Yes, it is Mr. Bingley. Jane mentioned there has been a change in command in the local garrison, but she gave no details. I assume that is why she could stop hiding. She has invited your aunt and me to her wedding, assuming we can obtain travel permits. The good news is that it will give me an earlier opportunity to discover the fate of your friend."

In her shock, Elizabeth could hardly spare a thought for Mr. Darcy's fate. "Did she say anything about me?" Her voice shook on the last words.

Mr. Gardiner looked at her sharply. "No, but it was a very short letter. She said nothing about anyone else in the family, either."

But the others had not vanished mysteriously as Elizabeth had. All those nights lying awake and fretting over what Jane must be suffering, wondering if she had been killed, and instead Jane had been planning her wedding! And without even waiting a decent interval out of grief or in hope of her sister's return? Elizabeth sank her teeth into her trembling lower lip.

Her uncle, apparently noticing her distress, said, "I am sorry, Lizzy."

"Oh, it is nothing," she said. How could she admit that she had wanted Jane to grieve for her? "I am merely sad to miss her wedding. When I left, I knew I would miss events like this, but I had not thought it would happen so soon."

Mr. Gardiner said slowly, "I admit I am puzzled, both by the events and the haste with which they are occurring. There must be more to the story than she is telling us. She might have said more had she known that you would be hearing the information from me."

"No doubt," said Elizabeth dully. She and Jane had always spoken of standing up at each other's weddings. Now she would not even be present.

"I will be able to tell you more after I see your family. Tell me, how is... Georgiana finding her stay? She said so little I cannot judge."

"Well enough, though she is still frantic with worry over William – Mr. Darcy, that is. Since I cannot keep her from speaking about William, I told Mrs. Landon that he is our brother, so I have been referring to him that way. When I see him again, I may have trouble remembering to call him Mr. Darcy."

"I hope I will be able to discover his fate when I go to Longbourn. But I am glad to see you have more hope that he is alive than you seemed to before."

Elizabeth hesitated. "I have doubts about my reasoning, but I have come to the conclusion that most likely he was arrested not because of Georgiana, but because of his efforts to protect me. If they thought he had committed treason, they would have arrested him for that and likely have taken all the servants in for questioning. Instead, they trumped up a murder charge – an excuse to get him into custody, if I am correct. My guess is that Captain Reynard wanted to punish him but needed an excuse because he knew Mr. Darcy was protected by more powerful Frenchmen. If that was the case, it would have been too risky to execute him. I may be wrong, but I pray I am not."

"That is a hopeful way to look at it," said her uncle. "But wait – is not this Mr. Bingley a good friend of his? Would he be planning his wedding if his friend had just been executed?"

Elizabeth shook her head slowly. "I would not think so. If Mr. Darcy were still in prison, he might go forward with the wedding, but I believe you are correct. That is a happy thought which may be of comfort to Georgiana. She is desperate to see him again." For at least the hundredth time, she reminded herself it made no difference to her. Whatever she might wish for in the middle of the night when she relived his kiss, Darcy could never be more to her than a friend. Perhaps someday that thought might not hurt as much.

"I hope it may provide her some relief."

Elizabeth still felt tears pricking at her eyes. To keep them from escaping, she said, "Of course, her brother may not be happy with me when he discovers I have distracted her from her worries by introducing her to forbidden fruit. He did not permit her to read novels, but she is devouring them now. Until now, her reading has been training for her future. Do you know what she said when I asked her what her favorite book was? Hume's *History of England*, all six volumes! Although she did spare a good word for Abbé Barruel's *Memoirs Illustrating the History of Jacobinism* since it has helped her to understand her enemies."

With a knowing laugh, Mr. Gardiner said, "No wonder she is happy to discover novels!"

Chapter Eight

Darcy reined in Hurricane at the top of the hill and feasted his eyes on the vista before him. Pemberley. Six years away and it still had the power to make his soul ache. God above, how he longed to gallop down the hill and enter those well-remembered rooms, to drink in the sight of the beloved items his mother had chosen for their home, to walk the portrait gallery and let the history of his family surround him...

No. He yanked the reins, turning Hurricane away. He should not even have come this close. If any of his staff or tenants saw him, they would expect him to stay, not to leave after one brief conversation. It would be his duty to stay, but right now his duty to England came first.

He set out for Lambton, a market town he had rarely visited in the past. If he gave a false name there, no one would be likely to detect it. Fortunately, the Royal Oak had both a room for the night and a private parlor available. The proprietor found a boy to carry his note to Mrs. Fitzwilliam at Pemberley, with only a slight snort on hearing the name rather than his aunt's former title.

Then there was nothing to do but wait. Wait and worry. Wait and cover three sheets of paper with ridiculously far-fetched possibilities regarding where Georgiana and Elizabeth might be, assuming they had not been imprisoned, attacked, or worse.

It felt like days rather than a few hours before a carriage pulled up in front of the inn. Darcy waited inside the private parlor. No one had recognized him so far, but being seen with his aunt might raise suspicions.

She sailed into the private parlor and kissed his cheek. "This is a surprise."

"Thank you for coming so quickly." Darcy tightened his folded hands. He was not looking forward to this.

His aunt said crisply, "I assumed this must be urgent, especially since you did not come to us at Pemberley." She had always been a step ahead of him.

"I need help. I was arrested by the French – the reason is unimportant – and, following my instructions, Georgiana disappeared to parts unknown. Unknown even to me, and now I need to find her."

"Georgiana? You mean…?"

"Yes, I mean *her*. I tracked her as far as I could, but now all I can do is hope she is spotted somewhere. If I set up too much of a search, it will draw notice. You told me once that Frederica has a network of people who collect information. That is what I need."

His aunt regarded Darcy placidly, but he knew that expression usually denoted deep thought for her. Finally she said, "Yes. I believe it is time for you and Frederica to work together. You can find her in London at 26 Leadenhall Street, across from St. Andrew Undershaft."

"I thank you." It was frightening how close he felt to begging his aunt for reassurance that everything would turn out well.

Darcy hesitated on the doorstep of the house on Leadenhall Street. This was not going to be pleasant, but it was his best hope for finding Georgiana and Elizabeth. He was not looking forward to confessing everything to Frederica, especially after all these years, but there really was no other choice. Hiring more men to search for Georgiana increased the risk of someone reporting Darcy's odd requests to the French. No, he needed Frederica's network of trustworthy Loyalists more than he needed his pride.

His mouth twisted as he knocked on the door. While waiting for a response, he flicked open his card case and pulled out a calling card. The door opened, but Darcy could see little of the man standing in the shadows beyond it.

Darcy proffered the card. "For the lady of the house." Those were the words his aunt had told him to say.

The shadowed man ignored the card. Instead he cocked his head to one side and drawled, "It may have been a long time, William, but I think we are beyond the calling card stage."

Darcy knew that voice. He stepped forward, shading his eyes, and peered ahead. "Kit?" he asked incredulously.

"You do remember my existence! I am honored! But I assume from your surprise you did not expect to find me here and no doubt would not have come here had you known. You need not worry; I have no more desire to see you than you do to see me. Still, I assume you must have some reason for deigning to call in this lowly part of town." Kit's insolent tone was as familiar as the little smile on his face, and he had lost none of his ability to cut through Darcy's defenses.

"I am here to see Frederica." Darcy hoped he did not sound as disconcerted as he felt. "You answer the door yourself now?"

Kit's upper lip curled. "We are not so high and mighty as you are. Only trusted people answer our door." He put an emphasis on the word 'trusted,' as if to make it clear that Darcy was not.

Darcy narrowed his eyes. "It is good to see you looking so well," he said evenly. "Is Frederica here?"

"Yes." Kit stepped back to allow Darcy to enter and called over his shoulder, "Freddie! You have a very special caller!" His tone was mocking. As they waited, Kit turned back to his brother with a bright smile that did not reach his eyes. "In the meantime, shall we get our usual conversation over with, the one where I ask to see Georgiana or at least to write to her, and you refuse without any good reason? There, I managed the entire conversation without you even having to say a word."

Darcy's breath hissed out through his teeth. "It is more complicated than that." He did not want to fight with Kit. His brother's complaints were perfectly reasonable, but he did not know the truth about Georgiana.

Fortunately, Frederica emerged from a room towards the back of the house. "William!" She hurried forward and embraced him. "What a lovely surprise!" She stepped back to look at him, and her smile faded. "But how did you find this place? No one should have told you where I was."

Darcy pulled the letter from his pocket and proffered it to her. "From your mother. And you need not worry; your secret is safe with me."

Kit interrupted, "But is it safe from all your high and mighty French friends?"

Darcy ignored him. "Freddie, may I speak to you privately?"

Frederica looked up from the letter she had been perusing, her brows drawn together. Her gaze flicked to Kit and back to Darcy. She said slowly, "Mother says this is about business, and I cannot exclude Kit from business simply because of this nonsensical quarrel between you."

"It is not nonsensical!" snapped Kit. "He sold out to the French, and he refuses even to let me write to my sister!"

"Fine," said Darcy. "We will all talk. I am tired of being blamed for something I cannot control. But it must be in private."

"Of course." Frederica opened the door to a room on their left.

Kit walked past her. Darcy waited for Frederica to go ahead of him.

Frederica laughed. "We do not bother here with all the nonsense about ladies and gentlemen and who walks through a door first." His cousin had grown more hard-edged in the years since he had last seen her.

He gave a slight smile. "That is your privilege, but I do still bother with it. Will you be so kind as to indulge me?"

"Very well." She preceded him into what must have once been the drawing room. It still held all the appropriate furnishings, but several of the chairs were covered with stacks of closely written pages and a map was spread across the tea table.

Kit drawled, "If we are to be proper, I suppose we must offer you something to drink." He held up a dusty bottle of wine and filled three glasses. "Not what you are accustomed to, but my allowance only goes so far." He handed glasses to Darcy and Frederica, then lifted his own with a challenging look. "Her Highness. God save her." He waited for Darcy's response with a smirk.

Through all the tension, it seemed somehow ridiculous to hear Kit, all unknowing, propose a toast to their little sister. Darcy lifted his own glass and said ironically, "God save her indeed, because I cannot always do it."

Kit stiffened. "What is that supposed to mean?"

This was not how Darcy had intended to begin, but he had not counted on seeing Kit and how savagely angry his brother would make him. "The reason you have not been allowed to see Georgiana, first by our uncle and later by me, is because you would have immediately recognized that she is an imposter. You have been serving England in your own way, and so have I. Yes, I sold out to the French, but it was because I had a different task: to keep one fair-haired nine-year-old girl safe, no matter what it cost me."

Kit snorted in disgust. "You are making no sense. How could she be an imposter?"

But Frederica, always the cleverest of the family, had gone pale. "Oh, no. I see it now. You know the story, Kit. Georgiana was a favorite playmate of the princess. Our fathers employed her to gain access to the princess when they stole her away, then they took two fair-haired girls across the country in a farm cart. When they reached Milford Haven, one

125

man and one girl boarded a ship to Canada. The other girl went to Matlock Park with my father where he told everyone she was Georgiana Darcy. Oh, God help us all!"

Darcy finished the story for her. "And three months later, the French took Matlock Park and your father suffered an apoplexy, so that little girl had to go to the only other person who knew her secret." He kept his eyes pinned to Frederica because he was afraid of what he might see on Kit's face.

Frederica tapped her cheek with her finger, a sure sign that she was scheming. "If she is here, that changes everything. With her to rally around —"

"Stop!" interrupted Darcy. "I did not come here either to tell you this story or to offer you her services. I came because she has been missing for a fortnight, and I need your help to find her."

Frederica ran her finger along the map. "They started in Hertfordshire, and you traced them as far as Oxford before losing the trail. Presumably they would not have gone back towards Meryton, but any other direction is possible. We have people to the north in Coventry and Birmingham. Stoke-on-Trent, too, if they were headed toward Scotland. Gloucester and Worcester to the west. The hard part is the South, since they could have gone anywhere. Bristol, Basingstoke, Reading, and London, of course. You have no other guesses where they might have gone?"

"I have followed all my leads." Darcy ticked them off on his fingers one at a time. "Elizabeth Bennet has an uncle in London, but her sister says that he knows nothing. My contact in Carlisle has not seen them. No horses meeting the description of mine have been sold at Tattersalls. I had someone check Bath since it is easy to take lodgings there and be anonymous. Your mother was the only other person whose name

Georgiana knew, but she was aware your mother was being watched. Still, I checked there, and your mother sent me here. I sent a man to Brighton because Georgiana had once mentioned wishing to see it. I have racked my brains and come up with nothing."

Frederick wrote a note on a scrap of paper. "Spas and resorts – a good idea."

"Why did you never tell me?" Kit's voice reverberated with fury.

Darcy took a deep breath and straightened. "Our father made the decision. You were but fourteen, wild and impulsive. It was too big a secret to risk."

"I grew out of that!"

"You did, but by then you were furious with me and considered me a traitor. It was safer to say nothing."

"You could have said something!"

"What? Something such as I wished I could explain it to you? Or it was not my decision, or that it had nothing to do with you, or that someday I would explain? I said all those things again and again, and they made no difference!"

"How do you think I felt? You and Georgie were the only family I had left, and you kept pushing me away!"

Darcy's fingernails cut into his palms. "You had Frederica, and during school holidays you stayed with her mother at Pemberley. That is more than I had. Do you think I enjoyed being the family traitor? That I liked working with the French? That it was enjoyable to deal with an out-of-control young girl all by myself, to keep her by my side constantly for six years? Six years! Six years of people spitting when I walked past them, looking down their noses at the traitor who betrayed his country. I have not even been to Pemberley in all this time because people there would notice the difference in her. Do you think I wanted to push you and all the world away? I did not ask for this duty. Do not complain to me. Freddie never got even a hint from her parents, did she?"

Frederica said calmly, "And you may be sure that, once I have a moment to myself, I will be furious with them. If only I had known, I could have prepared differently, been ready to go when she was old enough. But I also see that it was too important a secret to risk. Now, the two of you must either calm yourselves or leave me alone. It is your choice."

"Very well," said Darcy with a steadiness he did not feel. "What is your plan?"

Frederica nodded. "I will send word to our contacts in those places, asking them to make inquiries if anyone has seen your curricle and two young women, or a woman and a boy. It will take time; our messages are not sent directly to reduce the risk of exposure. If we should hear anything about her, where will you be? Darcy House?"

Darcy shook his head. "If I go to Darcy House, I will officially be in town, and that means I will be expected to be at the beck and call of various French officials. I would do better to find a lodging house and send you the address."

"Better not to go to a lodging house, or you will be reported to Lamarque's men," said Frederica. "You can stay here if you wish. There are few comforts, and it is not without danger from Lamarque's so-called police, but you are welcome as long as you stay out of the way of our business."

"I will do my best, but I have no idea what you actually do here except that it involves a great deal of paper." Darcy gestured to one of the stacks.

Kit gave a sharp laugh. "That it does."

"I cannot be expected to keep all the information in my head," said Frederica. "We do a variety of things. Kit handles the escape routes when someone needs to leave England quietly. I keep track of our network of sympathizers and the information they send me, the location of troops and armaments, how the arms depots are guarded, and so forth. Andrew, whom you will no doubt meet, puts out a newspaper that tells what is happening beyond the censored information the French give out. Kit and I both help with that."

Darcy raised an eyebrow. "Not *The Loyalist*?"

"The very same. You know it?"

"Everyone knows it. I am impressed."

"I am glad to hear it," said Kit dryly, "since you paid for quite a few issues."

Darcy looked at him with lively suspicion. "I did?"

"Remember when I begged you to help me settle my gambling debts? I had no debts, but we had run out of money for paper and ink. And no, I have no regrets about lying to you."

Darcy said nothing until he could be certain his anger was sufficiently under control. "I suppose I would rather it go to *The Loyalist* than to gambling debts."

Frederica said sharply, "Kit, stop trying to provoke your brother. He has given as much to the cause as you have, and if he lacked faith in you, I must point out that you also lacked faith in him."

"So did you," retorted Kit.

"In fact, I did not. I found it hard to believe he would sell out, but my mother told me so firmly that I was not to involve Darcy in my ventures that I suspected he had some other mission, most likely insinuating himself into the confidence of the French. If she could, I think she would like to keep the entire resistance in the family."

Darcy almost smiled. "Your mother, of course. I should have realized who was orchestrating this."

Frederica frowned as she read through her reports. "Still nothing. No reports of a curricle with a pair of matched grey thoroughbreds and a chestnut-haired woman and fair-haired boy or girl, nothing even close to a match. If they went north, they somehow managed not to be noticed.

There is a stable boy on the road from Oxford to London who remembers a particularly handsome pair of greys, but he did not see the carriage or the travelers. No one at the inn recalls two people meeting the description, but it is a busy coaching inn with high traffic."

It was a disappointment, but Darcy was becoming inured to failure. "It is little comfort, but I will have the opportunity to speak to Elizabeth Bennet's family in a few days. My friend Bingley is marrying her sister, and I have been invited to the wedding. Perhaps her sister may have more ideas of where Elizabeth might have chosen to go. It is not much to go on, but I will do what I can."

Frederica drummed her fingers on the table. "Kit is good at extracting information from people. Perhaps you should take him with you."

He would rather have the company of a spitting tomcat. "Meryton is several hours away. I would prefer to arrive there alive, thank you, and preferably without a black eye."

Tossing her reports aside, Frederica said with some exasperation, "William, I have worked with Kit for three years now. He is reliable, hardworking and loyal. He can also be stubborn, something he has in common with you. And yes, he does try to unnecessarily provoke you. You were twenty-one when your father left. Kit was fourteen. Think about that for a minute. This house is the first home he has had since the invasion. I wish he would stop needling you, but could you not manage to ignore it? He has felt abandoned by you for so long. He is not going to allow himself to rely on you overnight."

Darcy groaned. "Not another one! Georgiana is always afraid I will leave her, and now Kit feels abandoned." He managed to stop himself before he said something foolish, that perhaps he would like someone to rely on for once. "Very well. I will try." But he thought it unlikely to make a difference.

Not surprisingly, Bingley's wedding to Jane Bennet was small and rather subdued. Elizabeth's absence cast a palpable shadow over the celebration. Still, Darcy was happy to see Bingley, and he had miraculously managed not to argue with Kit on the road to Meryton.

There was an unexpected presence at the wedding, though. Darcy had not expected to see any French officers there apart from the youngest sister's husband, but across the church he saw his old friend Lieutenant Bessette. No, it was Captain Bessette now. What was he doing at this intimate wedding?

Once outside the church, Captain Bessette hurried to his side. "Monsieur Darcy!"

"Captain, it is a pleasure to see you again." Or it would be if his mere presence did not make it more difficult for Darcy to gain information from the new Mrs. Bingley. "May I present my brother, Mr. Christopher Darcy?"

Rigid, Kit barely returned the captain's bow. "Captain," he said coldly.

Captain Bessette's smile wavered.

Darcy glared at Kit. "Captain, I must ask you to make allowances for my brother. He is a Loyalist. Kit, Captain Bessette was instrumental in removing the former commanding officer here, a man who badly mistreated the local people, and he most likely saved my life along the way."

The captain laughed. "*Monsieur* Darcy is too kind! It was his intervention, not mine, which caused Captain Reynard's arrest. But I am very much in his debt for that, and for recommending my promotion. *Monsieur* Darcy, I think you will find the local people have fewer complaints about the regiment now."

"That is news I am glad to hear. Have you come for the wedding?"

"Yes, I was invited. Not what you might have expected, *n'est-ce pas*? But I have been courting Miss Mary Bennet." He lowered his voice. "After Miss Elizabeth Bennet disappeared, many people were most unkind to the family and treated the younger daughters as ruined. I recalled you had often visited Longbourn and thought you would not be happy with that outcome. Since I have made my intentions known, the family has been accepted in society again."

The man had found a clever way to repay the favor Darcy had done him. For Elizabeth's sake, he was glad of it. But wait – had not Elizabeth spoken of her sister Mary as plain and dull? Perhaps the captain had done the family two good turns, but it was certainly more repayment than Darcy had expected. "I am glad to hear it. I hope it pleases Miss Mary. I had thought she was not often in company where she would meet gentlemen."

With a knowing smile, Captain Bessette said, "I understand you. Miss Kitty is prettier and livelier, but someday I will bring my wife home to France. Miss Mary, she is a lady I can introduce to my mother, you know?"

"A wise decision," Darcy said. "I congratulate you on it. You will make her a good husband."

Kit made a hissing sound through his teeth.

Captain Bessette turned on him. "*Monsieur* Christopher, your brother is a good man. You Loyalists can look down your nose at those like him as much as you please, but your brother, he permitted Captain Reynard to beat him only so that he would have bruises to show to the colonel from London. That is why the evil man is gone. I was there. Your brother, he could have fought back, but he did not. Because of him, women here are no longer afraid to leave their houses and no one is being turned out or robbed of their earnings. How many Loyalists have done as much to aid those that are suffering?"

Darcy placed his hand on Kit's arm. "Captain, I thank you for your defense of my character, and for all the changes you have made here. All of us do our part in attempting to make the world a better place, even the Loyalists."

The captain chuckled. "You are more diplomatic than I, *Monsieur* Darcy! But I see Miss Mary is looking for me, so I must leave you." He clicked his heels together as he bowed, whistling as he walked away.

Darcy did not look at Kit. He did not want to see the disgust on his brother's face. "Come, I will introduce you to the family so that you can get on with your work."

The introductions were made outside the church. Kit promptly busied himself flirting with Kitty Bennet and charming Elizabeth's mother. Darcy was happy to leave that job to him, and even happier to avoid a discussion with his brother about Captain Bessette.

Darcy set off by himself towards Longbourn for the wedding breakfast, but a fashionably dressed man a few years older than him maneuvered to walk beside him. No doubt a favor seeker, but a wedding was not the place to be rude, so Darcy said, "It is a pleasant day for a wedding." The weather – the most neutral subject possible.

"Very pleasant indeed. Yesterday my niece Jane was concerned it might rain on her nuptials." The man said nothing further for a minute before adding, "I believe you are also acquainted with my niece Elizabeth. It is a pity she could not be here today."

Darcy gave him a sharp look. "I have that honor, yes."

A woman stepped up beside the man and took his arm. "Pardon me for interrupting. I fear I am becoming a little fatigued after our travels."

The man patted her hand. "I am sorry, my dear; I was not thinking. This gentleman and I were discussing the lovely weather. It would be a perfect day for curricle ride, would it not? With a pair of fine grey horses, I think. I recently met a young lady with just such a curricle; perhaps I shall ask her if I might borrow it someday and take you for a drive in the park."

The woman crinkled her forehead. "You know curricles are too high for me, my dear. Now a phaeton would be just the thing!"

The man now had Darcy's complete attention. A curricle with a pair of gray horses belonging to a young lady. It had to be a message for him.

Darcy wanted to grab him by the shoulders and demand to be told everything.

But apparently his wife knew nothing of the matter, so Darcy was unable to say anything directly. "I had a curricle with a pair of greys once, but it was not a high perch one. It had a clever compartment hidden under the seat."

"Why, so does my young friend's! I wonder if they came from the same maker." The man nodded slightly to Darcy.

Darcy returned the nod. The man did know something! Finally!

Mrs. Bennet elbowed her way through the crowd. "There you are, brother! Jane wishes to introduce both of you to her dear Mr. Bingley. Come with me."

Darcy could happily have strangled her as she took the couple away.

The room was filling rapidly. How was he to find a way to have a private word with the man? Darcy made his way across the room to Kit. "That gentleman over there with the bride, the one in the blue coat – I must speak to him alone. He knows something."

Kit's eyes lit up. "Finally! I have learned nothing useful so far. Let me see… Outside or inside, which would you prefer?"

"Outside. Too many people inside."

"Good thought." Kit peered out the window. "There is a little wilderness on the other side of the lane – wait there. Does the gentleman wish to speak to you or to avoid you?"

"To speak to me, it seems," said Darcy.

"That will make it easier. Go now, and I will send him as soon as I can."

Kit watched his brother leave and made his way across the crowded room to stand between Bingley and the man with the blue coat. They were conversing about the wedding. Bingley gave him a puzzled glance.

Finally there was a pause in the conversation. "Bingley," Kit said cheerily, "I have not yet had the chance to give you my congratulations on your wedding. You may not remember me after all these years, but you made quite an impression on me as a boy. Kit Darcy, at your service." He put out his hand.

"Darcy's brother?" exclaimed Bingley, shaking his hand with enthusiasm. "It has been years, has it not? Darcy had not mentioned to me that...that he had seen you recently."

Kit laughed. "You mean that he and I are on civil terms again? It is cause for astonishment, I grant you, but my brother and I have spent most of the last fortnight together, and we are both still alive."

"I am delighted to hear it," declared Bingley. Turning to the man in the blue coat, he said, "Darcy is a very dear old friend, and my wedding would never have happened if not for him. He made it possible for Jane to come out of hiding."

"She mentioned something of that to me," said the man. "That he had reported the officer who was threatening her or some such?"

"Yes, Darcy sent a letter about the man to his commanding officer, but what really did the trick was that Darcy allowed the man to give him a beating. His bruises were apparently a good argument, and his friend the general had the blackguard dragged off for court-martial. All of us are very much in your brother's debt."

Why must everyone tell him that story? If William was a hero in Meryton, what was it to him?

"We are indeed," said the blue coated man to Kit. "Is he here today? I would like the opportunity to thank him personally for what he has done."

Kit's mind jerked back to his task. "He stepped outside for some air. Would you like me to take you to him?"

"I would be most appreciative of it! Bingley, it has been a pleasure to meet you, and I look forward to knowing you better in the future."

As Kit led him outside, the gentleman thanked him for his assistance.

"It is a pleasure to be of service, but I must confess my brother asked my help in arranging this meeting. Come. He is in the little wilderness over there."

William was pacing impatiently beside a low stone wall, but he halted as they approached.

The man bowed to him. "Mr. Darcy, I presume? I am Edward Gardiner, Elizabeth's uncle. I had hoped I might meet you here, or at least discover news of you."

The uncle that Frederica's people had been watching? Despite his curiosity, Kit suspected William wished to keep his conversation private. "I will leave you then, gentlemen." Had that come out too sharply?

William's brows drew together. "You are welcome to stay if you wish. Mr. Gardiner, pray forgive my directness, but have you news of my sister?"

"I know where she is, if that is what you mean. My niece Elizabeth contacted me to request my help finding lodgings for them. She told me a most astonishing story." Mr. Gardiner tilted his head to one side, asking a silent question.

"It is a most unusual circumstance. My brother is aware of it as well," said William. "I have been hunting for them since my release and I cannot tell you how relieved I am to hear this news."

"Your, er, sister has been very worried for you, since the last news she had of you was that you were in French custody. I suggested leaving a letter at your townhouse, but she was quite insistent that nothing should be put in writing."

He wished Georgiana had not been quite so good about following his instructions. He might have found them much sooner. "We had planned for circumstances like these, although I never considered the possibility that I might be arrested for something completely unrelated to her. Where is she?"

"The two of them are staying with a widowed friend of mine in London who believes they are survivors of a fire that killed their parents. I would be happy to take you to them when we return to London tomorrow."

William pulled his shoulders back. "I would be greatly appreciative of that," he said evenly.

Kit might not have seen his brother much in the last six years, but he knew that look. "By which, Mr. Gardiner, my brother means, 'I have barely been sleeping from worry all this time and devoting every minute to finding my sister, and you want me to wait until tomorrow?'"

"Kit," said William in a warning tone. "Mr. Gardiner has done us a great service, and it is kind of him to offer to escort us there."

Mr. Gardiner looked at William and then at Kit, the corners of his mouth twitching. "Mr. Darcy, on this occasion I think I must choose to believe your younger brother. I cannot return to London sooner than tomorrow, but if you truly wish to mount your horses and ride pell-mell to Town straight away, I will tell you how to find the house. Your sister will not object; she has been losing sleep, too. I understand she is not accustomed to being separated from you for such a length of time."

William's smile was self-deprecating. "I fear I have been somewhat overprotective of her."

"Under the circumstances, who could blame you? Someday I would like to hear the story behind how such a young man ended up with this responsibility. Your sister attempted to explain it to me, but it was a bit garbled. But now I must go back inside before my wife starts questioning my absence."

"My deepest thanks to you. You cannot know how you have relieved my mind," said William.

"Oh, I imagine I could guess!" Mr. Gardiner told them the address, adding, "They are employing the names of Miss Elizabeth Gardiner and Miss Georgiana Gardiner. I imagine we shall be meeting again. Elizabeth knows how to contact me."

"I assume your wife is not aware of the situation?"

Mr. Gardiner cocked an eyebrow. "She is not. She is quite trustworthy, but it is safer for both of us this way."

Kit said ruefully, "You and my brother are going to be very good friends. I only know of it because he needed my help in hunting for them."

"A painful decision for him, no doubt, but the correct one," said Mr. Gardiner with a bow. "And now I will wish you both a good day, gentlemen."

As Mr. Gardiner walked away, Kit came to stand beside his brother. Adopting a tone of mock sternness, he said, "We can leave quickly if you wish, but not without taking our leave of Mr. and Mrs. Bingley first."

Darcy gave him a sidelong glance. "Well, if we must," he grumbled. "Let us get it done, then."

Kit eyed the townhouse at the address Mr. Gardiner had given them. It appeared prosperous but was located in an unfashionable part of town. An excellent choice, since no one would look for Miss Georgiana Darcy in this sort of place, much less for Princess Charlotte.

William straightened his waistcoat before knocking at the door. Kit had suggested changing clothes rather than presenting themselves at a stranger's house covered with the dust of the road, but his brother would not brook any delay. It was not how Kit would prefer to appear when calling on any lady, much less a royal one.

When a doddering butler answered the door, William said crisply, "Mr. William Gardiner and Mr. Christopher Gardiner to see the Misses Gardiner."

The butler smiled delightedly, apparently not having been taught that butlers should show no emotion. "Come in, come in! They will be most delighted to see you. Miss Georgiana has spoken of you often." Definitely not trained as a butler.

After he announced them, Kit allowed William to take the lead going into an overdecorated sitting room. Two young women in black sat near an elderly lady in a Bath chair whose hands were heavy with rings, but he had no time to notice anything more because the girl with flaxen hair shrieked, "William!" and ran across the room, heedless of obstacles, to cast herself into William's arms.

Kit stabilized a wobbling side table the girl had knocked against in her headlong rush. This was not how he had anticipated the princess would behave, and seeing her clinging to his brother, her shoulders shaking with silent sobs, gave him a queer feeling in the pit of his stomach. It was one thing to imagine William taking charge of the girl, rather in the manner of a stern schoolmaster, but this! Surely William would step away to greet her with more propriety. But instead William was speaking quietly in her ear.

Kit swallowed hard, produced his handkerchief and slipped it between William's fingers, taking excruciating care not to touch the princess's black-clad back.

The chestnut-haired young woman came towards him, her hands held out to him with a warm smile beneath her striking dark eyes. "Christopher, I am so happy to see you," she said as she put her hands in his. To his embarrassment, this complete stranger leaned forward and pressed her lips against his cheek. Before she withdrew, she whispered, "Lizzy."

It was clever of her to give him the hint since she could not be certain if he would know her name. He squeezed her hands. "What, so formal today, Lizzy? I cannot recall the last time you called me Christopher. What happened to 'Kit, do this! Kit, do that! Kit, do not pick mother's flowers! Kit, I will tell father what you did!'" He looked across the room at the beaming older lady. "I was a very henpecked brother."

Lizzy said, "Mrs. Landon, may I present my brother Kit?"

Kit made an extravagant bow over Mrs. Landon's hand. "I am charmed to meet you. I understand I must thank you for opening your home to my sister...sisters."

Lizzy was quick to cover his slip. "As for my other brother, he is that vague shape behind Georgiana. I will introduce you if Georgiana ever releases him."

"No need to worry about that, my girl," said Mrs. Landon. "After hearing so much about him from dear Georgiana, I already think of him as part of the family."

In a loud whisper meant to be overheard, Lizzy said to Kit, "I fear Mrs. Landon has guessed our family secret – that compared to William, you and I are but distant seconds in Georgiana's affections!"

Kit glanced backwards. Were their antics providing enough cover for William's unbrotherly behavior? At least now his brother had stepped back and was drying the eyes of the girl who was not Georgiana. For some reason, applying his true sister's name to her seemed wrong.

William whispered something in the girl's ear, and she spun around to face the others. "Kit!" she cried. "I did not even see you there!"

And then Kit was nearly bowled over as she ran into his arms, just as she had earlier with William. Instinct made him put his arms around her as he would anyone else in that situation. Still, she was not anyone else. Even if she were not royal, Kit would never embrace a lady he was not related to.

But she did not feel like a princess. He was quite certain that princesses were not supposed to feel so warm and soft in his arms.

At least she released him quickly, before he could think about how men had once been beheaded for doing the sort of thing he had just done. Perhaps it was just as well that William had not told him the truth about her until now. If meeting her could knock him off balance this easily now, he would indeed have had difficulty managing it six years ago.

He was certainly never going to admit even to himself that he had liked the way she felt in his arms.

140

She returned immediately to William's side like a puppy that would not stray too far from its owner, but now her cheeks were pink beneath her golden curls. She gazed up at William while he made conversation with Mrs. Landon.

Sweat prickled at Kit's brow. Good God, were they going to have to sit in this overcrowded room for half an hour and talk pleasantries? The idea had not troubled him before. Now it sounded like torture.

A hand touching his arm made him jump. It was his other brand-new sister, Lizzy, the one who did not terrify him.

She leaned close to him and said softly but with an emphasis on each word, "Just an ordinary fifteen-year-old girl. Nothing more. An ordinary girl, and young for her age in many ways."

"Am I that obvious?" he asked, attempting to sound amused.

"To someone who went through the same thing less than a month ago? Yes."

He looked back at the girl. Georgiana. Her name was Georgiana, and she was just an ordinary girl. Perhaps if he repeated this to himself a few thousand times, he might even start believing it.

Watching Kit Darcy, Elizabeth began to understand why Mr. Darcy had been so insistent that the princess should always be thought of as Georgiana. Kit's deferential attitude towards Georgiana would be all too easy for an observant person to notice.

But Elizabeth could hardly claim to be behaving normally herself, not since the moment she had spotted Mr. Darcy in the doorway. When she had seen him last, she had not yet admitted to herself the strength of her feelings for him. Now the sight of his familiar broad shoulders made her heart skip a beat and her mouth grow dry. Heavens, she had even envied Georgiana who could run and throw her arms around him!

But the most disconcerting part was that even as he embraced Georgiana, his eyes had been seeking her out, studying her with that familiar intent look. A very serious look, too – more as if she were a problem he needed to solve than that he was pleased to see her. And she felt it like a blow.

It was a relief to banter with his purported younger brother, if for no other reason than that she no longer had to see Darcy's eyes on her. Even then her awareness of him did not fade. Instead she felt his gaze in the prickling of her skin.

But, oh! What a relief it was to see him free and unhurt, to hear his deep voice speaking! Elizabeth's eyes kept stealing back to him.

She longed to ask what had happened during this month of separation, but if she did, it would only force him to make up a story. Mrs. Landon knew nothing of his arrest, and it would contradict the story Mr. Gardiner had told her.

After the prescribed half hour for a social call had elapsed, Darcy said, "I am sorry to say my brother and I must be leaving. Mrs. Landon, you have been tremendously kind to our sisters. I did not receive word of their presence here until a few hours ago, so I have had no time to arrange lodgings for us. Would you be so generous as to allow our sisters to continue to impose upon your hospitality for a day or two until I do?"

"I would be happy for them to stay as long as they like. They are both charming guests," said Mrs. Landon.

"William," said Georgiana in a trembling voice. "Can I not go with you?"

A shadow crossed over his face. "Kit and I are staying with a friend, and there is not room for all of us."

"But can we not be together somewhere else?"

Mr. Darcy said, "I will find lodgings for us as quickly as I can, and I promise to call on you again tomorrow."

As Georgiana's lip began to tremble, Elizabeth said, "Georgiana, before William leaves, would you like to show him the lovely rooms Mrs.

Landon chose for us?" She almost slipped and ruined everything by calling him Mr. Darcy. How did he manage never to forget the role he played?

"I would like that very much," said Mr. Darcy. Were his cheeks flushed? "Come, Georgiana. Will you show me where it is?"

A brief silence fell the over the sitting room after they left. Elizabeth broke it. "I am sorry for that scene, Mrs. Landon. It is not a judgment on your excellent hospitality but on Georgiana's nerves. She has never been apart from William for so long a time before. She hates it when he is away even overnight. Something almost happened to her during the invasion, something very bad, but William saved her from it and now, with the fire happening when he was away... Well, I suppose I should have foreseen she might have difficulty letting him go." Most of the story was true enough even if it was worded so as to deceive the kind Mrs. Landon.

"There is no need to explain anything, dear," said Mrs. Landon. "Both of you have been through a terrible experience, and it is no surprise she is easily upset. But enough about that." She beckoned her manservant. "I will leave you children to your reunion." She leaned back in her Bath chair as the servant wheeled her out of the room.

Elizabeth moved her chair closer to Kit's so they could speak without being overheard. "Who are you when you are not pretending to be Mr. Darcy's brother?" she asked him in a low voice.

"Kit Darcy," he said with an engaging smile. "William's brother."

"Oh!" That was the one answer she had not expected. "Forgive my confusion. He never mentioned a brother to me, but now that I think on it, Georgiana did say he had one."

"Georgiana never met me before today, and William has been ignoring my existence for six years now. I was not party to the family secret, you see." Bitterness tinged his voice. "But he needed my help to find you, so here I am."

An uneasy feeling ate at Elizabeth's stomach. Would Jane and her father feel the same sort of anger when they discovered what she had hidden from them? "I am sorry. I fear I have done much the same to my own family, abandoning them without a word and leaving them to worry about me. But I cannot see anything else I could have done." She swallowed hard. "It is a very bitter price to pay, choosing between my country's needs and the family I love, and I wish to God no one else should be put in this position." The words came out more fervently than she had meant them to be.

Kit nodded slowly. "William told me some of your story." He began to say something else, then stopped, and started again. "It surprised me to see, er, Georgiana's reaction to William," he said cautiously.

"It is disconcerting, is it not? But when you think of what she has been through..." Elizabeth leaned closer and spoke in a whisper. "She was an enormously indulged child who knew the entire country adored her and saw her as their best hope. Then one day, everyone she cared about disappeared, and she never saw them again. She was taken from the only home she had ever known and placed in the sole care of a stranger who had to teach her quickly to be reserved and withdrawn for her own safety. He has been the only person who knew the truth about her, at least the only one she ever saw, and he has been her sole dependence for years. If she lost him, she lost everything." She shook her head. "Poor girl. Sometimes the indulged, willful child returns for a few minutes, but at the slightest criticism, her confidence disappears."

"I see," he said slowly.

"Until now, she has had no woman in her life to teach her how to be a lady. Throwing her arms around an unknown young man, indeed! She and I will be having a discussion about that, I assure you." But she said it with warmth to lessen the impact of her criticism.

"I think she was just attempting to greet me in the same way she greeted William, to keep anyone from suspecting she had no idea who I was."

She smiled at his readiness to defend Georgiana. "I know. But while we have a moment, may I ask you what happened after your brother was arrested? Did my uncle tell you where to find us? Oh, I have a thousand questions!"

"I will happily answer what I can, but I am not fully in William's confidence." And it clearly pained him to admit it.

When Darcy and Georgiana did not emerge after a quarter of an hour, Elizabeth followed them upstairs to provide reinforcements. Much-needed reinforcements, apparently, as she found him helplessly watching while Georgiana sobbed into a handkerchief.

Elizabeth waved him aside and put her arm around the girl. "Come now, if you continue this way, your brother may start to think you are sorry the French did not hang him! Did he tell you what happened? Kit explained it to me. He said your brother was arrested for the only crime in the world he had not committed against the French. Once his friend here in London knew about it, he was released in a trice. Then he managed to trace us as far as the inn at Oxford, the one where we asked directions. We were too clever for him after that, though. You should tell him where we spent that night."

Georgiana sniffled, but she lowered the handkerchief a few inches. "We slept in a hayloft."

Elizabeth laughed. "Oh, just look at your brother's expression! He is thinking he made a terrible mistake in entrusting you to me!"

Now Georgiana giggled. "If Charles II could hide for a day in an oak tree, I can sleep in a hayloft! The nicest old couple helped us. They were so good to us, even sharing their food when they hardly had enough for themselves. And they took us in for no reason except that the French were chasing us."

All color faded from Darcy's face. "The French were chasing you?" He sounded half strangled.

"Yes, but we did manage to get away!" said Elizabeth with more than a hint of impertinence.

"They were no match for your greys," said Georgiana.

Darcy covered his face with his hands.

Elizabeth said in a loud whisper, "I think we are frightening your brother."

"Good!" retorted Georgiana. "After the way he scared us, he deserves it!"

"I quite agree. Now I suppose we should let the poor man leave, but I am warning you, Mr. Darcy, that tomorrow you had best be prepared to tell us all the details about Jane's wedding, including every last bit of lace she wore. Is that not right, Georgiana?"

"Yes." But her voice had lost all spirit again.

"And I will be here with you every minute until he returns," Elizabeth said firmly. "I promise."

Georgiana turned to Darcy. "You will be careful?" she asked in a very small voice.

"Very careful," Darcy assured her. "You have my word on it."

Darcy allowed his brother to stride ahead of him into Frederica's study where Kit raised a fist in triumphant salute. "We found her!" he said without preamble. Of course Kit would take all the credit.

Frederica's eyebrows rose. "She was at the wedding?"

"No, but Miss Elizabeth's uncle was there, and he knew where they were," said Darcy.

Frowning, Frederica shuffled through pile of papers. "The uncle we have been watching? But we know they are not in his house, and we had him shadowed day and night! Here it is – the list of everywhere he and his wife have gone. He goes straight to work in the morning and stays there, apart from visits to the bank and the dockyards to inspect incoming shipments. He returns home directly except once – no, twice – he stopped to bring a basket of fruit to a widowed friend, apparently a habit of long standing. Occasionally he and his wife attended a dinner party." She looked up at them questioningly.

Kit grinned. "The widowed friend has two young ladies staying with her."

Holding the paper closer to her face, Frederica said, "Yes, but they are in mourning for their parents and appear in genuine distress, according to the servants – but I should not have dismissed it. Poor work on my part, quite unacceptable. Where is she now?"

"Still at the widow's house," said Darcy. "I did not have your permission to bring them here, and it would have looked odd to take them away on a moment's notice. It may be best for me to remove them to the countryside rather than staying in London."

Frederica tapped the top of her quill against her lips. "I suppose you could bring her here temporarily. I would like to have a sense of her mettle. But in the longer term, too many people come and go through this house, and it would expose her to too much risk. Of course, everyone here must think she is Georgiana Darcy, even Andrew."

Darcy nodded. "A few days would give me time to make arrangements to go elsewhere."

Chapter Nine

Darcy pushed past Kit to hand Elizabeth out of the hackney cab in front of the house on Leadenhall Street. "I believe you may be familiar with this neighborhood, Miss Elizabeth." It was the first time he had managed to say something just to her since they had left Mrs. Landon's house. Kit had monopolized her attention the entire time, leaving Darcy to converse with Georgiana.

"Of course," she replied. "It is but two streets away from my uncle's house on Gracechurch Street. I should go inside without delay; there may be people here who would recognize me."

Darcy ushered her into the house. "The servants do not answer the door since they would not know who is to be admitted and who should be sent off with a false story." He peeled off his gloves and tossed them on a small table.

"I see." She removed her bonnet and gingerly hung it on a hook, glancing around as if at an unknown danger.

Georgiana studied her surroundings with frank curiosity. "There are three of you living here?"

"Most of the time," said Kit. "We have frequent visitors, though. People who work with us, people who need a safe place to hide until they can make their escape, and so forth." He raised his voice. "Freddie, we are here."

Frederica, dressed plainly as was her wont these days, emerged through the doorway. Her gaze skimmed over Elizabeth and fixed on Georgiana.

Darcy said, "Frederica, may I present Miss Elizabeth Bennet? Miss Elizabeth, this is my cousin, Frederica."

"First names only, please," said Frederica. "That is the rule here. We cannot be forced to reveal names we do not know."

Darcy cleared his throat. "And this, of course, is Georgiana."

Georgiana made a proper curtsy. "Lady Frederica."

"I no longer am permitted that title," said Frederica somewhat absently, still studying Georgiana. "Will you join me in the sitting room?"

Someone had made an attempt to tidy the room. The chairs had been cleared of the papers that usually covered them. But Darcy was too restless to sit after being forced to watch Kit flirting with Elizabeth in the carriage, so he stood by the mantel as Kit gallantly showed Elizabeth to a small sofa and sat beside her. He murmured something in her ear, and Elizabeth turned laughing eyes on him.

Sometimes Darcy utterly detested his brother.

It was not fair. First Kit had resented him for keeping Georgiana from him, and now he was determined to charm the one woman who managed to enchant Darcy. And this after Darcy had been burdened for years with the thankless task of acting as nursemaid to Georgiana! Now that same service rendered him unable to court the woman he loved. It was bad enough to forgo the future he desired for the good of England; watching his little brother steal Elizabeth right under his nose was a different matter.

Fortunately for Darcy's sanity, Elizabeth's attention turned away from Kit to Frederica, who was explaining about her work gathering intelligence from across the country. Georgiana appeared captivated by the recital.

"When will it be time to use all this?" Georgiana's eyes were bright.

"Never, perhaps," said Frederica soberly. "Everything we have learned will be useful in the event of an uprising, but it cannot take the place of other things we need. We can do nothing until we rid ourselves of the warships in the Thames, or their cannon will level London at the first sign of a revolt. We need some sort of army and enough ships to hold the Channel at least for a time. We are a long way from having any of those things."

"Then... then why do you collect all this information if you cannot use it?"

Frederica's voice hardened. "Because if we are not prepared to seize the opportunity when it comes, there will be no hope of throwing off the French yoke. We can wait for something to change – something that keeps Napoleon's troops in France from providing reinforcements, some terrible defeat for the French, or a mass uprising, though I cannot hope for that. It might be successful, but many Englishmen would be slaughtered."

Georgiana shivered. "No, I would not want that, either."

"Some of us wish to attack when Napoleon marches his army to Russia," said Kit.

"No!" His brother's words had torn Darcy's attention away from Elizabeth. "That would be a disaster."

"I do not recall asking your opinion, William." Kit's voice was ominous.

Frederica held out her hand. "Wait. He knows something. What is it, William?"

Darcy hesitated. "Napoleon has already made plans for the contingency of an English rebellion while he is in Russia. I do not know the details, but the French are to burn as many towns as possible and destroy all food stores as they retreat. He estimates that a quarter of the population would die of starvation and cold once winter sets in, and the survivors would be so weak that they could put up little resistance when the French return in the spring."

A heavy silence fell on the room. Frederica, looking ill, clasped her hand to her mouth and turned away. Kit muttered a curse under his breath. Elizabeth simply stared at him in horror.

Finally Georgiana said grimly, "Yes, that is exactly what Bonaparte would do. I have been reading his favorite book on tactics."

Her face ashen, Frederica asked in a low voice, "William, how did you come by that information?"

"A French general of my acquaintance told me about it when I was last in London."

"What charming company you keep," Kit sneered.

God help him, he was going to hit his brother if he did not stop. Apparently Kit's anger at him had not lessened after all. "In fact, he told me about it because I asked him what was troubling him," Darcy said icily. "He was very unhappy with the plan. He thought it barbaric and inhumane." It had been an unforgettable night. There had been tears in Desmarais's eyes. A few days later Darcy had left for Netherfield, more hopeless about the future than ever.

Frederica gathered her papers into a pile, but her hands were shaking. "Kit, William has done us a service by telling us this. None of our informants have reported anything about it."

"It is only known at the highest levels. I was told only after a great deal of brandy had been consumed. The troops were simply instructed to record the location of food supplies and to build stockpiles of torches around the country."

"Which is consistent with what our informants have said." Frederica's voice was heavy. "That means any uprising must happen without any warning, and the French troops must be encircled and isolated from their commanders. Even more reason why we need an army of our own."

Georgiana said, "I hid in a root cellar at a cottage we stopped at near Oxford. It was lined with stone and would not burn. Is there a way to encourage people to make secret stockpiles of food and seeds in places that cannot burn?"

Frederica's eyebrows rose. "An excellent idea." She reached for her pen and began to write.

"You had to hide in a root cellar?" Darcy tried not to sound as horrified as he felt.

The animation left Georgiana's face. "Only for a very short time while an army patrol rode past. They never even came to the house."

Elizabeth added, "This was just before the episode where we slept in a hayloft." Her amused tone seemed to lighten the tension in the air.

"I assume there is more to this story. How did this come to pass?" asked Kit.

"It is quite a saga!" said Elizabeth. She launched into a light-hearted description of her adventures with Georgiana, managing to make being pursued by the French sound rather droll.

The sound of a knock at the front door interrupted her tale. Frederica gestured to Kit. "Would you be so kind?"

"Of course." He rose and left the room.

Elizabeth continued, "I was very grateful for your fast horses, Mr. Darcy. They left the French in the dust."

"Freddie?" Kit's voice had an odd, tentative squeak to it. "Were you expecting your—"

"Her mother?" Lady Matlock swept into the room. "No, of course she was not."

Frederica appeared frozen in place, her face ashen once again. "Is something the matter? Is it one of my brothers?"

"No, and before you ask, no one followed us here. Richard made certain of that. I never knew that boy had such devious tricks up his sleeves."

Frederica's eyes widened. "Richard? I thought he was in Jamaica. Or is this another secret?"

"No, I was in Jamaica. I just returned." Richard stepped into the room gingerly, walking with a barely perceptible limp.

Darcy stared at him in disbelief and then hurried forward and shook his cousin's hand heartily. "Richard, I cannot tell you how happy I am to see you back."

"But why are you back?" Frederica demanded. "And Mama, I told you not to come here."

Lady Matlock waved a hand. "I am only passing through to leave Richard here. I have sent my trunks ahead to Darcy House, where I plan to stay – I hope you do not object, Darcy? – but with a warrant still out for Richard's arrest, he cannot go there. I thought perhaps you could keep him. You might even find some use for him."

Frederica, finally recovering from her shock, stood to kiss her mother's cheek. "I am glad to see you, of course. Richard may stay here if he wishes, but I doubt the wisdom of so many of us gathering here."

Richard said, "Darcy, it is beyond good to see you again. I know you were there when I was carried aboard the ship, but to tell the truth, I hardly remember that time."

"It is astonishing you remember any of it." The sight of Richard on a stretcher, frighteningly gaunt, his eyes over-bright with fever from his injured leg, still haunted Darcy. He had looked unlikely to survive the voyage, and Darcy had grieved for him for almost a year until he received the first letter from Jamaica. "You look to be getting around well. I still cannot believe they were able to save that leg."

"That?" Richard glanced down at his leg. "It was by no means certain for a time. Now it is hardly a problem except on uneven ground, and I can still ride better than you."

"Ha! So you would like to believe." But Darcy smiled, happy to be on the familiar ground of his cousin's teasing. The limp suggested walking might not be as simple as Richard made it sound, but if his cousin preferred to ignore his impairment, Darcy would respect his wishes.

But he would never forgive the French for maiming and almost killing his cousin, not in honorable battle but by imprisoning him as a hostage for his father's good behavior and neglecting his wounds until he was near death. Even then they had not released him; Darcy had paid thousands of pounds in bribes to spirit his cousin out of prison. And then he had no choice but to put Richard on a ship to get him out of England, even if it might have killed him.

A wave of revulsion at the unnecessary cruelty of the invaders nearly choked him. This was why he had done nursemaid service for years. Ridding England of their French oppressors was the important thing. "What brings you back to England now?"

Richard grinned. "Perhaps I missed you so much that I had to come back. But, as you know, I have a few debts I wish to repay, and working with the so-called government-in-exile was a waste of time. They do nothing but prattle about what they would like to see happen. I prefer action."

Frederica nodded. "I agree. I do not take direction from them because they have so little knowledge of what we are facing here every day, and even less sense for the sentiments of the people. Some of their directives have been pointless at best."

"Hear, hear," said Kit. "Not to mention months out of date."

"It is almost as bad," said Frederica acidly, "as discovering my own mother has withheld crucial information from me!"

Kit crossed his arms. "Not to mention that I might have understood why my own brother turned into a beastly tyrant overnight, rather than blaming myself all these years for having done something to cause it."

Darcy stared at his brother. Kit had blamed himself for Darcy's refusal to let him see Georgiana? He felt a surge of sudden sympathy for his annoying brother.

"Secrets are only secrets when they are kept," said Lady Matlock frostily. "Do you think I did not wish to tell you? But I could not justify the added risk to an already perilous endeavor. No, the only one of you to whom I owe an apology is Darcy."

"To me? I cannot imagine why." Darcy's head was still whirling over Kit's admission. He knew all too well the price of blaming himself for something he had no control over.

"To you. You never volunteered for this duty. I could not manage to care for Georgiana and my ailing husband at the same time, but after his death, I could have taken her to live with me again. It might have required a new identity for her, or I could have taken a house elsewhere. My only excuse is that I was tired and not thinking clearly for some time."

His infallible aunt not thinking clearly? Impossible. And Lady Matlock simply did not become tired. Ever. But beside him Georgiana's expression showed devastation.

Darcy put an arm around her shoulder. "Georgiana and I have muddled along well enough, have we not? After she became accustomed to me, I would not have wished to put her through another change. In any case, the French were watching you constantly. Sometimes it seemed I got most of my news of you through my French friends."

His aunt's lips tightened. "You might have told me. Although I suppose it is just as well I did not know that until now."

Frederica said sharply, "It is not pleasant to discover you were left out of secrets, is it?"

Lady Matlock lifted her chin. "Enough of this. We have all been working to regain our country, and that has meant keeping secrets from one another for safety. Now it is time to pool our information and move forward. I will not tolerate pouting about each other's secrets."

Dead silence met her words until Kit laughed gaily and said, "That is easy for you to say since you are the only person who knew both William's secrets and ours!"

It broke the tension, although Frederica still looked displeased. "Darcy, does this change your plans?"

"I was not aware I had plans beyond staying here for a day or two while I find a house to let."

Georgiana looked up at him. "Could we not return to Netherfield, especially now that Jane is living there?"

Darcy shook his head. "That might cause questions we do not wish to answer, and Miss Elizabeth could not go there safely."

Elizabeth's sudden pallor belied the briskness in her voice as she said, "There is no need to worry about me. I am not your responsibility. As you say, I cannot go to Netherfield, nor can I remain here. This house is too close to my uncle's home where I lived for several years after the invasion, and people in the neighborhood would recognize me. Lady Frederica, if there is a way in which I could be useful to your work without living here, I would be happy to do so. If not, the simplest thing would be for me to return to my original plan and go to Scotland."

"No!" cried Georgiana. "Can you not remain with us, at least for now?" The familiar fear was back in her eyes.

Darcy's heart soared at the idea of Elizabeth staying with them, but how could it happen after the impossible position he had put himself into by kissing her at Netherfield? That, added to causing her to leave her family and friends, meant by all the rules of honor that he owed her a proposal of marriage. But that was the one thing he could not offer, no matter how much he might wish for it in his heart, and it would be an insult to offer her anything less. He could not stay silent, though. "You would be very welcome to remain with us as Georgiana's friend."

Did a shadow cross her face at his words? Guilt and wretchedness ate at his stomach.

Frederica nodded. "I think you should all go to Darcy House along with my mother. That way we can consult as needed."

"As I said before, Darcy House is out of the question. I would be expected to dance attendance on the French and have little time for anything else."

"You have survived that before. You should take Kit with you, too. We have another courier we can use if there is an emergency."

Kit raised an eyebrow. "Do I have a say in this?"

Frederica said wearily, "It would not be forever, just until we know what our next move should be. And you would have the agreeable company of Georgiana and Elizabeth. I would feel better about having another man in the household when William is away."

Kit's eyes flickered towards Georgiana. "Very well, then, if it is agreeable to William."

"Of course." After all, Darcy could hardly say that seeing his brother spend time with Elizabeth was going to be as pleasant as walking barefoot through nettles. "If Miss Elizabeth does not object, at least."

Elizabeth did not appear happy. "I have not yet decided my course of action." But her voice lacked its usual sparkle. Had Kit's flirtation failed to move her?

"Good Lord!" Kit exclaimed. "We have totally forgotten to introduce you. You must think us all mad. Aunt, may I present Miss Elizabeth to your acquaintance? She has been caring for Georgiana since they left Netherfield. Miss Elizabeth, this is my aunt and my cousin Richard, late of Jamaica. And this, of course, is Georgiana."

With a curtsey, Elizabeth said, "It is an honor to meet you."

Lady Matlock bent her head in acknowledgment. "It is a pleasure. And Georgiana! How you have grown, dear child. I would not have known you."

Elizabeth whispered something to Kit, though her eyes were not laughing this time. He responded at length, gesturing with one hand as if giving directions.

Darcy frowned. If she needed to know something, why had she asked Kit, whom she barely knew, instead of him? The sight of their heads bent together raised bile in the back of his throat.

Richard's voice rumbled beside him. "It is hard to believe. Kit was barely a stripling when I last saw him. Now he is a man grown."

Darcy wished his brother were still a boy. "I have only seen him a few times in these years. I needed to keep him away from Georgiana. You know who she is, I assume." It was an effort to keep his eyes from following Elizabeth as she slipped out of the room.

"My mother finally saw fit to inform me as we were in the carriage on our way here. It was a great relief to me."

"A relief?" It was not how he would have expected his cousin to react.

"Your letters have been worrying me for years ever since I noticed that you never went to Pemberley, just London and one leased country house after another. I thought you could not bear to go home after everything that had happened. Once I knew who Georgiana was, it made perfect sense. But what of the real Georgiana, the one in Canada? How does she manage?"

Darcy winced. "I wish I knew. My father sent messages indicating she was doing well but without details, and after his death I eventually received word that she was willing to continue the imposture under the care of another English exile, a friend of my father's. Or at least that was how I interpreted the disguised message. I worry about her, and Kit has been fretting greatly since he learned the truth, but I know my father had a plan in place for her if something happened to him. I have to trust in that."

His cousin whistled. "That is an uncomfortable thing. If it is any help, I have seen the reports the government-in-exile receives about her, and it sounds as if she is well protected. Of course, we all believed she was the real princess, so I never gave it much thought."

Clasping Richard's arm, Darcy said, "You have relieved my mind greatly. I did not know Georgiana well, but she is still my flesh and blood. Kit was closer to her since they grew up together, whereas I was away at school when she was born and then at Cambridge during her childhood."

"If I had known, I would have paid more attention to those damned reports." Richard scowled. "I suppose you could not have told me any of this in a letter, but I wish I had known what was happening."

"I certainly could not put it in a letter or even say it in person. Until last month, I told no one at all. Now there are five of us in this room who know the truth, and it makes me uneasy even though I trust all of you."

Richard snorted. "You should try working with the government-in-exile. Their idea of keeping a secret is to tell everyone they know. It is a good thing they never knew of your task."

"A good thing, indeed!" Something about Richard's words tickled at Darcy's memory. "That reminds me. This may be unimportant, but I recently met one of Lord Wellington's former aides who asked me how to reach the government-in-exile. He had an urgent message for them about a man they should contact."

Richard's eyes brightened. "Who was it? I knew most of Wellington's staff."

"His name was Tomlin. Lieutenant Colonel Tomlin."

"Tomlin is a top-notch soldier. If he says it is important, it is." Richard tapped his fingers on his thigh. "Did he tell you who this man was?"

"Just that he was the harbormaster of Milford Haven."

"Hmm. Those fools in Jamaica will do nothing about it even if they receive the message. Perhaps I will look into it. If this harbormaster can put us in the way of getting a ship or two, it could make a big difference. We can do nothing while Napoleon holds the Channel."

Ten minutes later, Elizabeth had not returned. Darcy knew he should not go after her, but he did anyway. What was it about her that made him break all his rules?

He found her in the dining room, leaning over the table to read a copy of *The Loyalist*. Most houses had tablecloths; here there were always newssheets on the table.

He cleared his throat. "I saw you leave the sitting room. Is something the matter?"

She straightened, her expression guarded. "It had been many years since your family had been together. I did not wish to intrude upon your reunion, and I am sorry to have taken you away from it now." She did not sound pleased.

What should he say? "I have had no opportunity to speak to you alone since that day at Netherfield."

"You will have plenty of opportunities if Georgiana has her way and keeps me with her." Her tone was definitely cool now.

She was angry with him, but why? Was it because he forced her to leave her family – or because he had kissed her? If only he could have talked to her instead of disappearing!

He had to be careful, even if he would rather kneel at her feet and beg her to forgive him. "Georgiana does seem quite attached to you. I apologize for putting you in an awkward position by inviting you to Darcy House."

"An awkward position," she said bitterly. "That is one way to describe it, I suppose. How long do you think it will be before Georgiana is able to tolerate my departure?"

His mouth went dry. "I wish I could predict that, but I cannot. It is an uncomfortable thing, as I know well. I am sorry her fears are forcing you to make unpleasant choices."

"Oh, I imagine living at Darcy House will not be unpleasant." Her bitterness had changed to heavy irony. "After all, I will be living in luxury with my only duty being to reassure an excitable young girl. What could I possibly object to, apart from living in your house under your protection when half of Meryton already suspects I am your mistress?"

Her words hit him like a blow. He took half a step forward before the look on her face stopped him. "I know I have placed you in an impossible position. I cannot blame you for thinking ill of me; by every measure you have the right to have expectations of me, expectations I cannot fulfill."

She gave a harsh laugh. "I have no expectations of you. Georgiana has explained your unusual situation to me, so I know you are destined for far greater things than a simple country miss like me. Or perhaps I should say as I once was. Now I am not even that."

"Georgiana said that? I had not thought she realized the consequences of living with me. It is not something I have wished for." In fact, he had avoided thinking about it whenever possible.

"Of course not! Why would any gentleman wish to be elevated to the rank of royalty? I am not a fool, sir."

He recoiled. "Most men, yes, but I am no courtier. If it should come to pass, I will be forced into a situation for which I am ill-suited by nature. But at least if Georgiana is restored to her rightful position, she would be able tell the world what you have done for her. You would be able to return to Longbourn as a heroine with your head held high."

She turned away from him. "There is nothing for me at Longbourn. Lizzy Bennet is dead, and her disappearance has caused nary a ripple." Her voice was tight.

If only he could take her into his arms and tell her all would be well again! But it would not be the truth. "Your family has been deeply distressed since you left." It sounded weak even to him.

"Oh, yes. My dearest Jane was so distraught that she became engaged within days and celebrated her wedding inside a month!"

He could not bear it any longer. He came up behind her and put his hands on her upper arms. "No. It was not like that. Your sister was utterly devastated when you disappeared. Bingley had guessed I was a Loyalist and informed her he thought I had something to do with your disappearance, so I told her that although I did not know your location, I knew why you had left and had every reason to think you safe. That relieved the worst of her anxiety. As for the speed of the wedding, Bingley was anxious to have her safely married to him, and I suspect Jane was uncomfortable moving back into the bosom of your family after all that had happened. She missed you greatly on her wedding day and chose to have no one stand up with her in your absence."

Her head was bent, exposing the nape of her neck to him. It was dizzying to be so close to her, the scent of rosewater washing over him. But it was odd, too. She had always worn lavender in Hertfordshire, but of course she could not have taken anything with her when she left with Georgiana, certainly not her lavender water. He yearned to taste the porcelain skin of her neck where a few errant chestnut curls had escaped from her coiffure, but even more he longed to offer her comfort.

When she remained silent, he tried again. "I cannot blame you for being angry with me. I deserve the blame for placing you in this position. If I had only realized why I was being arrested, I could have spared you this. I assumed they wanted me for the crimes I had actually committed, not for something unimportant."

"Murder is unimportant?" Her voice was ragged.

"No, but they knew I was not guilty of anything more than detesting the man I was accused of killing. Captain Reynard merely wanted to punish me for..." Too late he realized his error.

"For what?"

"For standing between him and his desires." Before she could reply he rushed on. "But he underestimated the power of my connections, and now he is the one awaiting trial. Still, you have paid a very high price for my error." He dropped his hands from her shoulders. He had no right to comfort her.

She rubbed her arms as if to warm herself. "Not really. You changed my destination and the manner of my departure, but had you said nothing, I would have had to leave for Scotland in any case." She sounded grudging, as if she were determined to be fair even if she did not wish to be.

"Do you wish me to speak to Georgiana and ask her to allow you to leave?"

"Would it make any difference if you did? I have seen how deep her fears run. "

"Perhaps not, but I could try. Until now it is only separation from me which causes her anxiety." It felt strangely uncomfortable to share that role after all these years.

Elizabeth turned to face him. "It does not matter. There is nothing for me in Scotland. If I am of use here, I might as well stay."

It might be a grudging acceptance, but it was still an acceptance. More importantly, he would not have to bid her a final farewell, which would feel like ripping his own skin off. "On Georgiana's behalf, I thank you."

If only Elizabeth did not look so unhappy!

Elizabeth waited a decent interval after Darcy left her before she returned to the sitting room, and she needed every minute of the time to gather her composure. It was painful to keep him at a distance when she longed to be closer to him, to touch him, to tease him as she had in Meryton. But that was before she learned what lay in his future – and that she could have no part of it.

When his warm hands had rested on her shoulders, the temptation to turn to him had burned through her. But she knew the dangers of that from their brief kiss at Netherfield. Her desire to touch him was even more powerful now, for she had learned what it was to be without him and to fear never seeing him again. And he was also her strongest tie to her former life. Georgiana had barely known her before they fled Hertfordshire together.

To see his family come together, just when hers was lost to her, had been excruciating. At least now she knew Jane had felt her loss.

Finally she forced herself to return to the others. They had been joined by a newcomer, a lanky man with ink stained hands.

"Do come in, Elizabeth," said Frederica. "May I introduce Andrew to your acquaintance? He also lives here, and he publishes *The Loyalist*. I was just telling him the news that Princess Charlotte is back in England. I think it might be useful if readers of *The Loyalist* were made aware of that."

"It is such excellent news!" cried Andrew. "I can put it in the next edition, if you like."

Darcy shook his head. "That would be far too dangerous. If the French know to look for her here—"

Frederica said sharply, "William, keeping the princess as safe as possible is important, but it is of no use if we never rid ourselves of the French. Many of our people are losing hope we will ever regain our freedom, and this one piece of information, more than anything else we have, will give them something to rally around. It will be almost impossible for the French to hunt down one girl who recently arrived from Canada and has had plenty of time to disguise herself. It is worth the very small risk."

Darcy looked mutinous. "I still think it a poor idea."

"I do not suppose..." Andrew trailed off. "I do not suppose the princess would agree to make a statement for an article."

Frederica examined the papers in front of her, her eyes never so much as moving towards Georgiana. "I imagine she would be willing to reply to a question or two in writing. Nothing about her time in Canada, though – we would not wish to expose any of her contacts there."

"Of course not." He scanned the newcomers. "Also, should any of you have stories that would be of interest, I would be happy to hear about them."

Kit laughed. "You are so restrained tonight, Andrew! Usually that is the first question you ask on meeting someone new."

"It is true," said Andrew mournfully. "I am obsessed with it."

Frederica looked thoughtful. "Elizabeth might have a story for you. She comes from a town with an abusive garrison captain."

Andrew bowed in her direction. "Miss Elizabeth, if you would be willing to speak of it to me, I would be in your debt. It is often difficult for me to obtain accounts of specific problems outside London, and stories of that sort are useful for keeping up people's spirit of rebellion."

Finally, someone who wanted her for herself. Elizabeth relaxed enough to manage a small smile. "I would be happy to do so if you think it might be of use."

Lady Matlock said, "Perhaps not tonight, though. If Elizabeth is going to live with us at Darcy House, she had best go there with me today. We need an explanation why a gently bred young lady would be living in a house with two single gentlemen. The simplest would be to introduce her as my ward, and therefore under my protection."

"But I know nothing of you," Elizabeth protested. "Anyone would be able to tell we are complete strangers."

"Nonsense," said Lady Matlock briskly. "I have known you since you were a child and cared for you since the recent tragic death of your parents. Not too recent, though, I think – black does not suit you, so you should be out of mourning. Perhaps just out of mourning, thus requiring a trip to London to obtain new clothing for you. It would also explain my presence here after all these years. Yes, that will work well."

Elizabeth instinctively looked to Darcy to see his reaction.

His eyes warmed as he met her gaze. "Yes, my aunt is always like that. In half an hour you will be certain that you have in fact known her since childhood."

Chapter Ten

On his first evening at home, Darcy struggled to decipher a blotted letter from Bingley, but he could not concentrate on the task, not when Elizabeth was in the same house. All he wanted was to seek her out and bask in her presence. But that would only make matters worse, so instead he hid in his study.

When Elizabeth appeared in the doorway of the study, her shape silhouetted in the light from the hall, a weight seemed to lift from Darcy's shoulders.

"Mr. Darcy, I wonder if I might take a few minutes of your time."

"Of course." As far as he was concerned, Elizabeth was welcome to every moment of his time for the rest of his life. "Do sit down. Is there anything I can help you with?"

Now that she was closer, he could see the lines between her brows. Something was the matter; he was sure of it.

"I am sorry to trouble you with this. Georgiana is distressed. I have tried to assist her myself, but she will not tell me the full story and instead referred me to you."

"I pray you, do not apologize. You are not troubling me at all. What seems to be the problem?"

She twisted a handkerchief between her hands. "Georgiana feels your aunt dislikes her intensely, and therefore is unhappy about the prospect of her remaining with us. I have seen no evidence of dislike myself, but Georgiana says that is merely because she is too well-bred to show it. And here is where you come in. Georgiana says your aunt is right to detest her because of a horrible thing she did years ago. She will not tell me what it was, just that you have forgiven her for it and that I should ask you about it. Again, I am sorry to trouble you, but I am at a loss as to how to reassure her when she will not tell me the problem!"

Darcy raised his eyebrows. "The difficulty is that I do not know what it is either. My aunt has always seemed fond of Georgiana, and I am unaware of any problems between them. Perhaps it is some small thing Georgiana has magnified in her own mind. Did she give you any clues as to what it might be, or when it happened?"

Elizabeth shook her head. "I have the impression it was shortly before she came to live with you. The only other thing she said is that you forgave her for it."

Darcy drummed his fingers on his desk. "That tells me very little, since I have forgiven her many things." Because he wanted to see Elizabeth smile, he added, "Although there were a few temper tantrums at the beginning that I might not quite have forgiven even yet. Her tantrums were quite impressive."

Thankfully, she did smile. "I can imagine. She does tend to feel things powerfully."

The connection warmed him. "Indeed she does. Although I would not have wished it on you, it is a remarkable relief to share the responsibility for her with someone. I am thankful for all you have done

167

for her, especially because it had become increasingly obvious to me that I was unable to provide all she needed."

"I cannot understand how you bore it all by yourself for so long!" she exclaimed. Then she looked up at him archly. "And you had to tolerate all my misplaced impertinence about your politics."

"I liked your impertinence," he said softly. "I wanted more than anything to tell you the truth."

For a moment, as her fine eyes held his, Darcy became acutely conscious of the curve of her lips. Perhaps–

Elizabeth sat back, suddenly businesslike. "Taking care of Georgiana was your first duty, so you could not tell me. I understand that. However, this does not solve my problem. Do you think if we spoke to her together, she might reveal what is troubling her?"

Georgiana. Her presence stood between them, and he had to remember that – and stop wishing it was not true. This longing for Elizabeth would pass with time. He had his duty, and that would have to be enough. But if there was one thing he could not forgive Georgiana for, it was this, not some event long ago. "Perhaps we should try asking my aunt first. She might be more forthcoming."

"Very well. I have a question, too, on the subject of your aunt. I do not know how to refer to her. The French say we must not use her title, so I do not wish to risk a servant overhearing it. But I cannot bring myself to call her 'Mrs. Fitzwilliam,' and it sounds clumsy to be forever referring to her as your aunt. It makes me feel like a stammering schoolgirl." Even her slight petulance was endearing.

"The servants at Pemberley call her Madam as if it were her given name. It is one solution, and she is accustomed to it."

The corner of her lips crooked up, intensifying his urge to taste them. "I suppose that is as good as anything. Will the servants here do the same?"

"That will be up to the housekeeper. You may have noticed my servants are less than clever, and many are hard of hearing. I am certain you will understand why."

She raised her eyebrows. "How do you explain those odd hiring preferences to your housekeeper?"

Darcy's smile was warm. "She is aware of the need. She used to be the housekeeper at Pemberley, but came here because I needed someone whom I could trust to manage the servants and to watch for anyone asking the wrong sorts of questions."

Elizabeth tilted her head to the side. "But Georgiana told me no one else knew the truth."

"She is unaware Mrs. Reynolds knows her identity. So did my late valet, who had previously worked for my uncle, or I could never have managed this masquerade for as long as I have. He died shortly before I went to Netherfield." It had been a hard blow. Not only had Darcy been fond of Blackwell, but he had depended upon him to manage Georgiana when he had to leave the house. Had Blackwell been at Netherfield that fateful day, Darcy would have entrusted Georgiana to him instead of to Elizabeth. His chest tightened at the thought.

Lady Matlock was as much in the dark as Darcy. "I cannot imagine why she would think I dislike her. There is nothing I hold against her, apart from an unfortunate taste for green dresses when the color makes her look bilious. That can be remedied, though."

Elizabeth said, "It seems to be something from long ago when she still lived with you. She says she did something utterly unforgivable."

Lady Matlock shook her head. "I cannot recall anything. She was sometimes unhappy, but who would not be when taken from everything she knew? Perhaps she did not understand why I asked Darcy to take charge of her in my place, or..." She paused and sighed. "Oh, dear. I am afraid I do know. I told her at the time it was complete nonsense, but at one point she thought herself responsible for my late husband's apoplexy. He was displeased with her that day because she had behaved very badly, announcing her identity in the presence of guests. While we were able to convince them she had made up the entire thing, we could not allow her to continue in that manner. My husband scolded her, something she was not accustomed to, and she threatened to run off. Anyway, it all came to nothing, as these things so often do, but when he collapsed that night, she blamed herself. That was when we received word that Matlock House had been pillaged, which no doubt had much more to do with his distress than her antics."

Elizabeth looked thoughtful. "That could fit. If it were true, it would indeed be unforgivable, and if you could no longer care for her then, she might see that as anger. I will ask her."

"No," said Lady Matlock. "I will speak to her myself. Perhaps you might accompany me."

After casting a glance at Darcy, Elizabeth agreed.

Elizabeth wanted nothing more than some peaceful time alone in her room, but Mr. Darcy would no doubt be waiting for a report on the outcome of Lady Matlock's talk with Georgiana. Taking a few minutes to tell him about it was the right thing to do. However, having her heart give little skips of excitement at the prospect of talking to him alone was not the right thing at all.

The intimacy of walking into his candlelit study was a stolen pleasure. Nothing could ever come of it, but was it such a terrible thing to let the heat of desire pool within her in his presence? When he looked up from his book, his dark eyes betrayed a different kind of excitement, one that made her insides quiver. The chiseled lines of his cheekbones and his shadowed lips seemed to beg for her touch.

She folded her hands behind her back, keeping them out of the way of temptation. "The crisis has been averted. When I left, Lady Matlock had her arm around Georgiana. I think Georgiana believed her reassurances, but it took some effort."

"Good. Thank you for helping her. I had no idea this was troubling her. She has never confided in me the way she seems to do with you."

It was late, and even if the door was open, most of the servants were already abed. And she was alone with him. Her skin tingled. "In this case, she may have not felt she needed to since she thought you already knew. She thinks very highly of you."

Darcy stretched his arms out in front of him. "Sometimes too highly. She thinks I can protect her from everything, and as we have seen, I cannot. I always feel as if I am walking on eggshells with her, and that the wrong word or look will set off one of her anxiety fits."

His confession only made her warm to him more. "I know what you mean, but I thought it was merely my own clumsy words that were making things worse. It is a comfort, I suppose, to know I am not the only one."

"I cannot imagine you ever saying something clumsy." His dark eyes were fixed on her. "She is merely sensitive and easily frightened. I did not handle her well when she first came to live with me. I had little experience with children, least of all a high-strung and temperamental one."

Even when he was speaking only of Georgiana, his words felt oddly intimate, as if they could somehow reach inside her.

"I can only imagine! I felt ill-prepared to handle some of her moods, and I have three younger sisters. I do not know how you managed."

His lips turned up in a slight smile. "By making a great many mistakes."

No, the mistake was allowing herself to be drawn even closer to him when she should be doing everything in her power to stay away from him. But it was late and she was tired, and his warmth was such a relief after all this time away from everyone she knew and loved. Even the brief visits with her uncle had only reminded her how alone she felt.

Footsteps echoed in the hall outside the study. Kit stuck his head inside the door. "I say, William, do you happen to know..." His casual tone turned abruptly formal. "I apologize; I had not realized Miss Elizabeth was with you."

Her cheeks grew hot. What must he think, finding them alone together at this hour? "I was just leaving. Georgiana was upset earlier, but I think we have finally straightened it out."

"Upset?" Kit sounded shocked. Perhaps he thought princesses did not have such feelings.

"Yes," she said with a smile. "Your brother can tell you about it, but it is past time for me to retire." Even that sounded too intimate.

Darcy must have felt the same, for he took a step towards her before stopping himself. "Good night, Miss Elizabeth. Thank you for your assistance with Georgiana."

"It was my pleasure." Why did her every word seem to suddenly have a hidden meaning? "Goodnight, gentlemen."

Even when she was upstairs, she still felt the pull of Darcy's presence. She bit her fingers in frustration. Could she manage this intensity? Did she have a choice?

After four days in one crowded stagecoach after another, the interminable ride interrupted every few miles by French soldiers demanding to see travel permits – and in some cases, to receive bribes – Richard Fitzwilliam debated remaining at the inn at Milford Haven and sleeping for a day before seeking out the harbormaster. But it was still light, and he was restless, so he limped down the cobblestone street to the waterfront. A passerby pointed him towards the small building housing the harbormaster's office.

Inside a thin, dark-haired man, his bushy beard streaked with white, sat at the small desk. He did not look up from his account book when Richard entered. "Yes?" he asked crisply.

"I am looking for the harbormaster," said Richard. Something about the man was not right.

"That would be me. The name is Wisley." The harbormaster still seemed uninterested, but his voice – that was it. His accent carried the stamp of Eton.

"My name is Richard Fitzwilliam, and I am here on behalf of..."

Wisley looked up suddenly, pinning him with piercing, steel gray eyes.

Even when caught off guard after all these years, Richard's reflexes still knew what the situation demanded. He snapped to attention. The unplanned movement on his weak leg almost caused him to lose his balance, something that rarely happened these days. But his hand remembered how to salute. "Sir!"

"Stop that nonsense at once. I am just Wisley, the harbormaster."

"I thought you were dead. Everyone thinks so. Of course: Wisley, Wellesley—"

"Do not say it." It was clearly an order. "Come, Fitzwilliam, sit down and tell me what brings you here, since it seems I am not what you expected."

"Not at all, sir." Richard collapsed into the offered chair. "Good God! I am stunned. At least this explains why Tomlin thought it so important for the government-in-exile to contact an obscure harbormaster."

The steel gray eyes lit up. "The message was received after all! Tomlin will be pleased. We had begun to give up hope and think all our planning was for naught."

"Definitely not for naught, sir. There is an active Loyalist movement whose leader is in search of someone who knows how to command an army. Nothing would make them happier. I still cannot get beyond this – you, here at the ends of the earth!"

"Hardly that. Did you know that the packet boats for Ireland are based here? Packet boats are, of course, much smaller than warships, but they are fast, maneuverable, and carry cannon to defend themselves from privateers."

"Land and sea," Richard breathed.

"Exactly. I am not alone in this venture. I must introduce you to the captain of one of the packets, an old friend of mine by the name of Hamilton. Former Navy man, you know." He paused, a triumphant expression on his face, clearly waiting for a reaction.

Hamilton? Richard had never heard of a Navy man by that name. Wait – Hamilton. Emma Hamilton. His breath caught in his throat. "Is Captain Hamilton perchance missing an arm?"

"Very good! You always were a clever one, Fitzwilliam. You will meet several other old friends here in addition to Tomlin – Abercromby, Popham, Coote, and Harris."

Richard shook his head in disbelief. "That many? But how did you manage it?"

"The credit should go to the late Duke of York. During the last campaign, when Napoleon's troops began preparing for the invasion, he told his most trusted generals and admirals that if the worst happened, we should make our way here to regroup and plan. Sadly, he himself never arrived."

"I would ask why Milford Haven, but I suppose it is as close to the end of the earth as one can find in Britain."

"Precisely, and it has indeed proven a haven for us. But there is a time for planning and a time for action."

Ten days later, Richard returned to Leadenhall Street with two companions. Finding his sister buried in her usual piles of paper, he said, "Freddie, about that army and navy you were wishing for? Permit me to present to you the harbormaster of Milford Haven, whom you may have known once as General Lord Wellington. Lord Nelson, of course, needs no introduction. Gentlemen, this is my sister Frederica, the one with the list of every arms depot in England and the partisans prepared to blow them up."

Wellington bowed over Frederica's hand. "Madam, you are a lady after my own heart."

"You know I must go," Darcy told Georgiana for at least the fourth time. "Elizabeth, Kit, and my aunt will be here with you; and I will return as I always do." Her moments of panic when he went out for the evening had seemed to stop now that she had other companions, but apparently they were not completely gone. "Now take a deep breath and let it out slowly. You know how."

Georgiana followed his instructions for a few seconds, but afterwards her breathing became rapid and ragged again. Her knuckles showed white as she gripped Elizabeth's hand.

"Remember that calm thoughts help," said Elizabeth in soothing tones. "Just as we practiced before. Think of how William has always returned to you, even after he was arrested. You may depend upon him."

A shiver ran down Darcy's spine. The sound of his given name on Elizabeth's lips seemed to promise an intimacy that did not exist. Even though he referred to her as Elizabeth as often as Miss Elizabeth, she was always careful to call him Mr. Darcy. No doubt she had used his name now deliberately in an attempt to calm Georgiana. "I promise I will return tonight just as I always do," he said, trying to match Elizabeth's tone.

"And I will be here with you the entire time. I will even sleep in your room tonight if you like." Elizabeth rubbed Georgiana's shoulder with her free hand.

"You will not leave me?" Georgiana's voice hitched.

"Of course not. Remember what I said? You may depend on me, unless there are elephants or tigers involved. As I have heard nothing of elephants or tigers in London, you are quite safe. Now a few slow breaths, along with me. Breathe in and out."

Darcy could tell Elizabeth was teasing Georgiana to distract her, but how had tigers and elephants come into it? It seemed to help, so he ought to play along. "What about lions? Should we be concerned if there are reports of lions in London?"

Elizabeth raised an eyebrow as if considering the question. "No, I think not. Lions do not hold the same fascination for me. Kangaroos, however, are a different matter."

Georgiana managed a weak giggle, but perspiration still beaded her forehead.

Darcy squatted down beside her. "Is something the matter tonight? You did not seem to mind it when I left the last few evenings. Did I say something that frightened you?"

The girl shook her head, pressing the heel of her hand against her chest. "No, not you," she said weakly.

"Who, then? I am certain no one meant to worry you."

Georgiana dropped her chin. In a barely audible voice she said, "Our aunt quarreled with Elizabeth."

"Is that all?" exclaimed Elizabeth. "That was not a true quarrel, just a disagreement. When I have a real quarrel, I say far ruder things than that. Just ask your brother." Her smile took the edge from her words.

"But she said you were ungrateful, and you said you could not stay under these circumstances." Georgiana's breath caught.

"Oh, my dear, that did not mean I plan to leave, just that the circumstances had to change. I am not going away from you. And I daresay I truly am an ungrateful thing!"

Darcy tensed. Was Elizabeth thinking of leaving? "Might I ask how this came to pass?" His words must have come out more sharply than he had intended, for Georgiana shrank back from him.

"It was nothing of importance," said Elizabeth. "When we were at the mantua-maker, your aunt wanted to order more evening dresses for me, and I told her it was too expensive."

Georgiana whispered miserably, "That is not what you said."

"Now you mean to embarrass me in front of your brother!" Elizabeth teased. "Very well; if you want the full, unvarnished truth, I told her I could not accept expensive and unnecessary items purchased with your money, and that I wanted nothing more than a few simple dresses suitable for a companion." Her eyes sparkled at him, daring him to argue.

This was dangerous territory, given Elizabeth's fear of appearing to be under his protection. Should he agree that it was up to her what was purchased, or would that simply reinforce that even simple dresses were paid for out of his pocket? No, he had to follow her lead and make light of it somehow. He cleared his throat. Speaking in a dramatic version of his proudest tones, he said, "Ungrateful, indeed, Miss Elizabeth! I imagine my aunt was less concerned with whether you wanted those dresses than with the enjoyment I would receive by seeing you in them. It was very selfish of you to refuse."

Elizabeth laughed. "I am indeed very selfish! Still, your aunt agreed not to order the evening dresses, so I have no reason to leave. You have nothing to worry about."

"Nothing at all," agreed Darcy. His aunt had almost certainly returned to the milliner later with instructions to make the dresses anyway, but he would deal with that problem when it arose. "I will have to suffer my disappointment, consoling myself with the pleasure of admiring you in whatever dress you may choose to wear."

"And you say your brother does not flirt!" Elizabeth said dryly to Georgiana.

Darcy raised an eyebrow. "As I have said before, I am highly selective about it."

Elizabeth made a face at him. "Well, Georgiana, if I can manage to tolerate your brother's company, I can certainly deal with your aunt. Shall we let him go, then? I will be able to amuse myself for hours thinking of how much he must be suffering in the company of the odious French."

"And you will remain here with me and not leave?" asked Georgiana.

"I will stay right here with you." She rubbed Georgiana's hand.

Darcy tried not to let his relief show. After having Elizabeth in his house for even a few days, he did not know how he had ever made it through a day without her. Someday he would have to face that dilemma, but it would not be today.

There was no escape. Georgiana might have made her promise to stay, but somehow Elizabeth had to find a way to leave. Staying in the same house with Mr. Darcy was tearing her apart.

Whenever she saw him, she felt more drawn to him, and she knew he felt the same. He would walk into a room, an attentive question for Georgiana on his lips, bristling in response to a barb from Kit, or inquiring after his aunt's comfort – but only after his gaze had first settled on Elizabeth. She would look up to find his eyes caressing her silently, his face sporting a slight smile as if at a pleasant memory, or sometimes a twist to his lips that seemed to acknowledge the hopelessness of their situation. Those moments added light to her life, but that made no difference.

She could not stop her agonizing thoughts of him married to Georgiana. Her only consolation was the hope that such a fierce attraction must burn itself out quickly, but each morning the knot of anxiety in her stomach grew larger, and she had to work harder to smile as she forced herself to swallow her breakfast.

Her only relief came at dinnertime. Darcy usually dined with his French officer friends, not returning until after most of the house was asleep. Not Elizabeth, though. She could not force her eyes to close while she imagined what, or who, might be keeping him out so late. French officers were fond of the company of beautiful women, were they not? Even if Darcy did not go of his own desire, any man might enjoy looking at those lovely women.

Who could have guessed a mere glimpse of love could hurt so very much?

After a fortnight, she had to face the truth. Familiarity had not, as she had hoped, lessened her feelings for him. Instead it had only shown her how well-suited Darcy was to her. The final straw had been the easy rhythm they had settled into while calming Georgiana. It felt so natural and so right, but it could not change the fact that he belonged to Georgiana, not to her.

Even as she had reassured Georgiana she would not leave her, Elizabeth knew it could not work, not while the girl lived with Mr. Darcy. But at the same time, how could she break her word to Georgiana? It was an impossible situation.

She had to do something, so the next day she sought out Lady Matlock. "Your ladyship, I have been hoping for an opportunity to speak to you privately. I find myself in need of advice."

Lady Matlock showed no sign of surprise. "If there is any way in which I can be of assistance to you, I would be happy to do my best."

"I thank you. You have been very kind to me; in fact, everyone here has been very kind, welcoming me as if I were part of your family. But I am not one of you. I am a stranger whose path crossed with that of Mr.

Darcy, and I cannot remain as a hanger-on here forever. The difficulty is Georgiana's fear of separating from me. I hoped you might have some thoughts as to how I could convince her to let me go."

"You wish to leave, then?" Lady Matlock's eyes seemed to penetrate into her.

Elizabeth looked down at her hands. "I think I must."

"Not quite what I asked, but I sympathize. It would be wise for me to leave, but it has been such a pleasure to be with William and Kit, and to know Frederica and Richard are here in the same city, that I keep finding reasons to remain a little longer." She gave a light sigh. "What do you propose to do when you leave?"

"I thought to ask Frederica if there is any way I could be of use to her cause."

"And, of course, Frederica will say that the most useful thing you can do is to remain with Georgiana and help her learn to be a lady."

The problem was that Georgiana was always with Darcy, but Elizabeth could not say that. "She might have some other ideas. Failing that, I suppose Scotland is my best option. I hoped I might ask your ladyship for a letter of introduction to your son who lives there. Perhaps he could assist me in finding a situation as a companion or a governess."

"He would be happy to help you, of course. Still, it is interesting that you and I have been grappling with similar dilemmas. Mine, though, is how to separate Georgiana from Darcy. I had hoped your presence would ease her way, but that will not work if you are leaving."

Elizabeth should not care what happened to Darcy and Georgiana after she left, but she could not help herself. "Why would you wish to separate them after all this time?"

"Georgiana has become a young woman. It is not suitable for her to be living with a single gentleman. She needs to learn to be a lady, and that is something he cannot teach her. And, if I dare say it, Darcy has paid a high price for his guardianship. It has weighed him down, and, as a doting aunt, I would like to relieve him of the burden." Lady Matlock looked as if she were gazing at something in the far distance – or perhaps into the past.

"The war has weighed us all down in one way or another." How had she found herself attempting to comfort Lady Matlock?

The countess's eyes seem to clear. "Indeed it has. Now, what was I saying? Ah, yes, Georgiana. I had been thinking of taking a small house in the country where you and Georgiana could live with me. It would not be charity, as you would be providing an important service as Georgiana's companion. Equally importantly, she seems more inclined to follow your example than that of a woman old enough to be her grandmother. Is that a situation you would consider?"

Elizabeth bit her lip. It was a tempting offer. The idea of going to live among strangers in Scotland was frightening, and she had grown fond of Lady Matlock. "What of Mr. Darcy? Would he live there?"

Lady Matlock gazed steadily at her. "It is his company you wish to avoid, is it? If he has been attempting to take advantage of you, I hope you will tell me. You are here under my protection, and I will not permit inappropriate behavior towards you."

Elizabeth recoiled. "Not at all. He has behaved properly towards me." Apart from that memorable day at Netherfield which felt like several lifetimes ago.

"I am glad of that. He would not live with us, since the point is to avoid having a single man sharing the household with two unmarried girls. I daresay he would be a regular visitor, though. Georgiana would insist on it."

It would still be hard to see him when he visited, but it would be even harder to say a final goodbye. Perhaps it would be enough. She would not have to worry about encountering him every time she entered a room or wonder where he was each evening. "I would like to consider it, if I may."

"Of course, my dear. It is all contingent upon obtaining Darcy's agreement, of course."

Elizabeth wondered how Darcy would react when he learned of her role in the plan.

Darcy eyed his younger brother. Admittedly, the placid life at Darcy House must be tedious for a young man accustomed to skirting the law and daring escapes, but even so, Kit's choice to voluntarily remain in the room when Lady Matlock asked to discuss a serious matter was downright reckless. Poor Kit would no doubt end up entangled in some convoluted scheme as a result. Perhaps he did not recall how wily she could be, even if it was usually in a good cause, of course.

Darcy folded his hands. "How may I be of service to you, Madam?"

"I would like to discuss Georgiana's future. When you originally accepted her under your care, we hoped it would be no more than a year or two until the French were defeated. Unfortunately, it did not turn out that way, but Georgiana is no longer a child. It is not suitable for a young lady to be in your sole care."

Darcy examined her statement for traps before responding. "It has certainly been a more comfortable situation since you and Elizabeth have been with us."

"You have done an excellent job of educating her for her future responsibilities, but now she needs to learn to be a lady. And, while it is understandable that she has developed an excessive dependence upon you, we must begin to wean her away from her constant need for your presence."

Was that intended as a rebuke? "Her situation was an unusual one."

"Indeed. I would like to propose that we set up a separate establishment for Georgiana, much as you would have done had she been an ordinary girl, under my care and with Elizabeth as her companion. It would need to be nearby so Georgiana could have easy access to you, but I believe she could tolerate the separation under those conditions."

Darcy's hands gripped the arms of his chair, but he kept his voice neutral. "Georgiana's reactions can be difficult to predict. She could interpret this plan as a desire on my part to be free of her, and it could make her even more anxious." It was a reasonable answer, and he hoped his aunt could not tell that his response was more to the idea of losing Elizabeth than Georgiana.

To his surprise, Kit stepped up to his defense. "I do not think Georgiana is ready to leave William yet. He is her rock. Even Elizabeth is but a recent acquaintance in comparison. Yesterday it took both William and Elizabeth to calm her when she was in distress. Encouraging her independence is an excellent goal, but I believe she would do better remaining here with all of us for now."

Darcy was sufficiently glad of Kit's support that he did not consider why his brother might make such a strong statement. "A separate household in your care is a good goal, but I agree with Kit that it would be better taken slowly. If we were to attempt it now and Georgiana could not tolerate the separation, she might not agree to try it a second time later on."

Lady Matlock's serene expression faltered slightly. "She is almost sixteen. Anyone seeing her behavior towards you would find it odd in a girl her age."

Darcy could not argue with that, since his knowledge of fifteen-year-old girls was based solely on Georgiana. "That may be true, but it does not follow that an abrupt change will improve matters." He tried to sound calm, but if his aunt chose to insist on this plan, he would have little choice but to accept it. After all, Georgiana had originally been in Lady Matlock's care, not his. King George would never have approved placing her with a man of Darcy's age.

Lady Matlock pursed her lips. "I confess I had anticipated you would be eager to be relieved of the burden, but perhaps other aspects of the situation outweigh that. Nevertheless, she will not become less dependent on you when she is with you so constantly most days. Perhaps if you were away from the house more, she might learn to tolerate your absence better."

Other aspects of the situation? Was his aunt taking a shot in the dark or had she guessed his feelings about Elizabeth? "I could arrange to be away more during the day," he said slowly. He supposed he could go to his club. And he would strangle Kit if he tried to flirt with Elizabeth in his absence.

It was not fair. He finally had his family around him, and now they wanted him to leave.

Chapter Eleven

"I do wish I could have seen the Rosetta Stone," Georgiana said wistfully as they crossed the courtyard in front of Montagu House. "But even if the best exhibits have been taken to Paris, I am still glad we saw what is left of the Egyptian exhibit."

Even though they had visited the museum at an unfashionably early hour and Georgiana was wearing a deep poke bonnet which shadowed her face, Kit walked closer to her side than was proper, almost like a bodyguard.

Elizabeth bumped him with her elbow. "Kit, do stop hovering. It looks odd."

Kit flushed. An outing to the British Museum had seemed a fine idea when Georgiana had proposed it, but now that they were out among other museum-goers, all he wanted was to bundle her into a carriage and get her out of sight. William, damn him, looked as much at ease as he ever did. Perhaps he was so accustomed to the risk that he no longer noticed it. It had been over a month since Kit first met Georgiana, but he could not forget for a second that the safety of the heir to the throne was in their hands.

"It is most unfashionable of me," said Elizabeth in a louder voice, "but I have to say I prefer the Greek sculptures to the Egyptian antiquities. Even if the Egyptian exhibit is more exotic, I admire the purity of line of the Greeks. Why, some of those statues were so lifelike I could imagine them stepping down from their pedestals and inquiring about the time of day."

Georgiana said, "If they did, we would be glad to have William with us, as I am certain none of the rest of us could converse in ancient Greek!"

Still smarting, Kit added, "But then they would be discussing Greek odes for hours while we all fell asleep on our feet."

Elizabeth intervened before William could do more than glare at him. "I had not known you for a classical scholar, Mr. Darcy. I pestered my father endlessly to teach me Greek, but he did not have the patience for it. Nor, perhaps, did I, since I always preferred to be out of doors whenever I could! But I suppose it was not a practical accomplishment for a lady in any case."

"As far as I am concerned, it is not a practical skill for anyone," declared Kit. "What good will it do me to spend years learning to read Herodotus in the original when there are perfectly good translations available?"

William did not rise to the bait. "You never know when knowledge of the classics may turn out to be useful."

There was clearly no sport to be had in baiting his brother today. William had kept his word to their aunt and had gone out every day, but he had made an exception in joining them for this outing. Most likely he did not trust Kit to manage it himself. Typical William.

Kit kept his eye on the people around them, watching for potential dangers. They had arrived at the museum in a carriage, but with the plan of walking back since it was just over a mile to Darcy House. Again, it had sounded reasonable at the time, but now it seemed to leave Georgiana horribly exposed.

His worries magnified when they reached Oxford Street. A crowd of people stood on the pavement, held back from the street by a line of French soldiers. Kit's heart began to pound. Should they turn around and take a different route, or perhaps return to the museum and try again later? But they were already in the midst of the crowd, and they could not afford to look as if they were running away. Kit sidled closer to Georgiana. Elizabeth did the same on the girl's other side.

In his stuffiest voice, William said, "My good man, whatever is happening here?" He seemed to be speaking to a prosperous looking fellow beside him.

The man spat on the pavement. "Prince Jérôme will be coming through shortly." He sneered as he said the name. "Most likely that is his carriage approaching. Would that it could drive him back to France, or straight to hell!" A murmur of agreement came from around him.

Georgiana rose on her tiptoes, craning her head to see over the people in front of her. Elizabeth clasped her hand and whispered urgently in her ear.

Surreptitiously Kit felt for the knife hidden beneath his waistcoat. There was no escape, but as long as the soldiers took no notice of them, they should be safe. Dear God, if anything happened...

An open carriage, gilded and drawn by four horses, clattered down the street. Bonaparte's brother, the so-called Prince Jérôme, held himself proudly, ignoring the sullen crowd watching him. His two children sat beside him.

Georgiana tugged at Elizabeth's restraining hand. Her voice pitched high, she said, "Let me go! I want to see them."

Several people turned to stare at her – including two of the soldiers.

Then William pushed his way in front of Georgiana, sending her stumbling back against Kit, and pulled Elizabeth against him. Wrapping one arm around her waist, he said in a slurred voice, "What's a pretty girl like you doing here all alone? Waiting for me, perhaps? Come, give us a kiss, there's a good girl." He bent his head as if trying to kiss her.

Elizabeth struggled in his arms. "Unhand me at once, sir! You are drunk!" she cried loudly, pounding her fists on William's chest.

Kit grasped Georgiana's arms. "Swoon!" he hissed at her.

187

"But I—"

"I said swoon! Now!"

She collapsed against him.

Kit swept her up in his arms and pushed his way back through the crowd. "Pardon me...Sorry...my sister needs some air..." Behind him he could hear Elizabeth, now shrieking as she begged for assistance.

"Just a little kiss!" It was William's drunken voice.

His brother apparently had hidden acting talents. Kit decided to leave him to it. He carried Georgiana back towards the museum. Had there not been a hackney stand there? This time there would be no walking. Georgiana was going to sit inside a carriage where no one could see her, and that was final.

After a block he set Georgiana down. A couple walking would not draw attention in the way a man carrying a young woman would, and he had started enjoying having her in his arms more than he should. "I apologize for taking liberties with your person," he said stiffly.

Georgiana was looking down, making it impossible to see anything under her bonnet. She said nothing, but shook her head briefly.

They walked in silence until they reached the hackney stand. Kit made arrangements with a driver to take them to Grosvenor Square, a short walk to Darcy House. It was a habit now never to give his address to anyone. Frederica had taught him that.

He handed Georgiana into the hackney and sat on the bench beside her, taking care that there was a good foot of space between them. What was she thinking? Was she furious at him for telling her what to do? His shoulders slumped.

In a small, shaky voice, she said, "Are you angry at me? I cannot bear it if you are angry."

Kit let out an explosive breath. "No, I am not angry at you, although you did frighten me half to death. Soldiers were staring at you, and everyone knows what you looked like as a child."

"Those children are my cousins, even if they are half Bonaparte, and I have never even set eyes on them. I just wanted to see their faces."

The poor girl! But the risk had been unthinkable. "It is understandable, especially since you were taken unaware by their approach. But I beg of you to take more care in the future."

"I know. William always tells me that," she said sadly.

Just what he wished to hear, that he reminded her of his brother! What he needed was a reminder that he himself was supposed to be playing the role of her brother, not having distinctly unbrotherly thoughts about how her legs had pressed against his arm as he carried her. "There is no need to worry. Nothing happened, and you are perfectly safe."

"Only thanks to you." She moved along the bench until their arms touched. "I am sorry for what I did." She leaned her head against his shoulder.

Pleasure at her trust mingled with panic. What should he do? It seemed to calm her when William put his arm around Georgiana, but William did not have to fight off thoughts of her rosy lips. Carefully, as if moving too quickly might cause her to break into pieces like a porcelain shepherdess, he moved his arm to lie along the seat behind her.

She sighed and snuggled closer.

Brotherly thoughts! He needed to think brotherly thoughts, but the only thought he had about brothers was that William was going to kill him if he ever found out about this. He needed to remember that she was not another young lady of the *ton*, but a royal princess far above his station. Devil take it, why did royal princesses have to be warm and soft like other women? It was not fair.

The girl untied her bonnet and set it beside her. "Did you miss your father after he left?" she asked shyly.

Where had that come from? Kit cleared his throat, but his voice still sounded strangled. "Very much. I thought my father must not have wanted me since he did not take me. And, of course, I was certain

189

William did not want me." The summer scent of rosewater tickled Kit's nose.

"It is a terrible feeling, is it not? I did not believe at first that Lord Matlock had taken me for my own safety. It seemed ridiculous. I had always had guards around me. If I was in danger, why were there suddenly no guards? I was angry at my grandfather since I assumed it had been his scheme, and at my father for allowing me to be sent away when everyone always said the French could be defeated in a trice. I never had a chance to say goodbye. I hated everyone for a time, but mostly I just missed my family and my governess. Then, one by one, they were captured or killed." Her voice trembled. "I never saw any of my relatives again – not until today. I could not help myself."

She had been much younger than he when she lost her family.

He tightened his arm around her. "I understand. There is nothing that can take the place of family, but at least you are not alone now. You have William and Elizabeth, and the rest of us."

"Do I? Do I have you, Kit?" Soft fingers caressed the line of his jaw.

Good God! If she were any other woman in the world, he would think this an invitation to kiss her. But she was not any other woman. "Of course you do." His voice sounded hoarse even to his own ears.

"But is it for myself, for the person I am, or only because of what you hope I will become someday?" She pressed her hand against his chest.

This was not good, not good at all. William was going to tear him limb from limb, and he would be correct to do so. "We cannot do this." Why had that come out sounding like a question?

"I do not know about you, but I cannot live my entire life waiting for a tomorrow that may never come. I may never be more than I am right now. Can you not see that?"

The problem was that he could see all too well what she was right now. He made one last, valiant attempt. "You are still upset about what happened earlier."

"Oh, do stop it," she said breathily, and then warm lips pressed against his. Soft, tempting lips. Sweet, irresistible, *royal* lips. God help him, if there was anything left of him after William was done tearing him limb from limb, Frederica was going to pound him into the ground, pour lamp oil over him, and set him afire.

He could already feel the flames licking at him. He kissed her back.

"May I be of assistance to you, madam?" The fashionably dressed proprietress of the milliner's shop on Oxford Street approached Elizabeth.

"I hope so. I find myself in a difficult situation. The soldiers out there separated me from my brother, and now I am alone and without an escort. I wondered if you might have an assistant or a seamstress who could walk with me to my house near Hyde Park. I would pay generously for the service, of course." Elizabeth smiled in what she hoped was a winning fashion.

"Might I inquire who your brother is?"

"Of course. He is Mr. Fitzwilliam Darcy." Elizabeth was becoming altogether too practiced at lying.

"Mr. Darcy! I have heard fine things of him. I am certain we can assist you, Miss Darcy. Pray excuse me for a moment while I see who would be available to escort you."

Elizabeth hoped returning to Darcy House was the right choice. In keeping with her role in their impromptu drama, she had left Darcy without a backwards glance when several men pulled him away from her. But when she returned a quarter hour later he was nowhere to be seen, leaving her stranded in a part of London she was unfamiliar with. It seemed as if their visit to Montagu House had happened days ago instead of less than an hour.

Fortunately the shop assistant who was assigned to accompany her knew the route to Hyde Park and did not question Elizabeth's lack of knowledge.

They had not gone far before a familiar shape came striding towards them. Elizabeth turned quickly to the shop girl. "Oh, that is my brother! Thank you for accompanying me. Pray take these for your pains." She handed her several coins.

The girl bobbed a curtsey. "Thank you, madam." She waited until Darcy was within a few paces of them, then retreated back towards the shop.

Darcy's brow was furrowed and his face appeared shadowed, but once he reached her, Elizabeth could see a purple bruise along his jaw. "Elizabeth! Are you well? Did you run into any difficulties?"

"I? It appears you are the one who ran into difficulties, or at least into someone's fist." She lightly touched his jaw, wishing she could soothe the pain away.

He raised his hand to cover hers. "Nothing to speak of. Your rescuers carried me off to teach me a lesson. Where are Kit and Georgiana?"

Her relief at seeing him intertwined dangerously with the intimacy of his touch, even though they were on a public street. It had to stop. Withdrawing her hand, she said coolly, "I cannot say. They had already disappeared by the time I got away. I assume they are together." She resumed walking along the pavement.

Darcy caught up to her in two long strides. "Kit will keep her safe. I am sorry you were abandoned. You did a brilliant acting job even though I could give you no warning of what I planned to do, but I still owe you an apology for my crass behavior."

She looked away. "Hardly. We were both trying to create a scene, and we accomplished it. I just hope no one recognized either of us."

"I saw no familiar faces, but you are right. It was pure luck we were not caught out. It would have been extremely difficult to explain ourselves. My first thought was to claim my pockets had been picked, but that might have led to the arrest and imprisonment of some perfectly innocent soul. Instead I risked harming your good name. I wish I had been able to come up with something else." His voice was heavy.

With a lightness she did not feel, Elizabeth said, "Fortunately, that risk is limited since there is no actual Elizabeth Gardiner whose name can be ruined. If a problem arises, I could simply change my name again. It would be rather more difficult for you."

He frowned. "I wish things could be different for you, and I still regret my error that day which caused so many difficulties."

Why must he constantly put the blame on himself, no matter what she said? "You wish things could be different for me? Well, here is what I wish were different: I wish you would stop telling me how guilty you feel about me. I made my own choice about fleeing with Georgiana. You did not make it for me. I have made no demands on you and have told you I have no expectations. Yet you want me to offer you forgiveness and consolation, and I am tired of it."

He stared at her incredulously. "If you wish it, I will never speak of it again. But I will not pretend that I have no responsibility for your situation."

It was easier to quarrel with him than to allow herself to want what she could never have. "Where would I be if you had never come to Meryton, or if you had never asked me to take care of Georgiana? I would have had to set off for Scotland without a penny to my name because of Captain Reynard's advances. No matter what you did, I would have had to leave my home and my family. But because you asked me for help, I am in London instead of Scotland, living in luxury and with the support of your family, and I even have the consolation of being of some slight use to my country. If anything, you did me a service."

He shook his head. "But in Meryton we were friends, at least of a sort. Now you seem to want nothing to do with me."

She crossed her arms and hugged herself. "In Meryton we were obliged to spend time together. That is different from friendship." But it was not true. Darcy's arrival in Meryton had changed her life. He had made her want his love, and now she was reminded of that every time she looked at him.

That was the truth she could not speak. Involving her with Georgiana had not changed things between them. Kissing her had done that. There was no going back from that kiss.

And from the pained look on Darcy's face, there would be no going back from the words she had just said.

The breakfast parlor was the place where Elizabeth was most likely to encounter Darcy alone, so she had taken breakfast in her room for the last three days. She was not afraid of what he might say. No, it was the opposite. He might say nothing to her beyond the barest acknowledgement, and that would hurt her more than the unkindest words could.

Since their visit to the museum, Darcy had not directed a single word towards her beyond the minimum requirements of civility. He did not even look at her, which was worse. Before this, his eyes would always seek her out when he entered a room. Often his gaze had rested upon her for a time, and it had made her skin tingle and warmth pool in her stomach. Now she might as well be a piece of furniture, but he would not look away with such fierceness from an innocent table or chair.

She should be glad of it. His attention to her, no matter how intoxicating it had been, had only deepened the well of loneliness inside her. Now he was making his disdain for her clear, but instead of being relieved, she felt more alone than ever. She would have given anything for even a glimpse of Jane or Charlotte.

Now the sight of Darcy made her heart drop. She longed to tell him she had not meant what she had said, that they had indeed been friends in Meryton. But his studied avoidance kept the words inside her.

She did her best to hide her distress from Georgiana, who was blossoming in the company at Darcy House. The girl had not had a nervous attack since that evening at the beginning of their stay there. Her reconciliation with Lady Matlock seemed to have removed a burden from her, and she clearly enjoyed talking to Kit Darcy. Perhaps more people to trust had been what she had needed all along. Certainly the girl seemed more confident every day.

But she could not help but notice that for every bit of vivacity Georgiana gained, Kit seemed to fade away. He was as cheerful and flirtatious as ever, but when he thought no one was watching, his expression turned grim. He had taken to pinching the bridge of his nose, perhaps in unconscious imitation of his brother, when he was worried.

It was safer to worry over Kit than to dwell on Darcy's withdrawal, so when she caught him alone one day, she said, "You have seemed troubled of late."

Kit flushed. "Troubled? More restless, I would say. I am accustomed to working for the cause – helping people escape from the French, working on *The Loyalist*, compiling information. Now I can do none of that, nothing but watch as William goes off to meet with his French friends. Yes, I do understand why he does it, but it makes me feel as if we are accepting their control of England. I need to do something, not just sit in a luxurious drawing room and make conversation." His voice was taut.

"Could you not go back to working with Lady Frederica?"

"No," he said flatly. "She wants me here."

Interesting. It had indeed been Frederica's suggestion for Kit to join them at Darcy House, but would Kit do it simply for that reason? "So you and your brother can become better acquainted again?"

"She would like that, but it is a minor concern to her. For her, the cause is the only thing that matters."

"This was an assignment?" Elizabeth hazarded.

Kit looked away. "Yes. You have found me out."

Her throat tightened. "Spying on your brother?"

He gave her an odd look. "No. She wants a better understanding of Georgiana."

Elizabeth pursed her lips. "You have a hidden reason for all those hours of flirtation, then. You should be careful. She is inexperienced, and you could hurt her rather badly."

"Hardly," he said moodily, kicking at the gravel underfoot. "It is more likely the other way around. She knows perfectly well that nothing can come of it, regardless of my motivations."

The other way around? Was Kit worried that he would be hurt? "Surely you know that, too. But perhaps that is not much protection against wounded sensibilities."

He said nothing.

She tried again. "You are the only man she has ever come close to flirting with."

He let out an explosive breath. "She has an impressive natural talent for it, then."

This was dangerous territory. Perhaps a change of subject was in order. "You follow Lady Frederica's instructions? It is unusual to find a young man willing to take orders from a woman." Would that provoke him enough to distract him from Georgiana?

"I do not have to like it. I want the French out of England, and Freddie is our best chance for that, so I help her."

"Why is she our best chance?"

"She is unmatched when it comes to strategy, and she has the patience to keep her eyes on the goal rather than charging into action. Had I been on my own, I would have attacked the nearest Frenchman years ago and would have died a pointless death. She has more experience and knowledge than anyone else among us, by dint of staying alive longer."

A chilling thought, indeed. "Is that how she came to be the leader of the Loyalists?"

He shook his head. "Her brother first formed the network, but when the French caught wind of his plans, he had to flee to Scotland. He stopped at Matlock Hall en route, gave Freddie all his records, and told her to take his place. That was four years ago."

"He told his *sister* to take his place? How very forward thinking!" It was frankly astonishing.

Kit gave her an amused look. "You have spent all this time with my aunt and still cannot understand why her son would believe that the right woman can sometimes accomplish things men cannot? If I could put my aunt in charge of our group, I would do so in an instant. Freddie is much like her."

Elizabeth tilted her head. "Perhaps your aunt *is* in charge," she said thoughtfully. "Lady Frederica is one of her deputies, as is your brother, and perhaps also the government-in-exile."

Kit laughed. "An intriguing idea! You may have something there. Good for her – and now I feel better about our chances. If only she had an army hidden in her reticule!"

"That would be somewhat difficult to conceal," Elizabeth teased.

"But I should thank you. I do feel better now. If Freddie thinks flirting with Georgiana is the best use of my abilities, I will endeavor to recall that she is usually correct, even if I prefer action."

"If it is any comfort, I share your frustration. I long to help, too. Yes, I make Georgiana feel more easy and help her learn ladylike behavior, but it does not feel like that accomplishes anything. I wish I could *do* something."

Chapter Twelve

"We will be going on an outing to St. Paul's today. Georgiana has never been inside it," said Lady Matlock as she spread jam on her toast. "You need not feel obliged to come, Darcy. Kit will be with us."

As if Darcy would allow them to go alone with Kit after the near disaster on their way home from Montagu House! "I would be happy to accompany you." The question was why his aunt was making this effort to prod him into joining them. Had she picked up on the tension between him and Elizabeth and was attempting to force them to spend time together? That was unlikely to end well.

Georgiana clapped her hands. "I am so glad. We have been planning it for days, but it will be much more enjoyable with you there."

At least someone wanted his company. Elizabeth had made it perfectly clear she did not. He would never forget her reproof, so well applied: *In Meryton we were obliged to spend time together. That is different from friendship.* It rang in his mind until it had practically driven him out of his wits. He had imagined so much more than friendship between them, even if it had been impossible to act upon it.

He could not bear even to look at her. All the magic had gone from the bluebell wood – and his life.

This journey to St. Paul's in her company was going to be torture.

But on their arrival at the cathedral, the torture took a different form than he had expected, because the only thing worse than being with Elizabeth and knowing she disliked him was watching her walk away from him with Kit.

Kit had cheerfully announced that he and Elizabeth had an errand nearby and would find their own way back to Darcy House later. Darcy could have killed him happily, especially since Elizabeth seemed unsurprised by this plan. He tried not to grind his teeth when the two of them walked away, in earnest conversation with one another.

His aunt touched his arm. "I feel the need to sit in a pew for some private prayer. Perhaps you could show Georgiana around the cathedral."

Lady Matlock making a public display of piety when it was not a Sunday? Something was definitely afoot.

"Of course."

Georgiana seemed subdued, but it was difficult to tell since she was looking down. "Do you know where Kit and Elizabeth are going?" She sounded unhappy. Was she feeling as abandoned as he was?

He tried to sound calm, or at least not despairing. "They did not tell me, although I would guess they may be headed to Frederica's house. Leadenhall Street is not far from here."

"But why would they not take us with them? And why not tell us where they were going?"

If he had an answer to that question, perhaps his chest would stop hurting. He had not seen Kit flirting with Elizabeth much since their arrival at Darcy House, but he could not know what happened during the times he was away. His stomach churned. "I cannot say, but no doubt they will have an explanation later."

Georgiana sighed. "I suppose either they were going somewhere they could not take me, or perhaps someplace Kit thought you would forbid them to go."

He tasted bile. "Kit is a grown man and does not need my permission for anything he does. He has opposed me often enough that I cannot imagine he would hesitate to do so now."

The girl's shoulders slumped. "I wish my presence had not come between the two of you. Until I met Kit, I did not realize how much pain it caused both of you. I should have known, I suppose, but I did not understand."

"It was not your fault. I made the decision, and it was worth it to keep you safe." And every time Kit turned wounded eyes on him, he wondered if there might not have been some other way. "I do rather wish my aunt had seen fit to reunite us sooner than she did, though." He had not meant to say that.

Georgiana glanced back over her shoulder at the pew where Lady Matlock sat, as if she might somehow have overheard their whispers. "How odd. Someone is talking to her."

The fear that was never far from the surface when Darcy was in public with Georgiana made him swing around, reaching towards his pocket. As if he could draw a pistol in church! But it was just a woman with a shawl over her hair. No, wait – the figure was familiar. It was Frederica, dressed as an older lady.

He willed his pulses to slow. At least that explained why his aunt had been so eager for this outing. "That looks like Frederica. They must have arranged this meeting." Frederica had told her mother it would be safer if she did not return to the house on Leadenhall Street.

But that did not explain the odd disappearance of Kit and Elizabeth. And here he was, under the soaring nave, surrounded by the majesty of Sir Christopher Wren's masterwork, and all he could find in his soul was black jealousy of his own brother. It was wrong. If he himself could not find happiness in marriage, he should be happy if Kit did. But not with Elizabeth. Dear God, not with Elizabeth.

Elizabeth examined her hands in the Darcy House entry hall. "Perhaps I should leave my gloves on," she said with a laugh. "I do not wish to cause any difficulties."

Kit handed his own gloves to the butler. "My hands are even worse, so we might as well admit to it."

"I suppose so. But thank you for arranging it. I do feel better now."

"As do I."

A figure loomed ahead of them. Elizabeth caught her breath. Was Mr. Darcy angry at them? It had perhaps been improper for her to be out near dusk with Kit, but it hardly compared to some of the other improper things she had done since leaving Longbourn.

"Where have you been?" Darcy's voice rumbled.

Oh, yes. He was angry.

Elizabeth swallowed hard. She had no intention of allowing him to browbeat her. "We were folding copies of *The Loyalist*," she said defiantly, stripping off her gloves and displaying her ink stained fingers.

"Folding newspapers?" His voice was disbelieving.

"Yes. And writing an article for the next edition."

"Alone together all these hours?"

Kit drawled, "Hardly alone, but you are not my chaperone, William."

The corners of Darcy's mouth turned down. "No, but our aunt is responsible for Miss Elizabeth, and you may be certain you will be hearing about it from her."

"Fine," snapped Kit. "But it is still no business of yours." He brushed past Darcy and hurried up the stairs.

Darcy studied Elizabeth with a long, serious look, then turned away without a word, returning to his study.

Elizabeth followed him. Foolhardy, perhaps, given his unwillingness to speak to her in the last few days, but she did not want to be the cause of yet another rift between the brothers.

He was already seated behind his desk, pouring himself a generous helping of brandy, but he rose again on noticing her presence. His expression was unreadable.

She spoke in a low voice. "Kit was attempting to do me a kindness. I had told him how useless I felt since I could do nothing for the cause apart from sitting in a drawing room with Georgiana. He went out of his way to find a task I could do, and indeed I feel better for having accomplished something, even if it was something any child could do."

He frowned ferociously. "You told *him* that you feel useless."

"Yes, I told him that. Is there some reason I should not have?"

Darcy's lips tightened. "What is going on between you and Kit?"

She took a step backwards. "Is that what this is all about? Nothing. Not a thing. I have no desire to be anything but a surrogate sister to Kit, and his interests are firmly lodged elsewhere."

He frowned. "He has said nothing to me of another woman."

No doubt Kit assumed his brother was not blind, but if Darcy was oblivious to the growing tension between Kit and Georgiana, Elizabeth had no desire to be the one to tell him. With a brittle laugh, she said, "Nonetheless, you need not worry about Kit forming an unequal alliance with me." No, Kit's unequal alliance was quite different and even more hopeless. How would Kit react when he discovered who Georgiana would most likely marry? What a tangle this was!

He closed his eyes briefly and turned to face the fireplace, his elbow leaning on the mantle. "Inequality was not my concern." His voice was low.

Her heart was already aching. She could not afford to think of what his concerns might be. "In any case, now you know the truth and that your brother did not intend to annoy you. That is all I wished to tell you. If you are dining out tonight, I will see you in the morning." Assuming he was not out half the night and sleeping in till the afternoon.

He swiveled his head to look at her, his eyes haunted. "If I could... But it does not matter. I do not wish to quarrel with you. Georgiana has been in tears all afternoon, and I have been worried for your safety."

"Why was Georgiana upset?" Or was that his way of saying he was upset?

His chin dropped. "Because she saw her only two friends abandon her without a second glance to go off on a secret errand together. Because you are telling Kit your frustrations, and he is telling you about another woman."

Ridiculous! She and Kit had gone for walks before, but it had never seemed to bother Georgiana. And Georgiana did not even know what the two of them had discussed. Only Darcy knew that. He was the one who was troubled because she had confided in his brother.

But if Georgiana was jealous of Kit choosing to spend time with Elizabeth when he could have been with her, that might cause difficulties. Were her feelings for him even more engaged than Elizabeth had suspected? That was ill tidings.

Suddenly weary, she said, "It was not meant to exclude her. Kit did not invite Georgiana because he thought she would be safer with you. I will explain that to her." She curtsied and turned to leave. With her back to him, she finally forced the words out. "And I did not mean it that day when I said we were not friends. I was upset." After a moment of silence, she started out of the study.

"Please do not go."

Elizabeth stopped in her tracks.

"I never have the opportunity to speak to you these days. You are always with Georgiana and Kit."

She turned slowly to face him. "And you are always off carousing with the French." She had not wanted it to sound bitter, but she feared it had.

"Carousing? Hardly. And you know it is not my choice."

"What am I to think when you do not return home until the middle of the night, even on evenings when there are no balls? The theatres are not open that late." Oh, why had she said that? She had not wanted him to know she had noticed when he returned. Her cheeks began to burn.

"I do not go to balls or to the theatre. I have had to do so in the past, but not now." He paused to pour two glasses of wine from a decanter, ignoring the already poured brandy. Holding one out to her, he said, "Now I dine every night at the same place, often with the same people in attendance. There are many who seek an invitation to this exclusive group, but if they received it, they would find it excruciatingly dull. Conversation is the main entertainment. The general likes nothing better than a good argument, or perhaps I should say a spirited disagreement. Sometimes he talks until the early hours. I find it more tolerable than the early days when I needed to haunt social events to maintain connections, but I would rather be here with you. And Georgiana and Kit, of course."

A sip of wine did little to ease the dryness of her mouth. "Then why do you go so often?"

He made a face, as if he had found the wine to be sour. "Because the general's regard for me is powerful protection for all of us. It saved me when I was arrested. It saved your sister Jane from Captain Reynard. Someday it could make a difference for Georgiana. And it depends on me showing my regard for him. Therefore I do so, even when it means that I return home and feel as if..."

Elizabeth did not need words to understand his meaning. When he returned home, he found Georgiana, Kit, and Elizabeth forming a bond that did not include him – or so he thought. And then Elizabeth had taken Kit's side against him.

Impulsively she held her hand out to him. "Thank you for being so careful to keep us safe. I have done my best to distract Georgiana when you have been out, and Kit has helped with that. But it is not the same as when you are here."

His fingers grasped hers. "And what of you?" he asked hoarsely. "Have *you* missed me?"

She ought to say something light and teasing. No, what she ought to do was to leave the room. But how could she tear herself away when he was finally looking at her, truly looking at her, again?

"I..." She moistened her suddenly dry lips. "What is it you want from me? Apart from a companion to your sister, of course. Or is that my only value?"

"You know it is not." His voice was low and strained. "I cannot have what I want."

How could his words simultaneously relieve her and tear her apart? She had to stop this. "If you have made up your mind to sacrifice your future for Georgiana, you must let me go. No longing looks, no surreptitious touches, no standing closer to me than you ought. You cannot have it both ways."

"It is not something I chose, but something I cannot avoid. If it were left to me—"

"But it is your choice," she said furiously, the words she had been thinking for weeks spilling out of her. "If someday there is talk about you and her, then yes, it might be easiest if you married. But what would happen if you did not? She would still be queen. A few suitors might be frightened off by the gossip, but there are very few men who would turn down a kingdom even if she openly took a different lover every night. You have made it your duty to save her life, but why is it also your duty to give up your own hopes in order to save her from a little gossip?"

Darcy shook his head. "It is not that simple. Her position may not be secure."

"Not secure?" Elizabeth gave a disbelieving laugh. "With every man in England drinking daily toasts to her? Do not be ridiculous. It is your right to decide to sacrifice yourself for her sake, but do not expect me to agree that you have no choice. And because of the difference between her situation and mine, I am the one who will suffer for your choice. If anyone discovers I have been staying with you, I will have no reputation left, and, unlike Georgiana, I will not have most of the princes in Europe at my door. I will be ruined and without prospects. Do not expect me to feel sorry for poor Georgiana facing a bit of scandal." She had been longing to say this for days, but it gave her no relief.

"I never forget the price you have paid. Never."

She pulled her hand away from his. The contact had become unbearable. "And yet you do nothing about it. Perhaps that is another difference between Georgiana and me. Marrying her would elevate your status. Your children would be royalty. Even if Georgiana had not come into your life, you would not have considered marrying a penniless girl with no connections. It would be a degradation. I understand that. But pray be honest with me and admit it."

"No! Your circumstances have nothing to do with it. When I took Georgiana in, I accepted whatever consequences might come of my actions. I have a responsibility towards her. But I would like at least to be your friend, and for you to be content with your life here."

"Content?" She pushed herself to her feet. "Being forced to watch you and Georgiana every day, knowing the future you have chosen? How much would you enjoy sharing a house with me and my future husband? Yes, let us suppose I planned to marry Kit. Imagine how you would feel, faced with both of us every single day. Would you be content?"

He shook his head slowly but said nothing.

She had gone too far to stop now. "What will you do if nothing changes? If Frederica is right, it could be years before we get our freedom. Will you simply wait and do nothing forever? Will you still be caring for Georgiana when she is five-and-twenty? Thirty? Forty?"

"Elizabeth, my dear." Lady Matlock's elegant tones made Elizabeth feel like a thief caught in the act. "Forgive me for interrupting. Georgiana is quite distraught, and I wonder if you might have more success calming her than I have had."

Elizabeth flushed. Although Lady Matlock had made no acknowledgement of the compromising position she had discovered the two of them in, she was too perceptive to have missed the tension between them, but there was nothing to be done for it now. Elizabeth smoothed her skirts, more to hide her expression than because they needed it, then regretted it, wondering if the ink on her hands had transferred to her clothes. She would have to check later. "Of course. Where is Georgiana?"

"In her rooms. She will be pleased to see you." Lady Matlock's tone was not condemning, but it did not show particular warmth either.

"I will go to her straight away. Pray excuse me, Mr. Darcy."

He said nothing, only watched her as she left.

Frederica smiled warmly at Darcy when she opened the door at the house on Leadenhall Street the next morning. "William, how lovely to see you again. I hope you are well."

Darcy had never felt less well in his life. "We are all in good health at Darcy House. You look lovely today."

It was true. Her hair was up in an elegant twist with a few curls loose around her face and her simple sky blue dress was trimmed with ribbon, unlike the purely utilitarian dresses she had worn during his earlier visit. She also seemed more at ease.

Before allowing him to enter, she called back over her shoulder, "Doors closed, if you please." Then she turned back to him. "Forgive me. There are people here whom you should not see. But I assume there is a purpose for your call."

More secrets. He despised secrets. "I wished to speak to Richard if he is here."

"Yes, of course. I will bring him to you if you will wait here."

A minute later Richard limped into the front hall. "Darcy, this is an unexpected pleasure! Our public rooms are in use, and Freddie insists you should be kept apart from our current guests, but you are welcome to join me in my humble garret."

"Lead the way, cousin. Freddie is keeping secrets, I take it."

Richard waved away the comment. "Freddie is always keeping secrets. Did I tell you I took a trip to Milford Haven and followed up on that lead from Tomlin you passed along? It paid off handsomely, though I am not permitted to tell you how. But we are more optimistic than before."

"Freddie looks happier, I must say."

Richard paused half way up the second flight of stairs and turned towards him. "Love will do that to a woman," he said with a wink.

Frederica in love? "Do I know the fortunate gentleman? I assume he must be a gentleman since you apparently have not killed him yet."

"I wish I could tell you, but it is another secret. You will not disapprove, though. Even my mother would approve." He held open the door to a small room furnished with a simple bed, two chairs, and a desk. "But you look as if you have not slept for days."

Darcy lowered himself onto a wooden chair. "Close enough. Only one day, though."

"What is the matter? Is someone ill or in trouble?"

Darcy shook his head. There was no point in disguising it. He needed Richard's advice. "No. This is woman trouble."

With a low whistle, Richard said, "I think you had better tell me all about it."

"You may be sorry you asked. It is complicated." As briefly as he could, Darcy explained his dilemma with Georgiana and the challenges Elizabeth had presented to him the previous evening.

Richard listened without interrupting. When Darcy finished, he said, "Well, I think your Elizabeth is right about one thing. It will not matter if there is gossip about Georgiana living with you. Good God, think of her mother and father. They survived much worse rumors, and most of them were true. In fact, I would argue that marrying her would cause even more damaging gossip – that you had taken advantage of her impressionability to further your own ambitions."

"But I have no desire to be her consort!"

Richard held up his hand. "I know. I believe you, but others may not. The bigger question in my mind is why you think you have no right to marry the woman you love. What is holding you back? Is it her lack of connections? Is she unpresentable? After all, when this is all over, you will either be dead or in line for a peerage, so her connections hardly matter."

Darcy groaned. "I do not want a peerage for doing my duty."

Richard laughed, but with sympathy. "You ought to have considered that before you saved the life of the heir to the throne."

"Spare me!"

Despite the early hour, Richard produced a bottle from under his bed. "Jamaican rum. I developed a taste for it. You look as though you could use it." He poured a small amount of amber liquid into a cracked glass and handed it to Darcy. "I know you never wanted glory for yourself. But what of your family, of knowing your father and mother would be proud of you? My mother would be thrilled to have you made a peer, and I wonder if my father may not have had it in his mind to put one of his own sons in the place that has fallen to you. He was ambitious for the family, even if you are not."

Darcy took a cautious sip of the rum. "What is your point?"

"That you could bring honor and glory to the family name and be a power at court. You care for your Elizabeth, but she would have been a poor match for you even before this. Does your pride revolt at the idea of moving from rubbing elbows with royalty to marrying far beneath you? Can you see her as your duchess, or would your pride get in the way?"

Elizabeth had made the same accusation last night, and he had dismissed it. Now Richard, who had known him all his life, had raised it again. He did not want to think of himself as looking down on Elizabeth, but her life in Meryton had been a curiosity to him because it was so different from his own. He had been attracted to her against his will, even when he saw it as conflicting with his duty to Georgiana.

No, that was not it. Once, long ago, his pride in his station might have made him disdain Elizabeth and her family for their low connections, but after having to humble himself so often to the French, there was little of that pride left.

In Meryton he had ached to make Elizabeth his, but he had known it could never happen. Georgiana's secret had to be kept at all costs. In Meryton Elizabeth had been lively and teased him. When he had been hunting for Georgiana and her after their disappearance, he had imagined how joyful she would look and how her eyes would sparkle when he found them. But when he did, she was always either angry at him or keeping a distance, and her teasing and flirtation were reserved for Kit.

Whatever had been building between them in Meryton, he had destroyed it when he told her the truth about Georgiana. He had blamed himself for taking her from her family, but that was not his true regret. His true regret was that it had made him lose her, leaving an aching pit of grief inside him.

"No," he said abruptly, hardly aware that he was speaking aloud. "Her station in life does not stop me. It is that she does not want me now."

"That is hard to believe, given your discussion with her last night."

Darcy shook his head fiercely. "That is different. She would marry me because she has no other choice. When we first met, she liked me, at least when she was not furious at me for being a traitor. I could see joy in her eyes. Then I turned her life upside down by asking her to help Georgiana, and now the joy is gone."

Richard took a sip of rum and rolled it around in his mouth before answering. "And what have you done to bring the joy back?"

"How?"

"The usual. What does she like? Jewels? Pretty dresses?"

Her sister, who was out of her reach. Bluebells, which were out of season. Puppies.

Puppies.

After a night of poor sleep, breakfast had little appeal for Elizabeth. Calming Georgiana had not been difficult, but afterwards she had forced herself to face facts. Her feelings for Darcy were not going to lessen, and whether it was because of her family and low connections or that his feelings for her simply did not run deep, Darcy was determined to remain available to marry Georgiana. There had never been much chance he would change his mind – hardly any chance, in fact – but now she had to admit there was no hope.

Her head ached. Even the delicious hot chocolate served every morning tasted dull and hard to swallow. But it was the morning of her pre-arranged fortnightly meeting with her uncle, so she found the wherewithal to put on her spencer and walk out to Hyde Park.

Mr. Gardiner was waiting on his usual bench and greeted her with a warm smile, but after he had passed along all his news about their family, his expression became increasingly concerned. "You seem out of spirits. Is anything the matter?"

"Oh, nothing of significance," Elizabeth said quickly. "I have no reason to complain. After being frantic with worry over both my family and Mr. Darcy, and being solely responsible for keeping Georgiana's spirits up, you would think I would be delighted now that everything is fine and there are three other people to share the burden of entertaining Georgiana."

"But you are not delighted?"

"No." She scuffed her half-boots on the gravel underfoot. Could she keep him from guessing the true source of her distress? "Oh, some parts are lovely, like having Mr. Darcy's library to explore. But I still feel the emptiness. Georgiana cannot bear the idea of my leaving, and she reminds me every night of my promise to stay with her, but she does not need me any longer. She prefers Kit's company to mine, and her aunt gives her more instruction in how to be a lady than I do. I never thought I would miss mending clothes and carrying tea trays to the stable. Even when I lived with you, I helped with the children. Now I cannot even distract myself with writing letters, since no one must know where I am, and that makes me miss my family and friends even more. You must think me the most ungrateful creature alive."

"I might, if I thought loneliness and boredom were the worst you suffered. But I can tell there is something more. You only get those dark circles under your eyes when you have not been sleeping. What is the matter? Has Mr. Darcy or his brother tried to take advantage of you?"

Ready tears rose to her eyes, and she brushed them away fiercely. "No. Nothing like that." How could she tell him it was the exact opposite?

"Then what is it? Tell me the truth, Lizzy. I am worried about you."

Scuff, scuff, scuff. "No one is trying to hurt me, I promise you."

"Lizzy." There was a warning tone in his voice.

"Oh, very well, if you must know," she said, half resentful, half relieved. "It is sheer foolishness. I have feelings for Mr. Darcy, and he sees himself as promised to another lady. It is hard, and there is no way out of it since I have nowhere to go. I am completely dependent upon him."

Her uncle patted her shoulder. "I am sorry to hear it. I had hoped he might make you an offer, since he effectively took you from your family. Does he know how you feel?"

She kept her eyes on the path. "I believe so, and he is not without feelings of his own, but he remains set in his course."

"Perhaps I should speak to him. It was through no fault of his, but you were compromised by his behavior. He has a responsibility to you."

"No! He already knows that, but he has a similar responsibility to the other lady. And I do not want him to offer for me simply because honor forces him to it." Becoming one more of Darcy's many responsibilities would be soul-crushing.

"Are you certain? If he has feelings for you, he might be glad of the intervention."

She shook her head. "He is perfectly capable of making the decision for himself. If only I could leave him behind! Lady Matlock has said that someday she will take a house for herself, Georgiana, and me, but I do not know when, or if, it will happen. And I am too much a coward to go to Scotland when I have a warm bed here. I thought of trying to find a position as a lady's companion, but Georgiana insists she needs me. I have not sunk quite so low as to attempt my other idea, which is to ask Mr. Darcy for money to pay for nearby lodgings for me. But I fear it will come to that."

"I can help you a little," said Mr. Gardiner.

"Do you know what lodgings in this neighborhood cost? The rent is astronomical. And it would only be fair for Mr. Darcy to pay; after all, he is responsible for my circumstances. But it would make me feel like a kept woman, even though I would not be." She released a ragged breath which was closer to a sob than she would have liked.

"Have you spoken to, er, Georgiana about your dilemma? Perhaps she would be more willing to let you go if she knew how much it is costing you to remain."

"I cannot do that. Pray do not ask me why; I assure you it is quite impossible. And it is all foolishness anyway. Almost any woman in England would happily trade places with me and accept all this luxury and comfort in exchange for a little heartache." She did her best to sound light-hearted, but she doubted her uncle would be convinced.

He frowned. "I am not happy about it, but at present I can think of no better alternative. And there are certainly advantages to retaining Georgiana's affections. But if the situation becomes intolerable, you must tell me. Send a note to my office. No need to sign it; I will know who it is from."

"You are very good to me. I cannot tell you how much comfort it gives me to have this one small contact with my old life. Although I am sorry to be a worry to you."

He laughed. "Do not think twice about that! You have given me an opportunity many men would die for – the chance to help a certain someone in her time of need. It may not make a swash-buckling tale to tell my grandchildren how I bravely sought out lodgings for you, but you may be certain I will be proud of it all my life. And I owe that to you."

She sighed. "You are right. I forget that this is a privilege, too. I spend so much time convincing myself she is no more than a rather demanding young girl who is not yet out that I almost forget it is not true. I should try harder to recall why I am doing this."

It did help to have a greater purpose.

Elizabeth's headache that afternoon made her want to hide in her room, but instead she gathered her courage and asked Lady Matlock for some private conversation. "I wondered if you had thought more about your plan to take a house for yourself and Georgiana. I do not think I can remain here much longer."

"I am not surprised, my dear," said Lady Matlock. "Your conversation with Darcy last evening did not appear pleasant."

Elizabeth shook her head and immediately regretted it as the motion exacerbated her headache. "It was not."

"I am sorry. I can raise the question to Darcy again. Georgiana does seem less dependent on Darcy, but she has unfortunately attached herself to Kit instead. It would be better to remove her from here. I would prefer to see her getting to know Richard."

"Your son?" What had he to do with anything?

"Yes, although that is not why I chose him. He is the only man who knows her identity and is not believed to be her brother. He is not an ideal choice for her to marry, but there is no other choice."

Elizabeth's chin dropped. "You wish for her to marry him? She is far too young, and they do not even know each other."

Lady Matlock folded her hands together with a sigh. "Elizabeth, if Georgiana were to die tomorrow, who would become King George's heir? The true heir, that is, not Prince Jérôme who was appointed heir by Napoleon."

Elizabeth sucked in a breath, momentarily forgetting her own distress. "Her cousin. Princess Amelia's son by Jérôme Bonaparte."

"Precisely as Napoleon planned it. If his nephew becomes the true heir to the throne, the cause of independence will be well-nigh lost. Georgiana may be too young in many ways, but she must have children as soon as possible to protect the line. For that she needs a husband. If I could march her to the altar tomorrow, I would do it."

She could hardly believe her ears. Lady Matlock wanted Georgiana to marry Richard Fitzwilliam? "But your son, not Mr. Darcy?"

"My dear, the rebellion is years off and, with it, the time that we can declare William is not her brother. She needs an heir now. Besides, William is a fine man, but he would make a poor Prince Consort. Richard is not ideal, either, but he will manage it, if he lives long enough. I rather imagine that once the fighting begins, Richard will be in the midst of it."

Elizabeth struggled to remember the little she had seen of Richard Fitzwilliam. She had been too focused on Darcy, Lady Frederica, and Lady Matlock to pay much attention to him. Why had she never considered that he could be a solution to the problem of Georgiana's reputation? Perhaps because she had not known at first that Darcy had a cousin, and she never rethought the plan afterwards.

But it could change everything for her. Or it might prove her worst fears: that Darcy would not offer for her even without the pressure to marry Georgiana. Or did he know about it already? "Have you discussed this with Mr. Darcy?"

"Not yet. He has an unfortunate tendency to be sentimental about Georgiana, no doubt because he was so young when he took charge of her."

Elizabeth raised an eyebrow. "Sentimental? I would rather have said 'at wit's end.'"

"Therein lies the problem. Georgiana is a pleasant girl, and I would certainly prefer for her to be happy, but first and foremost she is the means to an end. England needs her. If that means she must bear her first child at sixteen, so be it. Darcy, though, would be worried about her happiness. We do not have that luxury."

"Could she not marry Kit instead? She might be better pleased with that."

Lady Matlock shook her head. "The marriage must be legal for the heirs to be legitimate. No one will agree to marry Georgiana Darcy to her brother Kit, and we cannot take the risk of changing her identity again, not when the French are hunting for a disguised princess."

"I suppose not." Poor Kit was not going to take this well.

"But this does not solve your problem. I will give it some thought, and perhaps I will discover a solution."

Elizabeth hoped it would be soon.

Chapter Thirteen

Elizabeth heard the front door open as she was practicing a duet with Georgiana. The easier part, of course, since Georgiana played far better than she did. And today she played even worse than usual because of her distraction.

Darcy had not returned home the previous night. He had sent a message to Georgiana saying that he had to attend to some important business out of town. What sort of business could take him out of town? Thinking of it made Elizabeth's stomach turn.

After their quarrel, Darcy had dined out and left before breakfast the following day, so she had not seen him at all. She had waited on tenterhooks all the previous day to see how he would respond to her. But he did not return home to dress for dinner, and he stayed out all night. How much more of an answer did she need? She had cried herself to sleep.

And now he might have returned. Elizabeth's fingers missed a note as she strained to hear the rumble of his voice. By the time she had found her place again, the sound of footsteps on the stairs indicated he did not plan to join them as he often did when he heard their music. He must be avoiding her.

Georgiana looked at her oddly, and Elizabeth quickly returned her attention to her playing. "Sorry," she whispered.

But her concentration was shattered, so at the end of the duet Elizabeth retired from the instrument and left Georgiana in sole possession of it. Instead she joined Lady Matlock in providing an audience for the girl, though she was barely listening to the music. Darcy could not avoid her forever.

A few minutes later Darcy, his hair damp, bounded into the room. Bounded? Kit was the one who bounded into rooms, not the proper Mr. Darcy. But this time he had definitely bounded in. He stood by the hearth, his elbow resting on the mantle.

Now that he was finally before her, she was suddenly afraid to know. What if she saw only distance and coldness in his expression? Her heart pounding, she forced herself to look at him.

And saw nothing. Although a slight smile curved his lips, all his attention seemed to be fixed on Georgiana's performance. Quickly Elizabeth looked away. She did not want to be caught staring at him like a lovesick girl. Disappointment stabbed at her. She should have known better.

Finally Georgiana finished her piece. Darcy applauded and said, "An excellent performance. Very moving." Then he added, "Miss Elizabeth, would you care to join me on a walk through Hyde Park? It occurs to me you have been deprived of your rambles in the countryside during your stay in London."

She could not believe her ears. Before her muddled brain could put together a coherent response, Lady Matlock said, "What a lovely idea. The fresh air will do you good."

"I would enjoy that very much, thank you." Her voice did not even tremble.

As she fetched her bonnet and parasol, she reminded herself not to let her hopes rise. After all, she now knew he was free from having to marry Georgiana, but he did not, and she could not be the one to tell him. That would seem like a demand.

As they departed from Darcy House, they passed an older gentleman about to enter his house next door. He gave Darcy a curt nod, but his upper lip curled and he did not touch his hat. Darcy nodded back but said nothing.

"What was that about?" Elizabeth asked after they were out of earshot.

Darcy shrugged. "Cartwright dislikes my politics. He was a close friend of my father, so I let it pass." But from the tone of his voice, his neighbor's disdain still stung.

"I am sorry you are subjected to that and most especially that I did the same to you."

"It was perfectly understandable, but enough unpleasantness. Even though it is near the fashionable hour, the park should not be crowded since so many people have left London to escape the heat. It can be more like a parade ground than a park much of the year."

He had considered her preferences? Surely that must be a hopeful sign. "Yes, a crowded park does not feel like a park at all." Then, unable to tolerate the uncertainty, she blurted out, "And a quiet one is much more suitable for delivering reprimands. Is that your intention in inviting me to join you?"

Astonishingly, he laughed. "Have I turned into such a duty-bound Puritan as that? I assure you the only reason I made the suggestion was because I wished to walk with you."

"Simply because you wished to? I am sadly disappointed in you, sir! I thought you far too serious to engage in activities for such a frivolous reason!"

"Now that is a well-deserved rebuke. I only decided recently on this new strategy of doing things simply because I wish to. I am even serious when I am deciding to be frivolous!" He smiled down at her as they entered Hyde Park. "Have you a preference for any particular walk?"

Happiness bubbled through her. How ridiculous to be so pleased simply because he was being considerate of her! "My only preference is not to be run down by feckless horsemen."

"We will avoid Rotten Row then. Did Kit take you there?"

"Yes. He wished to sigh longingly at the fine horseflesh on show there. I am not such an admirer."

He gestured towards a path on their right. "Then perhaps a stroll along the Serpentine will suit."

She glanced up at him through her eyelashes. "Georgiana was worried when you did not return last night."

"Did she not receive my message?"

"Yes, but she fretted anyway." And so had Elizabeth. Just when hope had returned to her, had she lost him to another woman? "But I am certain you had a good reason for your absence."

He smiled, looking oddly boyish. "I think so. I was arranging for a surprise. Perhaps later you will tell me if it was worth the trouble."

That certainly did not sound like another woman. With greater cheer, Elizabeth said, "I hope you do not expect me to question you about your surprise as many women might. I will not fall into that trap!"

"I would not expect you to, and I should have to resist if you did question me." Suddenly his face clouded over. "Oh, devil take it!"

Startled, Elizabeth asked, "What is the matter?"

"We have company," he muttered. "Follow my lead, I pray you."

Two men in highly decorated blue uniforms rode towards them. As they drew abreast, they reined in their horses and dismounted. The more decorated one tossed his reins to the other officer and strode up to Darcy and Elizabeth.

"Darcy, I can hardly believe you are here so close to the fashionable hour!" he said with a French accent. "And with a charming young lady!"

Elizabeth dug her fingernails into the palm of her free hand as she smiled.

Darcy bowed. "I had not anticipated the pleasure of your presence, sir. Miss Gardiner, may I present General Desmarais, whose timely assistance freed me from imprisonment in Hertfordshire and removed a very unpleasant garrison commander who had been terrorizing the local women? General, pray permit me to introduce my aunt's ward, Miss Gardiner, to your acquaintance."

General Desmarais? *The* General Desmarais, commander of all the French forces in England? Her happiness faded under a surge of old hatred.

"*Enchanté*, Miss Gardiner! Your aunt, Darcy, is that the famous Mrs. Fitzwilliam?"

Darcy said coolly, "As you say, General, or perhaps I should say *Monsieur* Desmarais, since you apparently object to titles."

"Ah, *touché!*" cried the general. "Do not worry, Miss Gardiner; I will not arrest him for insubordination. I have the greatest respect for Darcy's honesty. I cannot trust these Englishmen who pretend to be delighted by the presence of an army of occupation. No, I prefer a man who is not afraid to show his resentment and who makes it clear he only works with us because he has no other choice."

Elizabeth hoped her voice would remain steady. "Pray accept my gratitude for your assistance to Mr. Darcy and for taking an interest in the behavior of your subordinates."

"Ah, Darcy, she is as prickly as you were when we first met! No matter. I try to stop the excesses of my men when I can. We French are unhappy to be so far from our families, just as you English are unhappy to have an army of occupation, but that is no excuse for abusing our power. The Emperor has ordered us here, so we must all learn to rub along

221

together. And your Darcy, he tells me whenever I become – how do you say it? – too high and mighty."

Caught off guard, Elizabeth blurted out, "I imagine he would be quite good at that!"

Darcy's head swiveled towards her. "You do?"

Why did she suddenly feel breathless? She tried to cover her discomfiture with an arch smile. "If there is anyone your stern look cannot quell, I have yet to meet them. However, I must say adding General Desmarais to the list is a surprise."

"Ah, I like this one, Darcy! She knows how to tease you. I must study her technique."

Darcy snorted. "You, sir, are in no need of improving your ability to tease me."

The general leaned towards Elizabeth and said in a whisper clearly intended to be overheard, "Darcy tries so hard to convince us he has no sense of humor, but we are not fooled, Miss Gardiner, are we?"

She managed not to recoil from him. "Or perhaps it is part of a subtle plan of his, too deep for simple folk like us to fathom."

He threw back his head and laughed. "Darcy, I like this one! You must bring her to dinner tomorrow night."

Darcy raised his eyebrows. "I must? That decision would have to be made by my aunt – and Miss Gardiner, of course."

Elizabeth opened her eyes wide with mock innocence. "Too high and mighty, is that what you meant to say?" She regretted it instantly; this was the worst possible moment to allow her playful spirits free rein.

But the general roared with laughter again. "Precisely so, Miss Gardiner! Darcy, you say I will need the permission of your infamous aunt to invite her? Very well, I would like to meet her in any case, if she has finally come out of hiding."

"Perhaps seclusion would be a better word, but I warn you, her seclusion protected you as much as it did her. She does not always mince her words," said Darcy dryly. "Still, I will introduce you if you wish."

"But I may live to regret it? I confess a great curiosity about this redoubtable lady. Is she at home today?"

Darcy stiffened. "She is at Darcy House, but she has not been receiving callers or going about in society. This is purely a family visit."

It sounded like such a weak excuse that Elizabeth added, "In fact, she came here to order new clothes for me, and the opportunity to visit Mr. Darcy was an added incentive."

"Then I am unlikely to have another opportunity, am I?"

Darcy shook his head. "I know better than to think I can dissuade you."

"Shall I meet you at Darcy House in, say, half an hour?"

Darcy made a slight bow. "I will be at your service."

"Until then!" said the general. "Miss Gardiner, it has been a pleasure!" Taking the reins of his horse from his aide, he mounted and raised a hand in farewell.

As the two soldiers rode off, Elizabeth said, "If this is the usual result of doing what you wish, I can see why you would avoid it. I had not realized your French friend was General Desmarais himself. How can you abide spending time with him?"

Darcy looked away. "It is not as bad as you may think. General Desmarais is a decent fellow. If it were not for his position as an enemy of England, I would consider him a friend. He does not take offense at people who disagree with him or at those of us who love our country better than his. He will not be affronted when my aunt is frostily polite with him."

Elizabeth glanced around them before saying, "But Georgiana—"

"I agree; it would be best for them not to meet. May I suggest we turn back now so we arrive first and can give a warning?"

"I think that would be wise." The thought of what Georgiana might say in the presence of the French general was terrifying.

Darcy remained silent as they strolled back up the path to the park gate. Elizabeth was grateful for the lack of conversation. Her head was spinning from the unexpected encounter. Had the commander of the French forces truly been teasing, practically flirting with her? He had been responsible for so much misery, and yet Mr. Darcy called him a decent man and a friend. She could never be friends with a French soldier, much less their commander – and now he wanted her to dine with him! Did he want the same thing from her that all French soldiers seemed to want from Englishwomen?

She bit her lip. "I do not understand why he invited me to dinner." If only she could ask about the general's intentions more directly!

Darcy appeared surprised at her question. "He seemed to find you amusing. He enjoys the company of clever people who are not intimidated by his rank."

"But he only exchanged a few words with me."

"True, but you were with me, and he trusts my judgment." His eyes shifted away from her. "It is also possible he is playing matchmaker. He has told me often enough that I should marry."

"Oh." Her cheeks grew warm, but at least that explanation was better than the alternative. Finally she blurted it out. "Then he is not one of those officers who seeks out young ladies for his own purposes?"

"Good God, no! He is married and loves his wife dearly. She will be present at the dinner."

How vain he must think her to assume the general might be interested in her! "I am glad to hear it," she said hollowly.

"That is why I knew he would wish to stop Captain Reynard."

Should she apologize for misjudging his so-called friend? Better perhaps to say nothing. The mood between them had been ruined in any case.

As they left the park and turned onto Brook Street, Darcy cursed under his breath. "Look, he is there already!"

It could not have been more than a quarter of an hour since the general had left them in the park, yet even from this distance, he and his aide were visible standing in front of Darcy House. There would be no opportunity to spirit Georgiana away. "But he said…"

"I know," said Darcy flatly. "This is his idea of a joke, no doubt thinking to embarrass me. He does not know what is truly at stake."

"I suppose we must hope for the best." If worst came to worst, she could drag Georgiana from the room.

When they reached General Desmarais, Darcy said dryly, "I believe you are before your time."

"Of course I am," said the general affably. "It would take all the fun out of meeting your aunt if you had the chance to warn her in advance."

"I would by no means suspend any pleasure of yours. Whom shall I contact to remove your body after she is finished with you?"

The general chuckled. "I have survived a few battles in my day. Lead on, my friend!"

Naturally the gentlemen allowed Elizabeth to precede them into the sitting room. Her heart pounding, she contorted her face into a dramatic expression of horror as she walked in, hoping to give Lady Matlock, Georgiana, and Kit at least a moment's warning that something was seriously amiss.

"Elizabeth, whatever is the matter?" asked Lady Matlock.

Elizabeth stepped aside to reveal the uniformed general behind her. "Why, nothing, madam. During our walk in the park, we encountered one of Mr. Darcy's friends who is most eager to meet you."

Darcy said, "Madam, may I have the honor of presenting General Desmarais to your acquaintance? General, this is—"

"No," interrupted Lady Matlock. "You may not. I have no desire to make his acquaintance." She stared at the general for a moment and then turned away. The cut direct, given to the most powerful man in England. "Kit, do take Georgiana upstairs. She is too young to be in mixed company, especially company of this sort." She pronounced the last words with distaste.

"Of course." Kit bowed and escorted the wide-eyed girl from the room, giving the general as wide a berth as possible.

Darcy said, "The general has been a good friend to me. It was his intervention that brought about my release from prison, perhaps saving my life."

Lady Matlock's eyes flashed. "How very kind of him." Her voice was sharper than a knife. "He is also responsible for my eldest son fleeing to Scotland where he may yet be if he is not dead, for my second son's imprisonment and exile, for the disappearance of my daughter and the conscription of my youngest son, not to mention seizing everything my husband owned on mere suspicion, leaving him bedridden and unable to speak before going to an early grave. You will have to forgive me, Darcy, if I find his assistance to you does not outweigh all those others."

Darcy turned to the general. "I did warn you."

Lady Matlock was not finished. "If for this discourtesy, he wishes to introduce me to Madame Guillotine, he may do so with my blessing. Having lost my husband, children, lands, and station, I do not consider my life of any great value."

"Indeed you did warn me," the general said genially. "You may tell your aunt that I understand completely – and that her eldest son is indeed still alive and well in Scotland. I will leave you now. Good day, Miss Gardiner, Darcy." He bowed deeply in Lady Matlock's direction. "Good day, your ladyship."

"I will show you out." Darcy followed the general from the room.

Lady Matlock maintained her pose until they heard the sound of front door closing. A small smile played across her face. "It is been many years since I have had the opportunity to behave so badly. Apparently it is a skill one does not lose. A worthy opponent, too; did you notice he used my title at the end?"

Elizabeth sank limply into an armchair. "No. I was too preoccupied with fear of the punishment you were risking to notice such details."

"Well, yes, it was a risk, but I had to do something to draw his attention away from Georgiana. I daresay it worked quite well."

"It certainly distracted me!" Elizabeth's voice was still trembling.

Of course Lady Matlock would notice her discomfiture. "Why, did I frighten you? My apologies. I did not think it a great risk since I was aware of his fondness for Darcy." She poured a cup of tea from the tray and brought it to Elizabeth. "Drink this. It should still be warm."

Obediently Elizabeth took a sip even though she had no desire for lukewarm tea. No, what she longed for was to hide away from this topsy-turvy world. If only she could return to the time when she could make a tent beneath her bedcovers and pretend that the outside world did not exist!

After seeing General Desmarais off, Darcy walked slowly back to the sitting room where the ladies were waiting for him.

"Darcy! There you are," said Lady Matlock. "Would you like some tea?"

He massaged his aching temples. "I think something stronger is in order."

"Was he very angry?" His aunt sounded more pleased with herself than concerned.

"No, he was more amused than annoyed, having already heard you were a redoubtable character. And he is downright gleeful to have managed to glimpse 'the mysterious sister.' Perhaps I have made her too mysterious. I shall have to mention her more often."

Lady Matlock smoothed her skirts. "I am glad there will be no repercussions for my insolence. Now that is settled, I had best check on Georgiana and Kit. They have been alone together too long."

"Too long? It has only been a few minutes."

"My dear boy, it may have passed your notice that Kit is a handsome young man and Georgiana is a pretty girl, but I assure you, they are both aware of it."

"But she is his sister!"

"Is she? That is precisely the problem. You met her as a child, and after all these years, she feels like your sister, and she looks to you as her brother. Kit met a pretty young woman. Now, if you will excuse me..." She sailed from the room.

Darcy stared after her. That was a problem he did not need. Now he definitely wanted something stronger than tea. He poured a glass of wine from a decanter on the sideboard. "Would you like some?" he asked Elizabeth belatedly.

She shook her head without looking up. Something was odd about the way she sat hunched over, gazing into her cup of tea.

He set his wineglass on a small table and joined her on the sofa, his body angled to face her. "Is something the matter?"

Her only response was another shake of her head, this time barely perceptible. The teacup was trembling in her hands, so he took it from her and placed it on the tea tray. "What is it? Pray do not tell me you are perfectly well. Is there some way I can be of assistance to you?"

Elizabeth still would not look at him. "Not unless you can make my world return to its normal state."

What was its normal state? "Are you missing your family?" he hazarded.

She flicked her hand dismissively. "I always miss my family. But this – this is too much. Your aunt could have been signing her own death warrant."

"General Desmarais will not hold her words against her. He told me as much."

She turned her face to gaze at him, her eyes suspiciously shiny. "Do you not understand?" she asked, despair in her voice. "We had him in the same room as Georgiana. To you, he is a friend, but to me he is a powerful and dangerous Frenchman who could crown his career by discovering Georgiana is—"

Darcy laid his fingers over her mouth before she could say more – her warm, soft, tempting lips. "I know. That is likely why my aunt set out to draw his attention, but he would never have suspected anything. If I said she was my sister, why would he doubt it?" He lowered his hand before his fingertips could begin exploring her face of their own volition.

"It may seem natural to you, but it is all wrong for me! My father is a gentleman of no particular substance. I never laid eyes on a member of the nobility before I met your aunt. Meeting the French commander while walking in the park and being invited to dinner – this sort of thing does not happen to me. Georgiana is completely out of my sphere, and to cap it all off I was in the room with all of you while your aunt spoke treason! It is too much. And your aunt thinks she can fix it all by giving me a cup of tea." Her voice broke.

"You have done remarkably well." Sometimes praise helped when Georgiana was upset. "No one would know that you feel out of place. I did not even know it."

Apparently that must have been the wrong thing to say, for she bowed her head and covered her face with her hands, her shoulders shaking.

Desperately he sought for something to comfort her. What could console her when she felt the world had gone mad? Perhaps the truth was best. "It must seem very strange. We all feel out of place at one time or another. Do you remember the first time we met, when you were proud Titania surrounded by your court of puppies and I was mere Theophilus Thistle trespassing upon your bower in the bluebells? You are still Queen Titania to me, and you always will be. We were apart from the entire world that day, and that magic was more true than any inherited rank." Carefully he laid his hands on her upper arms. "All will be well again, Elizabeth. All will be well." His voice fell to a whisper.

She made a sound halfway between a laugh and a sob. "That is what I told Georgiana the day you were arrested in almost the same words. But I only said it to calm her, knowing it was not true. And it is still not true."

"Not yet, perhaps, but what feels impossible today will become easier with time, and I will do whatever is in my power to make you happy again. Are not some things better already? Your sister is able to live her life in the open and is married to a man she loves. Would you go back to the time when she lived in the stables and saw only you and Miss Lucas?"

She shook her head. "Of course I am glad Jane is happy. You should not pay any attention to me. I am simply overwrought."

It was even harder to see her pretend to be calm than to watch her tears. He tried another tack. "Elizabeth, when I arrived at Netherfield, I was at the lowest point I have ever known. I had not seen any of my family in years – not Kit, not my aunt, not Richard who had been my closest friend – and I saw little chance of that changing. Six long years of being alone with no one but Georgiana, of trusting no one, and we were even farther from gaining our freedom than when we had started. Everyone saw me as a traitor, just as you did. But now I have my family again. I am no longer alone with my secret, and I can hope that someday England will be ours again. But at the same time, all this has been purchased by taking you away from the family you love, and that should never have happened. But I promise you, what you are feeling now will end, just as it did for me."

It was not the whole truth, but he could not tell her that the moment which had changed everything for him had been meeting her in the bluebell wood. He did not have the right to tell her that, not yet. And he most especially did not have the right to brush her rosy lips with his own. But, like Theophilus Thistle helpless under the spell of the fairy queen, he did it anyway. For a brief moment he thought he could smell bluebells.

She stiffened – of course she did! What else could he expect? But as he tried to collect his wits enough to step away and apologize, the muscles of her arms relaxed under his hand, and she swayed towards him. Only a little, perhaps no more than an inch. Still, it was enough to make him lose his head, as surely as if the queen of the fairies truly held him in her thrall.

He had been starving for this, for her touch, for a kiss, and even more so for her tenderness. That need was all that allowed him to hold back the storm of passionate desire he had been denying since they met. For now it was enough to taste her sweetness. For now.

Except that someone was laughing.

Furious, Darcy whirled around to face the intruder, instinctively shielding Elizabeth with his body.

General Desmarais stood in the doorway, his thumb hooked in his sash. "Ah, Darcy, I cannot turn my back on you for a moment! I was just down the street when I recalled I had not asked your aunt's permission to invite Miss Gardiner to dinner. Now I see you may have something more important to discuss with your aunt than my so inconsequential dinner. Ha! I knew as soon as I saw you with her in the park that this one was special to you."

Mortified, Darcy said, "This is a private matter. I will be happy to ask my aunt your question."

His aunt's voice came from behind Desmarais. "What question is that?"

The general stepped back and bowed. "I wished to ask your permission to invite Miss Gardiner to join Darcy at my house for dinner." He chuckled. "Darcy will have a more serious question for you."

"Miss Gardiner may do as she pleases," said Lady Matlock icily. "Elizabeth, why are you hiding behind Darcy?"

Elizabeth stepped away from him. If her lips were rosier than usual, her expression was unruffled. "It is nothing, madam. General Desmarais misunderstood the scene he came upon and is hinting that Mr. Darcy owes me an offer of marriage. He does not, and even if either of us wished for such a thing, it would not matter. I am an orphan, and I will not be of age for almost a year. Under the Civil Code which your Emperor was kind enough to impose upon us, I cannot marry until I am of age."

"But no!" cried the general. "That is not true. Your guardian may consent for you, or a council of your other relatives."

Elizabeth's smile did not falter. "Alas, I have no surviving relatives, and Lady Matlock's guardianship of me is based on an informal verbal agreement and therefore it is not valid for the purposes of the code. I have looked into it. Besides, this was nothing but a foolish moment of comfort gone astray. Should you consider a mere kiss to require marriage as a remedy, I must warn you every single French soldier in England owes a proposal to at least half a dozen village girls."

"I would not be so impolite as to argue with a lady, Miss Gardiner, but dare I hope you will consent to accompany Darcy to dinner tomorrow? I think my wife would like you. She argues with me, too." His eyes twinkled.

"I will look forward to meeting her," said Elizabeth with a curtsey.

The general said, "Excellent! I will bid you *adieu* until tomorrow evening, then." He bowed and left the room, but his departing chuckle was distinctly audible.

Lady Matlock wore a calculating look. "Will he return to this subject at some point, Darcy?"

Darcy did not meet her eyes. "It does not matter." Desmarais loved to meddle and was almost certain to badger Darcy about Elizabeth, but he did not wish to give Elizabeth anything more to worry about. He had already done enough. It had been a wrench to hear her dismiss their kiss so lightly.

"It might be—"

She was interrupted by a loud crash from the direction of the kitchen, followed by a woman's voice shrieking, running footsteps, and barking.

Darcy shot to his feet. "Good Lord, I completely forgot!" He dashed for the door, but it was too late.

Resignedly he held the door open and allowed the puppy to charge past him. "My apologies. I had meant to surprise you when we returned from our walk, but then we were distracted. He must have heard your voice."

Puck was now gangly and close to his full size, but that did not stop him from jumping into Elizabeth's lap and enthusiastically licking her face. Elizabeth almost disappeared behind his bulk.

"Down, sir!" Darcy commanded.

Puck ignored him completely. Of course, that might have been because Elizabeth's arms were wrapped tightly around him.

"Oh, Puck!" Elizabeth's voice was unsteady. "What are you doing here?"

Darcy said, "Since you were missing your home, I thought you might like to have him here. I went to Meryton last night and asked your father if I could buy him. I said I had taken a fancy to him while I was at Netherfield." He held his breath waiting for her response. Would she be pleased?

Elizabeth buried her face in Puck's fur. The dog gazed up at Darcy, panting happily.

Darcy squatted down beside them. "Good?" he asked huskily.

She turned her head to face him. "Oh, yes." Puck rewarded her with another face lick. "Puck, when did you grow so big? But will he not be too much trouble here? You have so many lovely things that he could damage."

Darcy lowered his voice. "One of the grooms will take charge of training him and will have responsibility for his immediate care. He can be in the stables some of the time. As long as we do not try to keep him inside for extended periods, I think we can manage it."

"Thank you," she said softly, her eyes meeting his. And there was happiness in them.

Chapter Fourteen

The following afternoon Elizabeth paused at the top of the stairs to smooth her skirts one last time. After a deep breath, she started downstairs and halted just inside the sitting room door.

Georgiana gasped at the sight of her. "You look so beautiful!"

Darcy said nothing, but his eyes grew even darker as he stared at her. Something about his look made liquid heat pool in her stomach.

"You are very kind," said Elizabeth. "I never imagined I would wear a dress this lovely, but I fear I will be quite overshadowed at Carlton House."

"It is impossible not to be overshadowed at Carlton House," said Lady Matlock. "The house itself is so overdressed that no one short of royalty can compare. But I was right to order evening gowns for you."

Darcy took her hand and raised it, his eyes meeting hers as he brushed his lips against the back of her fingers. Even through a silk glove, the sensation sent prickles of excitement down her arm. "You will be the most beautiful woman there," he said huskily.

The carriage was already at the door. Lady Matlock said, "One of the maids will be chaperoning you on the journey, but Darcy tells me that a chaperone would not be welcome at the dinner. I have no worries, of course, since you will have Darcy by your side."

Elizabeth wanted to laugh. How could Darcy chaperone her when he was the man most likely to compromise her? But she did not care. She had been unchaperoned so many times since that fateful trip to Netherfield that one more hardly mattered.

The driver set them down in front of an impressive portico of Corinthian columns. Elizabeth took Darcy's arm and tried not to gawk as they entered the palatial residence of the late Prince Regent. The majestic ceiling of the cavernous entrance hall soared high above the expanse of marble floor.

One magnificent room followed another. The numerous swags of crimson velvet surrounding the showy gold plasterwork in the drawing room made Elizabeth dizzy, and she was grateful when they passed through it to a relatively subdued anteroom. "Your aunt was correct," she whispered to Darcy. "Even the most beautiful gown would be overshadowed." It was by far the grandest and most ostentatious building she had ever seen. How ironic it was – the Prince Regent had spared no expense when it came to building his personal residence, and now it served as General Desmarais's home.

"We usually meet in the anteroom because Desmarais and his wife dislike the overdecorated state rooms," said Darcy. "The emperor insisted upon having his commander take over the Prince Regent's house, but it is not at all to Desmarais's taste."

"I can understand that!" Elizabeth said. At least there was one thing she and the general could agree on.

The other dinner guests also showed restraint in their appearance. There were no French uniforms; even the general wore evening clothes. It was not a large gathering: two other couples, one French, one English, and the general and his wife.

Elizabeth could not decide which guests held less appeal for her – the French for being French, or the English for being traitors. Of course, they likely thought she was one, too. But Darcy made no pretense of sympathy to the French cause and no one commented on it. Perhaps they were accustomed to it.

General Desmarais introduced a warm, motherly woman as his wife. "This is Darcy's little friend, the one I told you about. I think his days as a single man are numbered."

"Do not tease poor Darcy," admonished Mme. Desmarais. "And Miss Gardiner is not yet used to your ways. He only means to help, you see. Darcy is so serious, *n'est-ce pas*? My husband wishes to see him laugh more."

The disarming affection between the general and his wife made Elizabeth lower her guard. Looking up at Darcy with an arch smile, she said, "I begin to wonder about your friendships, Mr. Darcy. The general seems to enjoy your company because you are prickly, resentful, argumentative, and occasionally insulting. Now his wife tells me you are too serious. Do all your friends hold you in such high esteem?"

The general roared with laughter. "She has you there, my friend! *Ma chérie*, do you see why I think she will be a good wife for him?"

"Mme. Desmarais, now your husband is teasing me," said Elizabeth. "I have already explained to him that I cannot marry until I am of age."

"Ah, did not Mrs. Fitzwilliam tell you? She should have received a document this morning naming her as your legal guardian." His eyes twinkled at her.

"General, you are full of surprises! Mr. Darcy, is he always such a busybody?" The words were escaped from her mouth before she realized what she had said. Had she truly just criticized the French commander to his face? She had to learn to think before she spoke.

"Incurably so," said Darcy, who did not seem disturbed by this new information.

Heat rising in her cheeks, Elizabeth turned back to Mme. Desmarais. "I grow ever more mystified as to why these gentlemen seek out each other's company."

"But they also have many things in common, my dear. They sit up talking until all hours, the two of them, whenever Darcy is in town."

They did? Elizabeth had assumed Darcy was only part of a larger circle of acquaintances. Was it possible he was the general's particular friend? A shiver went down her back.

The General clapped his hand to his chest in a dramatic manner. "Ah, *chérie*, you are not going to reveal our secret vice, are you? It will ruin our reputations. Poor Darcy will never be able to hold up his head in public if word gets out. It is a terrible, terrible thing that we discuss during those late nights."

Darcy leaned down and spoke in her ear. "We argue about Latin poetry."

Elizabeth's jaw dropped. Could he possibly be serious?

"Ah, Miss Gardiner, now you know our dreadful secret. I hope you will not hold it against Darcy."

She struggled to find her scattered composure. "I see you both have hidden depths!"

"Oh, you," said Mme. Desmarais to her husband. "You should greet your other guests and leave poor Miss Gardiner to me."

The general made a precise military bow to his wife. "As always, I can deny you nothing, *ma chérie*."

Taking Elizabeth's arm, Mme. Desmarais led her to a sofa and sat beside her. "You must not take my husband too seriously. He once dreamed of teaching classics at the Sorbonne, but the Emperor had other plans. I am not complaining; the Emperor has been very good to him. But sometimes I think my husband views Darcy as the student he was never able to have."

Elizabeth blinked. The supreme commander of the French troops in England dreamed of teaching Latin poetry? "He was not always a soldier, then?"

"Not at all! We French were not born with the ambition of conquering other countries, but when the coalition attacked us, we had to fight back. Now we follow our Emperor, and sometimes it leads us to surprising places. Who would have thought my Latin scholar husband would have a talent for military command?"

A new guest arrived, a young Frenchman. "I beg pardon for my tardiness. Monsieur Lamarque was beside himself today. He thought he was close to identifying the publisher of *The Loyalist*, but it proved to be a false trail. He is obsessed with finding him."

General Desmarais frowned. "A pity the man slipped through his fingers. The lies *The Loyalist* has been spreading about Princess Charlotte coming to England have been agitating the populace."

One of the other guests asked, "Are they lies, then, sir?"

"Yes, there is no doubt. Princess Charlotte is still in Canada. I have spies there who would inform me if she had left. This is just a ploy to give false hope to foolish people, and they will be the ones who will suffer when we have to repress their rebellions."

Elizabeth swallowed hard. She dared not look at Darcy. Had he known Desmarais had spies watching the real Georgiana Darcy?

"Enough politics!" Mme. Desmarais declared. "Dinner is ready, and I will not have you spoil your digestion with such unpleasant subjects."

Elizabeth kept her eyes down as Darcy led her into the dining room. It had been a sobering reminder that the amusing, affable lover of Latin poetry also wished to arrest, and no doubt hang, Frederica's charming friend Andrew, and he would not hesitate to kill Englishmen for their loyalty to their country. Vague nausea wound through her. How could she have forgotten even for a moment that Desmarais's hands were stained with English blood?

To Darcy's surprise, Elizabeth instructed the maid to ride outside with the coachman. Why did she wish to have no chaperone? He could see lines of strain around her fine eyes, so it was unlikely to be for any romantic reason.

When the coach swayed into motion, Elizabeth leaned back on the bench seat and closed her eyes. "Thank God that is over!"

Darcy spoke carefully. "I thought you did well. It must be difficult to be the new arrival when the rest of the group knows each other."

"I do not know how you tolerate it."

His heart sank. "I am sorry it was so unpleasant for you. Compared to some of the company I have been forced to keep, I find this group quite tolerable."

She turned her face away from him. "I had not realized you were such a particular favorite of the general's." It was an accusation.

Just when he had thought there might be hope for them. "I have never hidden what I do. I avoid mentioning Desmarais by name because people would beg me for favors if they knew of the connection, but you have always known I had friends among the French leadership. Did he say something that offended you?"

"Were you not offended when he spoke of taking reprisals against English rebels?" Her voice shook.

"No. It is a part of his duty that he hates. Did you not hear him? He was angry over the stories in *The Loyalist* because he feared they would lead to insurrection, and then he would have to take reprisals. There are many soldiers, both French and English, who think nothing of killing the enemy. He is not one of them."

"But he will still do it!"

"Yes, he will still do it, just as my cousin Richard killed French soldiers. If he had been ordered to take reprisals, he would have done it. Do you hate him for that?"

"Of course not, if he was ordered to do it. But this is our country, and they have no right to it!"

"The French did not start this war. We did. We invaded first, sending troops into France and taking Toulon, and we allied with other countries against them. Napoleon invaded us to stop us from fighting him. I want England to be free, but does that mean I must despise every man who had the misfortune to be born in France? They obey their Emperor as we obeyed our King and Parliament. If I hated every French soldier for doing their duty, should I not also hate English soldiers who did their duty in another country? Desmarais is a good man. He does not want anyone, French or English, to be killed. What more can you ask of him?"

Elizabeth did not respond, and her expression was hidden in the darkness.

"Elizabeth? Forgive me, I pray you. I should have spoken more temperately. I am too accustomed to the lively arguments at Carlton House."

When she remained silent, he reached out his hand and touched her arm. She did not shy away from him, but then he realized she was weeping.

What had he done? She had been upset since the previous day, and now he had made it worse – by defending Desmarais, of all things. He knew how she felt about the French. He was a fool.

He shifted along the bench until he could put his arm around her shoulders. Pressing his lips gently against her temple – stolen pleasure! – he murmured, "I am sorry. I never should have agreed to take you there. I had forgotten how it must seem to an outsider."

She pressed her handkerchief over her eyes. "No, you must forgive me for being silly. I do not know how you manage it, finding common ground with them rather than seeing them as enemies, but I cannot criticize you for it. I do not think I will ever have the forbearance to achieve that myself."

He breathed in the scent of lavender water. "At first I hated them all, but when I had to deal with them so often, I came to see them as individuals. How often has England invaded France over the centuries? I cannot begin to count. We call Henry V a hero for conquering France, but I doubt the French liked being under our thumb any better than we like it today. Centuries on centuries of war between our countries, until all we can see in a Frenchman is an enemy and not a human being who is a child of God. I have tried to teach Georgiana to see them that way, but I cannot claim much success."

For a moment he could hear only her soft breathing, but then she asked, "How long have you known General Desmarais?"

"Three years or so, since he was first put in command here."

"I will try to give him a chance for your sake." Her voice was shaky but determined.

He rested his cheek on her hair. "You are brave. I know it is not easy for you." If only he could take her fully into his arms and tell her everything that was in his heart! He sensed she would not stop him, but he would be taking advantage of her distress.

She shifted against him. Was she protesting the presence of his arm around her shoulders? Reluctantly he lifted it.

"No," she said softly.

Then, miracle of miracles, soft fingers touched his cheek and slowly drifted down to the corner of his mouth. Somewhere in the depths of his mind he registered that she must have removed her gloves, then he lost the ability to think as her finger traced the line of his mouth. Instinctively he caught her fingertip between his lips and nibbled it. Would she pull away?

He heard her sharp indrawn breath, then she whispered, "I am sorry I spoke so harshly that evening in your study. I know you did not wish to be caught in this dilemma, and we are both only human."

All too human at this precise moment, as his tongue tasted the sweetness of her fingertip. But he did not wish to frighten her by going too far, so he released her finger just far enough to press the lightest of kisses on the delicate pad of flesh. He was going to stop there; he truly was. But her soft skin intoxicated him and he could not resist brushing his lips down the length of her finger and pressing a kiss into her trembling palm. But that was all. He had to stop now, even though she had made no effort to pull away.

"You have nothing to be sorry for," he murmured into her hand. "I have been considering what you said." It was all he could say now without abusing the trust she had put in him, and it would have to suffice. Good God, he was trembling, too.

But surely if he could not permit himself to speak the words he wished, he ought to be allowed to show her how he felt. And how could he stop when she was allowing him to worship her hand, to caress her flesh with the intimacy of his lips? The longing to taste her drove him on. His tongue wandered along the creases of her palm, the heart line, the life line, drinking in the scent of soap and lavender. It still was not enough, even as he heard her gasp.

And he needed to distract himself from the clamoring of his own body. His torso was on fire where her side pressed against his, flames of desire licking through him and pooling in his groin. If her hand was this thrilling, his body asked, what would the rest of her be like? How far would she let him go? There was nothing stopping him from pressing her back until she lay on the upholstered seat and exploring her with his hands, his tongue, seducing her into allowing more and more...

In fact, he should be proud of himself for doing no more that kissing her palm, nibbling the mound at the base of her thumb and letting his mouth draw against it. He was restraining himself, so there was no real reason to stop, was there? Nor any reason not to draw his own fingers enticingly across the back of her hand. No reason at all. Even if he ached for so much more.

No reason to stop – except that the carriage had drawn to a halt, and the sound of the coachman's boots striking the pavement told him they had reached their destination.

But it was not enough, so he pressed his lips to the inside of her wrist. Her pulse raced against his lips. Then, with a superhuman effort, he drew her hand down until it laid by her lap. Even then, his fingers insisted on entwining with hers, just for the brief moment until the door latch rattled.

Then he was handing her out of the carriage, and if his hand clung to hers for several seconds too long, what of it? She was still wearing all her clothes, and her hair was not even mussed. He deserved sainthood for that, because he knew she would have allowed more. The thought made him groan in the back of his throat.

Elizabeth's melodious voice asked, "Have you injured yourself?"

The words brought him back to reality. They were standing in front of Darcy House, and the candles blazing in the sitting room window were a testament that his family had waited up for their return. "No," he said quietly. "I have never been better."

Elizabeth hugged herself as she snuggled under her bedclothes. Oh, how could she contain her happiness?

How astonishing it was that the dreadful strain of General Desmarais's dinner could transform into such intense happiness! Darcy had given no sign anything extraordinary had happened while Elizabeth answered Lady Matlock and Georgiana's questions about the dinner, his manner towards her just as it had been earlier that day. But when she had said she was retiring for the night, his gaze had scorched her. It had been as palpable as if he had run his hands down her body. What would it feel like if he did just that?

Yesterday had given her hope but not enough to be certain. After all, he had gone far out of his way to bring her Puck, but perhaps that might have been meant as consolation for other things he could not give her. But he had kissed her, too. Not that a man's kiss necessarily indicated that he meant to propose, but it had been a good sign.

Tonight's carriage ride had removed any question, though. His arm around her had made her yearn for more, and when she had found the courage to touch him...

She drew her hand out and held it in front of her. Who would have thought such powerful sensations existed? The spots where his lips had touched still tingled, even hours later, and the memory made heat pool deep within her. Combined with his admission that he was considering what she had said, it was practically a declaration. A thrilling, wordless declaration. She hugged herself again, happiness making her feel as light as air.

Her eyes misted. After all her worries, pain, and longing, everything was going to work out perfectly. Well, not perfectly; the loss of her family and home could not be repaired, and the French would still rule England. But she could live with those sorrows as long as she had Darcy.

It would make his family happy, too. Georgiana would be relieved for her own future and pleased to have more ties to keep her from leaving, and Lady Matlock would no longer have to worry over Georgiana living with her unmarried nephew.

Perhaps he would declare himself tomorrow. She held her hand to her chest and smiled.

The next morning, Darcy had been tempted to sulk when he discovered Elizabeth had already gone out with Kit and Georgiana. He had foolishly slept later than usual, no doubt due to lying awake for hours torturing himself with the memory of those moments in the carriage. But if he could not speak to Elizabeth this morning, he could still put his time to good use, so he told his aunt he had a pressing need to visit his solicitor.

That visit had been very satisfactory. The settlement papers were drawn up, ready to be presented to Elizabeth's uncle as soon as she accepted his proposal. Presented secretly, of course, but it was only proper for him to consult the one member of her family who was aware of her relationship to him. From his brief experience of Mr. Gardiner, Darcy thought he would be pleased.

But the greatest pleasure would be his own, when he could finally ask Elizabeth to make him the happiest of men. Perhaps they could try again to take a walk in the afternoon, this time steering clear of the populated parts of Hyde Park. But when he returned to Darcy House, the butler told him she was still out. Somehow he managed to subdue a fierce surge of jealousy. After all, Elizabeth had made her opinion clear on the subject of his brother.

He would wait for her return in the drawing room. His aunt was already there, and she quickly removed the reading spectacles she denied needing and closed her book. After greeting her, Darcy said, "I understand Kit and the young ladies are still out. This must have been quite an excursion."

"I believe so. They went to St. Paul's, apparently planning to meet Frederica there."

Darcy's annoyance over Elizabeth's absence transferred itself to his brother. "I wish he would not involve Georgiana in further dealings with Frederica. It is an unnecessary risk."

Lady Matlock said mildly, "Georgiana is already involved and has been for years. She needs to play her role."

The abrupt sound of the front door slamming made Lady Matlock raise her eyebrows.

A moment later Kit stood in the doorway, his hair disheveled and breathing heavily. "They are not back, then?"

A sick feeling began to grow in Darcy's stomach. "Georgiana and Elizabeth? Are they not with you?"

Kit collapsed into a chair without even bowing to Lady Matlock. Covering his face with his hands, he said despairingly, "Damn, damn, damn, damn, damn."

Lady Matlock said primly, "Christopher, your language!"

245

Darcy did not care about Kit's language. "What has happened? Where are they?"

"God help me, I think...I think they were arrested."

"Arrested? By the French?" Darcy demanded. His hands itched to grasp Kit's shoulders and shake him.

"Yes, most likely Lamarque's men."

Elizabeth and Georgiana in French custody? Bile rose in his throat. "Why? What happened?"

"I...I do not know precisely. I think they were with Andrew, working on *The Loyalist*."

Darcy could not trust himself to speak. Elizabeth, arrested by the French. Elizabeth, when he finally had a future with her. And Georgiana.

Lady Matlock came to sit beside Kit. "You need to tell us everything, from the beginning." It was her commanding voice.

Kit dropped his hands, revealing haunted eyes. "We went to St. Paul's together, but I thought someone was following our hackney. I assumed they must be watching me, so when Georgiana and Elizabeth left the carriage at St. Paul's, I made a point of getting back in. I got out at the Cheapside Market and darted between stalls until I was certain I had lost him, then I took a roundabout route back to St. Paul's. When I could not find them there, I went to the crypt where we store copies of *The Loyalist*. No one was there either, so I raced to Leadenhall Street. Freddie said she had spoken to the two of them at the cathedral and left them at the entrance of the crypt." Out of breath, he looked beseechingly at his aunt.

"Could they not have gone somewhere else with Andrew?"

Kit shook his head. "They would have waited for me, and there were papers scattered around the crypt. I asked two people nearby if they had seen any French officers. They both said no, but did not meet my eyes. I searched the crypt and found this." He produced a crumpled bit of paper. It looked like the twisted paper apothecaries used for doses of powdered medicine.

Darcy took it from him. Dread filled him at the sight of traces of powder inside. "What is it?"

"It held arsenic. Andrew always carried it in case he was arrested because he knew too much. Since he was caught with stacks of *The Loyalist*, he would have swallowed it as soon as he saw the officers." Kit turned his head to the side and covered his eyes.

Lady Matlock said briskly, "Or it might have been a headache powder."

"I tasted the residue. Sweet and metallic. It was arsenic." Kit's voice trembled.

In a strained voice, Lady Matlock asked, "Does Frederica carry arsenic?"

Kit nodded bleakly. "As do I. But it does not matter. If the French have Georgiana, we have lost everything."

If the French had Elizabeth...Darcy could not even complete the thought.

"Nonsense," said Lady Matlock, but without her customary energy. "She is but a symbol, and we do not even know whether they are in custody. They might have left before Andrew was arrested, or might have been questioned and released, or might have bribed their way to freedom. They could be making their way back here at this moment."

Darcy rose to his feet. "We must set up a search for them."

Kit shook his head. "Freddie ordered a search before she left, and she has people everywhere."

"Before she left?" asked Lady Matlock sharply.

"To go into hiding in case someone is forced to reveal the location of the house."

Lady Matlock turned to Darcy. "Could your friend General Desmarais help us?"

"It is too soon to go to him," said Darcy. "If they have been released, I do not want his attention drawn to their connection to Andrew. If we have heard nothing by morning, I will ask him." If they had heard nothing by morning, his world would have come to an end.

Chapter Fifteen

Two hours later, the butler interrupted Darcy's pacing to hold out a letter on a silver salver. "For you, sir, brought by a runner. A French runner."

Darcy snatched it and tore it open. Then he closed his eyes tightly, inhaled deeply, and slowly exhaled. Opening his eyes, he said, "I require a carriage to take me to Carlton House immediately."

"Yes, sir." The butler bowed and retreated.

Kit turned on Darcy. "Even now you obey as soon as Desmarais crooks his finger? Will you at least ask him about Georgiana?"

Darcy tossed the letter onto a side table. "No need," he said heavily. "He has her."

"*He* has her? Then I am coming with you!"

"No, you are staying here in case there is word from Elizabeth. He says nothing of her." But if Desmarais had Georgiana, most likely he had Elizabeth. Darcy's heart was pounding so hard he was half-surprised the others could not hear it.

"He is right." Lady Matlock's voice might sound calm, but her pallor told a different story.

"I will send word as soon as I can." Darcy strode out of the room before Kit could ask any more questions. He had no answers for his brother, only a terrible premonition of disaster.

The journey to Carlton House was a nightmare of fears and recriminations. Why had he allowed Elizabeth and Georgiana to go out with Kit? He should have forbidden them to leave the house! Could someone have recognized Georgiana, or had they been betrayed?

He had to calm himself. He would need all his wits about him when he spoke to Desmarais.

He was not shown in to see the general right away. That was a bad sign. Instead he was left kicking his heels in a tiny anteroom for what seemed like hours, but his pocket watch claimed it was only ten minutes. Ten minutes of acute agony, wondering what was being done to Elizabeth. If she was even still alive.

Finally a footman led him to the yellow sitting room. Georgiana, her eyes red and her face streaked with tears, huddled in a chair in the corner. Mme. Desmarais hovered over her, attempting to offer her tea.

As soon as she saw him, Georgiana half ran, half stumbled to him and threw herself into his arms. Playing the halfwit? "Oh, William, I have been so bad!" she wailed. "I did not mean to be bad. Elizabeth said you would not mind, but General Desmarais says you would mind very much. I am so sorry I was bad! Pray do not be angry with me!"

He patted her back. "I know you would not be bad on purpose," he said hollowly. "Are you injured?"

"No, I am well. They were a little rough at first, but once Elizabeth told them who I was, they were nice to me."

"What happened?" He had not meant to blurt it out, but he had heard her unspoken message: they had been nice to her, but not to Elizabeth.

Desmarais cleared his throat. "Perhaps you will be kind enough to join me in my study, Darcy." It was not a request.

"Of course." Darcy released Georgiana. "I will not be gone long."

"But..." Her voice quavered.

"Mme. Desmarais will be here with you. She is a very kind lady, I promise you, and she will not let you come to any harm."

Darcy followed Desmarais through the grand library and into a much smaller chamber also lined with books, far plainer than the state rooms. Darcy had only been there once before, the first time he had met Desmarais, when he had been brought in for gentle questioning. It did not bode well for today's interview.

Desmarais sat down in the heavy leather chair behind his desk. "Darcy, what do you know of this sad business?"

"Nothing. Elizabeth – Miss Gardiner – took Georgiana out this morning. They were going to visit St. Paul's, but they never returned. I have been frantic with worry. How did you come into this?"

The general ignored his question. "Do you know why they went to St. Paul's?"

"Elizabeth had never seen it before." It was weak, but the best he could come up with.

"Have you heard of *The Loyalist*?"

"Of course. Who has not?" Darcy fought to remain calm rather than demanding an answer about Elizabeth.

"They were found in the crypt with the man who publishes it. Your friend Miss Gardiner was folding copies while your sister was listening to treason."

Darcy shook his head. Would it look like credible disbelief? "Miss Gardiner folding a newspaper? She is a lady, not a laborer."

"She had ink stains on her hands. Darcy, I am sorry to say you were much deceived by her. She is under arrest for treason."

Breathe. He needed to breathe. "I cannot believe it. There must be some misunderstanding."

Desmarais placed his hands on his desk and laced his fingers together. "There was no mistake. She admitted to her crimes freely, and when I questioned her later, she did not hesitate to tell me she had been using you, hoping to gain information she could pass on to the rebels. She was proud of it. Her affection for you was nothing but a pretense. I am sorry." His voice was gentle yet firm.

"Where is she? I must speak to her!"

"She is in a prison cell, and no, you may not speak to her. It would only hurt you, my friend. If there had been even a shred of doubt in her story, I would tell you so. She fooled you, and that is all. She is apparently a very good actress."

But it was Desmarais who had seen Elizabeth's acting abilities, not Darcy. If only he could shout it out! But Elizabeth's only hope was for him to remain calm. Dear God, Elizabeth in a prison cell! He could not bear it. "I cannot, will not believe it. What are you planning to do with her?"

Desmarais sighed and rubbed his temples. "She will stand trial for treason. The evidence is overwhelming, and she has confessed. You know the punishment."

Death. Bile rose in his throat. "Merely for folding a newsletter? Half of the country has a copy of *The Loyalist*."

"Not whole stacks of them, all while chatting like an old friend with the man who publishes it, the one spreading the lies about Princess Charlotte being in England. He is fomenting an uprising, and she knows all about it."

"But does that crime deserve the same punishment as if she had killed a soldier? Surely there must be something you can do."

The general shook his head, his expression pained. "There are differences in the crimes, but the law says both are treason."

"But you freed Georgiana!"

"I did not free her; I merely took her into my personal custody. To her credit, the one thing your Miss Gardiner did right was to tell the soldiers who your sister was and your connection to me."

Of course she had, then she had confessed in order to distract attention from Georgiana. Just what he would have done in her position.

She would die for it, and he would never have a chance to tell her he loved her. "Into your custody? Does that mean Georgiana is still under arrest?"

"Even Lamarque has little appetite for imprisoning a half-witted child who did nothing more than listen to treason she could not understand. She is still charged with treason – even I am not above the law – but I have little doubt the tribunal will find her innocent. Until then, she must remain with me."

Disaster on disaster. Could Georgiana maintain her act day in and day out? If Desmarais even suspected the prize he held in his hand, it would be the end of everything he had worked for.

Without Elizabeth, he could hardly bring himself to care.

Georgiana needed protection. But how? "I am of course grateful you are providing her a safe place, but she will be terrified. She cannot bear being separated from me. She goes into a panic and often stops breathing when she sees a man in a French uniform, ever since the day when she was nine... but no matter. She has never spent the night apart from me unless Elizabeth was with her."

"I cannot release her to you. Does she have a maid whose presence might comfort her?"

"No. She does not like servants near her." Not near enough to guess her secret.

"Then all I can say is that we will do our best for her."

Elizabeth sentenced to death and Georgiana in the single most dangerous place possible. Georgiana's acting could not always be trusted, and Demarais was not a fool. Darcy tugged at his cravat, trying to relieve the suffocating pressure. "If my aunt were willing to come here to stay with Georgiana, would you permit it?"

Desmarais's mouth quirked up in amusement. "Your aunt, the one who refused to be introduced to me?"

A trickle of sweat ran down the back of Darcy's neck. "I understand. You cannot be expected to offer her hospitality under the circumstances." He must sound as defeated as he felt.

"She would be welcome, but will she bend her stiff neck that far?"

"For Georgiana's well-being she would. She lost her own daughter, you know." The familiar lie came out easily.

"Very well."

Somehow he forced out the words. "I thank you for your consideration and hospitality for my sister." But Elizabeth, his Elizabeth, was lost forever, all because he had come into her life and torn her away from her home.

"Of course. I wish I could do more."

Darcy could not help himself. "I have no right to ask it, but I beg of you to allow me to see Elizabeth, even for a few minutes."

The general sighed. "I am sorry. For your sake I will arrange for her to have a few comforts, and if you wish, I will ask for her sentence to be commuted to transportation. But I have seen what happens to women who are transported, and, were she a woman I cared for, I would rather see her hanged."

"Would I be permitted to go with her?" He had not intended to say that.

"Darcy, my friend, she does not deserve your loyalty. I wish I could make this easier for you, but there is no hope. You must try to forget her. Come, do you wish to speak to your sister again before you go?" It was clearly his final word.

"If I may." But the words were ashes in his mouth.

Darcy hesitated when he reached Brook Street. If only he did not have to enter Darcy House! Not that there was anything else he wanted to do, apart from throwing himself into the river, or perhaps boarding a ship to Canada – anything to leave this agony behind. But if there were the slightest chance his presence might help Georgiana, he had to stay. He would not deceive himself about Elizabeth, though. Her case was hopeless, and it was his fault.

Grimly he stepped inside the house.

Kit raced out of the sitting room to meet him. "Where is she?"

Attempting to keep a semblance of normality for the sake of the servants, Darcy handed his hat to the butler. "Georgiana is safe. Could we discuss this more privately?"

Kit flushed. "Of course." Once the sitting room door was closed, leaving Darcy, Kit, and Lady Matlock alone, he demanded, "What happened?"

If only Darcy could hide from everyone until this agony lessened! But this interview could not be delayed. "They were arrested along with Andrew. Georgiana is pretending to be a half-wit. Desmarais has her in custody at his house instead of prison. He says she will be found innocent." He turned to his aunt. "Since he could not release her to me, I asked if you would be permitted to stay with her. He agreed to that."

Lady Matlock nodded as if there were nothing extraordinary about the request. "Should I go tonight or wait until morning?"

"Tonight, if possible. Georgiana is distraught, and I was not permitted to speak to her alone."

"I will go immediately. My maid can pack a trunk for me to send later. And one for Georgiana, too, I suppose. What of Elizabeth?"

The black fog closed in on him. "To protect Georgiana, she confessed to treason and to spying on me. Desmarais will do nothing for her." Could they not guess the rest and spare him the agony of saying it?

"She is a brave girl," said his aunt, as if it were an elegy. "I will pray for her."

Darcy turned his face away. He could not trust his voice.

Lady Matlock paused at the door. "Kit, is there any possibility Frederica could help Elizabeth?"

"No. We have faced this before. It would be too risky and would almost certainly fail. Besides, we have no way to contact Freddie since she is in hiding. Until she sees fit to contact me, we are on our own."

"I see. Darcy, I will speak to you again before I depart." Lady Matlock left the sitting room.

Kit closed the door behind her. "Thank God Georgiana is unhurt! I was imagining far worse."

Darcy stared at his brother in disbelief. Before he could give into the temptation to murder him, Darcy said savagely, "Good night, Kit."

"Wait! I know there must be more to this. Is Desmarais treating her well? Will he permit us to visit her?"

Darcy shrugged. "I suppose he will. He did not say otherwise."

"I never thought I would be grateful that you made yourself one of Demarais's favorites, but you were right to do so. It saved everything."

After a long, serious look at his brother, Darcy spoke, enunciating each word carefully. "Kit, get out of this room before I kill you."

But Kit had never known when to stop. "I know. It is a damned shame about Elizabeth. Andrew Cobham is, or was, one of my closest friends, and he is not the first I have lost this way. One learns not to think too hard about it, or none of us could keep going."

Six years of constant caution made a thought stir in Darcy's brain. "Andrew Cobham? I thought you only used first names in case you were captured. Does he know who you are?"

Kit groaned. "You are right. Of course he knows my name; we were at Eton together. I will have to vanish too. Devil take it!"

Something fluttered inside Darcy's chest, then faded to nothingness. "Go, then."

Kit nodded. "I will be gone within the half hour. Tell Georgiana that... I am thinking of her." He opened the door and stepped out.

Involuntarily Darcy called after him. "Kit!"

His brother stuck his head back in. "What?"

"Be safe." Darcy's voice was thick.

A rare soberness made Kit look older than his years. "And you as well."

The next day, Darcy made the requisite call at Carlton House to see Georgiana. Apart from sitting very close to him, she seemed relatively calm. Lady Matlock chatted as if it were a normal social call, making no reference to the unusual situation. He took the cake Mme. Desmarais offered him, but he had no appetite for it. He had given his dinner last night to Puck and most of his breakfast.

Since the entire visit took place under the watchful eye of Mme. Desmarais, their conversation was limited. When Georgiana inevitably asked if he had heard anything about Elizabeth, Darcy told her only that she was under arrest. He was relieved when the prescribed half hour was over and he could depart.

He went straight to his solicitor, Mr. Baer, and explained Elizabeth's circumstances to him.

Mr. Baer removed his spectacles and placed them on his desk. "It is a sad story and all too common. What is it you would like me to do?"

"I would like to engage a barrister to defend her." If there was anything he could do, no matter how unlikely it was to help, he had to do it.

The solicitor sighed deeply. "Not possible. She will be tried in a French tribunal, if you can call it being tried. She will be brought in, the charges will be read, and the sentence pronounced."

Darcy had feared as much, but the confirmation robbed him of breath and drove another dagger into what was left of his heart. "Can you determine what prison she is being held in?"

"Possibly. It may do you no good. The accused are not allowed visitors, and while you might be able to bribe your way in, the odds are against it."

"I would still like to know." Even if it proved purposeless, at least he would know where she was.

His guilt drove him next to Gentleman Jackson's boxing saloon. Boxing was not his preferred sport, although he could do a creditable job at it. Today he welcomed the blows and the bruises he received, and was sorry when the Gentleman told him he had to stop.

He returned home aching and sore. After his years alone with Georgiana, it had been a delight to have his family around him again. Kit's insouciance, his aunt's gentle management of everyone, Georgiana's music. And Elizabeth's laughter. Above all else, Elizabeth's laughter.

Now it was but a house, empty of all save servants, and inside Darcy there was a deep, dark chasm where happiness had once been.

He raised his head at the sound of scratching. Puck skittered across the floor and did his best to climb Darcy's leg. To the undoubted horror of his butler, Darcy sat down on the floor of the hall and let the puppy clamber all over him.

It was what Elizabeth would have wanted.

The butler looked displeased as he entered Darcy's study. "Sir, as instructed, I have been telling callers you are not at home. Mr. Bingley has been very persistent, and now he says that if you do not see him, he will remain at the door until you do. He is beginning to attract attention from the neighbors. I felt I should inform you."

Someday, when he would not have to keep secrets any longer, Darcy would hire decent staff rather than the least clever ones he could find. He could not bring himself to care about either the embarrassment or Bingley's ill manners. Those things might once have been important to him, but not now. Still, Bingley must have something of great importance to tell him. He might as well be done with it. As long as Bingley did not ask him about Elizabeth, it would be bearable. Barely.

He would try not to hate Bingley for being able to marry the woman he loved.

"Show him in." Normally he would straighten his coat and check his appearance, but not today. No doubt he looked as if he had slept in his clothes. To think that once upon a time that would have bothered him!

Bingley appeared equally ill-kempt and his pallor was striking. "Thank you for seeing me. I apologize for making a nuisance of myself."

"Bingley, I regret that you were kept waiting. I just learned of your presence."

"I am so sorry, Darcy. I know it is inadequate. What I did was unforgivable, but I did not know what else to do. But I had to see for myself that you were unharmed."

"Bingley, what are you talking about?" He had no patience for dramatics.

"You do not know?"

"Obviously not."

Bingley rubbed his hands over his face. "Some soldiers came to question Jane about Elizabeth's whereabouts. Something about an article in *The Loyalist* they thought she might have written. Jane denied knowing anything, but they did not believe her. They were going to arrest her and force her to talk. I could not bear it, so I took them aside and agreed to tell them what I knew if they would leave Jane alone."

No. It could not be. Not Bingley. "What did you tell them?"

"That Elizabeth had left with your sister and you would be the most likely to know where she was. I did not tell them anything else about you, I swear it! Nothing about your, er, activities. They left Jane alone, but they put a guard on us, so I could not write to you. This morning they said the guard was no longer needed. I had to come to see if they had harmed you."

That was why the arrests have been made. They must have been following Elizabeth, not Kit, and it was Bingley's fault. They had been betrayed by his friend.

But there was no point in saying anything now. It was too late. Dully he said, "As you can see, I am perfectly well."

"I... I am truly sorry. If they had threatened me instead of Jane, I could have borne it. But she has suffered so much already, and she is in a delicate condition. What else could I do?"

Was Bingley really so innocent? "You could have misled them."

"I... I did not think of that. I would not even know what to say."

"Apparently not." It was fortunate for Bingley that Darcy was too numb to be angry. "Go back to Netherfield and take care of your wife."

"But something is the matter. Are you in trouble with the authorities because of this? Is that why you would not see me?"

Something snapped inside Darcy. "Something is indeed wrong," he said savagely. "Elizabeth and Georgiana were arrested yesterday for treason, and Elizabeth is to be hanged. You will have to forgive me if I am not in the mood to receive callers."

Bingley gasped. "No! It cannot be true."

Darcy's mouth twisted. "You may believe that if it gives you comfort."

"Oh, God – is it because of what I did?"

"It may well be, but you need not worry. She gave them a false name when she was arrested, so your dear Jane will never learn the truth and can continue to believe her sister is somewhere in Scotland."

"I... I... Is there nothing that can be done?"

"Do you think I have not tried? For God's sake, Bingley, go away and leave me in peace."

"If that is what you want. But I wish..." Bingley did not complete his sentence. He shuffled out of the room, his head down.

He should have said nothing at all. That was what Elizabeth would have wanted.

Darcy had thought nothing could possibly make him feel worse. Another new loss to add to the list – Elizabeth, Desmarais, and now Bingley. One more of his few friendships ruined beyond mending.

He deserved to lose all his friends. If he had not given in to the temptation that night at Netherfield when he had given the address to Mr. Tomlin, Bingley would not have guessed about his role, and he could not have sent the French after Elizabeth. Why, oh, why had he done it? He had known the dangers. He had spent six years avoiding taking even the smallest risk – until he met Elizabeth.

But why had the French sought out Elizabeth in the first place? It was not surprising they had managed to see through the anonymity of her article, but why would they care? They usually ignored stories like that. Why would they be interested now?

Of course. They did not care about the article. They only wanted someone who could lead them to Andrew. Desmarais had said it himself – the paper was causing too much unrest with its reports about Princess Charlotte being in England. Elizabeth's arrest was nothing but an afterthought.

That only made it worse.

The following day, Desmarais stopped in during Darcy's visit with Georgiana. "Darcy, it is good to see you. Will you dine with us tomorrow night? It will be a small gathering, quite informal."

Darcy could hardly bear to look at him. "I thank you, but I must decline. I am not of a sociable disposition at present." He had never refused one of the general's invitations before. He should not be risking it now, but he no longer cared.

Desmarais's genial face clouded over. "I am sorry to hear it. Can I perhaps persuade you to join me for a glass of port in the library?"

"It would be my pleasure," Darcy said woodenly. He had no choice. Desmarais's word was law in England.

"Very well." Desmarais's tone told Darcy he had understood his meaning.

Darcy trudged behind him through the ornate library. He should not hope for news, since the only news would be bad.

The general poured two glasses of port and handed one to Darcy. "So," he said, almost gently. "Is our friendship to be ended then?"

Darcy set down his port untasted. "I am very grateful to you. Without your efforts, Georgiana would be in prison and facing a death sentence. I can never repay that debt."

Desmarais settled himself in his favorite leather armchair and sipped his port, as always taking a minute to appreciate the fine wine before he spoke. "That was not what I asked, but it is, I suppose, an answer to my question. I am sorry for it. Another casualty of this damned war."

"I understand you have to behave in accordance with your laws, regardless of my sentiments on the matter." Darcy could not even bring himself to care how bitter he sounded.

With a sad shake of his head, Desmarais said, "Not regardless of your sentiments, but despite them. To think I had wished to see you fall in love someday! But not like this. Not like this. She does not deserve you. She deceived you and she is proud of it."

A sensible man would have said nothing, but anguish had undermined Darcy's good sense. "No, she did not deceive me. I knew her views perfectly well and that she was in contact with the Loyalists. I made no effort to stop her. She put on an act for you because she knew her case was already hopeless, and she wanted to protect me from suspicion. Now you may arrest me as well."

The general held up his glass and examined the color of his port. "Darcy, I have always known where your sympathies lay. Your family is a hotbed of rebels. Your father fled with Princess Charlotte. Your uncle was in communication with the government-in-exile prior to his apoplexy, no doubt abetted by your charming aunt. Your brother has been up to his neck in the Loyalist movement for years. I can overlook his little rescue missions since he has not been captured on one of his jaunts to the Scottish border, and his mistress seems to limit herself to making useless lists. You yourself have no doubt wished us to perdition a thousand times, but you have faced reality and obeyed the law."

"And this is where it has brought me." He should not be saying these things, not when Desmarais held Georgiana's safety in his hands. But the Frenchman was an honorable man; he would not punish Georgiana for Darcy's sins. "Have you hanged her yet?"

Desmarais winced. "She has not yet been sentenced. The men who were with them are still being put to the question."

Darcy's heart skipped a beat. "Is she being questioned?" He could not bear it.

"Of course not. I told you I would see to her comfort. Besides, she seems to know nothing of their leader, the mysterious Frederick. He is the one we seek."

They would seek a long time before it occurred to them that the mysterious Frederick was a woman, one who cared about nothing but making useless lists. "Thank you."

"But she must have something to hide. Did you know Gardiner is not her real name?"

Of course. Lamarque's men had been hunting for Elizabeth Bennet and found Elizabeth Gardiner instead. "Yes."

"Why is she using a false name?" It was the tone Demarais used when he was questioning someone.

"So that no one would find her and return her to her family. They are not Loyalists."

Desmarais nodded. "As I suspected. That is what I told Lamarque when he asked. I thought it wiser to give him an answer than to have him attempt to obtain one from her."

An icy chill ran down his spine. "I appreciate your efforts."

"Ah, I dislike seeing Lamarque questioning women. He enjoys it too much." Desmarais took a long sip of port. "Again, I am sorry I cannot help more, doubly so if what you say is true and she does care for you. But there is nothing I can do beyond hoping that someday you and I may begin anew."

"Would you be able to forgive the man who allowed the woman you loved to be executed?" Darcy said harshly.

The general's calm demeanor did not change. "No, most likely not. It is perhaps too much to expect friendship when I have my duty to the Emperor and your loyalty lies elsewhere. But I wish you well, and I will continue to work to restore your sister to you. It is a pity your Miss Gardiner dragged her into this."

Darcy jammed back the words that threatened to spill out. He was the one who had dragged Elizabeth into this. It would do no good to say it and would only expose Georgiana. He could not afford to antagonize Desmarais, not when there might still be the slightest possibility of helping Elizabeth, even if only to make her suffer less during her last days. "I understand. This situation is neither your fault nor of your making. You are simply the embodiment of the French occupation. That is the true cause of it. If—"

"Stop!" Desmarais commanded, holding up his hand. "You are skirting close to treasonous speech, and I have no wish to be forced to act upon it."

It was a sobering reminder. Desmarais was Napoleon's man before he was Darcy's friend. "Of course. My apologies," he said stiffly.

Desmarais clapped his shoulder. "It is nothing."

Darcy hesitated. "Does Lamarque know about my brother?" He would have to find a way to warn Kit. He could not bear to lose Kit, too.

Desmarais shook his head. "Lamarque's answer to any hint of trouble is hanging, so I do not share my intelligence with him. I think there are better ways to solve problems. Now go see that sister of yours. She speaks of you constantly."

Darcy inclined his head. "Yes, General."

"Miss Gardiner?" It was a woman's voice, one with a French accent, at the barred door of her cell.

In no particular hurry, Elizabeth stepped down from the stool which allowed her to gaze out the tiny window. The crowded street, busy with London's poorest, would not have been an appealing scene in normal circumstances, but now it was the most interesting thing in her life. She had learned to entertain herself by making up stories about the passers-by, creating conversations with them in her head. It helped to keep despair at bay.

After seeing no one but her gaolers for days, it took her a moment to recognize her visitor. "Mme. Desmarais, how kind of you to visit." At least she could show the Frenchwoman that she still remembered her manners.

The lock rattled as the guard turned the key in it, permitting Mme. Desmarais and her maid to enter. The maid carried a basket. Dare she hope it might contain decent food?

"Good day, Miss Gardiner," said Mme. Demarais. "I hope you have been as well as one might be under the circumstances."

"I am quite well, I thank you." Elizabeth gestured to the single rickety wooden chair which graced her cell. "As you can see, my accommodations are more comfortable than they might be. I suspect I have your husband to thank for that." Once she might not have considered this small, whitewashed cell with rudimentary furniture to be remotely comfortable, but after a single night in a Newgate cell, it was paradise.

"He has not mentioned it to me, but I hope you have been treated well."

"Far better than a traitor deserves, I imagine," said Elizabeth. "I am surprised to see you here." Shocked would have been a better description. Why was Mme. Desmarais there? They had only met once on the evening she had dined at Carlton House, hardly enough to be considered more than acquaintances. But there were many things she wanted to know about, and this would likely be her only opportunity to get answers.

Mme. Desmarais gestured to the maid's basket. "I have brought you a few comforts – some cakes, a book, and a copy of Ackermann's *Repository*. I hope it will make the time pass more quickly for you."

A book? She would give almost anything for a book, even if it were Fordyce's *Sermons*. "It is kind of you to be so generous, especially to a traitor."

Mme. Desmarais smiled with the same warmth she had shown at Carlton House. "I cannot blame you for loving your country more than mine."

Elizabeth managed a laugh. "I fear I am but a poor excuse for a Loyalist! If one is to be hanged, should it not be for some dramatic attempt at freeing one's country? I shall go down in history as the fearless woman who was hanged for folding newspapers."

"Is that what you were doing? Dear Georgiana becomes distraught whenever that day is mentioned, so I have not dared to ask her. But I am glad to see your sense of humor is intact."

Elizabeth seized on her words. "You have seen Georgiana? I have heard nothing since your husband took her away."

"Oh, yes. She is with us at Carlton House. My husband arranged for her to remain in his personal custody until he can arrange for her freedom."

The relief was so profound that Elizabeth could hardly speak for a moment. "I am glad to hear it. Thank you for caring for her." There were so many other questions she wished she could ask, but just knowing Georgiana was safe was enough for now.

"She is a dear girl. But you must be wondering why I am here. I am hoping to beg a favor of you."

Elizabeth gestured to indicate her cell. "I cannot imagine what would be in my power to do for you, but I will be happy to try."

Mme. Desmarais lowered her voice. "It is a very simple matter. Would you be willing to write a note to Darcy, telling him that you want him to eat?" She sounded mildly aggrieved.

This time Elizabeth's laugh came without effort. "To eat?"

"He has not been eating, you see. I have had my cook make his favorite tarts for when he comes to visit Georgiana, but he will not touch them, and his man tells me Darcy has been feeding his meals to your dog. He looks terrible, and my husband is fretting about it. Darcy will not listen to me, but I thought if you were to ask him, it might be more successful."

"I would be happy to do so." There was so much she wished she could tell Darcy, but even this small thing was a connection of a sort.

Mme. Desmarais beamed. "I knew you would! My husband, he is not certain whether you actually cared for Darcy, but I could see you did on the night I met you."

"I do care for him. Very much." Elizabeth blinked back tears.

"I know. These men, they are such a problem sometimes, are they not?" She turned to the maid. "Marie, can you give Miss Gardiner the pen and paper?"

"*Oui, madame.*" The maid unloaded the basket on the plank that served as a rude table.

"May I ask you one thing?" asked Elizabeth impulsively. "Can you tell me when my trial will be? It is hard, waking up each day not knowing if it is the last." Her voice barely trembled.

Mme. Desmarais looked crestfallen. "Alas, I do not know. The tribunal meets once a month, but I cannot tell you when it is."

A chill ran down Elizabeth's spine. It had already been ten days.

When Darcy arrived for his daily visit to Carlton House, the footman did not take him to Georgiana but instead to a worried-looking Mme. Desmarais. "Madame, is there a problem?"

"Yes, there is a problem, the same one I take you to task for every day. You have not been eating."

Of course he had not been eating. Food choked him and tasted like ashes. How could he forget that Elizabeth had nothing but prison fare to eat? She was most likely going hungry rather than eating the vile concoctions that passed for food in gaol. "I assure you I am in perfect health, but I will try to eat more if you wish." He did not mean it, but it seemed only polite to agree.

"That is what you have said every day. Since you will not listen to me, perhaps you will listen to someone else." She held out a folded sheet of paper.

He had no energy for these games. He took it because it was less trouble than refusing. There was no seal or writing on the outside.

"Open it, you silly boy. It is from your Miss Gardiner."

Darcy's breath caught. He unfolded the letter with trembling hands.

> *My dearest William,*
>
> *Does it shock you to hear me address you so? One of the few benefits of waiting to die is that I need no longer care about propriety. Therefore I shall say whatever I wish, and you may despise me if you dare! But I have little time, and a mission to fulfill.*
>
> *Mme. Desmarais tells me you are not eating. You must eat, you know – if not for yourself, then because of the people who need you. If you do not care for yourself, how can you care for Georgiana? You may find this difficult to believe, but Kit needs you, too, although he would rather die than let you see it. But please eat for my sake, even if you have no appetite or taste for food; I need to believe you are well and caring for yourself. I can tolerate my lot as long as I know you are well.*

Madame is waiting, so my time is short. I pray you will find happiness again someday, for you deserve it more than anyone I know. Do not blame yourself for inviting me to London; it has been a privilege to have had the opportunities you have given me. I would not trade the last few months for anything. There is so much I wish to say, but no time.

Think of me when you see bluebells, and my spirit will be there with you.

Your Titania

The last words blurred before Darcy's eyes. He turned away from Mme. Desmarais, clutching the letter as if it were his only hope for salvation. But nothing could save him. He had lost Elizabeth, and even if she forgave him for leading her to her death, he would never, ever forgive himself.

Rubbing the heel of his hand against his eyes, he struggled to breathe, like Georgiana in the midst of one of her nervous fits. The ache in his chest seemed to press against his ribs, but he knew better. He was an empty hull with nothing inside him but a dark void, a place that had once been filled with love and Elizabeth's laughter. And bluebells.

Think of me when you see bluebells.

As if he would ever be able to think of anything else.

But the magic would not be there the next time he visited a bluebell wood because the magic was Elizabeth, lending life and sparkling joy to everything she touched. And soon she would be gone, her spark of vitality and her future stolen by a length of rope.

He had not cried when his father and sister left him to go half a world away. The news of his father's death had brought no tears to his eyes. He could not remember crying since the morning he sat by his mother's deathbed on a sunny spring day when the bluebells were in bloom. He had thought there were no more tears left inside him.

He had been wrong.

The click of the door latch sounded behind him. Mme. Desmarais must have decided to give him some privacy. Fortunate Mme. Desmarais, who had spoken to Elizabeth, had been in the same room with her, breathed the same air she did. He would never have those privileges again.

All he had was this brief letter. He read through it again, hearing Elizabeth's voice in his mind. Even while waiting to be hanged, she managed to find humor.

My dearest William...

How could three small words simultaneously fill a void in his soul and stab him in the chest like a knife twisted in his heart? If only he could turn the clock back and have her say it to him a fortnight ago, it would have been one of the finest moments of his life. If only he had realized earlier that he need not tie himself to Georgiana forever, he might have had the chance to see her lips shaping the words. Now it was too late.

He ran his finger over the words she had written as if somehow that would reach her. There was a faint round spot below the last paragraph – was it a tear? He pressed his lips to the spot, that tiny bit of Elizabeth that was all he had left.

For all he knew, they might have hanged her today after Mme. Desmarais's visit. Her body, the neck at an unnatural angle, might be piled on a heap of other executed traitors.

Think of me when you see bluebells.

The sharp pain in his chest would not relent. He bent forward, resting his hands on the windowsill, but it made no difference. Nothing could help this agony of loss. An empty future of darkness loomed before him. All those years of being alone but for Georgiana, a few months of glorious respite, and now it was back.

But he had to compose himself. Georgiana might walk in at any moment. He could do this; after all, he had managed to hide his feelings from the world for years. He had to do it.

Once more he pressed his lips to the letter and secreted it in the pocket nearest his heart.

His duty waited for him. It was all he had left.

.

Chapter Sixteen

Three days later, the sound of knocking distracted Darcy's attention from a steward's report. He was only pretending to read it in the hope the words would somehow sink into his skull, even when he could not care enough to read a complete paragraph. Everything distracted him – the sound of a maid moving in the next room, the crackle of the fire, a fly buzzing at the window, and above all the omnipresent crippling ache of grief and guilt.

How could he think of crops and roof repair when he did not know if Elizabeth was alive or dead? It was an additional cruelty of the French to keep their proceedings secret. He might never know when the end had come.

His butler entered with a card on a silver tray.

"I am not at home," Darcy said dully. "You know that."

The butler cleared his throat. "General Desmarais is here to see you, sir."

With an oath, Darcy pushed his chair back from his desk. It was not the butler's fault; he could not refuse an order from Desmarais. "I will see him in the sitting room." Did his presence mean the worst had happened, or was this another ill-fated attempt at remaining friends? He could not even look at the man without seeing in his mind's eye the image of Elizabeth's body dangling limply from a gibbet. The now-familiar nausea rose in his throat.

The sitting room was empty, of course, bereft of the presence of Elizabeth and his family. Darcy had not entered it since the day of the arrests. Now he stood stiffly in the middle of the echoing room.

Desmarais strolled in. "Thank you for seeing me, Darcy."

As if he had a choice. "It is my pleasure. May I offer you a chair?"

"Thank you." Desmarais chose Kit's favorite chair and stretched out his legs. "I will not be staying long. I have just come from speaking with Lamarque about your sister. He has agreed to drop the charges against her rather than to set the dangerous precedent of finding a prisoner innocent." His lip curled in distaste.

"Thank you. That is good news." Now he braced himself for the bad news. The worst news.

Desmarais rubbed his hands together as if to clean them. "Lamarque agreed that Miss Gardiner will, of course, be found guilty and condemned to death, but her sentence will be postponed indefinitely."

No. He would not allow himself to hope. It would only hurt more in the end. "What does that mean?"

"I could explain it in pretty words, but put simply, she will live as a hostage for your good behavior. We have several such hostages. As long as you continue to support our regime, she will remain safe. I told Lamarque the truth – that I feared her execution would drive you into the arms of the rebels. We cannot afford a Northern uprising at present. He agreed she might prove more useful among our other, ah, guests."

He did not dare to believe it. "My cousin, Richard Fitzwilliam, was held as a hostage. He suffered greatly and nearly died from the experience."

"That was in the early days of the invasion when each commander made his own rules. We are no longer so barbaric in our methods."

"But she will remain in prison indefinitely." Elizabeth might prefer to be hanged.

"No, no. Not free, but not imprisoned. We have better accommodations for our guests. She will be aboard the *Neptune* with several other ladies. They have several cabins to themselves and the freedom to walk on the deck. It is not luxurious, but neither is it uncomfortable."

The *Neptune*, anchored in the middle of the Thames, was only accessible by boat. A natural prison for ladies, since they never learned to swim. "Will I be allowed to visit her?"

Desmarais hesitated. "Soon. After she has had a chance to settle in. You may write to her and send her books to pass the time. The other ladies net purses and paint watercolors, and one even has a small harp. No embroidery, I am afraid – the needles, you understand. She will be allowed some of her own clothing and toiletries. Everything will be searched before being given to her, including letters, I am sorry to say. It is not ideal, but better than losing her forever, I hope."

"And what must I do in return?" His stomach clenched. What if the price were to betray Kit or Frederica?

"Nothing more than you have been doing all along. Cooperating with us and keeping the peace." Desmarais looked at him expectantly.

"This is a permanent arrangement, with no hope of her release?"

Desmarais shrugged. "If England becomes more accepting of us, if Lamarque is recalled to France, if at some point your loyalty is considered proven or you render a great service to the Emperor – who is to say what might happen? There is always hope, my friend."

It was so little to go on, but Elizabeth would be alive. He could see her from time to time. The lead weight that had been crushing his chest since her arrest eased just a little.

The general stood, straightening his dress sword. "And for the sake of God, Darcy, you must eat something. Otherwise Miss Gardiner will hardly recognize you when you visit her. You will be skin and bones if you do not eat."

"I will eat. I promise you." He would do it, too, no matter how it choked him. He owed Desmarais far more than that. Lamarque would not have agreed to give up one of his prisoners so easily; the general must have made concessions to him to obtain this bargain. He ought to find a little gratitude in his heart; very few friends would do as much for him, especially after he had spurned Desmarais's efforts at maintaining their connection.

It was hard, but he would show his appreciation somehow. "Thank you."

Darcy hurried downstairs to meet Georgiana and Lady Matlock on their homecoming from Carlton House. "Welcome home." Darcy tried to sound cheerful and failed abysmally.

His aunt calmly kissed his cheek. Georgiana stood behind her, her posture rigid and her hands balled into fists.

"Georgiana, what is the matter?" he asked.

She attempted to respond, but her breaths were coming in such quick gasps she could not speak. Instead she buried her face in her hands.

Darcy put his arm around her shoulders and guided her into the sitting room. "What is this? There is nothing to fear now. You are safe. It is all over, and you are free." It was even mostly true.

Lady Matlock said, "She is frantic about Elizabeth. The general never mentioned her to us, and we thought it unwise to ask. Has she been sentenced yet?" She left the second possibility unsaid.

"She is still alive. Although she was found guilty, they decided to keep her as a hostage instead of hanging her."

Lady Matlock's eyebrows shot up. "Indeed? I had not realized your influence extended so far, but I am glad of it."

Georgiana's shoulders were shaking now, but her breathing began to ease.

To give her time to recover, Darcy said, "I hope you were comfortable at Carlton House."

"I was comfortable enough, but it was difficult for Georgiana," said Lady Matlock. "She had to play a role the entire time, and Carlton House itself brings up memories for her."

Of course. Carlton House had been Prinny's residence, so Georgiana had been born and reared there. "That must have been difficult. I am proud of you, my dear, for keeping your composure so well all these days."

Lady Matlock said briskly, "I was not idle, either. I must speak to Frederica. I have a good deal of information she will find useful."

He had been afraid of this. "That may not be possible. She and Kit have both gone into hiding, so you are on your own. Also, some of what you learned is likely to be false. Desmarais tests people that way."

"He told me nothing. He knows my sympathies. These are things I overheard or that Mme. Desmarais let slip. For example, she said—"

"Stop!" Darcy commanded. "No more, I pray you."

Georgiana froze in mid-sob.

Lady Matlock wore a well-bred look of faint surprise. "What is the matter?"

Darcy ignored her. "Georgiana, you have done nothing wrong. I was speaking to my aunt."

"Oh." The girl fished out a handkerchief and began to dab at her eyes, her shoulders hunched.

"But this is something I must tell both of you. I do not wish to know anything about the Loyalists, including what Frederica and Kit are doing, where they are doing it, or what you have discovered or done for them. I want to be left in complete ignorance of it. Elizabeth's life depends on my cooperation with the French. I need to be able to swear I know nothing about what any of you are doing."

With a long, serious look, Lady Matlock said, "And what of Georgiana? Must that arrangement change?"

"Of course not. Georgiana is my sister, and I will do whatever is in my power to keep her safe. Any change in that would draw attention."

Seeing Georgiana's white face, he added, "Besides, I would miss her too much. It has been far too quiet here, and I am glad you are back."

The girl made a weak attempt at a smile. "But Kit is gone?"

"I am afraid so."

Her face crumpled. Darcy should have expected it. No sooner had she begun to rely on others than Kit and Elizabeth had vanished. This time he shared her feelings of loss.

"A bosun's chair?" Elizabeth shaded her eyes to examine the warship looming over her. "How will a chair help me climb aboard?"

The sailor who had rowed her to the ship said, "It is not a real chair, *Mademoiselle*. Just a board tied with ropes like a swing. You sit on the board and the crew will hoist you up."

She eyed the contraption dubiously. "Very well. I hope you will fish me out of the river if I fall in."

"No one ever falls. Just hold onto the ropes on either side..." His voice trailed off as he looked down at her bound hands. "Never mind. It is very safe."

Compared to dangling from a gallows, the bosun's chair was no doubt extremely safe. And the ship was no higher than the trees she had climbed as a girl, though her hands had not been bound then. She would not give the French sailors the satisfaction of seeing her fear, so she perched herself in the center of the so-called chair. "Well?"

The board bounced against the side of the ship several times as she was hoisted up, then two French sailors assisted her over the rail. There were ropes everywhere, running from the ship to the masts, and cannons on runners. The deck shifted under her feet. Being aboard a warship was a new experience. Today had abounded in them.

There was a quick exchange of French between the sailors. Elizabeth caught General Desmarais's name but little else. It had been a long day. A very, very long day. But she was alive, which was more than she had dreamed of, and out in the open air for the first time since her arrest.

She followed a young lieutenant along the deck to a hatchway. Four elegantly dressed ladies, each carrying a parasol, stood a short distance away, looking as out of place on the ship as tropical birds in a winter storm. One of them pointed to her bound hands and whispered to the others, who tittered.

Elizabeth supposed she must look a sight. Who could hope for more after a fortnight in gaol, wearing the same dress she had been arrested in and having nothing but her fingers to comb her hair? But she smiled cheekily at the ladies. She had nothing to be ashamed of.

Steep steps led down to another deck with a low ceiling. Several doors stood on each side of a narrow corridor. "Officer's quarters, *Mademoiselle*. They have been made over for use by the ladies. Not what you are accustomed to, perhaps, but they are the best we have." He opened a door small enough that he had to bend down to enter. "This will be your cabin."

Elizabeth peered inside the tiny space. A pair of bunks lined one wall, with a small wardrobe and a washstand against the other.

"Your possessions have already been brought aboard. Hortense, who is the maid for all the ladies here, has unpacked them." He gestured past the cabin. "Beyond this bulkhead is a stateroom for the ladies. Shall I send for Hortense to assist you?"

"Thank you, that would be lovely. Is it possible to have an ewer of water? Fresh water, that is." Washing the prison grime from her hands and face would be an incredible luxury. "Oh, and if you please..." She held out her bound hands.

"Of course, *Mademoiselle*." He produced a knife from his belt and sawed at the rope until it parted. Just like that, she was free. "I will fetch Hortense."

Elizabeth rubbed her wrists where the ropes had chafed her skin. Slowly she turned in place, taking in her new surroundings with the low ceiling and curved walls. A month ago she would have found it confining. Now the simple pleasure of being able to walk from one room to another seemed the epitome of freedom.

A strikingly pretty young woman with red hair appeared through the door in the bulkhead. "Oh! You must be the new guest." She made a face as she said the last word. "I am Mrs. Hayes. I am in the cabin next to yours."

"I am glad to meet you. I hope you will tell me where to find everything and how things work here."

"Of course! I will be happy to do so." Her delight was obvious and infective. "What would you like to know first?"

"Could you show me where my clothes are? I cannot tell you how much I am longing for a clean dress. And a hairbrush – I have been dreaming of hairbrushes!" At the woman's shocked look, Elizabeth said, "I am not always so odd, I assure you. But after a fortnight in gaol, things I once took for granted seem like a luxury."

"In gaol?" Mrs. Hayes gasped. "Oh, no! How did you – but I suppose I should not ask. I can tell from your accent you are a lady, so I cannot imagine how you came to be in gaol."

"It is not a secret. I was arrested for treason. This morning I was sentenced to be hanged by the neck until dead, then they told me I was coming here instead. I still cannot quite believe it." Elizabeth ducked her head to enter the cabin.

"Treason? What did you do?"

"I was helping to prepare copies of *The Loyalist* for distribution." Suddenly it seemed beyond ridiculous, and she began to laugh uncontrollably. Then, to her horror, her laughter turned into tears. She sank down on the bunk and covered her face with her hands.

"I am so sorry. I did not mean to upset you." The other woman pressed a handkerchief against her hand. It was the cleanest cloth Elizabeth had touched in days.

Gulping back the tears, Elizabeth said, "It is just so strange. I have been guilty of things the French would consider terrible crimes, but they were going to hang me for folding newspapers!"

Mrs. Hayes gave a hesitant smile. "Strange indeed! But come, my dear, let us find you a clean dress to wear." She squeezed past to open the small wardrobe. "Shall I help you out of your dress?"

"Thank you. The lieutenant said he would send a maid, but I cannot bear to wait."

"You should not wait. Hortense is far more interested in flirting with the sailors than in us. You will be fortunate if she is here within the hour."

"Then I am doubly grateful," said Elizabeth ruefully. She turned her back to allow Mrs. Hayes to undo the buttons. "And I assure you I am not usually a watering pot."

Her new friend smiled indulgently. "If a few tears are all that comes after a fortnight in gaol, I consider you very calm indeed!"

"You are very kind." It was an enormous relief to be able to speak to a sympathetic woman her own age.

Hesitantly her new friend said, "But if I might give you some advice, I would not mention what you have just told me to the other ladies aboard the ship. They are very proper and are fond of their own importance, and it is not pleasant to meet with unkindness from those you must spend every day with."

"I fear I may already have made a poor impression on them. They saw me with my hands bound as I came aboard. But if they think badly of me for opposing French rule, I have no desire for their good opinion."

The other woman looked down at Elizabeth's hands. "You poor dear! Once you are dressed, I have a special lotion that will help those wrists of yours. And I will be your friend in any case. The others do not approve of me. I was an actress, you see, before I was fortunate enough to catch the eye of my husband."

"An actress! I hope you will tell me about it someday. I know it is a difficult life, but it must be exciting to become someone else when you step upon the stage."

"It is like nothing else. But wait, I still do not know your name."

"I am Miss Gardiner, but I pray you to call me Lizzy." She was tired of responding to a name that was not her own.

"And I am Molly. I may not be very proper, but I am overjoyed to have a new friend. There, now you can step out of the dress. That shift must go, too." She untied the stays and tugged the shift over Elizabeth's head. "Here is a clean one for you. Which dress would you like? This blue one, perhaps?"

"Anything that is clean!" The new shift felt like heaven.

"Very well, the blue one. Does it fasten up the back? Yes, I see it does." Molly held out the dress for Elizabeth to step into. "If you are unmarried, who are you being held hostage for? For the rest of us, it is our husbands. Is it your father?"

"I assume it must be Mr. Darcy. He is a friend, and I am his aunt's ward."

The other woman raised her eyebrows. "He must be a very good friend if he will change his behavior to keep you safe."

Elizabeth tried to undo the damage. "His sister is very attached to me." No, that just sounded foolish; his sister would have been a more useful hostage in that case. "Yes, he is a good friend. A very good friend."

Molly gave a knowing smile before turning her attention to the buttons. "Perhaps more than a friend?"

"Perhaps. I think so. I thought he was about to make me an offer. Now, of course, that is out of the question." Her voice shook. Good heavens, was everything going to make her cry today?

"I do not mean to pry," said the other woman with obvious dismay. "I am too curious for my own good, and I cannot resist seeing romance everywhere. I promise not to tell anyone."

"It is not a secret as much as something I have not been allowing myself to consider. I miss him so very much, you see."

"Oh, I understand." Molly paused. "The other ladies here will tell you I only married my husband for his money, but that is not true. Truly, I would have been willing to marry a man for money, but I do love him. They cannot understand how I can love a man old enough to be my father, but no man has ever treated me with such tenderness and respect, and he was devoted enough to me to offer marriage instead of *carte blanche*. I am just a poor girl from the docks who was fortunate to find a position as an actress, but he treats me like a queen. How could I not love him?"

"That is true love! My Mr. Darcy is young and handsome, but like you, that is not what I love about him. I love him because he cares so much about everything, from his younger brother who tries hard to provoke him to a puppy met by chance. He even cares about the French – well, a few of them, at least."

"I am glad you understand." When Mrs. Hayes smiled, her face lit with extraordinary brilliance. She must have been a marvel on the stage.

"But your story sounds remarkable, almost like a novel. I do hope you will tell me more of it. I love stories. While I was in gaol, I kept my sanity by making up stories. Perhaps someday I will write them down." Elizabeth smoothed her skirts. Clean clothes at last! She sat down to peel off her stockings.

"This may be your opportunity. There is little to do here, so you would have plenty of time."

Until now, Elizabeth had not considered her future aboard the ship. It had been enough simply to be alive and out of gaol, but sooner or later she would want more. If she could find something satisfying to do, it would be easier to tolerate the monotony. Georgiana was no doubt distressed over her absence; perhaps she could write out a fantastical adventure in India for the two of them, or any of the stories she had distracted herself with over the years. She smiled. "Perhaps I shall."

"Oh! I did not see this before." Molly held out an envelope. "It was with your clothing."

The seal was broken, but the letter contained two sheets of paper written in Darcy's close handwriting. She caught her breath, half eager to read it and half afraid. Mme. Demarais had clearly believed Darcy was suffering from her loss, and the commutation of her sentence was clearly for his benefit. But she had wondered how much of his distress had been for her and how much for Georgiana. Now she might find out the answer.

"I see this is a special letter, so I shall leave you to read it. If you wish to find me afterwards, I will be in our stateroom."

"Thank you for everything. I appreciate the welcome more than I can say." But she could think only of her letter.

Elizabeth closed the cabin door behind Molly and opened the letter with trembling hands.

My dearest Elizabeth,

As you see, I am taking permission from your letter to address you with equal intimacy. There is no point in protesting that you only called me your dearest William when you assumed I would never have the opportunity to reply, since I intend to seize any advantage I can. I have been silent too long already.

I am told this letter will be opened and read prior to reaching you. Once I might have allowed that to limit me rather than to allow other eyes to see my tender words to you, but no longer. As far as I am concerned, the entire world is welcome to know my sentiments about you, so I will write as if yours are the only eyes that will read it.

I only received the news yesterday that your sentence has been changed. There are no words to express the relief it has given me. I hope you are being treated well aboard the ship. If there is any comfort you wish for, be it a particular book, a favorite food, or some article of clothing, it would be my very great privilege to send it to you. I have already chosen several books for you, and Georgiana is taking great care in selecting the clothing we will send to include your favourites since she longs to be able to help.

Georgiana misses you almost as much as I do. She returned home yesterday from an extended stay at Carlton House under General Desmarais's supervision. You are well aware of how easily confused she is, and will not be surprised that the change was a great shock to her, even though my aunt attended her throughout her stay. She misses Kit as well since he has gone to stay with friends for a time.

Puck also misses you. He has been my near-constant companion since your arrest, as I have spent almost all the time home, the circumstances making my disposition more unsociable than usual. But I am glad to have Puck since he reminds me of our first meeting. He is settling in here and even obeys my commands most of the time. Very well, he obeys them some of the time. I have discovered on our walks in Hyde Park that it is dangerous to allow him within scenting distance of a duck. Ducks are apparently irresistible to him, and when he sets off after one, his ability to listen disappears entirely. Fortunately for the ducks, he only wants to demonstrate his prowess, releasing them after he catches them, so the park has not been completely denuded of ducks.

You will notice I have said little of how I miss you. I do not have words for that either, and if I tried to express it, you would quickly come to the conclusion that I am in dire straits without you – and you would be correct. During the day I am able to appear in tolerable spirits, but I miss the music of your laughter, the rapier of your wit, and the joy and lightness you brought to this house with your presence. None of this is anything compared to what you have suffered, but be assured it is heartfelt. There is much more I would tell you, and will do so when I am permitted to visit you.

I remain, as ever, your adoring subject,
Theophilus Thistle

Elizabeth pressed the letter against her heart.

Puck had found something on the banks of the Thames – a rag caught on a stick, it appeared. As always, the river was full of debris and refuse, a foul odor rising from its waters.

None of it troubled Darcy. His eyes were fixed halfway across the river where the *Neptune* and the *Achille* rode at anchor, their rows of cannon pointed directly at London. Just one salvo from those guns would reduce much of the city to rubble. Through the sooty fog, Darcy could just see letters picked out in gold on the bow, but even when he squinted he could not make out details of individual figures on the deck. Damn this fog!

Even if he could not see her, Elizabeth was nearby, alive and well. It would have to be enough.

Puck trotted up to him, his stick proudly held in his mouth. Darcy ruffled his ears. The puppy lay down beside him and chewed energetically on the stick.

"Are your eyes good enough to see her?" Darcy asked the dog. "Perhaps next time I should bring opera glasses."

Puck responded with a whimper. Even the puppy could sense his mood.

"I could not agree more," said Darcy heavily.

"Welcome aboard, gentlemen," said the naval lieutenant with a heavy French accent. "The ladies are on the quarterdeck. Pray permit me to guide you to them."

"Thank you." Darcy wanted nothing more than to rush to Elizabeth's side, but he turned to the soberly dressed man behind him. "Perhaps you might remain here until I have spoken to the lady."

"Of course," said the magistrate.

Darcy followed the lieutenant across the spotless deck of the *Neptune*. Everything on the ship was clean and shining, from the masts to the railings. The crew must have a great deal of time for cleaning, since their only other duty was to be prepared to level London in a barrage of cannon fire. The cannons looked spotless, too.

Darcy scanned the quarterdeck as they approached it, his pulse quickening. Two ladies carrying parasols watched their approach, but even from a distance he could tell neither was Elizabeth. Finally, as he climbed the set of steps to the raised quarterdeck, he spotted her. She stood next to a red-haired lady, their backs to him as they gazed over the stern.

At the sound of his footsteps, she turned, her guarded expression blooming into one of heartfelt delight. She hurried towards him, her hands outstretched, but when the lieutenant cleared his throat, she skidded to a stop just a few feet from him. She held out her hands to the lieutenant instead, her palms facing up.

The lieutenant nodded. "Mr. Darcy, I will need to see your hands, too. It is protocol."

"We must show that our hands are empty," said Elizabeth. "They do not want me to slip anything to you, or vice versa."

The lieutenant added, "Apart from touching hands, you must keep a hand's breath apart, and no whispering."

Darcy frowned. "I was already searched on shore, so you need not worry."

The lieutenant shrugged. "So is everyone, yet the rules still apply."

Then Elizabeth took his hands, and Darcy lost all interest in the lieutenant and his ridiculous rules. All that mattered was the sparkle in her eyes and the smile curving her tempting lips. Joy rose inside him, a flame that only burned in her presence. The circumstances did not matter. He was with Elizabeth.

He had not even bowed to her. As he gazed into her bewitching eyes, he said the first thing that came to his mind. "Greetings, proud Titania."

Her lips twitched with amusement. "Theophilus Thistle, I welcome you to my new realm."

"Puck misses you. As do I."

She squeezed his hands. "He is still with you?"

"Yes. He reminds me of you. He stays in the house with me most of the time."

"And eats your food, if Mme. Desmarais is to be believed! And are you well, and your family?"

Darcy nodded. "We are all in good health. Georgiana wanted to come with me today, but I thought all the uniforms would upset her." And the last thing he wanted was Georgiana aboard a French warship.

"Pray tell her my thoughts are with her." Elizabeth loosened her grip on his hands. "Come, let us sit on that bench by the rail. I want to hear everything that has happened."

"Very well." But Darcy only released one of her hands. He did not care how improper it looked. Her touch was a lifeline to him. "Did they tell you I was coming today?"

"No, but I am so glad of it!" Her eyes searched his face. "You have lost weight. Mme. Demarais was correct."

"A little. But I am eating more, if for no other reason than that General Desmarais said I would not be allowed to visit you if I did not."

Elizabeth lowered her voice. "I assume he was responsible for the change in my sentence?"

"Yes. But I do not know what happened between your arrest and your release, and I pray you will tell me so I can stop imagining every possible horror that might have occurred." He held his breath. Terrible things happened in the London gaols.

Her eyes clouded over as if she were in pain. "I should have known you would fret. I assume Georgiana has told you about the arrest? After General Desmarais took her away, the rest of us were put in a cell in Newgate. They are every bit as disgusting as everyone says, but I was too busy caring for Andrew to mind." Her expression grew somber. "He had taken arsenic as soon as he saw we were to be arrested. He said he was a terrible coward when it came to pain, and he knew too many secrets. He was very brave, and seemed at peace with his choice, but he suffered greatly."

Darcy could do no more than press her hand. "I am sorry." And Kit carried arsenic, too.

Elizabeth took a deep breath. "General Desmarais came to interview me then, and I am afraid I said a great many unpleasant things to him, including that I had duped you."

"He told me. I knew why you must have said it."

"Later I was put in a cleaner cell by myself. They said it was at General Desmarais's orders. Having just confessed to treason five times over, I was grateful for that consideration. Then it was merely dullness for days until I went before the tribunal to be sentenced. I was waiting my turn at the gallows when Colonel Hulot took me away and brought me here." She shivered.

"Your treatment here – how is it?" He had to know everything she suffered.

"We are treated well. We can walk on the quarter deck when the weather permits. It allows me some exercise, even as the days become cooler. One of the other ladies has become a good friend – that one over there, the beautiful one with the red hair. She is the wife of—"

"No names," the lieutenant said sharply.

Elizabeth sighed. "In any case, I like her very much. And two of the other ladies were taken off the ship a few days ago, and that gave me hope that someday it might be my turn."

"Truly?" It was the best news he had heard in years.

"Truly, though I do not know why they were released. And thank you for sending me books; I have enjoyed reading them."

An ensign approached them and bowed. "The magistrate wishes to know if you will require his services."

Elizabeth looked quizzical. "You brought a magistrate?"

"I will need a few minutes first," Darcy told the ensign, suddenly anxious. He turned his body to face Elizabeth, cradling her hand between both of his. For a moment he studied their entwined hands, then looked up at her. Would she be unhappy about his presumption? "This may seem very abrupt, but I do not know when I will be permitted to visit you again. I would like to marry you. Now. Today."

Her lips parted and she searched his face. "Now? Would you not prefer a wife who is free to live with you?"

He touched her lips with one fingertip, a stolen pleasure. Pitching his voice low, he said, "If you are my wife, it makes you a more valuable hostage and encourages the French to keep you alive. At the moment, their belief that you are important to me rests solely on Desmarais's word, and if anyone thought I had lost interest in you... I do not even wish to think about it. And..."

"And?" she echoed.

He tightened his hold on her hand. If only he could take her in his arms! But he had to convince her with his words and nothing else, and pretty words had never come easily to him. "It makes no difference that I cannot live with you since I will never marry another woman while you live, or even after. From the first time I saw you enthroned in the bluebells, you have been the only woman for me. If I never saw you again, that would not change. By giving you my name, I can make you safer, but it will also give me happiness and peace to know you are my wife. My dearest Elizabeth, I beg you to grant me the privilege of being your husband."

Her eyes were suspiciously shiny, but she did not look unhappy. "I hardly know what to say. If you are certain this is what you want and that it is for the best, I do not wish to waste any of our precious time together discussing the advantages and disadvantages. I will take your word for it. I do not understand how you have arranged it, but my heart has been yours for months, and now you may have my hand." She raised their joined hands, smiling tremulously.

Joy spread in him until he could feel it even in his skin. "Thank you," he said softly, pressing his lips against the back of her hand. "It must be a civil ceremony, in keeping with French law, but I hope someday we can celebrate it in church in the English manner." He waved to the ensign to fetch the magistrate.

She tightened her grip on his hands. "French or English, it does not matter. The only thing that matters is that you wish to marry me."

There was some sort of commotion on the main deck, but Darcy did not care, not when he could stare into Elizabeth's fine eyes.

"*Mon Dieu*!" said the lieutenant, snapping to attention.

Elizabeth appeared equally oblivious. "Does your family know you planned this?"

"My aunt. She signed the papers on your behalf, now that Desmarais made her your legal guardian. I also told our friend, Mr. Gracechurch." He shaped the words 'your uncle' silently with his lips. "And Desmarais knows since I needed his permission to bring the magistrate. I thought it safest to say nothing to Georgiana, especially since I did not know if you would agree."

"And if you had told her, she would have wished to attend. I hope she has not taken my absence too badly."

"No worse than I have, my love." How freeing it was to say the words!

Elizabeth blinked rapidly. "I have missed you so. In my cell, I spent hours thinking of all the things I wished I had told you when I still had the chance. My pride seemed a foolish thing in hindsight." She straightened suddenly, staring beyond him. "Were you expecting company?"

Darcy followed her gaze and laughed. Nothing could upset him, not now, not even one of Desmarais's little tricks. For a group of three people stood there: Desmarais himself, his wife and an older man who looked somehow familiar. "Not at all. I did not realize we would be making a party of it," he said to Elizabeth.

Mme. Desmarais approached them, her husband standing a few paces back. "Miss Gardiner, I hope you will forgive this terrible presumption. I cannot imagine you have fond feelings towards my husband, but our sons did not live long enough to marry, and it would mean a great deal to us if you permitted him to be present today for Darcy's wedding. Of course, if you object, we will respect your decision. It is your wedding, after all."

Elizabeth shook her head. "You are welcome to join us." Her voice trembled.

"I thank you," said Desmarais. "I have taken the liberty of bringing the Lord Mayor, Sir Matthew Hayes, to perform the ceremony instead of the man you brought. Usually he delegates the duty to his magistrates, but I thought he might be willing to make an exception on this occasion."

Mme. Desmarais added, "And because you are an old romantic."

What did it matter who married them as long as they were married? But if Desmarais wished them to be married by Sir Matthew, Darcy had no objection. "Sir Matthew, I am honored."

Elizabeth's friend, the one whose name he was not permitted to know, took several hesitant steps forward, her gaze not on Desmarais, but on the Sir Matthew. Suddenly Darcy realized where he had seen her before: on Drury Lane. It had been a great scandal when the Lord Mayor had become besotted of a beautiful actress and married her despite her past. Then, after less than a year, he had started attending events without her. The gossipmongers whispered that she must have run off with a handsome footman. Apparently they had been wrong.

Sir Matthew, evidently experienced with the process, showed his empty hands to the lieutenant before approaching his wife.

Yes, Desmarais was definitely an old romantic. And Darcy wished they would all leave so he could be alone with Elizabeth.

Chapter Seventeen

Elizabeth rested her fingers on the paper she had just signed. Elizabeth Darcy. That was her name now.

Darcy – her husband! – slipped his arm around her waist. "How much time is there before I must leave?" he asked the lieutenant.

"Ten minutes. And there is to be hand holding only, none of that." The lieutenant gestured towards Darcy's arm.

Only ten minutes and then another fortnight before she could see him again? The thought made Elizabeth's throat ache.

"Come, they are newlyweds!" admonished General Desmarais. "It is a special occasion."

"The rules have no exceptions, sir," said the lieutenant stiffly.

Desmarais's eyebrows rose. "Indeed? And who made these rules?"

"Monsieur Lamarque, sir."

Darcy once more held her hand, but took full advantage of the lieutenant's distraction to brush his lips on the inside of her wrist.

A pleasurable tingling rushed up her arm. "I still cannot believe we are truly married," murmured Elizabeth.

"Indelibly, my dearest, loveliest Elizabeth. Till death do us part." He watched her intently.

"It is just a surprise. You have had time to accustom yourself to the idea of our marriage." Her tongue felt oddly thick as she said the words.

"You will have many years to grow accustomed to it." Darcy traced his finger along the lines of her palm. Apparently if all he was permitted to do was to hold her hand, he intended to make the most of it.

General Desmarais asked the lieutenant, "Who is in command of this vessel?"

The poor young man looked like he wished to sink through the deck. "Captain Rigaud, sir."

"And I believe Captain Rigaud and the *Neptune* have been seconded to my command. Is that not so?"

"Yes, sir. Exactly so."

Desmarais nodded. "Is Monsieur Lamarque in your chain of command?"

"No, sir," the lieutenant squeaked.

"Then why do you insist upon following his orders over mine?" Desmarais sounded as if this were no more than a discussion over the dinner table. "You may speak freely, Lieutenant."

The boy licked his lips. "Monsieur Lamarque, he is... frightening."

"Ah, now we come to it. Did he threaten you?"

The lieutenant stared at his feet and said nothing.

"Of course he did," said Desmarais genially. "Lamarque is constitutionally incapable of giving an order without making a threat. Nonetheless, he is aware he cannot touch any man under my command. Do you understand?"

"Yes, sir."

"Good. Then let us consider why we keep these ladies as our guests. It is because we wish their husbands to cooperate with us, yes? All these ridiculous rules of Lamarque's – no embraces, no kissing, no moments alone together – do you suppose these rules make their husbands more eager to be more cooperative with us?"

"N...No, sir."

"Correct. We wish to make them happy. They should be treated as honored guests. As long as it does not endanger the ship or interfere overly with its operations, there is no reason to deny their requests."

Elizabeth whispered to Darcy, "Does he always give orders in the form of lessons?"

"Whenever he can. He says men are better about obeying orders they understand, but I think he simply enjoys it."

"The poor boy is going to have nightmares tonight."

Darcy surreptitiously nibbled her ear. "If it allows me more time with you, it will be well worth it."

Desmarais continued, "Now that we have determined there is no reason our guests must be supervised at every minute, perhaps you and I may continue this discussion on deck." He strode from the stateroom trailed by the lieutenant.

Molly darted across the room and closed the door. Her eyes dancing with mischief, she announced, "I have an idea. I think we should all close our eyes and keep them closed."

Darcy's face almost split from the width of his smile. "Mrs. Hayes, that is a truly inspired idea, and I intend to put it into action straight away. And should I forget and open my eyes for a moment, I am certain I will be blind to everything but my lovely wife." He ostentatiously squeezed his eyes shut.

"Hear, hear," murmured the mayor appreciatively.

"I suppose I did promise to obey," said Elizabeth archly as she closed her eyes.

A warm hand tenderly cradled her cheek, tipping her face up. Her lips began to tingle even before she felt the pressure of his against them.

Darcy's masculine scent of spice and pine wafted over her, taking her back to the memory of his intoxicating kisses the day they had walked in the park. Once again his tongue teased her lips apart. A jolt of pure need made the world recede, everything but the sweet pressure and taste of him, leaving her longing for more.

Her hands crept around his neck as he began to explore her mouth, probing and tormenting her with increasing ardency until she could not hold back her own response. Each dancing thrust added to the ache building within her, and she strained her body against his as if that might somehow ease it.

Now his arm was around her, his hand exploring her back before settling tantalizingly at her neckline. The explosion of sensation as his fingertips caressed her exposed skin made her gasp.

With a low growl of satisfaction, Darcy drew her onto his lap. The new pressure of his strong thighs against hers made her shudder with need and longing.

Now his lips were tracing the lines of her jaw, nibbling at her earlobe, brushing her neck until settling on the tender spot between her collarbones. Oh, this was sheer torment! Exquisite, agonizing torment, and she hoped it would never stop. Her head fell back, giving him the freedom to nibble, to taste, to torture her with overpowering desire.

A crash of thunder dragged her back to reality. No, it was not thunder, just thunderous pounding at the door.

She scrambled off Darcy's lap and touched her hands to her hot cheeks. What must she look like?

Darcy, his eyes dark with desire, tucked a stray lock of her hair behind her ear. After a last quick kiss, he strolled to the door and opened it to reveal Desmarais. "Why, General," Darcy drawled. "You should have knocked more loudly. I could barely hear you."

Desmarais clapped Darcy on the shoulder. "I am certain you did not! Now, gentlemen, might I request a few moments of your time?"

"Of course." With a regretful glance back at Elizabeth, Darcy followed Demarais and Molly's husband.

"Well, that was an unexpected pleasure, if shorter than I would prefer." Molly plopped down beside her. The neck of her dress had somehow slipped completely off her shoulder, and one side of her hair had come down.

To think she had worried about her own appearance! Firmly shutting her mind to what Molly and her husband might have been doing, Elizabeth straightened her friend's dress. "Turn around and I will see if I can salvage something from your hair."

Molly obeyed. "What do you suppose the general is telling them? I hope they are not in trouble."

Elizabeth pulled the few remaining pins from Molly's hair. "I doubt it. General Desmarais seems to enjoy giving pleasant surprises. At least he does to Darcy, but it must be more general than that or he would not have troubled to bring your husband today. I cannot see that he benefitted from it otherwise."

"I certainly did," said Molly with a sigh. "I thought he would not be allowed to visit for another week. And now you are married, too! It is a shame you cannot consummate it, but at least you will have something if they continue to allow this much privacy."

"Yes." Her body still ached with desire, but she would not have given up those few minutes in his arms for anything.

She had just managed to make Molly's hair remotely presentable when the gentlemen returned. Their husbands. The sight of Darcy made the fires in her burn hotter.

Apparently it had not been bad news, for the mayor was beaming and Darcy – well, he was not precisely beaming. He looked more like a hungry tiger who had been promised a particularly tasty gazelle for dinner. Elizabeth smiled. Perhaps she should write Darcy as a tiger in one of her silly stories for Georgiana.

Molly's husband whispered something in her ear that made her give an unladylike whoop and throw her arms around his neck.

Elizabeth turned raised eyebrows on Darcy. "Has something happened?"

Looking suddenly shy, he cradled her hand in both of his. "Desmarais has ordered a change in the rules for visiting you. Now I can come here once a week instead of once a fortnight, and instead of being limited to an hour, I can..." He paused, his cheeks flushing. "I can stay until the next morning. If you are agreeable to it, of course. I know it was not what you expected when you agreed to marry me today, and there is no reason—"

Perhaps Molly had the right idea. Elizabeth cut off Darcy's stream of words in the most efficient way possible.

"Propriety is well enough for lovers who are free to spend every evening together, but I do not care to waste my few precious hours with my dear husband following foolish rules for propriety," Mrs. Hayes declared to the two gentlemen at dinnertime. "Instead I propose we dine in a Shakespearean tavern."

"A Shakespearean tavern?" asked Darcy blankly. It was odd enough sharing the stateroom with the other couple, but Desmarais had made clear they were not to retire until the watch changed at eight bells, since otherwise the sailors would be too interested in what was occurring behind closed doors. The other hostages had eaten already in what was mysteriously called the first dog watch. Ships seemed to have a language of their own. But how did a tavern come into it?

"Yes. Imagine, if you will, that Sir John Falstaff is sitting over there, a buxom barmaid on his knee, enduring a ribbing about his exaggerations from Prince Hal. In the other corner some knavish looking fellows are singing a drunken song. Now it will be totally fitting if I sit on my husband's knee and kiss his cheek." She suited her actions to her words. Her husband's arm snaked around her waist as he returned her kiss – on the mouth.

Darcy's lips quirked. "I can see the appeal, but I do not know if Elizabeth—"

"Lizzy thinks it is an excellent idea, as you will see if you turn around." Molly gestured to the door.

His jaw dropped. The neckline on Elizabeth's dress had not been that low before, had it? And her hair had definitely not been dressed in that alluring manner, with a long twist of chestnut hair loose over her shoulders, tempting him to run his fingers through it. And the arch turn of her lips sent a shock of desire straight to his groin.

"Very fetching, Mrs. Darcy." He allowed his voice to drop on the last words.

Her smile widened. "I hope you do not mind a tavern setting. It could have been worse. Molly might have insisted on the witches in Macbeth rather than tavern wenches."

"I am perfectly happy with this choice." Happy, shocked, astonished, charmed, and very, very desperate to touch her. How far would she allow this to go? He patted his knee invitingly.

To his utter delight, she perched on it and laid her arm around his neck. She might not be quite as relaxed as her friend appeared to be, but her eyes were alight with pleasure. It was completely inevitable that he would have to press his lips against her delectable neck.

"Well?" asked Molly.

"Very well indeed," said Darcy. "It seems you have many excellent ideas." Any idea that allowed him to touch Elizabeth qualified as brilliant in his mind.

Sir Matthew chuckled. "She does indeed."

"You astonish me, Sir Matthew," Darcy said. "I was under the impression you were a poker-faced prig and a high stickler." Somehow the insult seemed completely benign in this setting.

"Only in public," said Sir Matthew austerely. "And before I met a woman who taught me to take pleasure in life. But if you should ever mention any of this, I will deny every word of it. And I was under the impression you were a French sympathizer."

"Like you, only in public. It helps protect my many Loyalist relations. But then the French arrested the woman who taught me about happiness." He pressed his lips against Elizabeth's. Oh, the pleasure of it!

"He is both," said Elizabeth in an unwontedly serious voice. "A Loyalist at heart, but a sympathizer with everyone, French or English. Until I learned better, I thought him a traitor. Even once I knew his sympathies, I could not understand it until I was here on the *Neptune*. He has the ability to look at his enemy and see not a monster, but a human being like himself. I am trying to learn some of his philosophy."

Sir Matthew's eyebrows rose. "Indeed. And in honor of sympathizing with our enemies, I will propose a toast that surprises even me." He picked up his wine glass. "To General Desmarais, long may he rule – over the *Neptune*!"

For some reason it seemed outrageously amusing. After they all drank, Darcy added, "And to his views on how to keep us cooperative."

"Especially those," said Molly emphatically.

Darcy pulled Elizabeth even closer as he drank. It gave him a most enticing view, but more importantly it held her close to his heart.

Sir Matthew set down his wine glass. "Speaking of false impressions, Darcy, would you be offended if I offered some unsolicited advice about having a wife aboard the *Neptune*?"

"Not at all." Perhaps he might know ways to arrange for more communication.

"Assuming you have not yet done so, I would advise you to delay announcing your marriage. Keep it a secret for now."

Darcy stiffened. "Why is that?"

Sir Matthew grimaced. "Because otherwise every old biddy in society will call on you, solicitously asking when she can meet your lovely wife, and since we are forbidden from telling anyone where our wives are, you will have no answer. Then they will make up their own answers, and they will not be pretty. You will be the subject of gossip columns, and everyone will think the worst of your wife. Secrecy would protect her good name as well as your own."

Darcy looked at Elizabeth. At her slow nod, he said, "That is sound advice. I thank you."

Molly stretched languorously. "It has been quite unpleasant for my husband, but less of an issue for me since I had no reputation to be harmed if everyone believed I ran off with a footman. You should take care, Lizzy."

Elizabeth laughed. "If I ever am fortunate enough to leave this ship, I will tell the gossips I spent all my time acting out scenes from Shakespeare, writing wicked stories, and pretending to be a tavern wench."

Their dinner arrived then and Elizabeth moved to sit beside him. But it was still a delight to be able to stroke her cheek or kiss her whenever he chose. The wine flowed freely, adding to the warm haze.

How odd it was that he could be both anxiously anticipating his wedding night, yet feeling more relaxed and content than he could recall being for years. Elizabeth's presence accounted for much of it, of course, but there was something more. It was not Molly's tales of her days on the stage or even the occasional Shakespearean monologue she performed for their pleasure, nor was it Sir Matthew's obvious pride in his wife and the sly jabs he made about their French overlords. It was not even Elizabeth's easy laughter as she teased him about Kit's sulky resentment until he found himself telling tales of his clashes with Kit, redone as amusing tales of dealing with a wayward younger brother. He even poked fun at himself by relating how he had attempted to deal with Georgiana's first episode of nerves, frantically racing about trying one remedy after another until it finally occurred to him to simply talk to her. And the others had laughed, just like friends.

That was it. He was among friends and not playing a role. Sharing the experience of the hostage situation created a bond, and Molly's antics had stripped down the reserve customary to meetings with strangers. He could just be himself, his one secret set to the side, no false face, no requirement to maintain a positive connection as there was with Desmarais.

This is what he had hoped to experience at Netherfield with Bingley, but while Bingley accepted him easily, Darcy still had to play the role of French sympathizer, and he had been too caught up in worry about Georgiana to relax his guard.

Yet here he was with Elizabeth, the daughter of a poor country gentleman, Sir Matthew, a goldsmith who had been elevated to his current position, and Molly who had grown up on the docks and graced the stage. All people he would once have considered beneath him. True, the stigma of trade connections had been wiped out by the invasion when the French had upended English society with their *égalité* and *fraternité*, but he still could not have pictured this scene before tonight.

By God, it was good to be among friends!

But when he finally stood in the door of Elizabeth's tiny cabin, some of his usual reserve returned. Good Lord, the French lieutenant had not been jesting when he warned Darcy about the narrowness of the berth! But as Desmarais had pointed out, a sufficiently motivated man could make do with almost anything, and there was no question his motivation to make Elizabeth his at last was more than sufficient. But could he make it pleasurable for her under these circumstances?

There was barely room for both of them to stand. They would have to sidle past each other. If he stretched out his arms, most likely he could touch both walls. And when he closed the door behind him, it was also completely dark.

He cleared his throat. "Are you certain about this? I have taken you by surprise, and you have not had your mother to prepare you for tonight."

Elizabeth laughed. "You are very thoughtful, but you need not worry. While I may be quite inexperienced, the last fortnight in Molly's constant company has taught me a great deal, some of it quite shocking. A few things she told me might even shock you!"

Darcy's lips twitched. "I am shocked already." He touched her chin with his fingertip and traced a line to the sensitive notch at the base of it, allowing his finger to linger there briefly before continuing slowly down to the delightfully immodest neckline of her tavern wench dress.

"That she would tell me such things, or that I would listen?"

He hooked his fingertip under the fabric and heard her gasp. "Not on her part. A little, perhaps, on yours, but since I am likely to be the beneficiary of your new knowledge, I am certainly not complaining of it."

"Once I would have been shocked, but in gaol I had a great deal of time to reflect on experiences I would never have. Until today I thought the closest I could ever come to sharing your bed would be to learn what might have happened if I did." Her voice was grave.

Darcy abandoned his sensual efforts and gripped her arms. "How hard was it for you, in truth?" If only he could see her face!

Her hair brushed against him as she bent her head and did not speak for the space of several breaths. "Very bad," she said softly. But then she brought her hands to each side of his face. "But I will not allow it to ruin our wedding night. Tonight is just for us."

"For us," he echoed.

Her hands moved down to his neck. "You are too formally dressed. How do I untie this cravat?"

He chuckled. "Allow me to assist you, proud Titania."

As he undid the knot, her hands slipped inside his coat.

Chapter Eighteen

Since her enforced stay at Carlton House, Georgiana's old anxiety had returned whenever Darcy was absent. To reduce her worry, he returned to his old custom of reading the newspaper in the sitting room rather than in his study so she could be with him. Not that the newspaper contained much of what might be called news, but occasionally he could glean bits of information from the scraps the French saw fit to allow English newspapers to print. The absence of news from Spain likely indicated the war on the Spanish front was not going well.

"Kit!" Georgiana leapt to her feet and hurried forward.

Darcy set the paper aside before rising. Kit stood in the doorway, a serious expression on his face.

Just as Georgiana appeared ready to embrace Kit, Lady Matlock cleared her throat. The girl checked herself and held out her hands instead.

Kit took her hands in his, but he seemed reluctant to do so, and he released them quickly.

The light in Georgiana's eyes seemed to dim. "I am happy to see you are well," she said formally.

Lady Matlock said, "Christopher, it is past time you made an appearance. I have some important information to relate to you."

Not this again! Darcy shook his brother's hand. "Kit, I am glad, too, but I must absent myself from any political discussion. Pray do not consider it a slight. The ladies can explain to you why I do not wish to know of your activities."

Georgiana bit her lip. "They are holding Elizabeth hostage."

Kit turned to his brother, his expression finally showing something. "Oh, I say. She is alive? I am glad of it."

"As am I," Darcy said. "Now, if you will excuse me—"

Kit held up his hand. "Not yet. There is something you must know. The French are already aware of it."

It must be something grave to leave his laughing brother so pale and serious. "What is the matter?"

Kit opened his mouth, closed it again, dropped his chin and covered his eyes. "I cannot do this," he muttered, as if to himself.

Now truly worried, Darcy asked, "Are you in trouble? Do you need help?"

Kit shook his head and straightened, his face white and showing a determination Darcy had never seen in him before. He took a step towards Georgiana and dropped to one knee as if he were preparing to propose marriage to her. Surely he must know better than that, even if he did have feelings for her.

Instead of taking her hand, Kit bowed his head. His words were barely audible and half despairing. "Your Majesty."

Darcy stiffened. Georgiana, or rather Princess Charlotte, was Her Highness. Only the queen would be Her Majesty.

Lady Matlock's skirts rustled as she sank into a deep curtsy, the one only used in the presence of the monarch.

Oh.

Darcy ought to bow at the very least, but one glance at Georgiana's raised chin, ashen face and tear filled eyes told him she needed a brother more than another subject. He hurried to her side and put his arm around her.

She pressed her face against his shoulder. Poor girl. More than either of her unreliable parents, she had loved her grandfather the king, the one who had always adored her. Even after all these years, it must be a terrible loss to learn of his death. Damn Kit! Why could he not have broken the news more gently?

Looking down on his brother's bowed head, the reason was suddenly obvious. Kit had become too close to Georgiana. Now he had to establish a distance between them. It was one thing to flirt with a disguised princess who might never take her rightful place. Doing so with a queen regnant was another story.

The girl lifted her head, leaving a damp spot on Darcy's lapel. In a high voice that was almost steady, she said, "Do stop that, Kit, and Lady Matlock as well. Within these walls, nothing has changed."

Slowly and stiffly Kit got to his feet, his expression bleak. Darcy narrowed his eyes at his brother. If he said, "As Your Majesty wills," Darcy would make certain he regretted it.

Instead Darcy took the lead. "Nothing has changed. Until you say otherwise, you are Georgiana Darcy, I am your brother, and you are among your own trusted family."

Her shoulders relaxed. Glancing at Kit, she repeated fiercely, "Nothing has changed. Nothing." She took in a deep breath but retained a tight grip on Darcy's hand. "Nothing. Except that now I have a war to win."

Lady Matlock said briskly, "Very true. Perhaps we would be more comfortable if everyone took a seat."

But despite what Darcy had said, nothing could be the same again. Some reflexes could not be overridden, so no one moved until Georgiana seated herself.

Kit sank onto the nearest sofa. How could she say nothing had changed? She was queen now. His queen. There had always been a gulf between them, even if he had pretended otherwise for a time, but now that gulf was a gaping chasm. He could not forget that, no matter how much it hurt.

The uncomfortable silence persisted until Charlotte – he could no longer think of her as Georgiana, and he needed to learn to think of her as Her Majesty – jumped to her feet and marched over to him. He attempted to stand, but small hands pushed down on his shoulders. What was he to do? Propriety demanded he rise; obedience insisted he sit. Charlotte's determined expression settled the matter. He sat.

Leaning towards him, she whispered in his ear, "If you do not stop all this nonsense this very moment, Kit Darcy, I will kiss you in front of all of them, and if you do not kiss me back, I will have you strung up for high treason. Do you understand?"

The icicle stabbing into his chest seemed to melt. She had not changed. With something that was almost a smile, he met her eyes for the first time, then slid to one side of the sofa and patted the space beside him. She sat down with a little huff.

"Better?" he asked quietly.

"Much."

Lady Matlock's cool gaze suggested she had not missed their byplay, nor was she pleased with it.

"Kit, I wonder how you came to be aware of this news. Do you know any details?"

Pleasing his aunt was the least of Kit's worries. "We intercepted a messenger from France. His Majesty apparently fell over the railing of his balcony. He died instantly and did not suffer." He glanced at the girl beside him. "That was three days ago. We do not know why the French are keeping the matter secret or how long they plan to do so, but that seems to be their intention."

Lady Matlock nodded. "I would do the same in their position. They know England is ripe for an uprising. With everyone believing that Princess Charlotte has returned, they would be asking for trouble if they attempted to crown Jérôme Bonaparte now. As long as everyone believes

King George is alive, they can keep the peace until they are in a better position to defend themselves."

"That is what Frederica thinks," Kit said. "She hopes we can be ready to take advantage of the moment when the news finally breaks, but it is a question of how quickly we can prepare."

"Did not Frederica say it was too soon for an uprising?" asked Lady Matlock sharply.

"She indeed felt that way," Kit said carefully. "But certain things have recently changed. I apologize that I am unable to discuss the specifics."

Darcy's brows drew together. "Is Richard still with you?"

Kit met his brother's eyes. "Yes. In fact he is, er, responsible for locating those specifics I cannot explain. But Frederica has a request for you, William. When the moment comes, we will need to be certain Desmerais cannot reach his troops. Would you be able to locate him and keep him somewhere safe, either in Carlton House or elsewhere?"

Darcy's expression turned grim. "No. I want nothing to do with this."

"The success of the uprising may depend on it," Kit urged. "Many lives may also depend on keeping Desmerais away. I am not asking you to kill him."

"You are correct that lives would depend on it, including a life I value highly. You will have to find someone else." William's words held a sharp edge, one that had denoted danger in the past.

Kit forced himself to plow ahead. "No one else has your freedom of access to Desmerais." Surely William would see reason.

A voice beside him spoke, still a little high-pitched. "Do not press him. William, I think it would be best if you left us."

William inclined his head. "I thank you." He picked up the newspaper he had been reading when Kit arrived. At the door, he looked back over his shoulder. "By the way, Kit, Desmerais spoke to me about you."

This was not good news. "My apologies. I have tried to keep the family name out of my work."

"It does not matter. Desmarais knows you are helping fugitives escape to Scotland, and he overlooks it for my sake. He said you keep a mistress who rarely leaves the house, and his only interest in you is that he believes you take your orders from the mysterious Frederick."

The French had known what he was doing all the time? And where he and Frederica had lived? Good God! Kit's hands clenched into fists, but he could not let his anger show. Better to cover it with amusement. "I cannot wait to tell Freddie she is my mistress," he drawled. "It is a good thing that we have abandoned the house on Leadenhall Street. Your dear friend would likely be less amused by my current activities."

"I only mention it because I thought you would wish to know what information he had. I do wish you well, Kit, even if I cannot help you with Demarais." Darcy leveled a serious look at him and left the room.

Kit blew out a long breath. Dammit! Everything depended on that one small piece of the plan. "Frederica will be livid," he said, more to himself than anyone else.

"Did you know that Georgiana and I spent the better part of a fortnight at Carlton House?" asked Lady Matlock, seemingly idly. "I took note of a great many things, including the number of guards, where they were stationed and when they were changed, when the servants were present, and when the general and his wife liked to be alone together. Perhaps more importantly, I befriended Mme. Desmarais, who has been lonely here in England. It would be quite unremarkable if I were to call on her."

Could it work? His aunt could be more subtle than any of them when she chose. But after a moment Kit shook his head. "Those schedules would be very useful, but Frederica would never permit us to put you in danger's way."

His aunt raised a delicate eyebrow. "Must you tell her I would be taking Darcy's place?"

"She would flay me if she discovered it!"

"Then it is fortunate you are not easily cowed, is it not?"

Did she not know her own daughter?

Beside him, Georgiana – no, Charlotte - said, "It is my will that Lady Matlock should take on William's role, and that Frederica should not be informed of the change. You may tell her so, should the question arise."

Kit sighed in defeat. He could pretend nothing had changed, but everything had changed.

Even though the day was chilly and the wind brisk, Elizabeth suggested spending part of Darcy's visit on the quarterdeck. On such a day, the least private part of the ship allowed for the most private conversation since it was difficult to for anyone to overhear them when the wind was snatching away their words.

"Does Georgiana enjoy my letters?" Elizabeth asked. "Or does she think my little stories foolish? Since she cannot write back, I have no sense of it."

"She adores your letters, especially the stories. I hope it is not tedious for you to write such long letters."

She rubbed her hands together for warmth. "Not at all. I enjoy writing the little tales of India, and since you sent me that book of travels in India, they are even slightly accurate. I do not know what I would say to her otherwise. How often can I write that I walked the quarterdeck and spoke to the same three ladies as I did yesterday and every day?"

"I depend on your letters and wish to hear it all, even if every day is the same. But Georgiana does need distraction."

"Is something the matter?"

Darcy grimaced. "Since your arrest, her anger and bitterness at the French are worse. She misses you badly and blames them. I worry about allowing her to speak to anyone but my aunt for fear of what she might say. And then there are other matters weighing on her."

"Kit's absence?"

"Only in part." He leaned close and spoke directly in her ear. "Do you recall hearing about the old man she is so fond of, the one who planned to leave his estate to her?"

An old man. What old man did Georgiana know? And the only thing she was to inherit was England. "Oh! The one who has periods of madness?"

"The very one. Apparently he died recently, but his family has kept it a secret to protect the inheritance. Kit heard about it somehow and came to tell her."

Good God! The king was dead, and no one knew of it? That meant Georgiana was now the queen. A shiver went down Elizabeth's back. "That must be difficult for her."

"Very much so. She feels the loss of him, and her new responsibilities are weighing on her."

"And on you, I suspect."

He sighed heavily. "Yes. In most ways nothing has changed, but it feels different. And she is more impatient now. She wants something to happen and is frustrated knowing that it may be years before it does."

"Poor girl. And you still have not told her we are married?"

Darcy shook his head. "She might say something where servants can hear."

Elizabeth gazed out over the Thames. "It is strange for me to think that no one there knows about our marriage, since of course everyone in my own little world on this ship is aware of it."

"I wish everyone knew. Sometimes it hardly seems real to me. I go about my days as a single gentleman, and I feel as if I dreamed it. It is a relief to come here and not have to pretend."

"What of General Desmarais? You need not pretend with him."

Darcy shrugged. "I am attending dinners at Carlton House again, but except for Colonel Hulot, who brought you here, none of the other guests know. Desmarais is...well, it is difficult."

"How so?"

Darcy's voice was low. "He wants everything to be the way it was between us, and I cannot do it. I know perfectly well he did everything in his power to save you and Georgiana and paid a price for it. He would have done more if he could. Yet I still feel as if I cannot forgive him, even though he has done nothing wrong."

Elizabeth rubbed his hand. "You can no longer pretend you are not on opposite sides of the war."

"Yes, that is it exactly. Desmarais knows it, too. One night when someone referred to me as a supporter of the French, Desmarais laughed and said I was not a supporter at all, but a Loyalist who had the good sense to recognize when his side was defeated." Darcy fell silent.

"I hope it will become easier with time. It is hard knowing I owe my life to him, yet being a prisoner."

Darcy spoke in her ear once again. "It may be that nothing will come of it, but he has written to Napoleon and asked him to recall Lamarque. He even sent his wife to Paris to plead his case."

Shocked, Elizabeth asked, "Because of me?"

Darcy shook his head. "No. Lamarque has frightened the people of London with his spies, senseless arrests, and hangings, and as a result, many people who had grudgingly accepted French rule are now muttering about revolt. Desmarais is worried Lamarque's behavior may set off a rebellion."

"Is it true?"

"Who can say? It is true there is more unrest now than there was a year ago before Lamarque arrived. I am hardly an impartial judge, though, since he is the one holding you here."

Elizabeth bent her head. "No," she said quietly. "But that is the least of his crimes. At least I am alive and can be with you on occasion."

Molly descended on Elizabeth as soon as she emerged onto the quarterdeck. "Why have you been hiding in your cabin all morning? Usually you are outside long before I am. I hope this means you have been writing." She struck a dramatic pose. "I am dying to know what happens next to Princess Rosalinda."

Elizabeth held up her hands. "I fear I have failed you. Last night's dinner does not seem to have agreed with me, so I have been keeping to my bunk."

Molly eyed her dubiously. "It seems as if many dinners here have disagreed with you of late." She laughed. "Or should I perhaps blame your virile husband for your suddenly sensitive palate?"

Elizabeth opened her mouth to respond, then closed it again. Surely Molly must be mistaken. It had been but a month since her wedding, and with Darcy's visits limited to once a week, it was highly unlikely. "I think it is the cook's fault," she said firmly.

Molly pointed a finger at her. "Then you have no excuse not to write the next chapter. You cannot leave poor Princess Rosalinda in the hayloft forever, not with her evil uncle in pursuit."

It was fortunate that Molly could not guess that Princess Rosalinda's adventures had not sprang purely from Elizabeth's imagination. "Very well, I shall do my best to get poor Rosalinda out of the hayloft today."

Molly dropped her voice. "The superior ladies are listening. They may call your story foolishness, but they cannot wait for the next chapter either." She gestured with her head towards the two other hostages.

Elizabeth laughed. "Only because they are so very bored since their fancy friends were released." Both she and Molly had attempted to tease one of the sailors into confiding why two of the hostages had been released, but the Frenchmen were either ignorant of the reasons or unusually closemouthed. Not that it would make a difference in her own case since, unlike the others, she had committed a crime, but it might mean hope for Molly.

And Elizabeth wanted Molly to leave, even though she would miss her new friend desperately. Staying on the *Neptune* was as much of a death sentence as being arrested for treason had been. It just would not happen as soon. It might take years, but sooner or later the Loyalists would rise up against the French and, as Frederica had said, their very first step would have to be destroying the two warships in the Thames. Elizabeth had never told Molly about their fate. After all, what good would it do for her to know there was a sword at their throat?

Molly crossed her arms. "I suppose I cannot object to sharing Princess Rosalinda with them – as long as I get to read it first."

Secretly flattered by her friend's insistence, Elizabeth said, "I promise you will always get it first."

Elizabeth seated herself gingerly in a gilded chair. After three months aboard the *Neptune*, the ground on land seemed to be moving under her, and after months of seeing nothing but the simple lines of the ship where everything was wood, rope, or water, the colorful ornamentation of Carlton House hurt her eyes.

From behind his desk General Desmarais waved away the guards who had escorted her from the ship. "I hope you do not object to my wife joining us since you promised this was not a political matter."

"Not at all." In fact, she was grateful for the other woman's presence.

"Good. I value her opinion in personal matters."

Mme. Desmarais smiled at her. "What my husband means is that he cannot bear a woman's tears, and I am here to defend him if you should happen to start to cry."

"I must apologize in advance, then. I will do my best, but of late, almost everything makes me cry. It means nothing; yesterday I cried over a bird in flight." Elizabeth strove for a light tone.

Mme. Desmarais's eyes widened. "Oh, dear. Oh, dear."

The general's brows drew together as he studied his wife. "What is the matter?"

"Nothing, nothing. Let us see what Mrs. Darcy has to say."

"Very well." He did not appear satisfied by her answer. "How may I be of assistance to you, Mrs. Darcy?"

Elizabeth swallowed hard. "Thank you for agreeing to see me. I do not know if you can help me or not. I have a problem, and I wished to ask you about it before I speak to Mr. Darcy."

Desmarais's eyebrows crept up. "Darcy does not know about this problem? Am I expected to keep it in confidence?"

She dropped her eyes. "I am not in a position to dictate terms."

"Even more curious. May I ask what this problem is?"

"It appears I am increasing," said Elizabeth bluntly, the ever present tears starting to well in her eyes. Somehow she managed to blink them back.

The general smiled. "You are *enceinte*? That is not a problem, but a cause for celebration."

"For my husband, perhaps, who will be glad to have a son or daughter," said Elizabeth. "Less so for me, since presumably my baby will be taken from me."

"Oh, dear," murmured Mme. Desmarais.

Desmarais picked up his quill and absently tapped it on the edge of the desk, once, twice, thrice. "That is indeed a problem."

Elizabeth plunged ahead. "I know there is little to be done about it. My concern is for Mr. Darcy. When I tell him, he will be unhappy about the situation and will want to find a way to change things. I imagine he will fret about it and eventually he will turn up on your doorstep in the hope you could help him. I wish to spare him those distressing days and

315

the disappointment by telling him right away precisely what we can and cannot expect. That is what I hope you will be able tell me."

"What information are you seeking?" *Tap, tap, tap.*

"Will the baby be taken from me as soon as he is born, or will he be permitted to remain with me for a short period of time? He will have to live with his father, I know, but will he be permitted to visit me?" She managed to speak with no more than a tremor in her voice.

Mme. Desmarais silently pressed a cup of tea into her hands.

That small kindness was more than Elizabeth could bear. Turning her face away, she covered her eyes with one hand. "I am sorry," she choked out. "I will not take any more of your time. Perhaps you could send me your response."

General Desmarais said slowly, "You do understand, I hope, that you are not my prisoner, but Lamarque's. As such I have only a limited amount of say over your situation."

Intent only on escape, she bobbed her head and stood up. Suddenly burning pain engulfed her hand. Good Lord, she had scalded herself with the tea! Quickly she set down the teacup and blew on her hand to cool it, but the pain intensified.

Mme. Desmarais took her hand and examined it with a tutting sound. "*Mon cher*, pray be so kind as to send for some cool water. You may leave this to me. I will take care of her."

The sound of receding footsteps indicated the general's departure.

"Your poor hand!" said Madame. "I am so sorry. I should not have poured the tea when it was still so hot. Do sit down, my dear, and you may cry as much as you like now. I did the same thing when I was *enceinte*. Everything made me cry."

"You are very kind," said Elizabeth woodenly. "It was entirely my fault for being so clumsy."

"Nonsense. Oh, here is the water. Put your hand in this bowl and it will feel better."

"I should return to the ship." Even though the water did ease the pain.

"If you wish." Mme. Desmarais sounded sad. "I think you would be more comfortable if you allowed me to put a tincture and bandages on it, but it is up to you. I only wish, for Darcy's sake, that you did not hate us quite so much."

Startled, Elizabeth looked up. "I do not hate you, only what you represent. I want my country to be free."

"Will hating us make that more likely? No, do not bother to answer. We are none of us free. Your king and your Parliament worked for their own best interest, not yours, and it is the same in every country. Your king is more German than English; is a French emperor so much worse?"

Elizabeth stared down at the reddened skin of her hand. "A French emperor who sends our young men off to die in foreign lands for the greater glory of France? Who taxes us down to our last penny to pay for his army of occupation?"

"Those things are unfair, I agree, but it is all a matter of degrees. Did not your Parliament send off young men to die? When we first came here, the poorhouses were full of people on the brink of starvation, all so the taxes could pay for ridiculous buildings like this one. It is very beautiful, but me, I look at the gilt and the painted ceilings and wonder how many Englishmen suffered and died so your Prince Regent could feast his eyes on it. In France we have at least tried to stop these abuses, but that also made England our enemy." She handed a small cloth to Elizabeth. "Here; you may dry your hand, and I will let you return to the ship unmolested by my lectures."

Elizabeth lifted her hand from the water, but did not take the towel. "Mr. Darcy has said many of the same things," she said in a low voice. "And you are right that our government was far from perfect. I should not judge people simply by the country they were born in, and you and your husband have been very generous to me."

Mme. Desmarais said more briskly, as if she regretted her earlier outburst, "We strive to do our best in a very imperfect world. My husband will do what he can for you."

"I know it cannot be much." Elizabeth hesitated before meeting Mme. Desmarais's gaze. "If you are still willing to bandage my burn, I would appreciate it." Would the Frenchwoman accept her peace offering?

"I am glad. Those miasmas on the river cannot be healthy for injuries." Mme. Desmarais gestured to a servant. "Bandages and oil of lavender, if you please."

When the servant left, the Frenchwoman said, "I would like to ask you something, just between the two of us, woman to woman. I cannot promise anything, but if my husband should happen to find somewhere you could be held with your child, would you be willing to give your parole not to attempt to escape?"

If her hand had not hurt so much, Elizabeth might have laughed. "Madame, just between us, woman to woman, I know how to swim. I am rather good at it. I could have slipped over the side of the *Neptune* any moonless night and swum to shore, but I know if I did, Mr. Darcy would suffer for it. Yes, I would give my parole."

"Good. Do not get your hopes up, but I will see if anything can be done. I do not like this idea of separating a mother and child."

Tears once again welled in Elizabeth's eyes. "Thank you. Thank you very much."

The young naval lieutenant came to the ship's sitting room with a message. "Mrs. Darcy, you are wanted on deck."

"I am?" What was the meaning of this unusual request? "Who wants me there?"

"A soldier." He shrugged, as if to indicate the unimportance of any member of the army rather than the navy.

Elizabeth put aside the latest sheet of *The Tales of Princess Rosalinda.* "Very well."

"I will come, too," said Molly. Suspicion flashed in her eyes.

"As you wish."

Elizabeth followed the lieutenant up to the quarterdeck. The morning fog had finally blown off, though it remained chilly.

A blue-coated officer bowed to her and held out a letter. "From General Desmarais."

Her heart started to beat faster. Was the news good or bad? The envelope was sealed, though letters were regularly opened and read before being delivered. Special rules must apply to the general. She broke the seal with her finger to find a letter written in a neat, feminine hand that must have belonged to Madame Desmarais.

> *My dear Mrs. Darcy,*
>
> *My husband informs me he has made alternate arrangements which may suit you better after your child is born. You would be in his custody and would have your own suite of rooms at Carlton House. You would have the freedom of the gardens and of Carlton House itself, except on those occasions when formal events are taking place. I am sorry to say, on the insistence of M. Lamarque, these same limitations would apply to your child. Your husband would, as always, have the freedom to come and go as he pleases in Carlton House, but could not take up residence. Should he at some point wish to remove your child from Carlton House, you would be required to return to the ship and to—*

A deafening blast knocked Elizabeth off her feet. Fire rained down around her.

Chapter Nineteen

Darcy handed his hat and gloves to his butler. "Is Miss Georgiana in the drawing room?" He had purposely kept his visit to his solicitor short to reduce her anxiety.

"No, sir. Your aunt has taken her out."

Odd. They had planned to be at home all day when he left. "Where did they go?"

"They asked for the carriage to take them to Carlton House, sir."

And yet more odd. While they had called on Madame Desmarais once before, they had waited for an invitation. One did not simply drop in to Carlton House. "I see."

"Mr. Christopher was here for a short time, but he had to leave."

Kit had been there? His brother had only returned to Darcy House twice, each time on a mission. What had he wanted today?

A foreboding seized him. "Was he here before the ladies left?"

"Yes, sir. They did not decide to go until just after his visit."

Kit had come, then Lady Matlock had decided to call at Carlton House. Could she possibly be taking his place in Frederica's plan to distract Desmarais?

No. She might do it, but she would not take Georgiana with her. That would be far too dangerous. Unless she had some purpose of her own as she so often did.

Darcy snatched back his hat and gloves. "I am going out again."

Most likely Lady Matlock had gone to attempt to obtain some sort of information for Kit and nothing would happen to Georgiana, but he could not be sure. And there had been some odd groupings of men on the streets as he rode home. If there was any possibility that this was the long-awaited uprising, he had to get Georgiana out of Carlton House before she ended up with her head in a noose.

"Darcy, what a lovely surprise," said Mme. Desmarais. "Your aunt had not mentioned you would be joining us."

Darcy shot a poisonous glance at Lady Matlock, who looked as imperturbable as ever. "She did not know it. When I discovered she and Georgiana had gone to pay a call here, I decided to join them."

And just in time, after what he had seen in the streets, now that he was paying attention. Men loitering and refusing to meet his gaze, lowered voices, and almost no children on the streets. Carlton House had less than half the usual number of guards, and there were few servants in the halls. It was going to happen. And the worst part was that he could not see a safe way to extract Georgiana from the situation. If the streets were on the verge of erupting, she would be safer here than on the streets. What in God's name had his aunt been thinking to bring her along?

Georgiana wore her half-wit face, but her eyes darted from side to side. No, this was not a social call.

Mme. Desmarais said, "Would you care for a slice of almond tart, Darcy? It is the one you are so fond of."

"That would be pleasant." Darcy doubted he could eat a bite, but it would look odd if he refused it, especially as Mme. Desmarais still worried about whether he ate enough. "No one can match your cook's tarts."

"More for you, *mon cher*?" the Frenchwoman asked her husband, who shook his head brusquely. "Pay no attention to him, Darcy. He is fretting because of some nonsense about a fire at the barracks."

That explained the paucity of soldiers guarding Carlton House. "I hope it will be easily extinguished."

"Mme. Desmarais, before Darcy arrived you were telling us about the new fashions from Paris," said Lady Matlock. "Are they truly wearing laced bodices now? How very medieval."

"The laces are more decorative than anything. They only gather some of the fabric in the front to create an illusion of depth. The gentlemen like it, of course, since it does tighten the bodice."

Lady Matlock said, "I would not wish to see Georgiana wearing such a thing."

"Of course not! She is much too young for that sort of fashion."

Darcy forced himself to take a bite of almond tart, every muscle in his body tense. What was Lady Matlock planning?

Lady Matlock kept the conversation going as a church bell began to toll in the distance, joined a few minutes later by another, then another. Was that the signal? He prayed Elizabeth was safely below decks away from any fighting. The Loyalists might already be boarding the ships to prevent the cannons from being shot.

Now the church bells were coming from all directions. Somewhere outside a man shouted. Darcy could not make out the words, since the room faced the garden. Desmarais frowned and signaled the footman standing by the door, who bowed smartly and departed.

"Is something the matter?" asked Mme. Desmarais.

Her husband replied, "Unlikely, my dear. A rabble-rouser, no doubt."

Lady Matlock said placidly, "It is not unusual for more than one church to ring the bells if someone well-respected had left this world. I hope it is no one I know."

"I hope so!" cried Mme. Desmarais.

Now the shouting was closer, and a man's voice bellowed, "The King is dead! Long live Queen Charlotte!" A volley of gunfire followed.

Mme. Desmarais froze halfway through lifting her tea cup.

Desmarais jumped to his feet. "Pray pardon me. I must leave you."

"I think not." Lady Matlock, who had chosen the seat nearest the door, now stood between him and the only exit from the room. She produced a small pistol from her bodice and cocked it. "I apologize for this extreme discourtesy, but I must request that you sit down, General. Please keep your hands in plain sight. You as well, Darcy. I do not want to have to shoot you, either."

Darcy stared at her in astonishment, but placed his hands on his knees.

An expression of incredulity passed over General Desmarais's face. Then he smiled and took a small step forward. "Surely, Madame, there is no need for violence."

"Stop right there!" Lady Matlock commanded. "I assure you, sir, that I know how to use this and I will do so if I must. And while I myself am accounted no more than a reasonable shot, the young lady behind you never misses."

Desmarais look back over his shoulder to where Georgiana stood, her shoulders back, pistol in hand. Carefully he held his hands out, palms facing Lady Matlock, and retreated to sit beside his wife. "I applaud your courage, Madame, but you have no hope of succeeding. My soldiers know what to do in case of an uprising, even if I am unavailable."

A thunderous boom sounded to the east. Lady Matlock said in a conversational tone, "Do you suppose that was the Deptford Armory? We will know soon enough, I imagine. It is, of course, possible we may lose, but I have been given one simple task: to make certain you remain in this room. I do not intend to fail. Georgiana, my dear, if you would be so kind as to lock the door?"

Georgiana sidled towards the door, keeping her pistol trained on Desmarais, only lowering it long enough to turn the key in the lock. Another explosion followed, then an even louder one, and a series of shots and more shouting.

Desmarais looked sadly at Darcy and gave a deep sigh. "*Et tu,* Darcy?"

Before Darcy could speak, his aunt said, "In fact, no. He was asked to lure you to a secluded spot, and he refused. He did not know I volunteered to take his place. But I would not look to him for assistance if I were you. He has some loyalty to you, but he will not betray his family."

General Desmarais's upper lip curled. "How kind of him to keep his own hands clean, but he still came here today to take part in this little ambush. I had thought better of you, Darcy."

Since Darcy had to keep his hands in plain sight, he could not clench them into fists. Instead he dug his fingernails into his thighs. It was true; he had done nothing to stop this. His loyalty was to England.

"Yes, Darcy, how *did* you know what we planned?" asked his aunt.

"You made no effort to cover your tracks. The servants told me Kit had come to speak to you, then you ordered the carriage to take you to Carlton House. It was obvious what you planned. I came after you in the hope of stopping you before you put Georgiana's neck in a noose. What in God's name were you thinking to allow her to help you?" Darcy demanded. "If this uprising fails, she will die!"

"I am well aware of that," Lady Matlock snapped.

"Then why did you bring her?"

"She insisted. Do not move, General; I am quite able to keep my pistol trained on you while I quarrel with my nephew."

Darcy could not believe his ears. "Because she insisted? You could have locked her in her room!"

Lady Matlock's eyes darted towards Georgiana. "She was very insistent. Commanding, one might even say."

Georgiana said, "I have my reasons for wishing to be here, William."

"Reasons or no, I would have locked you in!"

"Your concern for your sister is touching," drawled General Desmarais. "I am glad to know my safety was of no concern to you. It will save me from regret over losing your so-called friendship."

Darcy glared at him. "You told me to cooperate with you. I did. I never agreed to stop someone else's uprising for your sake."

Lady Matlock shook her head sadly. "Darcy, do calm yourself. General, it is only out of courtesy to Darcy that you have been taken alive instead of shot on the street – at substantial risk to both Georgiana and me, I might add. I took that risk because you had been kind to Georgiana. Holding you at gunpoint may seem a poor repayment of the hospitality you showed us, but I assure you, you would have liked the alternative less." She pursed her lips. "But I do apologize for behaving in such an ill-bred manner when I have received nothing but courtesy from you. You have made it difficult to maintain my illusion that all Frenchmen are villains."

"It is kind of you to say so." Mme. Desmarais's voice was a trifle unsteady as she observed Georgiana through narrowed eyes. "Not a halfwit, then, Miss Darcy?"

The girl raised her chin. "Not a halfwit, and not Mi—"

"Georgiana!" Lady Matlock's voice cracked like pistol shot. "This is not the time. You agreed to follow my lead."

The girl subsided but looked mutinous.

"Your ladyship, how long do you intend to hold us prisoner?" Desmarais spoke in a light, social tone.

"Until I receive other instructions, or, failing that, until your soldiers arrive to take me to prison. I hope it will not be too long. I am not as young as I once was."

Desmarais leaned back, apparently relaxed. Then he bellowed in a voice fit to carry over a battlefield, "*Aidez-moi!*"

Lady Matlock could move surprisingly quickly for a woman with grown children. In an instant she was behind Desmarais's chair, her pistol pressed to his temple. "Georgiana, watch the door."

Nothing happened. Outside, cries of "*Vive l'empereur!*" and "*Vive la France!*" began to be outnumbered by shouts of "Queen Charlotte!" and "For England!"

A knock at the door made Georgiana jump. Lady Matlock called, "*Qui est là?*"

"Richard. Let me in."

Lady Matlock hesitated. "What day were you born?"

"December 17, during a snowstorm," growled Richard.

Lady Matlock nodded to Georgiana. "Let him in. He would have lied if he were being held prisoner."

Georgiana worked the lock until the door opened. Behind it stood Richard wearing the Carlton House footman's livery.

Richard stared at the girl, clearly taken aback by her presence. He managed a stiff bow to her.

Lady Matlock said frostily, "You took your time in arriving. My arm is quite fatigued." She switched her pistol to her left hand and shook out the right.

Richard reached across and took the pistol from her. "If all goes well, Kit will be here to take my place soon. He is my second in command, but I did not trust him to infiltrate this place. Kit would still have qualms about knifing an innocent servant, so I put him in charge of the street fighting instead. Madam, I must say your schedules were worth their weight in gold."

Desmarais glanced at Darcy. "Another relative? Now I am paying for my leniency to your family," he said bitterly. "The Emperor warned me I was too trusting. I should have listened to him."

Richard turned on Desmarais with unconcealed fury. "What leniency? If there were not ladies present, I would tell you precisely how viciously your soldiers treated me when I was their hostage. If it were solely my decision, you would be dragged through the streets behind a cart until you were dead, and I would still consider it an inadequate punishment."

"Richard!" admonished Lady Matlock. "There is no call for rudeness."

Caught between Desmarais's accusations and Richard's hostility, Darcy said, "Richard, General Desmarais was not in command then. General, this is my cousin, Colonel Richard Fitzwilliam."

"Lieutenant General Fitzwilliam, actually," said Richard. "Wellington has been handing out field commissions rather liberally."

"Wellington?" said Desmarais coldly. "I suppose that explains a few things."

"Wellington on land and Nelson at sea," said Richard with relish.

In the distance, a familiar voice shouted, "Where are they?" It was Kit.

"In here!" called Georgiana.

Kit skidded to a stop outside the door and strode in, holding a pistol and wearing a shockingly red frock coat. A smile grew on his face. "Oh, well done!" Then he spotted Georgiana standing beside the door. "Good God, what are you doing here?"

"Never mind that," said Richard. "Report."

"London is ours," said Kit. "We hold the city and the bridges. The armories in Deptford and Greenwich have been destroyed, and the remaining French troops have taken refuge in Westminster Abbey. The crowd there is restless, and I cannot say what will happen."

Richard nodded. "Good. I will take over for you, then. You know what to do here. Are your men outside?"

"Yes," said Kit. "Waiting for you."

With a nod, Richard strode out, his limp barely showing.

Kit turned to Desmarais. "General Desmarais, Lord Wellington will be here within the hour to accept your surrender. Do you wish to give me your parole, or must I have you bound?"

Desmarais laughed harshly. "You will have to forgive me if I do not take your word about the situation." He held out his hands, wrists together.

Kit signaled to someone outside, and a man entered with a length of rope. Kit said, "Bind the general's hands."

"No," Georgiana said firmly, her head held high. "He is not to be bound."

Kit hesitated. "It would be safer—"

Georgiana shook her head. "He arranged my release from prison and saved my life. I pay my debts."

His brows drawn, Kit looked at the general, then back to the girl. With a sigh, he waved off the man with the rope. "Stand outside the door in case I need you."

General Desmarais tilted his head and studied Lady Matlock. "You give in to her when she insists. Now he does the same. Why, I wonder, do both of you take orders from a girl?" He turned to Georgiana. "How old are you, child?"

She lifted her chin. "Sixteen."

A disbelieving smile touched his lips. "I had you under arrest in my own home, and I let you go. Perhaps I deserve what the Emperor has in store for me."

Mme. Desmarais put her hand on his arm. "What do you mean?"

He shook his head. "I will explain later – if there is a later. Darcy, this young man with the unusual taste in clothing, he is your brother? A real one?"

The scorn in Desmarais's voice hurt, even though Darcy had done nothing to be ashamed of. "He is my brother, yes." And his frock coat was a truly appalling shade of red. Kit usually had better taste than that.

A man with his arm in a blood-stained sling entered and handed Kit a scrap of paper.

After scanning it, Kit turned to Desmarais. "Victory beacons have been lit in Chatham, Dover, and Portsmouth."

"Again, I will need more assurance than your word," said Desmarais coldly. "I assume you have taken the *Achille* and the *Neptune*, since I have not heard the cannon."

Kit nodded. "Both ships are at the bottom of the Thames."

"No!" cried Darcy, horrorstruck. He jumped to his feet. "Devil take it, Kit, Elizabeth is on the *Neptune*!"

Kit flinched. "Elizabeth was there? God, William, I am sorry. It had to be done; we could not allow the ships to fire on the city."

"Are there survivors?" demanded Darcy.

Kit glanced at Lady Matlock before responding. "They fired the gunpowder stores," he said apologetically. "The hulls exploded. No one could have survived."

Desmarais's mouth twisted. "Darcy, I apologize for suspecting you of involvement in this. Pray forgive a bitter old man."

A quiet sob from Georgiana was the only thing that broke the silence.

Horror and cold, empty darkness. Had Elizabeth felt any pain? Had the explosion killed her or had she drowned? It hardly mattered; she was dead, and she would have been alive if he had never entered her life. And Kit, the brother he had finally rediscovered, saying it had to be done. Would Darcy ever be able to look at him without recalling this moment?

He shouldered his way past Kit to the door, blindly seeking escape to a place where he could contemplate the wreckage of his life in private. Only the sound of his aunt calling his name halted him.

"Darcy, I must beg you to remain. Georgiana and I will require your escort to return to Darcy House, especially given the tumult in the streets."

He wanted to refuse. How could anyone expect him to do his duty now? But he had not the wherewithal to reject her request. Without a word, he crossed to the window where he could at least turn his back on the others. How could the late afternoon sun still be shining on the neatly trimmed courtyard garden?

Waiting for news of Elizabeth's execution had been a nightmare, but the reality was even worse. He had been given a bit of hope and a moment of happiness, and now it had been snatched away. Elizabeth was gone. Bingley had betrayed him, Desmarais had failed him, and now Kit had joined the ranks of those who had destroyed the woman he loved. What remained to him? Richard, the cousin he had not seen for five years, and then just for a brief meeting? Pemberley, where he had not set foot for even longer, where the servants and tenants must feel he had abandoned them? His other friends had either died in the invasion or turned their backs on him for cooperating with the French.

The conversation continued behind him, but it was a blur to him. Darcy stirred only when someone spoke his name. No, not his name. He had said Major Darcy. Tiredly he turned, ready to correct him, but the man had been speaking to Kit. Kit, a major? Ridiculous.

Tears still in her eyes, Georgiana said, "A commission, Kit?"

Kit colored. "Not precisely. Wellington said I was a major, so I am a major, at least for now." He glanced at his shoulder and ruefully pulled a mass of gold braid from his pocket. "I was supposed to put on these epaulettes once the fighting began, but it slipped my mind completely."

Georgiana shook her head. "That is why your coat is red! I wondered at that; it is not a color you usually wear."

"My tailor said the same, albeit with somewhat stronger words, but I could hardly tell him it was because of a shortage of red uniforms."

Georgiana took the epaulettes from him and shook them out. "How do they go on? Oh, I see the pins. Stand still, Kit." She had to reach on tiptoe to pin the first epaulette to his shoulder.

She was untangling the second one when Wellington, wearing a real red coat, strode in. Kit attempted to salute, a difficult operation with Georgiana pinning an epaulette on his shoulder. Wellington gave him a quick nod and said, "I hear London is ours."

"All is well, sir, and done in accordance with your plans. We lost a few men in a skirmish near Aldgate, and more at the barracks – a dozen Englishmen, some forty Frenchmen. An entire troop was taken down near the Tower by a mob of Londoners using their bare hands and kitchen knives, and many lone soldiers met the same fate. Jérôme Bonaparte, the so-called Regent, has barricaded himself inside Hampton

Court. The palace is surrounded by loyal Englishmen, and there is no escape possible."

"Good. Let him rot there." The older man's eyes scanned the room, settling on Desmarais. "General Desmarais, I presume?"

Demarais inclined his head. "General Wellington."

"The day is ours. Your ships at Great Yarmouth, Chatham and Portsmouth are in British hands, or failing that, sunk. Lord Nelson holds the channel. We await word from the north, but I do not anticipate problems there. I call on you to surrender and to order your troops to lay down their arms before more of them lose their lives."

Desmarais stood unmoving for a minute and then turned to Darcy. "I seem to have a shortage of servants at the moment. Darcy, might I impose upon you to bring me my sword? It is in my study; you know where to find it." He would have used the same tone to ask for cup of tea.

From a great distance, Darcy managed to nod. At a signal from Wellington, one of his soldiers trailed Darcy as he left the room, crossed the library, and triggered the latch on the door to the study. The dress sword rested against the side of the desk. It was heavier than he had expected.

He returned and gave it to Desmarais.

"I thank you, Darcy." Desmarais took the sheathed sword in both hands and held it out to Wellington. "I will order my men to disarm. I will give you my parole that I will make no attempt to escape, on the condition that you guarantee the safety of my wife."

Wellington took the sword. "I am happy to guarantee her safety. We do not make war on women or children. I accept your parole and return to you your sword."

The standard theatre of surrender.

It was true. The French were defeated. It was everything Darcy had dreamed of for years, and now he did not even care. He would give anything to turn back the clock.

"Kit." Lady Matlock's voice sliced through the resulting silence. "With England restored to us, I believe there is an important introduction you have forgotten to make." She looked pointedly at Georgiana who was placing the last pin on Kit's epaulette.

Kit met Georgiana's eyes briefly. Then he stepped away from her and made a formal court bow, the dramatic effect somewhat hindered by his epaulette slipping sideways off his shoulder. "Your Majesty, may I have the honor to present to you General Lord Wellington, commander of your troops – such as they are. General, you are in the presence of Her Majesty Queen Charlotte Augusta."

Mme. Desmarais let out a squeak. "But she is Miss Darcy!"

Wellington looked stunned.

Georgiana – no, Charlotte – her back straight and chin lifted, said, "General, I... We thank you for your efforts on our behalf." Her voice barely trembled.

"Your Majesty, it is my signal honor to serve you and England." Wellington finally made his bow and glared at Kit. "What in God's name were you thinking to allow her to be here?"

"We have already had this discussion," Lady Matlock said. "Since she is here, you might as well make use of her presence. It seems the crowds outside are restive. Perhaps Her Majesty could appear briefly before her subjects so they may be assured of her presence and safety? The colonnade overlooking the street might be suitable."

Kit sighed. "General, are you acquainted with the Countess of Matlock? She has no doubt planned every detail of this already."

Wellington nodded. "Madam, if you are Lady Frederica's mother, I must assume we are in very capable hands. It would be an excellent idea to help settle the populace, if Her Majesty is willing."

"I... We are willing." The girl took a deep breath and then spoke in a rush. "There is one matter which must be addressed first. In France, all power resides in the Emperor. We are not so benighted here in England, where we believe power should reside in a lawfully elected government.

Since we lack that government at present, it falls to us, as Queen Regnant, to command the formation of a government. We entrust this responsibility..." Her voice faltered for a moment, "... to a committee formed of Lord Wellington, Lady Frederica Fitzwilliam, and Mr. Fitzwilliam Darcy, with elections to be held within the year."

Kit exclaimed, "Oh, well done!"

She gave him a sidelong glance. "I have had six years to plan that speech."

Lady Matlock hurried forward to stand before her. Somehow producing a tiara from her reticule, she set it on the startled girl's head. "Now you look like a queen."

Darcy forced his voice to work. "I am honored by your offer, but I must beg to decline."

Georgiana – no, Charlotte – looked surprised and dismayed, but Lady Matlock was the one to respond. "We can discuss this later. Right now the people need to see they have a queen and an army. Or at least a general and a major." She bustled all of them from the room.

As soon as they were gone, Mme. Desmarais's composure slipped. Tears began to tumble down her cheeks, and she covered her face with a handkerchief, her shoulders silently shaking.

Desmarais put his arm around her. "There, there. It will not be so terrible, *ma petite*. You will see."

"Yes, it will, and you know it! Oh, *mon Dieu, mon Dieu!*"

Darcy returned to his window, staring out to give them at least the illusion of privacy. He tried not to overhear their low French conversation. It was simpler than usual to avoid it, since the ghost of Kit's voice kept echoing in his ears. *It had to be done.*

Elizabeth might even have agreed with Kit. Darcy could not. He rested his forehead against the gilt window frame. He hated gilt.

"Darcy, my friend," said Desmarais. "I must ask a very great favor of you. In all likelihood, Wellington will ransom me to France, where I will meet that fate the Emperor reserves for generals who fail as spectacularly as I have. Even if my wife does not share my fate, she will be left a pauper and an outcast. She would be safer in England under a false name than in France. Would you be willing to provide her with a very modest income and protect her from retribution?"

Darcy turned slowly. More duty, but he did owe Desmarais a great deal. "It may be difficult—"

Desmarais interrupted, his voice cold. "It is no matter. Pray forget I said anything."

"No, that is not what I meant. I would be glad to arrange for a place for her to live and an income. The protection part is more difficult because I do not plan to remain in England. I will be turning Pemberley over to my brother. Still, I cannot imagine Georgiana – the Queen – would allow your wife to come to any harm."

"Leaving England? Ah, *mon frère*, now I understand you completely. May I inquire where you will be going?"

Darcy shrugged. "Canada, at least at first. I have a sister there – a real one, that is, the one you have been watching for the last six years."

"If you could see your way clear to it, Canada would be a better place for my wife than England. No one there will care about my sins."

Could he never escape the past? "If it is your wish and hers, I would be honored to escort your wife to Canada."

Desmarais closed his eyes. "I thank you. You have relieved the heaviest of my burdens. Heaven will reward you for your kindness."

A deafening tumult of cheers from outside prevented Darcy from responding. Wellington must have presented Charlotte to the crowds. At least someone was happy.

A quarter of an hour later, Kit, Lady Matlock, and Charlotte returned to the sitting room. She was unquestionably Charlotte and not Georgiana this time. Georgiana would be frightened, but Charlotte was laughing, her cheeks flushed and her eyes bright. She looked like a stranger.

"That was exciting!" the girl confided. "I was worried at first, but the crowd cheered every time I waved my hand or smiled. And who could not smile under these circumstances?"

Darcy might never smile again. He suspected General and Mme. Desmarais felt the same.

Kit was smiling, too. "You were perfect. No one could have done better. I, on the other hand, have just been demoted. An hour ago I was responsible for taking the entire city, but Wellington says now my only duty is to keep you safe and to form a royal guard. I think I like this job better."

More proof that Darcy's role was at an end. He had been the one responsible for Georgiana's safety; now that she was transformed to Charlotte, he was no longer needed. She was Kit's responsibility now.

The girl looked up at Kit. "You will be perfect at it. It will keep you from running off, too."

"I never wanted to run off."

She seemed to be almost bursting with energy. Her feet carried her to Darcy's side. "Oh, William, I wish you had been there! You would have been proud of me."

"I am proud of you," he said stiffly. "I could hear the cheers, and I knew they were for you."

Her face fell despite his efforts to disguise his feelings. "William, are you angry that I suggested you should be part of the government planning? You would do such a good job, and there is no one I trust more. And after all you have done, you deserve to be part of the victory."

He could not bring himself to spoil her triumph. "Thank you for considering me, but I could not give it the attention it deserves. Pemberley needs my attention after all these years."

"Cannot your steward take care of Pemberley? He has done so for years, after all. I would be much happier to have you close by."

"I am sorry, but I cannot." He could not even invent a good excuse for it.

Desmarais's tired voice was soft. "He cannot do it because he is planning to make a new life for himself in Canada. He intends to give Pemberley to his brother. I am sorry, Darcy, but if she is queen now, she needs to know the truth."

Darcy could not bear to see her reaction, so instead he looked at Kit, whose dropped jaw and wide eyes were almost comical.

Small fists bunched themselves in his lapels. "No! I beg you, no! I cannot bear it!" Her breathing had gone shallow and rapid in the familiar pattern. "I cannot do it without you."

He patted her back, glaring at Desmarais over her head. "You underestimate your own strength. For a long time, I was all you had. Now you have Lady Matlock, Kit, Frederica, Lord Wellington, and soon you will have dozens of courtiers and ladies-in-waiting. The entire population of London adores you already. You will hardly even notice my absence." After all, she seemed not to have noticed Elizabeth's death for more than a few minutes.

"They are not the same." She was gasping for breath now. "They will leave, just like everyone else. Even Elizabeth left, and now you want to leave, too."

She was beginning to sag against him. With a frustrated sigh, he scooped her up in his arms and carried her to a fainting couch. "Lie still now, and try to breathe more slowly. You know how. In and out, slowly."

Mme. Desmarais, even under her own terrible stress, was the first one to the girl's side. She wiped the cold sweat from her forehead and crooned calmingly to her. "All will be well, *ma petite*. All will be well."

Kit seemed frozen. "A doctor! We must send for a doctor instantly!" He sounded frantic.

Darcy spared him a disgusted look. "There is no need. This has happened many times before. Rest and reassurance are all she needs." It had not been this bad for a long time, but there was no point in saying so now.

Lady Matlock perched on the side of the fainting couch. Taking the girl's hand in both of her own, she said in a quiet but businesslike manner, "Now listen to me, my dear. I am about to tell you something very important, so you must listen carefully. Men are not like you and me. When a man suffers a great loss, his mind stops working and he says the most ridiculous things. In a few days, they usually come to their senses. In the meantime, you must be generous enough to offer sympathy, but clever enough to pay little attention to what they say and wait for the storm to pass."

Georgiana's ragged breathing did not stop her from speaking. "Not William. He is not like that."

"Hush, *chérie*, your aunt is quite correct," said Mme. Desmarais. "All men are like that, including Darcy."

"Just a minute," said Kit. "Not all of us—"

Lady Matlock turned a look on him that would have frozen the fires of hell. "Are you disagreeing with me?"

The new Commander of the Royal Guard scuffed the edge of the carpet with his boot. "Er... no, madam. Of course not."

The countess gave a nod of satisfaction. "Then you should make yourself useful by sitting with Her Majesty and talking to her. William, go back to Darcy House. You are not helping here, and since Kit is now protecting Her Majesty, he can protect me at the same time."

"I want to go back to Darcy House, too," said the girl plaintively.

"You must discuss that with Kit, but in any case, you cannot leave this place until you have sufficient guards. Darcy, I told you to go."

Darcy strode out of the room without a word. How dare his aunt treat him like a child, especially at a moment like this? He was the one who had kept Georgiana safe. He was the one who knew what to do when she was upset. He was the one...

He was the one who had lost Elizabeth.

His anger drained away, leaving an empty pit of despair.

An odd assortment of men stood by the front door. They did not carry themselves as either servants or soldiers did. Presumably they were Kit's men. Darcy pushed his way through them, grabbed his hat and gloves, and strode out into the courtyard.

Outside the shouting and cheering were much louder. Through the growing dusk he could see the crowd of people beyond the Carlton House gates. Another obstacle he would have to pass.

They had spotted him. Several were pointing in his direction.

Darcy stepped back inside the house. "I will have to leave through the postern gate. One of you must come to lock it behind me."

Most of them snapped to some semblance of attention, obviously pleased to have something to do. Three trailed behind him as he marched through the state rooms and into the courtyard. How many men could it take to relock a gate?

Thankfully, the alley beyond the postern gate was quiet. Darcy made his escape, circling around the crowd on Pall Mall.

Usually the streets of London would be starting to empty by this time of day, but today was different. Even in this fine part of town, small groups of men were prowling the street, challenging all comers, lest a disguised Frenchman sneak by. The body of a French soldier in the gutter was almost covered by the refuse that had been thrown at him. Several doors, even those of fine townhouses, had been defaced with a large red T. T for traitor, Darcy supposed. How much violence would there be tomorrow as loyal citizens took revenge into their own hands? Most likely there would be a T on his own door.

It was full dark by the time he reached Darcy House. No red T on the door – that was one minor blessing. He opened the door, only to be greeted by two of his own footman holding cudgels in an obvious threat.

His butler hurried forward. "My apologies, Mr. Darcy, but there have been ruffians wandering the streets. I thought it best to be prepared."

The hollowness inside Darcy left him nothing for polite conversation, so he only nodded tersely.

"If I may ask, sir, were you able to find Miss Darcy? We have been worried for her."

What possible answer could he make? His staff would learn soon enough who Georgiana truly was, but he could not bear to make the explanation. "She is unhurt." He could not say the same for himself.

Chapter Twenty

The banks of the Thames were disreputable enough during the day. Visiting it at night was unwise at best. At his valet's insistence, Darcy took the precaution of leaving his valuables at Darcy House and secreting a small pistol in the pocket of his greatcoat. It would do no good if some footpad decided to slip a knife between his ribs but taking it with him was easier than explaining that he did not really care about his safety. All he cared about was getting as close as possible to the spot where Elizabeth drew her last breath.

He took Puck because the dog had loved Elizabeth, too. But he knew the truth: he needed the dog for his own comfort.

His coachman declined to leave him after dropping him by the river. "You'll not be able to hail a hackney or chair in this part of town, sir."

"It may be some hours before I wish to return." If he ever wished to return.

"No matter, sir. Mr. Jamieson would expect me to stay."

Carrying a small lantern, Darcy picked his way along the riverbank until he found the rude bench he had sat upon before. The mist rising from the river was almost as much a hindrance to visibility as the darkness. Puck did not care, running in circles around Darcy and pausing to stick his nose into the river.

Darcy sank down on the bench. He could see nothing of the river. The darkness and mist hid any sign of the sunken warships. Was the Thames deep enough to cover the tall masts?

But what did any of that matter? Elizabeth was gone, the bright spark lighting her eyes quenched forever. One day someone might stumble upon her body, but if she had been trapped in a cabin, her remains would spend eternity within the shipwreck. There would not even be a grave for him to visit.

And he was the one who had led her to this spot. It had been all his doing. The worst part was remembering how much he had enjoyed having her in London, her teasing in the drawing room, their walk in Hyde Park, listening together as Georgiana played the pianoforte.

Elizabeth had paid the ultimate price for his moments of pleasure. If he had not persuaded her to remain in London, she would be safely in Scotland now. He should have considered the danger to her, but he had grown complacent after hiding Georgiana in plain sight all these years. He had been a fool.

Puck butted his head against his leg. Darcy absently scratched him behind the ears. "What are we going to do without her?" he asked the dog in despair. "Our Titania is..." He could not even say it, not even to a dog in the dead of night. The queen of the fairies was supposed to be immortal, but her magic had failed.

The dog made no answer apart from leaning his head into Darcy's hand. After a brief nuzzle, the dog stood stock still, sniffing the air, and lifted one paw.

"Oh, no." Darcy grabbed the collar around Puck's neck. "No duck hunting for you, not tonight. And no amount of whimpering will make me change my mind. It is back to the carriage for you."

But as Darcy stood, Puck lunged away, leaving his collar dangling in Darcy's hand, and raced off down the riverbank. Darcy called after him, but there was no response. With a curse, he grabbed the lantern and followed the dog.

How would he ever find Puck in the dark? Fear stabbed at him. Why had he been such a fool as to bring the dog with him? First he had caused Elizabeth's death, and now he had lost her dog.

He shouted Puck's name as he clambered over piles of flotsam, scraping his hand badly on something sharp. Some hidden detritus tripped him, and he landed on his hands and knees in the filthy riverbank mud. "Damned dog," he muttered as he scrambled for safe footing.

This was a hopeless chase. Puck could leap over obstacles Darcy could barely fight his way past. The dog could be half a mile away by now. Hopelessness warred with helplessness in him, but he could not lose Elizabeth's dog, too.

Just as he was about to give up, he heard a familiar bark. "Puck! Where are you?"

Another bark, but no nearer. Darcy wiped his muddy hands on his trousers and pressed onwards. It sounded close by when Darcy collided with a decrepit pier jutting out into the Thames, knocking the breath out of him. He bent over, hands on his knees, until he recovered enough to push his way onto the pier.

Puck barked again, this time sounding as if he were standing beside him. Darcy turned in a slow circle, holding the lantern high, but saw nothing. Where was the cursed dog?

The barking was coming from under his feet. The idiot dog must have burrowed under the pier. Darcy tried to swing himself down on the far side, but his coat sleeve caught on a nail. He attempted to free it with no success. "Puck? Are you there?"

"William?" It was a woman's voice, one he knew deep in his soul.

Darcy's sleeve ripped as he jumped down into mud up to his ankles. He did not care. "Elizabeth! Is that you?" He thrust the lantern forward into the pitch black under the pier.

She was huddled with Molly Hayes against one of the piles that supported the pier. Her hair hung down in damp, bedraggled locks, with mud smeared on her arms. He could not see the expression on her face because half of it was hidden behind Puck's head as he enthusiastically licked her. Darcy had never seen anything so beautiful.

Dropping to his hands and knees, Darcy pushed his way past Puck and pulled Elizabeth into his arms. "Dear God, Elizabeth! I thought you were dead!"

"I almost was. William, you are so very...so very...warm." Her voice was weak, and she was icy cold in his arms.

He released her just long enough to strip off his greatcoat. "Put your arms in here." He pulled the coat tight around her and embraced her again. "And your hands against my chest. It will warm them."

"But Molly..."

"I am warmer than you, Lizzy, for you have been allowing me to be in the most protected spot," said Mrs. Hayes stoutly, but she was also shivering.

This was no time to think of appearances. Darcy removed his frock coat and held it for her as she struggled into it.

How long had they been sitting here in the night mist, soaking wet? "What happened? How did you escape the *Neptune*? Were you thrown clear?"

"I jumped. When the *Achille* exploded, I knew the *Neptune* would be next. Everyone was at the rail, trying to see the wreckage through all the smoke. Then...what was I saying?"

"It does not matter. All that matters is that you are alive."

"She saved my life," said Mrs. Hayes. "She grabbed my hand and told me there was no time to explain and we had to jump clear. We made it to the opposite rail. I lost my nerve once I was standing on the railing, but Lizzy jumped and pulled me with her. We hit the water – no one ever told me that it hurts to land on water from a great height! – and of course we sank down deep, and everything exploded around us, like a storm of wood and nails and worse things." She shuddered. "But I grabbed onto the nearest piece of wood, and by great good fortune, it was that barrel."

She pointed towards the water's edge. "With its help, we were able to get to the surface, but I was certain we would drown."

Elizabeth said, "There was smoke everywhere, and we were coughing out water, and it was hard to breathe, like Georgiana during one of her attacks."

"But the tide was going out," continued Mrs. Hayes. "It took us with it. Elizabeth could have swum to shore, but she would not leave me. By the time we made it here, it was dark, and we decided we should hide until daylight."

Puck had clambered onto the pier, and now found himself with his favorite people within easy reach. Enthusiastically he began licking first Darcy's cheek, then Elizabeth's.

Darcy tried to push the puppy away, but only half-heartedly. "Puck, you deserve to eat off gold plate for the rest of your life for what you have done tonight. But I do not need dog slobber all over my face."

Elizabeth gave a muffled giggle. "I do. The river water is foul and disgusting. Being licked by a dog is a great improvement."

The foggy, dreamlike quality was beginning to fade from Elizabeth's mind by the time Darcy managed to get the two women up to the nearest street. "Where are we?"

"Somewhere east of the Tower, I think." Darcy glanced up and down the street, keeping a supportive hand around her shoulder.

"But what of the curfew? If the French soldiers find us, they will know I came from the ship."

"Curfew?" He sounded puzzled, which was odd given how many years the curfew had been in place. "Of course, you do not know. London has been liberated; the only French soldiers left have taken asylum in Westminster Abbey."

She stopped so abruptly that he staggered. "Is it true? We are free? What happened? I knew the uprising must have started, but is it over already?"

Darcy's brows drew together. "I do not know the details. Once I heard the *Neptune* was sunk, I stopped listening to the rest. But it is over, and Demarais has surrendered. Kit will be able to tell you more; he was in the midst of it. Wellington is commanding the forces on land and Lord Nelson has the fleet."

"Wellington? Nelson? I thought they were long dead! Oh, this is the best news!"

"I beg to differ." Darcy's hand cupped her cheek. "Finding you alive is the best news."

If Elizabeth had not been so cold and so wet, she could have lived in that moment forever.

A boy ambled past them. What was he doing awake at this hour?

Darcy hailed him. "Ho, boy! Do you want to earn a shilling?"

"What? Yes, sir, if you please."

"I left my carriage on St. Katharine's Way. Can you run there and tell the coachman that Mr. Darcy says he should come here?" Darcy looked around. "Wherever here is."

The boy's eyes grew wide. "Cor! Are you really Mr. Darcy?"

"Did I not say so?"

"*The* Mr. Darcy? The one that hid the princess all these years?"

Elizabeth, seeing Darcy stiffen, said, "Yes, he is that Mr. Darcy."

"Cor! Wait till I tell my mates! I'll fetch your carriage in a trice, sir!"

"One moment! Is there a respectable public house nearby where I can take the ladies in the meantime? They are cold and wet."

The boy squinted at the women in the darkness. "Oh, sorry. I thought they were men in those coats. Bad night for swim, innit? But you can go to the Royal Oak down there at the corner, the one with the candles in the window. It's me mum's place, and she'll take care of you."

"Good. Now off with you."

The boy took off at a run.

"Where do you suppose he heard about me?" Darcy took Elizabeth's arm and steered her toward the pub.

Elizabeth's teeth started to chatter. "I have no idea."

"No more talking. We must get you warm."

Molly said, "Wait! What was that about the princess?"

"I will tell you later," said Elizabeth. "When we are warm."

The inn was lit only by a few candles and a dying fire, but the light dazzled Elizabeth's eyes after so many hours of darkness. Half a dozen men and women sat at tables in the tap room. A woman in an apron rubbed a rag over one table while several late customers tarried over their ale at another. The hum of conversation ceased abruptly as they entered.

Uncaring of the staring customers, Elizabeth hurried toward the fire, followed closely by Molly. Ah, heat! She only wished it could warm both sides of her at once.

The aproned woman bustled towards them. "Now, what's all this, then? This is a respectable house, this is, and I won't have no strange folks coming in at this hour and up to no good."

Darcy said stiffly, "My good woman, we are quite respectable. Your son has gone to fetch my carriage and he suggested we could wait here."

The woman seemed to waver, perhaps owing to Darcy's cultured accent, but it was not surprising she would have doubts. Darcy hardly looked the gentleman in his shirtsleeves and with mud covering his boots and knees, two bedraggled ladies wearing his coats and no doubt reeking of the stench of the Thames, and a half-grown puppy trailing behind them.

The hostess placed her hands on her hips. "Anyone can say they have a carriage, but I won't believe it until I see it. Now out with you."

"Aw, let them stay," called out one of the patrons. "It's not every day we have a new queen."

Wanting to sob at the very idea of going back out into the streets, Elizabeth took a shot in the dark. "He is Mr. Darcy." It had worked with the boy, after all.

The woman took a step back. "Not *the* Mr. Darcy?"

"Yes," said Elizabeth helpfully. "The one who hid Princess Charlotte all these years. He just saved our lives by fishing us out of the river. We were on the *Neptune* when it exploded, you see." She tried to ignore Darcy's stiff look of incredulity. If it meant she could stay by the fire, she would be willing to say almost anything.

A man with a bushy beard said, "But… But the lady on the *Neptune* is supposed to be dead. Miss Gordon, or whatever her name was."

"I am Miss Gardiner, and I came very close to dying, I assure you." She had become accustomed to being Mrs. Darcy, but if Miss Gardiner could have a place by the fire, she would use the name.

The innkeeper gasped. "The one who escaped with the princess and hid in a hayloft?"

"The very one. Georgiana – that is what we called the princess when she was in disguise – she said that if King Charles could hide in an oak tree all day, she could hide in hayloft all night." Elizabeth exchanged a wary glance with Darcy. How could these people know all these things?

"Well, that's different, then! Come with me, ladies, and you too, Peg Jones. We must get these ladies dry and clean. George Mason, you tend the bar and get Mr. Darcy something to drink." She herded Elizabeth and Molly behind the bar and into a blessedly warm kitchen. The other patrons were already crowding around Mr. Darcy and asking questions.

In the kitchen, a startled looking barmaid clapped her hand over her mouth at the sight of them. The hostess set her scurrying to fetch a bowl of water and towels and the woman called Peg to find dry clothing.

Dry clothing! It sounded like heaven.

Elizabeth managed to wash her own face and hands, but then the hostess took over her care personally, stripping her down to her shift and drying her hair. Molly, clearly considered a lesser personage, was left to the mercy of the barmaid.

Peg Jones miraculously produced two dresses in everyday brown and shifts to go with them. "Not what you ladies might be used to, but at least they are dry."

Elizabeth looked at the simple wool dresses, tears of gratitude in her eyes. "I cannot tell you how grateful I am. This is perfect, and I will be proud to wear it."

"As will I," said Molly.

"And who might you be?" asked the hostess, as if noticing Molly for the first time.

"Molly Hayes," she said humbly.

Elizabeth said, "Mrs. Hayes is the Lord Mayor's wife."

The poor barmaid shrieked as if horrified that her humble hands had touched the Mayor's wife. "I did not know!"

The hostess seemed less impressed, or perhaps the rescuer of the princess simply rated higher than the Lord Mayor's wife. As she began to dress Elizabeth, she asked, "What is she like, the little queen?"

What would common people want to know about her? Presumably not about her occasional petulance or fits of nerves. "She is a little shorter than I am, with flaxen hair, and when she is thinking hard, she always wraps her finger in one of her ringlets. Her hair is short, though, barely to her shoulders, because we had to cut it when we escaped."

"Is it true she dressed as a boy?" Peg Jones's eyes were wide.

That was an easy question. "Only when there was no other choice. She was very brave about it, and ready to do anything that would serve England and its people. She did make a fetching boy, though."

The women sighed happily. "And Mr. Darcy's brother, is it true he is mad with love for her?"

Good Lord! Where in heaven's name had they heard that, when it was only a few hours since London had been won? "I cannot repeat his confidences to me, but he is her most fervent supporter."

"Ooh, is he handsome?" ventured the barmaid.

"Oh, yes. He is dark-haired like his brother and has an engaging smile."

"I do hope the queen will take pity on him. After all, he has loved her for such a long time."

For a long time? Kit had not known Georgiana half a year! But now Elizabeth knew the source of all this information. No matter who had repeated the story to these particular women, Lady Matlock clearly was already preparing the populace for Georgiana – Charlotte – to marry Kit. With the overthrow of the French, Lady Matlock would have changed her plans for the queen's future as quickly as she might change her gloves. Richard Fitzwilliam was out of the picture and Kit was in. What must Kit think of his new role in this saga?

Finally they were dry and presentable, if appearing more like common women than usual, and Elizabeth had learned that good strong ale tasted much better than river water. Of course, almost anything would.

Back in the taproom Elizabeth discovered Darcy seated at a table with the other patrons, holding a tankard of ale and still answering questions with surprising amiability. Puck sat as his feet. When he rose to his feet on seeing her, his eyes were warm.

"I missed you," he said softly when he reached her side. "The carriage is here."

While the ale-drinkers huddled together in earnest discussion, Darcy paid the proprietress several times what the service required. Elizabeth promised to return the clothing as soon as possible. Then, recalling what Georgiana had done after their night in the hayloft, she pulled a silver ring from her little finger and handed it to the woman. "This is to remember tonight, and you may show it to prove we were here. The princess gave it to me."

"Oh, Miss Gardiner, I couldn't!" But the hostess was staring at the ring as if it were a holy relic.

"I want you to have it, and if the princess... the queen were here, she would say the same."

"Bless you, miss, and God bless Her little Majesty, too."

The man who had been appointed barkeeper rose from the huddle, stuck his thumbs in his waistband and addressed the hostess. "We've been talking here, and we think that in honor of today, and what the queen said about hiding in the hayloft like King Charles in the oak tree, this pub should be called The Royal Hayloft instead of The Royal Oak." A murmur of agreement followed from the others.

The hostess's expression lit up as she turned to Darcy and Elizabeth. "I hardly dare ask it, but would you mind it?"

Fighting back the urge to laugh, Elizabeth said, "I would be honored."

With poker-like solemnity, Darcy said, "You will need a new sign, then." He added two more coins to the pile.

Biting her lip was the only way Elizabeth could keep a serious countenance, but when the coach pulled away from the inn, she could no longer repress her mirth. Between bursts of laughter, she managed to say, "I felt as if we were characters in some old story like the tales of King Arthur. I half expected Sir Lancelot to ride up."

Darcy looked down at her with an arrested gaze. "I thought I would never hear your laugh again."

Molly cleared her throat as if reminding them she was still there. "Lizzy, about Princess Rosalinda and the hayloft," she said pointedly.

"Er, yes. Princess Rosalinda and Princess Charlotte do have a great deal in common, I am afraid. I wish I could have told you before. Do you remember when we first met, I said I was guilty of doing far worse things than folding newspapers? Now you know just how much worse!"

"Perhaps you should tell me the story now since everyone else in London seems to know more than I do," Molly teased.

The tale took up the duration of the journey to Mansion House, where Darcy delivered Molly into the hands of the tearfully grateful and none too sober Lord Mayor, still awake despite the church towers tolling midnight and already dressed in mourning black. As he embraced his wife, he said, "Darcy, if there is ever anything I can do for you, no matter what it is, I will be happy to do it. I owe you everything. When I heard the news about the *Neptune*, I thought my world had ended."

Once back inside the carriage, Darcy gathered Elizabeth into his arms and said, "His gratitude is misplaced, since I did nothing more than deliver her to him. But I do understand how he feels. I still cannot believe you are alive and here with me."

"And that we are free of the French," said Elizabeth, stifling a yawn. "It may take some time for me to truly believe that." She rested her head on his shoulder. How long had it been since she had felt as safe and happy as she did at that moment? If only she could remain in his arms forever! "I have not even thanked you for finding me."

"Puck deserves the credit for that." Darcy nodded to the sleeping dog on the opposite bench. Normally Puck was not permitted onto the carriage seats, but tonight Darcy would allow him anything.

"Well, then, I thank you for thinking to bring Puck to search for me."

Darcy's arms tightened around her. "I did not expect to find you. I had already sent servants to ask if there were any survivors from the ships, and they reported there were none. But I simply could not stay away. I had to be near you." He pressed his lips against the part of her forehead he could reach. It was true – she was alive, and soon she would be living with him at Darcy House as his wife. He had tried to avoid imagining that or it would have been too painful to awaken to an empty bed every morning.

Elizabeth's breathing was slow and even. Had she fallen asleep? Darcy held perfectly still to avoid awakening her. She must be exhausted, and she needed rest if she were to avoid taking a chill. And this way he could bask in the sheer indescribable joy of holding her close. He was the most fortunate man in the world.

"Elizabeth, my dearest, loveliest Elizabeth."

She barely heard Darcy's words through the veil of sleep, but the tenderness in his voice drew her. Without even opening her eyes, she tilted her face up to him. Oh, the pleasure of his kiss! Perhaps they could stay in the carriage forever, just like this.

She did not even care when the carriage came to a halt, not until she heard the click of the door latch as it opened, followed by it being firmly closed. She straightened abruptly, now wide awake. Had Darcy's coachmen actually caught them kissing? "Oh, dear."

"Oh, dear, indeed." Darcy did not sound in the least bit regretful. "It is safe to open it now, Symons."

When the door opened this time, the coachman's eyes were firmly fixed on the ground. As he put down the steps, Symons said, "This is as far as we can go, sir. I think you may need to deal with this."

Elizabeth stuck her head out. They were still a short distance from Darcy House, but despite the late hour, Brook Street was filled with people, some carrying lanterns. A line of men with rifles stood at the end of the block.

Darcy descended from the carriage and strode up to the nearest armed man. "What is this?" he demanded.

The fellow said, "Sorry, sir, nobody comes in without the major's approval."

"This is Major Darcy? Go ask him then." Darcy bit out.

"Nonsense!" It was the hearty voice of Mr. Cartwright, Darcy's neighbor, the one who had scorned him over his politics. "Darcy, pray allow me the very great privilege of shaking your hand. I could not be prouder if it were my own son. You, there, let Darcy through. He is the one who hid the princess."

Elizabeth was already beginning to tire of hearing this.

The armed man straightened abruptly. "Sorry, sir. My mistake, Mr. Darcy. You can go straight through."

The crowd inside the barrier was already turning towards Darcy. Mr. Cartwright called out, "Make way for Mr. Darcy!"

Elizabeth scrambled out of the coach, shutting the door quickly to keep Puck inside. Darcy held his arm out to her, even if she did look more like a servant than his guest.

The armed man looked askance. "Who's the lady, sir?"

"I am Miss Gardiner, and I am not dead," said Elizabeth. If everyone knew all the details anyway, she might as well save time. All the details except her marriage, that is.

"Another blessing on this blessed day!" exclaimed Cartwright.

The crowd parted in front of them. Several women sat on a stoop, cutting up French flags by lantern light and sewing the scraps into the familiar flag of Great Britian. Another flag flew beside the door of Darcy House, this one a roughly sewn jumble of red, blue and yellow. Elizabeth squinted at it. Was it supposed to be the royal standard? Someone must have been busy.

A woman near Darcy asked, "Is that truly Miss Gardiner from the *Neptune*?"

Darcy placed his arm around Elizabeth's waist and turned to face the crowd. This was a question he was happy to answer. "She has been known as Miss Gardiner, although she was christened Miss Elizabeth Bennet, daughter of Thomas Bennet of Longbourn. But I am proud to announce that her correct name is Mrs. Darcy and has been these last three months."

Scattered cheers were interrupted by shushing noises. "Her Majesty is trying to sleep!" hissed one fellow.

Darcy held the door for Elizabeth. His wife. Coming home with him.

The door was barely closed behind them when a cloud of white fabric and golden hair raced down the stairs and barreled into him with such force he staggered. "Thank God you are back! I was so worried!"

Returning her embrace, he said, "Georgiana – or I suppose I should say Charlotte or Your Majesty—"

"No!" The girl's face was buried in his neck, but her voice was perfectly audible. "You must call me Georgiana, just like always."

"Well then, Georgiana, you might want to let go of me long enough to see who—"

"Elizabeth! Is that truly you?" Kit dashed down the stairs almost as quickly as Georgiana had. He was still dressed in that ridiculous red coat, but his hair looked as if birds had been nesting in it. "You are alive!"

"Oh, Elizabeth!" cried Georgiana, tears filling her eyes. "I am so glad, so glad!" She started to embrace Elizabeth but drew back at the last second, her nose crinkling. "You smell horrid."

"Essence of River Thames. It is still in my hair," said Elizabeth with a laugh. "I believe I shall go back to lavender water; I do not care for this new scent."

Kit clasped both her hands. "Thank God you are safe! William was out of his mind when he thought you were dead – even wanted to leave England completely." He gave Georgiana a worried look, as if he wished he could take back the words.

"But now you will stay, will you not?" pleaded Georgiana.

"I will have to. I just announced to the world that Elizabeth and I are married, and I do not believe my wife wishes to emigrate." And he never planned to let her leave his side.

"Married?" Georgiana asked in disbelief. "But how?"

"We married secretly on board the *Neptune*," Elizabeth said with a smile. "Almost three months ago."

"And you did not tell me?" Georgiana sounded hurt.

Darcy smiled. "I am sorry. Perhaps I have learned the habit of keeping secrets too well, even when I should not."

Elizabeth patted Georgiana's arm. "I hope you will be happy for us anyway. I am so very glad to see you again. I would not leave here for all the tigers and elephants in the world."

"You cannot leave now that you are my sister. I never thought it could happen." Georgiana wound a ringlet around her finger. "Although I suppose you cannot be my actual sister since William is not truly my brother. But it will be just like being sisters, will it not?"

Kit sidled over to Darcy. "I should warn you, she drank quite a bit of brandy. She was so upset when she discovered you were not here, and nothing I said would calm her," he said in a low voice. "I have no idea how you and Elizabeth manage it."

Georgiana tugged at her ringlet, clearly deep in thought. "I know! We will be true sisters after all. After I marry Kit, that is." She smiled beatifically.

Kit's jaw dropped, leaving him standing with his mouth open. "I... I..."

Elizabeth said, "I would not worry too much. It is the brandy speaking, no doubt."

Georgiana gave her a puzzled look. "No, it is not. I decided it months ago. Kit is the logical choice, and I like him."

Kit raked his hand through his hair, leaving it even more disordered, and turned a helpless look on his brother. "Can you explain it to her?"

Darcy shook his head. "Perhaps we could discuss this in the morning."

"What? This is insanity! You know perfectly well she cannot marry me."

Georgiana bit her lip. "If you do not wish to marry me, I shall not insist." Her voice shook.

"It has nothing to do with my wishes," said Kit desperately. "You cannot marry me. I am no one. You must marry a prince, whether I like it or not."

355

The girl shook her head fiercely. "No. England should not have a foreign Prince Consort, not now, so I must marry an Englishman. And I need to produce heirs, since if something happened to me, Jérôme Bonaparte's brats will have a claim on the throne. I must marry quickly. Why should I take time hunting for a husband when I have a perfectly good one right here?"

"But your marriage is a matter of state, not just a personal preference. You are not even of age!"

"What difference does my age make? There is no Regent until we have a government to choose one. Perhaps... Lady Matlock, would you be so kind as to serve as my Regent until then?"

"Of course, dear, though you hardly need one," said Lady Matlock.

"May I marry Kit?"

"Yes, and I agree you should do so quickly. Kit, pray close your mouth before someone mistakes you for a fish."

Kit sank down to sit on the steps, his head in his hands. "I cannot believe this! And none of you even seemed surprised."

Georgiana sat beside him and patted his knee. "You simply need time to become accustomed to the idea. It will not be so bad, you will see."

Kit turned his head towards her, keeping his hands up so no one else could see his face. "I never said it would be bad."

The girl beamed. "Oh, good. You were starting to worry me!"

Lady Matlock said, "Perhaps we can sit down as we discuss what should happen tomorrow morning. I am too tired to stand for long, and Elizabeth looks half asleep on her feet."

"It is the morning already," muttered Darcy.

The mantel clock chimed once as if to agree with him.

Chapter
Twenty-One

Elizabeth had grown accustomed to the rocking of her bed on the *Neptune*, but it was not moving when she awoke. Was it an unusually calm day on the river? It also seemed softer than her bunk on the *Neptune*. But she could hear the sailors drilling as usual – or did she? The voices were shouting orders in English, not French, and no footsteps pounded overhead.

Her eyes flew open. Where was she? Pushing aside the luxurious bedclothes, she sat up and stared at the unfamiliar inlaid furniture and chinoiserie walls. She was still wearing the brown wool dress from the pub.

She shivered as the previous day came back – the exploding ships, fighting to stay afloat in the Thames, the respite at the pub, and finally Darcy House. But she did not recognize this room.

"Good morning, Mrs. Darcy. Would you like your hot chocolate now?" The cheerful maid was unfamiliar to her.

"Er...yes," said Elizabeth. "Am I correct in thinking this is Darcy House?"

"Mr. Darcy's own room, madam. Mr. Darcy carried you here when you fell asleep downstairs. He said you would want to bathe this morning, so I took the liberty of ordering water to be heated. Should I have your bath prepared now?"

"A bath would be heavenly." Elizabeth rubbed her arms as she got out of bed. "I do not recall seeing you here before. Are you new?" She would have remembered this girl. Darcy House servants, selected for their lack of curiosity, never showed this kind of initiative.

"Yes and no, madam," said the young woman. "I work for Mr. Cartwright next door. Most of his staff is helping here today. When your Mrs. Reynolds found out last evening she had to feed and house two dozen soldiers, she begged our housekeeper for assistance. Mr. Cartwright found out about it and asked for volunteers to help here, and of course everyone volunteered. It is such an honor! Shall I help you out of that dress?"

"Thank you. It is good of Mr. Cartwright to be so generous," said Elizabeth.

The maid made quick work of the fastenings on the simple wool gown. "I have never seen him so happy! As soon as he heard the news, he began organizing the neighbors. Everyone is helping to provide food or housing soldiers, and each house sent footmen to be in the royal honor guard. Major Darcy is drilling them now. And every woman on the block, from the mistresses of the houses to the lowest servants, is sewing tabards for the footmen so they will match, and new royal standards, too. My own mistress cut up her yellow satin dress for the first standard." The girl giggled. "It did not turn out very well, being made in such a hurry, but it was flying two hours after Her Majesty arrived, and that is what mattered."

Elizabeth shrugged out of the dress and started on the ties of her shift. Her stays must still be at the pub. "And all this had to be done in one night?"

"Of course!" said the maid eagerly. "Those French monsters will see how we honor Her Majesty. What if she wishes to go out today, and we do not have the royal guard ready? All England is watching us!"

"Of course," said Elizabeth solemnly as she stepped out of the scratchy shift. "Somehow I assume Lady Matlock must be part of this, too."

"Oh, yes. Her ladyship is meeting with General Wellington, Lady Frederica, and some other gentlemen about regaining control of the country, or some such matter. Lady Matlock told Mr. Cartwright that when he had everything on the block under control, he should begin planning the coronation. The coronation! Can you believe it? And to think we are actually in the same house as the queen! This is the most exciting thing that has ever happened to me."

The girl helped her into a satin dressing gown Elizabeth did not recognize. Of course; her own must be on the bottom of the Thames, along with all the possessions she had not been wearing and the manuscript of *The Tales of Princess Rosalinda*. A pang stabbed her. All the sailors she had come to know, the awkward lieutenant who missed his sweetheart in France, and the last two proud hostages – all gone in an instant. The lieutenant's sweetheart would wait for him in vain. Those annoyingly ever-present tears pricked at her eyes.

The girl finished buttoning the robe. "There. That is much better. Mr. Darcy wishes to speak to you before you bathe. May I send him in?"

Elizabeth's heart skipped a beat. "Yes, do let him in."

Her husband was coming to see her, and she was wearing nothing but a dressing gown with her hair loose about her shoulders. And still smelling of the Thames. How unromantic!

Then Darcy came in with all the assurance of a man entering his own bedroom. He stopped short when he saw her, his eyes darkening and a flush rising in his cheeks. "Elizabeth." He sounded half-strangled.

Suddenly worried, she asked, "Is something the matter?"

"No. Not at all." He shook his head as though to clear it. "The maid must not have realized that we have not yet..."

Her spirits lifted. "Not yet lived under the same roof as husband and wife?" she asked blandly.

The corners of his lips twitched. "Something like that." His voice was husky.

She touched the tip of her tongue to her dry lips. "I understand you carried me here last night. I apologize for falling asleep during the discussion."

He shifted his feet. "After the day you had, I am astonished you lasted that long."

Unable to resist the longing building inside her, she took a step towards him. "This is your bedroom, I assume?"

"Our bedroom," he corrected. "I slept in the dressing room last night, or what little of the night was left once I came upstairs."

"We could have shared the bed."

"Elizabeth," he growled, reaching out a hand and running a lock of her hair through his fingers. "You had been nearly killed, half drowned, half frozen, and altogether exhausted. I wanted you to rest. And I did not trust myself to keep that resolution if you were within arm's reach. I am only human."

Heat pooled in her belly and spread downwards. "I see."

Darcy cursed under his breath. "One of Wellington's men was supposed to take me to Carlton House half an hour ago, but I could not bear to leave until I had spoken to you, not after nearly losing you yesterday. He is still pacing the floor downstairs, and I fear if I even touch you, he will still be waiting an hour from now."

Now her mouth was so dry it was hard to form words. "Why are you going to Carlton House?"

His lips twisted. "I am to meet with Desmarais and Wellington's man to determine how best to manage our many French prisoners. It is a rather urgent question, since some of our people have decided to take justice into their own hands."

"That sounds important." And she did desperately need a bath. She placed her palms on his chest, causing him to suck in a deep breath. "I will give you just one kiss, and after that, we must wait until tonight." She tipped her head back and brushed her lips against his.

How could such a slight touch bring pleasure through her whole body?

He covered her hands with his. "Tonight, then. You have more self-control than I do."

"And I have a bath waiting which will finally allow me to remove the last of the river stench. That cannot happen soon enough."

Darcy groaned as though in pain. "Now I truly must leave, or I never will."

She cocked her head to one side. "Did I say something I should not have?"

"Bath. You. In the same sentence. Have mercy on me, I pray you."

Her cheeks burned. "Tonight, Theophilus Thistle," she said firmly, pointing towards the door.

"Tonight, proud Titania," he whispered.

The lower floors of Darcy House reminded Elizabeth of a busy market day, with people coming and going in all directions and a buzz of conversation everywhere. The dining room was filled with a jumble of what must be soldiers, given the amount of weaponry they carried. In the breakfast room, three uniformed officers argued over a map spread on the table. Servants and messengers bustled through the hall. The change from Darcy House's normal placidity was shocking.

In the drawing room, Georgiana practiced her music in solitary splendor.

"Elizabeth!" the girl squealed, jumping to her feet and running to hug her. "I still cannot believe you are truly here. I wanted to see you when I awoke, but William would not let me. He said you needed to rest, but I could not understand how you could possibly sleep through all this din."

"I do not think cannon fire over my bed could have awakened me. But I do feel as if I have come back to a completely different house." Elizabeth gestured around her.

"It is very strange, is it not? And odd – there are so many people, and none of them will talk to me beyond 'Yes, Your Majesty' or 'No, Your Majesty.'"

"Perhaps they are all too busy talking to one another," said Elizabeth tactfully.

"They are certainly doing that! My aunt – except she is no longer my aunt, is she? – Lady Matlock, Lady Frederica, and General Wellington are deciding the future of the country, which French laws still apply, and whether Parliamentary boroughs should be changed. I wanted to take part, but Lady Matlock said my presence was making Wellington nervous. The breakfast room is military headquarters, but that is only temporary. Mr. Cartwright is arranging to put them in his house and re-billeting the soldiers in other houses."

"It sounds as if Mr. Cartwright has been very busy."

Georgiana giggled. "Lady Matlock says he is the majordomo of the Brook Street Palace, but he starts to stutter whenever I speak to him."

"The Brook Street Palace?" Elizabeth could not help laughing.

"General Wellington called it that in jest, but somehow the name has stuck. Lady Matlock wanted us to remain at Carlton House now that I have declared myself, but Wellington said I had to return here until he could install me at Hampton Court. Anything less would draw attention to the fact that Jérôme Bonaparte is still there and I am not. But I was just as glad to come back here anyway, although it is not much like home anymore." She sounded wistful.

"It does seem strange."

Georgiana bounced up and down on her toes. "But now that you are ready, shall we go outside? I would like to thank the neighbors who helped us last night."

Elizabeth suppressed a smile. "A very kind thought, but I believe it would be more proper for them to come to you now." Lady Matlock must have failed to include lessons in royal protocol in Georgiana's instruction in ladylike behavior.

"Nonsense. That is what my father or grandfather would have done, but I have no intention of being that sort of queen. The people need to see I am alive and that I care about them." She grabbed Elizabeth's hand and tugged her towards the door.

"You must at least have a guard!" Elizabeth protested.

"Oh, very well. Kit is out in the street anyway, and it is his job to guard me."

No doubt that explained the sudden desire to go outside.

As the girl tied on her bonnet, she said, "Oh, I invited your aunt and uncle to call if they wished. William was sending them a message saying that you were alive, so I asked him to add that. They may be too busy, of course."

Elizabeth laughed. "You do realize that an invitation from the queen is the equivalent of a command, do you not?"

Georgiana's fingers stilled on the laces. "Oh, dear. I had not thought of that. I hope it will not be too inconvenient for them. I just thought they would want to see you."

Taking pity on the girl, Elizabeth said, "I shall be extremely glad to see them in any case, so I thank you for inviting them." But she would have to remember that Georgiana's uncertainty had not disappeared.

"Oh, good. What is your uncle's Christian name?"

"Edward. Why do you ask?"

"No reason. I was just curious."

The butler bowed so deeply as he opened the door that Elizabeth feared for his balance, but she was glad to get outside. The buzz of conversation and footfalls in the house was making her head ache.

The bright sun made her blink, and she tugged down her bonnet brim to shade her eyes better. The street was busy with small huddles of men and women conversing, some with faces she vaguely recognized. A makeshift barricade of loose bricks and stones stood at each end of the block, leaving a narrow pathway where people and carts could enter and leave. A rifle-toting guard blocking one opening shifted aside to allow a laborer with a large parcel through.

Elizabeth trailed Georgiana to the pavement where Kit was drilling a dozen footmen in new, slightly mismatched tabards. No one seemed to be paying attention to the two of them until Georgiana touched Kit's arm.

When Kit turned to see who it was, he started to smile. Then, apparently remembering himself, he signaled to his troops and gracefully shifted into a full court bow. In ragged unison, the troop of footmen fell to one knee. Like ripples in a pond, the people nearest them bowed and sank into curtsies, followed by those beyond them, until Georgiana was surrounded by a frozen tableau.

Elizabeth wondered frantically if she should join the obeisance. What was the protocol for a person accompanying the queen from one room to the next? She had never given the matter the slightest thought. She would have to ask Lady Matlock.

"As you were, I pray you," Georgiana said clearly. "I am glad to see so many of you here. I wish to thank each of you who has provided assistance and support to Darcy House, and therefore to me, during this time of great change."

The tableau broke apart as people straightened, but all eyes remained on Georgiana. The girl had forgotten to use the royal 'we,' but from the elated expressions of those nearest them, her subjects might have been equally delighted if she had recited nursery rhymes.

Georgiana spoke softly to Kit, and he ordered two footmen to stand directly behind her as he escorted her from one group of people to another. Elizabeth watched as she said a few words to each person. Whatever other fears Georgiana might have, she was by nature perfectly suited to this task. Elizabeth was happy to hold back and watch. Her morning hot chocolate had not settled well in her stomach. She had not felt ill in the morning for at least a fortnight and had hoped that indisposition was past, but apparently not.

Still, when a pair of familiar faces appeared by the barricade, Elizabeth forgot her discomfort and hurried forward. Tears of happiness filled her eyes as she waited impatiently for the guard to admit Mr. and Mrs. Gardiner.

As much as she loved her uncle, Elizabeth had missed the motherly care of her aunt. As she embraced Mrs. Gardiner, both of their cheeks were wet, and even Mr. Gardiner's eyes were shiny.

"Oh, Lizzy," cried Mrs. Gardiner. "This is a day of wonders indeed! Is this where you have been all this time? How I have fretted over you!"

"Here or aboard the *Neptune*. Has my uncle told you everything?"

"Indeed I have," said Mr. Gardiner heartily. "Mr. Darcy's note this morning likely preserved my life. Your aunt was not pleased with me for keeping so many secrets!"

Then Georgiana came up beside her, looking more like a young lady than the queen. Mr. Gardiner, recognizing her, made his bow, and Mrs. Gardiner followed suit a bit belatedly, her cheeks flushed a delicate pink.

Georgiana said, "Mr. Gardiner, we thank you for coming so promptly."

"It is my very great honor, Your Majesty. May I have the further honor of presenting my wife?"

"Mrs. Gardiner, it is a pleasure. Elizabeth has told me so much about you." Turning to Kit, Georgiana added in a voice intended to carry, "When I was fleeing for my life, Mr. Gardiner risked his own to bring me to safety and to help me find Mr. Darcy again."

Kit's look of confusion was understandable, since he already knew this quite well, but he dutifully replied, "Mr. Gardiner, all England owes you a debt of gratitude."

Georgiana's eyes danced. "Major Darcy, your sword, if you please."

"I beg your pardon?" asked Kit blankly.

She held out her hand. "Your sword." It was definitely a command.

Furrowing his forehead, Kit drew his sword and held the hilt out to her.

The sword point dipped as she adjusted to the unexpected weight of it. "Mr. Gardiner, if you would be so kind as to kneel," she said crisply.

Elizabeth's eyes widened. Surely she was not planning to... Just then her stomach churned again. Light-headed, she caught at her aunt's elbow to keep her balance.

Stunned, her uncle obeyed, bowing his head. The spell-bound crowd pressed closer.

Georgiana used both hands to steady the sword as she tapped first one shoulder, then the other, and back again to the first. "For extraordinary services to the crown, you will henceforth be known as Sir Edward Gardiner. You may rise, Sir Edward."

A murmur of approbation rose around them.

Her uncle's voice was unsteady. "I thank Your Majesty. I do not deserve the honor, since I did no more than my duty, but I will always do my utmost to serve you."

Sweat broke out on Elizabeth's brow as her queasiness plummeted to full-blown nausea. Somehow she kept a smile pinned to her face for her uncle's sake.

Georgiana was speaking again to Mrs. Gardiner – no, her aunt would be Lady Gardiner now. In an oddly detached manner, Elizabeth wondered how her mother would receive this astonishing news. She had complained bitterly for weeks after Sir William Lucas was knighted.

Her mother. Lydia. What would happen to her youngest sister now that her so-called husband was most likely a prisoner?

366

A sudden, powerful cramp made her clutch her mid-section. "Kit," she said through clenched teeth. "Help me back to the house, I pray you."

His brows drew together as he offered her his arm. "What is the matter?"

"Ill." It was all she could force out. She managed to totter along for what seemed to be an enormous distance while stabbing pain clenched her stomach. If only the cramping would ease! Finally her feet decided of their own accord to stop moving.

Kit peered down at her. "Can you walk?"

When Elizabeth shook her head miserably, he picked her up and carried her inside.

Darcy hurried up the steps into Darcy House, excited as a schoolboy to see Elizabeth again. His happiness was such that he was not even troubled by the various strangers who seemed to have encamped in his house.

But where was his family? The sitting room was empty, and it was too early for dinner. At last he found his aunt in the study examining a sheaf of paper, her detested spectacles unable to hide the lines of fatigue in her face.

"Oh, it is you." His aunt did not even make an attempt to hide her spectacles, a sure sign of exhaustion. "Did you and General Desmarais reach any conclusions?"

"A few, but I would like to see Elizabeth first. Where is she?" He had not meant to be so abrupt, but he could not stand another moment's delay before he held her in his arms.

"In bed. She is ill."

Darcy recoiled. "Ill? What is the matter?"

"What do you expect after she took a dunking in that cesspool we call the Thames? Truly, it was not a question of whether she would fall ill, but when."

Fear coiled inside him. "Has the doctor been called?"

"Been and gone. He says she should be fine, but she will be in discomfort for the next day or two." His aunt removed her spectacles and added pointedly, "He also says it should have no impact on her condition."

"Her condition? What does that mean?"

"It means, if I am not mistaken, that Elizabeth is increasing," said Lady Matlock dryly. "The doctor seemed to believe I was already aware of this. I see it is a surprise to you as well."

A surprise? It was more like being having a bucket of cold water dumped over his head. Could it be true? "Pray excuse me. I wish to see my wife."

He bolted from the room and took the stairs two at a time. When he reached his room, Darcy strode directly to the bed where Elizabeth lay. An enameled basin sat beside her on the counterpane. Her pallor was a shocking change after her morning blushes.

Her lips formed a weak smile. "William," she said softly.

He perched on the edge of the bed and took her hand in his. "My poor love. I am so sorry."

"As am I," she said with a mere shadow of her usual teasing. "The doctor says it is my own fault. I should not have gone swimming in the Thames. He was not amused when I asked if I should have drowned instead."

"I am very glad you chose to swim."

Her eyes grew unfocused. "John Lucas must have been smiling as he looked down from heaven. He taught me to swim one summer, along with his sister Charlotte. He saved my life."

For that, Darcy would even forgive the late John Lucas for retaining a spot in Elizabeth's heart.

He stroked a damp curl away from her forehead. Should he wait before asking her? No, he could not bear it. Hesitantly he said, "Is there... is it true that you are..."

Her eyes shone up at him. "Did General Desmarais let it slip? I had hoped to tell you myself."

"No. The doctor said something about it. But Desmarais knows, too?"

She started to nod and then put her hand to her head. "Yes. I asked him for help, and he was very kind to me. He was going to find a way for me to stay with our baby, but that does not matter now. In any case, I hope you do not mind."

"About the baby? Far from it. Nothing could make me happier."

She closed her eyes. "Good."

His heart went out to her. "My poor love. Is there anything I can bring you for your present relief?"

"My aunt has been taking excellent care of me." She made a weak gesture towards the window, her voice little more than a whisper now. "She had the misfortune to call precisely when I took ill."

Darcy looked up to discover Mr. Gardiner and his wife sitting by the window. At least he assumed it was Mrs. Gardiner. Their introduction at Bingley's wedding had been so brief he could not recall her face. Mr. Gardiner was peering at a heavy tome while Mrs. Gardiner sorted through a stack of papers.

Mrs. Gardiner said, "Mr. Darcy, it is a pleasure to see you again. Our arrival here was eventful to say the least, but I am happy to be of assistance to Elizabeth."

Darcy glanced at the piles of paper. "It appears that is not the only assistance you are giving. Was it Lady Matlock or Lady Frederica who conscripted you?"

"Both, actually, with the assistance of Her Majesty," said Mr. Gardiner dryly. "I had not realized how dangerous it was to make an appearance here."

Elizabeth turned her head to the side. "You should tell him what happened. I am too tired."

"And I still can hardly believe it!" said Mrs. Gardiner with a touch of amusement. "They called my husband in and quizzed him about his business, what countries he trades with and how he expected that to change now that we are Napoleon's enemy again."

Mr. Gardiner chuckled. "I could only think they suspected me of some malfeasance, but that made no sense when your sister – pardon me, the queen – had just honored me far beyond my merit. Then her ladyship asked if I was still willing to serve my country, and when I said I would be happy to do so, she told me I was the acting Minister of Trade." He shook his head with the memory of it. "I told her I was unqualified, and she said I was more qualified than she was. That, and a proven history of loyalty to the queen, seemed to be all that was required."

Mrs. Gardiner pointed to the heavy book. "Hence the necessity of refreshing his memory about Napoleon's Continental System and the embargo."

"I must say, Mr. Darcy, that your aunt is an altogether extraordinary woman," added Mr. Gardiner.

"She is indeed," Darcy said.

Elizabeth plucked at his sleeve. "There is one thing you could do for me." The lines of pain on her face broke his heart.

"Anything. Anything at all."

"Write to my family. Tell them what has happened." She closed her eyes again.

"Of course. I will do it tonight." He caressed her hand. If only he could take away her pain!

"Thank you. Now... go."

Mrs. Gardiner hurried to the bedside and laid a cool cloth on Elizabeth's forehead. "Edward, you should leave, too. I will tell you both when she is well enough to see you again."

"But..." protested Darcy.

Mrs. Gardiner waved him away. "You need not worry. These episodes are unpleasant, and I doubt Elizabeth wants witnesses. Quickly, now."

When they left the room, Mr. Gardiner shook his head bemusedly. "Do you ever have an odd feeling that this must be a dream and tomorrow you will wake up and discover it is gone?"

"Frequently," said Darcy quietly. But Elizabeth was here with him, and she was carrying his child.

The sound of retching behind the door made him wince in sympathy.

Chapter
Twenty-Two

A beaming Sir William Lucas strode into the sitting room of Longbourn, waving a newspaper at the inhabitants. "Your Lizzy! Your Lizzy is a heroine!

Mr. Bennet clutched both hands to his temples. "Softly, my friend! I indulged in too many toasts to the Queen's health last night."

"Then you have not yet heard!" Sir William thrust the newspaper into Mr. Bennet's hand and pointed to the middle of one column. "There! Start there."

Mr. Bennet felt in his pocket for his spectacles. Finding none, he held the newspaper a few inches from his eyes. "Good God!"

Sir William chuckled. "Keep reading, keep reading."

Mrs. Bennet touched a lacy handkerchief to her eyes. Fretfully she said, "I am sure I am as happy as anyone else about Queen Charlotte, but oh, my nerves! With the French gone, Longbourn will be entailed away again, and I will be left to live in the hedgerows after Mr. Bennet's death. And what shall become of poor Lydia now that her husband was taken away?"

"Good God!" Mr. Bennet looked up at Sir William. "Can this possibly be true?"

"You have read it yourself!"

Mrs. Bennet moaned, "What is it? My nerves, oh, my nerves!"

Mr. Bennet gave her the newspaper. "Read it for yourself. I cannot credit it."

With an air of being much put upon, Mrs. Bennet took it. Her lips moved as she read. "Oh, that girl! Always finding a way to be in the middle of trouble! Why could she not stay here as her sisters did? The shame of her name appearing in a newspaper! My poor nerves!" But she continued to read it.

Sir William looked shocked. "My dear lady, your daughter is a heroine! You should be proud of her."

"Oh! Oh!" cried Mrs. Bennet, fanning herself. "Look at this! She is married to Mr. Darcy! That clever girl! Just think of it! Mrs. Darcy – how well it sounds. And such pin money she shall have! Oh, I must tell my sister Phillips at once!" She hurried from the room.

Mr. Bennet retrieved the newspaper she had dropped. "Well," he said dryly, "I hope Lizzy's success in capturing Mr. Darcy will help my dear wife to forgive her for her impudence in rescuing Princess Charlotte."

Kitty jumped to her feet. "*Lizzy* rescued Princess Charlotte? Then this is all her fault!"

Mr. Bennet winked at Sir William. "No more handsome officers with charming accents, you see."

"Do not fret, Miss Kitty," said Sir William. "Having a sister who is the particular friend of the queen may bring you better suitors than common French soldiers. And just think, our Lizzy is with the queen herself!"

Darcy kissed Elizabeth's forehead. "You have a special visitor, my love. May I bring her in?"

"As long as she will not be shocked to find me in bed." Elizabeth sounded more like her usual lively self now. "Who is it?"

As he held the door open, her sister Jane peeked into the room.

"Jane!" Elizabeth pushed back the counterpane and stood up, holding out her arms. Her head spun, and she clutched the bedpost.

Moving quickly, Darcy caught her other elbow and eased her back to sit on the bed. "You can greet your sister from there," he said sternly.

"Spoilsport," she teased, but then her arms were around her sister. "Jane, dearest Jane! Thank you, thank you for calling. I have missed you so much!"

"Oh, Lizzy." A tear ran down Jane's cheek. "But what is the matter? You are ill?"

"Recovering from the aftereffects of my dunking in the Thames. Today is the first time I do not feel ill, only weak as a baby. And speaking of babies, am I to be an aunt soon?" She glanced significantly at Jane's swollen abdomen.

A pink flush rose in Jane's cheeks. "Yes, but that is old news."

"Not to me! Is Mr. Bingley here?"

A shadow crossed Jane's expression. "He is waiting for me beyond the barricade. He thought it was better that way."

"Better? How?" Elizabeth sent a questioning glance at Darcy.

A line appeared between his brows. "Perhaps I should speak to him and invite him in."

"Would you?" Jane's words sounded like a plea.

"Of course." Darcy bowed and left.

"Is something the matter?" asked Elizabeth.

Jane glanced back over her shoulder. "They quarreled, but I do not know what it was about. My dear Bingley has taken it very hard. But you – you must tell me everything that has happened. I simply could not believe it when Bingley showed me the newspaper! I had tried so often to imagine what could have been so urgent as to make you leave without a word, but in my wildest imaginings, I never came close to this."

"I do not think anything less would have sufficed. I will never forget the moment when Mr. Darcy told me the truth."

"To think that she visited me so often in the stables! Had I known who she was, I could never have kept my countenance. How do you do it? What do you say to her?"

With a rueful smile, Elizabeth said, "Very much the kind of thing I always said to her. At first I could not forget for a moment who she was, but as I saw what a struggle everything was for her and helped her through her fits of nerves, she began to seem more like a difficult younger sister whom I needed to manage. It feels so odd now when I see everyone bowing and behaving as if she is on a higher plane of existence than we mortals are."

"Fits of nerves? The queen?" Jane sounded horrified.

"Do you not recall how easily frightened she was? She is an odd mixture of parts, half willful, half terrified, as anyone would be faced with the constant fear of discovery all these years."

"Still, to think you have been with the queen all this time! I want you to tell me everything that happened. All I know from the newspapers is that you slept in a hayloft, were arrested, and imprisoned on the *Neptune*."

Elizabeth settled back against the pillows. "I hardly know where to begin. Mr. Darcy told me the truth just minutes before he was arrested..."

Darcy set a glass of brandy on the small table beside Bingley. He would have handed it to his friend if Bingley had not been so openly avoiding his gaze. Bingley had not looked him in the face since Darcy had found him outside the barricade and invited him inside. It had taken four invitations since Bingley refused the first three.

Bingley might never forgive him for his harsh words, but for Elizabeth's sake, Darcy would do his best to heal the breach. "Did you receive my letter when Elizabeth's sentence was commuted?"

"Yes. But you need not pretend to any warmth towards me. I do not expect it, nor do I deserve it. If you want to tell Jane what I did, go ahead. Elizabeth is bound to mention it sooner or later in any case."

Darcy shook his head. "Elizabeth does not know you played any role in her arrest, and I see no reason to change that. But if she did, she would understand your desire to protect her sister."

Bingley tugged at his cravat as if he found it difficult to breathe. "You would not have done what I did."

"How can you say that when the fault was mine for becoming careless enough that you could guess what I was about? If I had not been so indiscreet, you would not have known anything to tell them about Elizabeth's whereabouts. Any blame should rest on my shoulders, not yours."

Bingley turned his face away. "You would not have told the French anything. Nor, I imagine, did Elizabeth give the French any information when she was arrested."

"In fact, she confessed to a great many crimes, some of which had never occurred. I learned later that some of the Loyalists, including my own brother, carried arsenic at all times in case they were arrested. They were aware the French could make them talk. Anyone is susceptible to the right pressure."

Bingley spun on his heel and crashed his fist against the window frame. "Do you not understand? I have to live with the knowledge that I betrayed her, and even if she is alive and free now, I imagine there were others arrested with her who were not so fortunate. Their deaths will always be on my conscience. Until two days ago, I thought nothing could possibly make me feel worse than I already did, then I learned Georgiana's true identity. Our queen could have died because of my cowardice, and her blood would be on my hands. Do not try to make me feel better. I do not deserve it." He seemed to choke over his words. "I do not deserve my wife's love."

Darcy had never seen his friend like this. "Stop it, Bingley! You are blaming yourself for things that never occurred. Only your wife can determine whether you deserve her, and I would guess she does think so."

Bingley's eyes flicked around the room wildly. "Not if she knew what I had done."

Darcy took a deep breath and made his own confession. "Everything that has happened to Elizabeth, every sorrow she has felt from leaving her family to being sentenced to hang, is my fault. If I had never involved myself with her, none of it would have occurred. I knew the risk. At that first dance, I knew my attentions to Elizabeth could put Georgiana at risk, and I did it anyway. And Elizabeth has forgiven me. That is why I know Jane would forgive you."

Bingley clenched his hands into fists. "Shall we see? Where are they?"

Darcy hoped this was not a terrible mistake. "Upstairs. I will take you."

Bingley followed him to the room where Elizabeth now reclined in bed, still pale but sipping some wine, with her sister sitting beside her.

"Mr. Bingley!" Elizabeth exclaimed as they entered. "How kind of you to join us."

Bingley said abruptly, "There is something I must tell you. Both of you. It was my fault you were arrested. It happened when French soldiers came to Netherfield to ask Jane if she knew your whereabouts. When she denied knowing anything, they were going to arrest her and put her to the question. I made a deal with them. In exchange for them leaving Jane alone, I told them Darcy knew how to find you. Your arrest, your imprisonment, the death of your friends – it is all my fault."

There was a moment of stunned silence, then Elizabeth gave a gurgle of laughter. "Not another one!"

Bingley stared at her. "What do you mean?"

"You and Darcy are just alike. He is always telling me everything is his fault. It was his fault I had to leave my family. His fault I was all alone. His fault my reputation was ruined. His fault I was held hostage. No doubt he also thinks it was his fault that Napoleon invaded us, and I am certain he would blame himself for the French Revolution, were it not for the fact that he was only six years of age at the time!"

Darcy had never loved Elizabeth more than at that moment. "I was a very precocious six-year-old."

"You see, Mr. Bingley? Everything that happened to me was because in 1805 Napoleon tricked our fleet into haring off on a wild goose chase to the West Indies, leaving the Channel unprotected so he could invade us. Unless you caused that event, I am afraid it is not your fault. Your most important task was to protect Jane, and you did that."

But Jane Bingley's lower lip was trembling. "Is this why you have been so distant and unhappy all this time? Is it, Charles?"

Bingley nodded. "I have hated myself, and I knew you would hate me, too."

Jane stood and advanced on him like an avenging angel. "I have been miserable these last two months. I thought you must have met another woman and regretted marrying me."

Bingley gaped at her. "Of course not! Marrying you was the best thing I ever did. I have not even looked at another woman since I met you."

His wife's lips thinned. "Then you should have told me what happened!"

Darcy elbowed Bingley. "I believe the correct response is that you were an idiot and you will try to do better next time."

Bingley looked from Jane to Darcy and then back again. "I am an idiot, and I do not deserve you. But I love you more than anything."

Just then a flaxen-haired whirlwind blew through the door. "Jane!" exclaimed Georgiana in delight. "I just heard you were here. Mr. Bingley, it is a pleasure to see you."

Jane froze, her mouth open to respond, and dropped into a low curtsy. Bingley's bow was uncharacteristically awkward.

"Oh, do stop it!" the girl exclaimed. "When we are in private, I pray you to dispense with all that nonsense."

Jane's smile looked forced. Bingley's fingers were moving nervously.

Georgiana linked her arm in Jane's. "Come, Jane, I wish to hear everything you have done since I last saw you in the stables. We can pretend we are back there and drinking that horrid tea, but we do have better tea this time."

Jane shot a terrified glance at her sister.

Elizabeth said, "As you see, Georgiana has changed greatly from the nervous girl you first met."

Georgiana's animation fled. "Did I say something wrong?"

Elizabeth smiled. "Not at all, dearest. You are simply more exuberant than you used to be. It is a good thing, though perhaps a bit surprising to someone who has not seen you in some time."

"Oh. I suppose so." But Georgiana looked doubtful.

"And, of course, Georgiana has also been deprived of companionship these last few days, with Lady Matlock single-handedly resurrecting the government and Mr. Darcy's younger brother attempting to create a royal guard from mismatched footmen. Naturally she is delighted to have a visitor."

Georgiana's expression brightened. "Oh, yes, I must introduce you to Kit. He is very busy, as Elizabeth says, but one good thing about being queen is that he cannot be angry if I interrupt him."

"Too true," said Elizabeth. "But despite all these royal pleasures, I think you are also missing being plain Georgiana Darcy."

The girl wrinkled her nose. "Is that horrid of me?"

"Not at all," said Elizabeth. "It is very understandable, and you will be a better queen for having an understanding of what it is like not to be treated as royalty. I only mention it so that Jane may understand she is having tea with plain Georgiana Darcy, not Her Majesty Queen Charlotte Augusta."

"Oh, yes, if you please!" said Georgiana. "No one ever says anything interesting to the queen."

Jane said valiantly, "I will be happy to visit with my old friend Georgiana. Lizzy, shall I return for a few minutes before I leave?"

"I would like that very much." But the circles under Elizabeth's eyes looked more pronounced now. Finding the energy for visitors had clearly cost her something.

Jane cast one last panicked look back at her as she left with Georgiana.

Darcy took the chair Jane had vacated and gestured Bingley to the other.

"I do not know how you manage it!" exclaimed Bingley. "Talking to her that way, I mean. I could not possibly tease her now that I know who she is. I still cannot believe that Princess Charlotte herself lived under my roof all that time! Or how you managed to hide it for so long."

Darcy relaxed a little. "I hope you are not angry with me for keeping it secret."

Bingley shook his head vigorously. "Not in the slightest! I never want to know another secret. It is too dangerous. But no one in Meryton believes me when I say I did not know." He sounded aggrieved.

Darcy chuckled. "Poor Bingley! I will try to make it clear that I never took you into my confidence – or anyone else, for that matter."

"Please do! The main reason we came to London was to see Lizzy, of course, but we decamped from Netherfield in haste to escape all the neighbors who converged on us, wanting to be told every word Georgiana ever said. I would not be surprised if they have turned Netherfield into a shrine by the time we return. If only you could have seen them! Surreptitiously touching the furniture or the door handle she might have touched! One day of it was all I could tolerate."

Elizabeth had leaned back against the pillows and now said dreamily, "I can imagine. I have seen how differently people view me now, as if I were some sort of special being because of my connection to her. But I

380

have been so many different people in the last few months that I have almost forgotten who Elizabeth Bennet was."

Darcy said warmly, "Elizabeth Bennet is Mrs. Darcy."

Elizabeth smiled. "I certainly am. Mr. Bingley, would you be offended if I close my eyes as you talk? My strength is not what it should be."

"Perhaps I should leave you to rest," said Bingley.

She shook her head. "Not yet, I pray you. I would very much like to hear news of my family. Jane did not seem to wish to speak of them."

"Oh." Bingley suddenly appeared not to know what to do with his hands. "They are all well. Lydia is back at home now. She returned to Longbourn when her husband and the garrison were captured, but Mary elected to remain with her husband in captivity."

Seeing the question in Elizabeth's expression, Darcy asked, "Did she marry Captain Bessette then?"

"A month ago. It surprised everyone when he began to court her, but she seemed very happy. I do not know what will happen to her now. Women who married French soldiers are not being treated kindly."

Darcy leaned back in his chair. "Hopefully that will change soon. It is not yet announced, but French soldiers who married English women will be given the option of swearing loyalty to the queen and remaining here instead of returning to France when the exchange of prisoners for the Englishmen conscripted by the French is arranged."

"Not Lydia's husband," Bingley said with certainty. "He will return to his other wife in France, or I miss my guess. Mary's husband, though, might choose to remain. He is a decent fellow."

"Indeed he is," said Darcy. "Captain Bessette will soon be taken to London to assist General Desmarais in his new task – convincing our French prisoners to cooperate with their captors. They are more likely to listen to their own officers, but there are few French officers whom we can trust to be honest and keep their word, and he is one of them. We hope to make the soldiers work on rebuilding some of what they have destroyed while we wait for Napoleon to reclaim them."

Bingley wrinkled his brow. "It is a good plan, to be sure, but I am surprised the French are still willing to work with you, Darcy."

Darcy kept his face expressionless. "Many of them are angry at me, of course. Some prefer to direct their anger against Wellington and the Englishmen who actually fought them. General Desmarais has known me for years and understands why I made the choices I did." It had not actually been that simple, but Darcy doubted Bingley was prepared for the full explanation. Desmarais had not rejected him outright, but there were painful tensions between them. Colonel Hulot, who had attended many dinner parties with Darcy at Carlton House, refused to speak to him now. Darcy might be a hero to the Loyalists who had despised him, but it had come at a price.

"I thank you for the news of my sisters, but something is not right at Longbourn. Is it Kitty or my parents?" Elizabeth sounded weary.

Bingley glanced helplessly at Darcy, who nodded his permission. "It is nothing serious. Just that your parents have not responded to the news of your adventures as one might have hoped."

Elizabeth did not look surprised. "How so?"

"Your mother was upset at first, especially with the loss of Lydia's husband, but she has forgiven you everything since learning you had married Darcy. As for your father, he is..." Bingley hesitated, as if searching for a kind way to break the news.

Elizabeth said flatly, "He is angry and speaks cuttingly to anyone who dares to disturb him."

"Well, yes. And since your family has also been deluged with callers, he is being disturbed quite often."

Darcy took Elizabeth's hand and spoke softly. "I am sorry, my love."

"It is what I expected," said Elizabeth. "No one likes being left out of a secret of this magnitude, and not everyone takes it as gracefully as Mr. Bingley has. I suspect my father feels I treated him badly and robbed him of his chance to be a hero, while at the same time glad that he did not have to bestir himself to help."

Bingley sat up straighter. "Actually, his grievances are mostly with Darcy. Sorry, old fellow! His constant complaint is that Darcy took more care in asking him for a puppy than for his daughter."

"I would have been pleased to ask his blessing. As it was, I could only do the next best thing and ask Mr. Gardiner. I will write to Mr. Bennet with abject apologies for my presumption and tell him only my duty to the queen could override my desire to ask his permission," said Darcy with distaste. "I had planned to speak to him anyway to extend an invitation. I have made arrangements for us to have a proper English wedding in four days – assuming you are well enough, my love. Bingley, I hope you and Jane will be able to attend."

Elizabeth opened her eyes. "You were able to get a license?"

"Unfortunately not. No one at Doctors' Common has the authority to issue them yet, so until they do, clergymen are being directed to honor the French paperwork."

"But the paperwork for our French ceremony has my name as Elizabeth Gardiner. Correcting that was the whole purpose of the second ceremony."

Darcy smiled. "It turns out our paperwork was all in order after all. I called on my very good friend the Lord Mayor and explained our dilemma. He miraculously found the document we both signed before the wedding stating that Elizabeth Gardiner had been christened Elizabeth Bennet."

Elizabeth's brows drew together. "But there was no such document."

"There is now, though your signature has faded completely away, and you will have to sign it again. He is going to help Frederica and Wellington, too, since they also married under false names." Darcy shook his head, still astonished at the match. Wellington might be fifteen years older than Frederica, but he clearly made her happy again. She deserved that after all these years. Of course, Richard had claimed it was her only chance to marry a man who was as fascinated by the location of arms depots and troop movements as she was.

Elizabeth nodded. "Molly always said her husband was a kind man. Dare I hope she is in better health than I am?"

"Yes, I saw her briefly. When I told her of your illness, she said that, having spent her early years on the docks, she has already experienced all the illnesses the Thames had in store. But she insists you must rewrite the story of Princess Rosebud."

"Princess Rosalinda," said Elizabeth with a weary smile. "I think everyone must already know how that one ends."

Charlotte Lucas affixed the Darcy sapphires around Elizabeth's neck and stood back to examine her handiwork. "There. All ready for your wedding. I am so glad I arrived in time to assist you."

Elizabeth admired her reflection. "Far better than my first wedding. That did not include sapphires or even a pretty dress."

From the doorway, Darcy said, "You looked beautiful beyond my dreams anyway."

"Mr. Darcy!" cried Charlotte. "You are not to see the bride before the wedding!"

"But we are already married, are we not?" retorted Darcy. "My love, have you asked her yet? Georgiana is impatient for her answer."

Charlotte turned a suspicious look on Elizabeth.

Elizabeth shook her head. "Not yet. Do I have time to do it before we must leave?"

Darcy consulted his watch. "We have a quarter hour yet."

Elizabeth took her friend's hand. "Very well. This may come as a shock, Charlotte, but Georgiana wishes to offer you a position as lady-in-waiting. She thought you might be more likely to accept if I asked you."

Charlotte paled. "Me? But she barely knows me, and I am no one!"

"You may have only met her for a short time when you both visited Jane at the stables, but you are one of the very few people who knew her first as Georgiana Darcy. That is of more importance than you might imagine. Now everyone who meets her sees only the queen and what she might do for them, not the girl who has been through a difficult and painful few years. She needs people around her who can recognize that side of her. I hope you will accept because I wish to see more of you, and, quite frankly, having another sensible person to share her care would be a tremendous relief."

Charlotte narrowed her eyes. "Are you teasing me, Lizzy?"

"I am quite serious, and so is Georgiana – I mean Her Majesty. But I will understand if you do not wish to leave your family and Meryton behind."

Charlotte hesitated, then a determined look filled her eyes. "If the queen wishes it, I would be honored to accept."

Elizabeth hugged her. "I am so glad!"

Epilogue

"Not again!" Kit slumped down in his chair.

Elizabeth gazed at him sympathetically. "You might as well give in with good grace. We have done everything we can. Every newspaper tells us that Major Christopher Darcy is now Christopher, Duke of Sussex and soon to be Prince Christopher. We have encouraged clergymen to pray from the pulpit for Christopher Darcy. We have even sent out servants to pubs to buy a round of drinks in honor of the future Prince Christopher. It makes no difference. To the populace you will always be Kit Darcy."

"But Prince Kit sounds ridiculous. I am not a schoolboy," Kit protested.

Elizabeth could not quite suppress a smile. "Prince Christopher does sound more stately, and I can understand your preference for it. But England first fell in love with you as dashing Kit Darcy. Her Majesty Queen Charlotte Augusta is every inch an intimidating royal to them, but Prince Kit is the younger brother of all England. You humanize the queen. Kit, it is rather embarrassing how much people adore the very idea of you. They want to use your nickname because they love you."

Kit groaned. "They only think they love me. None of them have any idea of who I truly am. I feel like an actor playing a role all day long."

"So do we all," said Darcy. "I had thought once England was ours, I could stop pretending to be someone I was not. But no, it is even worse now because everyone thinks I am some sort of hero."

Elizabeth turned soft eyes on her husband. "You are a hero. Just not for the reasons they think."

"I think I was happier as an underground Loyalist and expecting every day to be killed by the French," grumbled Kit. "At least I had a purpose then. Now I am just a toy soldier on display."

"Kit, listen to me," said Elizabeth. "You do have a purpose. You and Georgiana, or rather Charlotte, are the glue that holds England together after the French tore us apart. You are serving your country."

"It is true," said Georgiana – the real Georgiana Darcy, late of Canada. "I came to England after the French were defeated, but there was still fighting between Englishmen. Neighbor against neighbor as they tried to reclaim their old lands and goods; the North turned against the South; Loyalists trying to dispossess those who had been forced to work with the French. The one thing they all had in common was that at the end of the day they would lift a glass together to Queen Charlotte and her Major Kit. Without a working government, England could easily have fallen into civil war, but the two of you are the symbol that held us together."

Elizabeth clapped her hands. "Well said!" She still did not know this new Georgiana well. It was challenging to suddenly have two flaxen-haired sixteen year old sisters who answered to both Georgiana and Charlotte, but apart from that, the two girls had little in common. Georgiana Darcy had not yet lost the hint of a Canadian accent, but she moved and spoke with the smooth confidence that showed years of practice at being royal. There were hints now and then that she did not always feel the confidence she portrayed – perhaps something she did have in common with the real Charlotte. Still, if the two girls were to walk together into a room of complete strangers, everyone would think Georgiana Darcy was the queen, not the excitable, playful girl William had protected all those years.

"I still say it is not fair," grumbled Kit. "We defeated the French, but Desmarais gets to live in peaceful obscurity at Pemberley tutoring local children in Latin, while we have to pretend to be something we are not. Sometimes I wonder if we truly are the winners."

Darcy said mildly, "I can assure you Desmarais was as uncomfortable with his fame as you are. He was simply more practiced at it."

"And Frederica," Kit continued. "She did much more than I did, but few people know of her except as the Duchess of Wellington."

"Freddie always did prefer to stay in the shadows," said Darcy. "But I agree with you. She has been very fortunate to be spared the fame she deserves."

Elizabeth, her hand on her swollen abdomen, said tartly, "William, you are as bad as Kit. Georgiana – the one who wears the crown, that is – has been nagging me about your title, and she swears that if you do not choose one, she will give you so many you will not be able to walk for the weight of all the chains of office."

William raised an eyebrow. "I am looking forward to the title of 'Father.'"

"I could not quite hear that," said Elizabeth pointedly. "Kit, did it sound to you as if he said Earl of Curbar and Viscount Castleton?"

Kit's eyes lit with mischief. "I could have sworn he said Marquess of Derby, too."

Elizabeth shook her head judiciously. "No, I am certain I would have heard it if he had said Marquess."

"Very well," said the royal Georgiana from the doorway. "Curbar and Castleton it shall be. You are very unkind to me, William. Giving out honors is the best part of being queen."

Kit muttered good-naturedly, "I thought it was being able to tell people what to do."

"No, silly," retorted the queen. "But I came to announce I have completed the plans for my new Order, and you will all be invested in it tomorrow after our wedding."

Elizabeth's eyebrows shot up. "All of us?"

"Yes. It is a most unique order. I have been burning to tell you for weeks. The Order of the Hayloft will be second only to the Order of the Garter, and it will be given exclusively to those people who knew my true identity while I was in hiding, regardless of their sex or rank. The four of you, Frederica, Lady Matlock, Sir Edward Gardiner, Mrs. Reynolds, and of course Mr. and Mrs. Simmons, since it was their hayloft in the first place. All of you will receive a special privilege, which is to abstain from all public acknowledgement of me as queen – no bows or curtseys, no 'Your Majesty.'"

Kit laughed. "You mean just like it is now?"

"Oh, stop it, Kit! I am serious."

"Mrs. Reynolds will never be willing to ignore your royal courtesies," teased Kit. "She is too proud of them."

"She managed it quite well for six years!"

Elizabeth pushed her bulky body up from the chair and kissed the queen's cheek. "Thank you. That is very touching. Who would have imagined that the night we spent in a hayloft would become the most beloved symbol of your reign?"

"I admit I was not so fond of it at the time," said the girl. "I was picking off bits of hay all the next day. Hay itches!"

Kit raised a glass of wine. "To the royal hayloft."

Elizabeth's eyes suddenly widened. "I may have one small problem with your plan." Her voice was tight.

The queen's brows drew together. "What is it? Do you think people will be offended that I am including women?"

"No." Elizabeth squeezed her eyes shut and then reopened them. "I do not think I will be attending your wedding tomorrow after all."

"But you must! Are you unwell?" asked the girl.

Darcy jumped to his feet. "What is the matter?"

Elizabeth placed a hand on her bulging stomach. "It appears the future Viscount of Castleton, or perhaps the future Lady Charlotte

Darcy, thinks he or she should take precedence over a royal wedding. I do not think I am in a position to argue."

Darcy paled. "But it is not supposed to be for another month!"

A smile flickered across Elizabeth's face. "You will have to take that up with your son or daughter. And I suspect you will be able to do so tomorrow."

Tomorrow was going to be a very busy day.

Historical Note

I have kept the discussion of history, both real and altered, in this book to a minimum in order to avoid interrupting the story line, but a great deal of historical research about the Napoleonic period went into this book. In addition to the fictional invasion of Great Britain, I have employed one deliberate historical inaccuracy. In 1805 Arthur Wellesley had not yet received the title of Marquis (later Duke) of Wellington, so he would have been known as General Wellesley, not General Wellington. I took the liberty of using his later title in this book because many readers would not recognize Wellesley as the same person as Wellington. I have used the term 'England' in place of 'Britain' in the story since that was the general usage at the time.

Napoleon came very close to invading Great Britain. From 1803-1805 he had an army of 200,000 men known as the *Armée d'Angleterre* trained and ready in Channel ports, along with a purpose-built flotilla including 2,000 invasion barges to carry troops. Many historians believe he would have succeeded in conquering England if he had been able to cross the Channel, and during that time the British lived in terror of the possible invasion. Napoleon's grand plan depended on gaining control of the English Channel briefly by drawing off the Royal Navy with a feint. The French and Spanish fleets were to break out from the British blockades at Brest and Toulon, sail across the Atlantic with the British navy in pursuit, and quickly return to destroy the few remaining British ships in the Channel. In reality, only the Toulon fleet managed to break the blockade and follow the plan, so half of the British navy remained in place to defend the channel.

After this failure, Napoleon turned the invasion force into the basis of his *Grande Armée* and marched them east on the Ulm Campaign. Contrary to popular beliefs, the invasion had already been called off by the time of the Battle of Trafalgar in October 1805, a victory which cemented British control over the Channel but did not prevent an invasion. For the purposes of this book, I have assumed that Napoleon's feint worked. There is a hidden irony in Nelson's self-blame for having been ill during this time; he was in fact in charge of the blockade at Toulon which the French broke, and he fell for Napoleon's trick and followed the French fleet across the Atlantic. In my altered history backstory, Admiral Collingwood's fleet failed to maintain the blockade at Brest as they did in reality, leading to the channel being left undefended.

The fictional conditions in occupied England are based on those described in French-occupied Prussia and Germany, including the very high taxes on the population in accordance with Napoleon's plan to have occupied countries pay for their own occupying forces, as well as for his wars. The story of Jérôme Bonaparte marrying George III's daughter Princess Amelia was based on the true story of his life. Napoleon created the Kingdom of Westphalia, declared his brother King, and married him to a princess of one of the constituent states to improve his claim – even though Jérôme's first wife was still alive and the pope had refused to annul his marriage. His tenure as king ended with the invasion of the Prussian and Russian armies. The use of warships with cannon pointed at cities was a tactic Napoleon used elsewhere to keep rebellion in check. Putting hostages aboard was my own invention.

The discovery that Princess Charlotte Augusta of Wales was indeed the exact age of Georgiana Darcy during the Pride & Prejudice years inspired much of the plot of this book. The real Princess Charlotte was very popular with the people and far more of an outrageous, impulsive madcap than I have portrayed her. Her love life was outrageous as well: her first infatuation at age 14 was with an illegitimate cousin who rode beside her carriage every day and would sit in private conversation with her at unseemly length. When he was called away, his place was taken by the handsome Lt. Charles Hesse. Charlotte's mother blatantly encouraged this romance, passing letters between the two and encouraging Lt. Hesse to sneak into her own rooms at Kensington Palace for illicit meetings with her daughter. She went so far as to lock Charlotte and Hesse into her own bedroom and said, "I leave you to enjoy yourselves." Charlotte was then but fifteen.

Princess Charlotte had several other tempestuous romances in her teen years and a widely publicized episode when she ran off to escape an unwanted marriage. My Charlotte's choice to deliberately induce Kit to kiss her was not only in character, but downright tame for the historical princess. The real Charlotte did not have an anxiety disorder to the best of my knowledge; I created that in order to keep 'Georgiana' calmer than Princess Charlotte ever could manage to be without completely mangling her real personality. Charlotte never became queen owing to her untimely death in childbed, the result of medical malpractice and frequent bleedings and purgatives during her pregnancy to reduce her 'spirits.' If not for that, we would have had the Age of Charlotte instead of the Victorian Age. For more details and references on Princess Charlotte, please see my blog post about her at Austen Variations. www.austenvariations.com/the-other-princess-charlotte-2/

All my French characters in England are purely fictional, including General Desmarais. Napoleon's generals had a high fatality rate, with almost 50% of his over 2,000 generals killed or seriously wounded, leaving many openings for deserving officers to be promoted. I have pulled pieces of Desmarais's story from the biographies of other Napoleonic generals. The Loyalist military leaders in Milford Haven are all historical characters.

Still, even an obsessive amateur historian will miss details and context, and no doubt I have mistaken some important details. All historical errors are my own.

Acknowledgments

As always, I could not have written this book without the assistance of many people. Dave McKee, Nicola Geiger, MeriLyn Oblad, and Susanne Barrett gave feedback on the final version and saved me from many typos. David Young helped with the historical side and corrected my limited French. Sarah Rakhmanov came up with the perfect title for this book even before she knew what Darcy was concealing. Many readers at Austen Variations gave encouragement and helpful opinions on the first part of the book, and didn't give me too much grief when I left them hanging with the discovery of Georgiana Darcy's true identity.

My family, as always, deserves endless thanks for their patience and support.

About the Author

Abigail Reynolds may be a nationally bestselling author and a physician, but she can't follow a straight line with a ruler. Originally from upstate New York, she studied Russian and theater at Bryn Mawr College and marine biology at the Marine Biological Laboratory in Woods Hole. After a stint in performing arts administration, she decided to attend medical school, and took up writing as a hobby during her years as a physician in private practice.

A life-long lover of Jane Austen's novels, Abigail began writing variations on Pride & Prejudice in 2001, then expanded her repertoire to include a series of novels set on her beloved Cape Cod. Her most recent releases are the national bestsellers *Alone with Mr. Darcy* and *Mr. Darcy's Noble Connections, Mr. Darcy's Journey*, and *Mr. Darcy's Refuge*. Her books have been translated into seven languages. A lifetime member of JASNA, she lives on Cape Cod with her husband, her son and a menagerie of animals. Her hobbies do not include sleeping or cleaning her house.

Abigail's website: www.pemberleyvariations.com

Also by Abigail Reynolds